RELICS - OMNIBUS

NICK THACKER

Relics: Omnibus

Turtleshell Press (www.turtleshellpress.com)

Copyright © 2017 by Nick Thacker, Turtleshell Press

All rights reserved. This book or any portion thereof
may not be reproduced or used in any manner whatsoever
without the express written permission of the publisher
except for the use of brief quotations in a book review.
Printed in the United States of America
First Printing, 2017

Nick Thacker
Colorado Springs, CO
www.NickThacker.com

PART ONE_

MYERS_

It was the second day of his new life when Myers finally remembered that he'd forgotten everything.

He had spent the first day running, though he wasn't sure why. When he finally crashed outside an old stone temple, his body had given in. He was done.

The morning found him just as the night had left him. Cold, broken, and afraid. But it was the unique *flavor* of fear coursing through him that ultimately startled him awake.

Myers stood, his back cracking from the stiffness of sleeping on hard-packed dirt. He almost laughed. This wasn't how a forty-three-year-old man should spend a night.

Forty-three?

He had no idea.

This was yet another thing he couldn't remember. He looked down at his body and saw a wobbling, exhausted frame of a man easily in his sixties.

How many years has it been?

He knew his name, his hometown, his parents' names. A few other things, but that was it.

So he started running again.

It was a stumbling type of run, one that would have made his track coach in high school yell at him. He remembered that man's face better than his own — creases above his frown lines from years of pushing students to their limit. He felt some sort of tugging as he tried to bring the memory into focus.

He took many breaks, stopping to rest his hands on his head to maximize his air intake. He walked to the top of a small rise — the highest point he could see — to get his bearings.

Having no idea where he was, or where he'd started from, it was as good a plan as any.

And he loved plans. That much he could remember.

The rise revealed what he needed to see: there was no direction that would provide anything other than open sunlight and miles of dry, cracked earth, except for one.

About three-quarters of a mile away he could see a broken, deserted city. Crumbling spires stretched into the sky, but their tops, if there were any, were hidden behind clouds of brown dust.

He sat down, staring at the city. The remains of a rock wall extended across his field of vision and back over the horizon, leading him to believe it was at one time a border for the city. In front of it stood a chain-link fence, taller and much sturdier than the wall. The city itself was on a rise similar to his, though much larger.

Myers reached the outskirts of the town — or what was left of it — ten minutes later. He gasped for air, but kept his dirty, swollen feet shuffling forward. At some point yesterday he'd wrapped them with two halves of his torn button-down gray shirt, leaving on the thin, cheap white undershirt, and the thread was already wearing thin. He felt every pebble and grain of sand as they landed, but he didn't stop.

There would be no answers here for him. He already knew that somehow, but he pushed forward anyway. *Stick to the plan.*

A tall fence loomed over him as he neared the edge of the town. It was rusty, and a crooked sign had been mounted on one of the locked sides of the chained swinging gate.

Istanbul.

Nothing else. No welcome, no instructions. Just a label.

Odd.

He reached a blistered hand up the gate and felt the rough chain links on his fingers. He applied a little pressure, but the gate remained stationary.

Myers shook it, hoping the gate would remember that it was supposed to be open. It jangled with the motion, creaking as the heavy lock and chain clanged against the two halves.

He looked up, assessing the climb. There was no barbed wire on top, but the fence was certainly higher than it appeared to be from afar. Myers shrugged and started climbing.

He wasn't sure when he'd climbed a fence like this last. Probably as a young boy. Flashes of memories exploded through his mind: climbing a fence to get a baseball, climbing a fence to run from a dog, climbing a fence with friends — hollow faces now in the memory — though none were helpful. He moved steadily, his weakened body keeping pace surprisingly well.

I must be in decent shape when I'm not stretched to my limit, he thought.

He reached the top and took his time shifting his weight over to the other side of the fence. When he began descending, he had a moment of vertigo that passed quickly.

At the bottom he stood for a moment looking back up the high fence to revel in his accomplishment then turned and walked into the city.

There was still a half-mile gap between the gate and rock wall and the first of the buildings, so he used the extra time to formulate some sort of loose plan.

Will there be people here? Will they be friendly?

In a moment of insight he looked around him for something to use as a weapon.

Just in case.

He found a fist-sized rock with a sharp protrusion on one end. *Brutal, but it would have to do.*

The buildings in front of him, except for the two spired towers, were identical. They formed an avenue around the open space between them, facing each other from each side of the road. Farther down, the buildings rose in height until he could see two- and then three-story buildings. They were abandoned, but remnants of activity were visible behind each of the dust-covered windows.

Televisions, ultra-thin and long dead, hung behind windows, facing the street. Shops displayed their dust-covered wares on counters, still waiting to be sold.

In one particular building, Myers noticed a small toy display case tucked into a corner. All of the toys were dolls of some sort, some plush, some plastic. All of the toys were covered in a thick layer of dust, painted the same pale brown as everything else.

He reached a juncture in the road, stopped, and peered both directions. He had no plan — at least not one that involved more than 'walk into the city' — and that drove Myers crazy. He felt adrift, lost, and not *just* because he was, literally, lost.

He chose left. It was an odd sensation, not 'deciding' to turn. He just *turned* and his feet began walking. His body seemed to agree, so Myers went along for the ride.

His feet were now caked in dust and dirt, and he was sure he'd need to stop and rest soon, so he started looking for an out-of-the-way home or storefront he could bed down in for the rest of the day and night. As the thought of sleep came over him, he looked up to find the sun directly above.

Noon. I must be getting old.

He walked for another hour, still unsure of the proper plan. *Look for another person, or seek shelter?* When he came to a bridge over a dried-up river, he decided to call it quits. A small kiosk stood next to the bridge, each side of it covered with windows. It would make a decent lookout if he needed it.

He brushed a circle of dust from each window, providing him with an unobstructed view in every direction, and entered the kiosk.

Inside Myers found a desk mounted to three walls, a chair in the middle, and little else. Postcards and brochures advertising sights and historic landmarks of the area, long since forgotten, were strewn about the floor. He slid the chair to the far side of the kiosk and sprawled out on the ground. The cool concrete felt fantastic on his sunburned neck and back, and he fell asleep before he could assess the wraps covering his feet.

MYERS_

Myers slept in fits, tossing and turning as his back found every small crack, rock, or piece of trash spread over the floor of the kiosk. He was sweating, even though the absent sun had cast the city into a cool, dry night. During one particularly long waking stretch, he tried to take a mental assessment of his condition, but he had no idea how to do that.

He started with his feet, wiggling his toes and rotating his ankles. *To see if anything is broken*, he told himself. His feet worked, though they were near the end of their ability to provide support to the rest of his body. He assumed sleep would help, so he mentally wrote it off as minor stress. He had no idea if that was a medical term, or if it was even true. He imagined a doctor standing over him, arguing; Myers silently tried to justify each of his decisions to the invisible medical professional.

He moved upward from his feet and continued the absurd pseudo-medical self-assessment. *My legs are sore, sunburned. I need to get some rest and see if I can find a pair of pants tomorrow. Maybe shoes as well.*

The common diagnosis when he reached his stiff, burned torso was 'you need rest,' so he concluded that a proper medical examination would have to wait. He needed to sleep.

The next time he woke up was from the silence. It was heavy, deep, and constant. It was an odd thing to be forced out of restful, much-needed sleep because of *silence*, yet that was the only thing that made sense. He knew it wasn't from a noise — there hadn't been anything like that since he'd entered the city. Myers realized he hadn't even seen so much as a bird.

So the silence woke him. He shot upright and looked around. For the briefest of moments he was back at home — wherever that was — at a desk. He saw the old, hardwood antique splayed out in front of him, covered with papers that were illegible. A beautiful craft lamp sat on the corner, surrounded by photos. He couldn't see the subjects of the pictures, nor could he make out any other features of the room. In the split second the scene was depicted in front of his eyeballs, it seemed as though the desk was floating in empty space.

But he knew it wasn't. He knew at once, even as the darkness from the creeping night seeped in and found him alone in the kiosk, that it was a *memory*. It was a vision from the past. *His* past.

He struggled to manifest it once again, but it was now toying with him. Just out of reach, just beyond the conscious mind, the memory nagged at him and threatened him. *I'm right here, but if you try to catch me I'll be gone,* it said. He almost screamed.

To not have any recollection of the past years was a new feeling for Myers, and one that he thought might be the worst possible emotion he'd ever felt. It wasn't like not knowing something, like never having learned that the earth was round or that it orbited the sun. It wasn't like not understanding something, either, like quantum physics or plumbing. Those were reconciliations people made with themselves. They chose, more or less, what things they wanted to know and what things to ignore.

But to *not be able to recall something you knew*, something that was close to second nature, was a totally new experience for Myers. He'd always had a fantastic memory, to the point of being labeled eidetic or having a photographic memory numerous times growing up. He remembered those times, sitting in class and watching as the other students struggled to recollect an important fact or date from their textbooks. He had no problem seeing in his mind's eye the teacher or professor nodding their head in confirmation as a younger Myers Asher answered a tough problem correctly, just from the sheer luck of remembering the obscure fact needed to find the solution.

Those memories, from long ago, were still there. Myers had an older brother who'd died in a car crash when Myers was seventeen. It tore his family apart, and the memories around that event and the emotions he felt were still very much inside him.

He tried to remember, again, the desk. It wasn't critical, that much he knew. The desk was just a strong association in his mind, to something he couldn't recall. There was nothing particularly special or stunning, or even significant, about the desk other than that it was *his* and he had remembered it, at least fleetingly.

He moaned. The pain from laying on his shoulder had finally caught up to him, reminding him that even if his mind couldn't remember his age, his body could. He stood, stretching once, then returned to the relative comfort of the cool concrete floor. He brushed aside some pieces of paper and pebbles that had gathered near him and tried again to remember his past.

The last memory he could muster before everything went blank was of a party. He watched the playback of the scene from a third person point of view. He and his wife, Diane, were holding hands and yelling toward him, at something he couldn't see. They raised their clasped hands and he could see fuzzy outlines of other people raising theirs in response. The party was for him — about him, but he couldn't remember *why* they were celebrating. It must have been the last memory he had before everything was wiped, and some of this one had gone with it.

Myers sighed, knowing that it was a losing battle. He wasn't sure if the soreness, exhaustion, and sunburn played a part in the amnesia, but he knew it couldn't help. He decided to listen to his earlier diagnosis of getting rest and forced himself to fall asleep.

RAND_

Jonathan Rand stepped into the hallway and began the long, arduous journey to the coffee pot at the other end. It was tucked away into a closet-turned-break room, which meant that it housed little more than a table with a percolator, some styrofoam cups stacked next to it, and hardly enough room for one person to 'take a break' inside of it at any given time.

Rand really was at end of the earth. Especially for a high-tech company like Vericorp. Rand's current employer was a state-of-the-art server optimization and cloud storage giant, but out of geographic necessity, it had to maintain offices in places like Umutsuz.

Rand resented it, but the System was in charge of reassignment, and there was nothing he could do to change that. He neared the end of his trip and swung left, into Roan Alexander's office.

"Cup of coffee?" he asked, before he'd even been noticed by Roan.

Roan looked up, his permanent state of annoyance reflecting on his face. "Uh, what? Yeah, sure, I guess."

Jonathan took the opportunity to jab his friend. "Hey, buddy, if you're deep in something important, feel free to —"

"I'm not," Roan said. "I never am. You know that. Nothing here is ever 'important.'"

Jonathan didn't even need to nod in agreement. Of course he knew that — it was all anyone here ever talked about. 'Washed up programmers find solace in community' was the topic du jour every day. They'd been reassigned at about the same time, Roan from what was left of Silicon Valley and Rand from Austin. Both cities had been all but abandoned in recent years, leaving only low-tech manufacturing and distribution companies behind. When Jonathan had first arrived at

Vericorp, he was stunned to see the narrow, dimly lit hallways inside the old, decrepit facility tucked away in downtown Umutsuz.

Roan Alexander was the first person he'd complained to about it, and quickly found a kindred spirit in the quiet, perpetually on-edge developer. Roan had racked up quite a career as a "bug squasher," using his uncanny ability to find and annihilate errors, bugs, and glitches in software in just about any computer language. He'd been sought out by every major tech conglomerate as a contractor, but when the System called him out to Umutsuz, he was forced to close his local consulting firm and ship out.

The two men both had a professed love of coffee, and Jonathan would often find Roan leaning against the wall in the tiny break room, silently sipping the drink with his eyes closed.

Roan stood up from his desk and followed Jonathan across the hall. They each poured a cup and returned to the hallway.

"So, anything exciting in the world of System Analysis?" Jonathan asked.

Roan shook his head. "Not unless you think watching a computer find, isolate, and repair its own bugs sounds exciting."

It didn't. Jonathan already knew his friend's line of work — it was somewhat of a joke among System assignees like them to recognize their uselessness in the 'new world' of System-based administration. Programmers, developers, and IT folks all had some usefulness to the world at large, just not enough to do anything remotely considered 'fun' with their skill set. New assignees that showed up often jumped into their new work with the vigor of a recent convert, only to find that their job, now, was only a fuzzy reflection of their past career.

Jonathan wasn't bitter. You couldn't be, in this type of work. He'd had his moments, like anyone, but he was generally grateful to still have a job. At least that was something.

Roan, on the other hand, never missed an opportunity to gripe about one thing or another. His resentment matched Jonathan's, but Roan was much more vocal about it.

"Yeah, no, I definitely don't," Jonathan answered, perhaps a bit too late. Roan was already moving back toward his open door and desk.

"Huh?" Roan asked, not even turning to look back at his friend.

"Oh, nothing, I —"

Jonathan didn't bother. 'Assignees,' like him and Roan and a handful of the others on their floor, could be picked out of a crowd solely from the disinterested looks on their faces. They tended to be restless, disconnected, and even flighty, and Jonathan was glad he wasn't in charge of managing them all. He started thinking about their manager, Felicia Davies.

"Hey, what do you think about Davies' reapportionment of the servers from B-Wing?" Jonathan asked.

Roan looked at him and shrugged, then sat down at his desk and sipped the coffee, his eyes closing.

I already put him to sleep. "Yeah, me too. Sorry, mindless chitchat, huh? Nothing I can possibly conjure up would make this place any more bearable. We can at least bitch about her, then."

Roan raised one eyebrow, implying a question. *What happened?*

"Well, she's been all gung-ho about this reapportionment for the last two weeks, and every time she brings it up she seems like she's just found the Holy Grail or something."

"She's a lifer, man. 'Anything for the System,' you know how it is."

"Yeah, I know, but she can't *really* think it's going to make a difference, right?" Jonathan asked. He leaned against the doorframe of Roan's office as he finished the last sip of coffee. It was too hot, but he didn't notice. He wondered how much else he'd forgotten how to notice over the past three years.

"She seems to think so. Why?"

Jonathan frowned. "I don't know. I guess… I just think there's something else going on. These 'improvements,' I mean. They're… obvious."

"Not sure why the System missed them?"

"Yeah, exactly. And why they're popping up more often now. Last week there were *three* modular adjustments to rack spaces. God, *three*. Before that, we hadn't had *one* in over three years." He took a breath, thinking. "And every time we find something, it's like a party. Everyone freaks out like we brute-force cracked an encryp."

"People like their job," Roan said. Jonathan loved that about the man — he couldn't be moved; couldn't be swayed into more than slow apathy.

Jonathan grinned. "Right, I *definitely* believe that. Seriously, though. Don't you think those 'improvements' are odd? Back-to-back like that, and something the System missed?"

"No. No, I don't care that much."

"Yeah, I know, man, I'm just talking. Thinking out loud. Let's grab a drink later?"

Roan lifted both his eyebrows this time, a rare feat, and answered. "You got it. See you then."

Jonathan walked the rest of the way down the hallway and entered his office again. It was well-appointed, at least compared to the others. He had a window, and a couple cushioned chairs. There were never visitors, not down here. But they came with the office, so he didn't have them removed.

He plopped down into his chair and waved his hand over the screen to wake it. It was almost as he'd left it fifteen minutes ago, with a minor change: the blue progress bar that he'd left at 26% was blinking at 100%. A dialog window had popped up over that telling him the update was complete.

Finally, a small ticker at the bottom of that window displayed a clock counting upward, timing how long ago the update had finished. "Update completed: 17 seconds."

Perfect timing. The seconds clicked upward, and Jonathan leaned back and waited for the next update request to ding into his inbox.

Each update had to be manually performed — a human, sitting in front of a computer screen, had to click each update to begin the process, wait for it to complete, and then wait for the next one to appear.

It was the epitome of mindless work, but it was *his* work. The System had decided it needed him, if only for this brainless task, each and every workday. For the honor of providing the System this crucial role, Jonathan Rand would be paid handsomely: 79,500 Current per annum.

500C shy of hitting the next tax bracket, so he was grateful the System had the decency to leave it there.

But still — it *was* mindless work, and certainly something he could teach a kid to do.

The next update *dinged* into the inbox, and he clicked it and started the process. He read the undecipherable label, an annoying habit he'd found himself in.

B67458RA34

It told him nothing, except that a reassignment was involved. "RA." The rest of the numbers and letters were always useless content, only there for logging purposes in the System's records. They weren't even chronological.

"Reassignment," he said to himself as he leaned back in the chair and watched the progress bar count upward. "Wonder who's getting fired today."

Jonathan swiveled left and right, another habitual dance he'd developed after three years of mind-numbingly dumb work, and closed his eyes as he waited for the installation to finish.

MYERS_

It must have been only fifteen minutes later when Myers awoke once again. *A noise.* A shuffling sound, then silence.

He looked out the peepholes he'd made on each side of the kiosk, trying to discern movement in the darkening sky. It was either already dusk or there was some sort of storm blowing in. He couldn't tell.

Another slight shuffling sound caught his attention from behind him, and he turned as silently as possible. He waited an entire minute before moving again. *Probably a rat or small animal,* he told himself.

The shuffling sound did not return, and he was again alone with only his thoughts to keep him company. He was already lowering himself back down to the floor to try to sleep through the night when the glass exploded behind him.

The glass in front of him followed immediately after, and Myers instinctively ducked farther down below the windows.

It was only then that his brain processed what had just happened.

A gunshot.

Someone had shot at him, and missed, blowing out the front and back windows of the small kiosk.

Myers panicked, curling up into the corner of the tiny building. *Maybe they'll leave,* he thought. As soon as the sentence entered his mind, he knew it was ridiculous.

They'd taken a calculated shot at him, and they would have gotten him — probably right in the back of the head — had he not decided to lay back down and go to sleep. He also realized he had likely given away his position by scrubbing the glass clean in small circles on each window.

He cursed to himself, then tried to assess his situation. *I'm a sitting duck in here, and they're either going to try to kill me again or come see if I'm dead. Either way, I'm dead.*

The safer plan — if there really was one — was to try to make a break for it.

He stood up into a crouch, calculating his escape. To his advantage, the shooter was behind the kiosk — the glass at the rear of the small building had blown slightly before that in the front. Assuming the attacker was far enough away, and mostly behind him, that meant he could at least run out the door and straight forward, using the kiosk as cover to give himself a few precious seconds to get away.

He didn't have time to develop a more in-depth plan. He made a run for it, moving out the door and into the cooling evening air as fast as his tired, old legs would take him. Myers kept running, the dry riverbed on his right, winding through the city.

When he felt safe enough to turn, he tried to move left abruptly enough to throw off anyone chasing him. The turn hurt his knee, but the pain would have to wait.

He'd almost reached the next street when a bullet smashed into a stone wall, directly behind him. The sound of the actual gunshot followed a half-second behind, both alarming Myers that his getaway had been foiled and allowing him to realize that the attacker was far enough away that it was difficult to get a solid bead on him.

He slid into the alley, taking only a moment to catch his breath. The attacker knew where he was, but he was far enough behind him that he was safe for now, and out of sight. But he couldn't stop. Not now.

Myers kept running, though it was merely a slight jog by now, and even that was stretching it. He slowed to a walk, realizing that he was traveling almost the same speed as when he was 'running.'

"Hey."

The voice came from behind him, and Myers almost fell to the ground. He turned, raising his hands above his head. "D — don't shoot." His voice was raspy, almost inaudible.

"I'm not going to shoot you. I — "

The voice stopped as its owner stepped into the remaining light of day and saw Myers up close.

"Oh, holy…"

The man talking was young, easily under thirty, and Myers was first struck by his eyes. They darted left and right, but it was clear they didn't miss a thing. His body stood ramrod straight, knees slightly bent and ready to spring into action.

"What? Who are you?" Myers asked.

"Don't worry about that yet. You need to get out of here. Why'd you come here?"

"Come where?"

"*Here,* idiot. Istanbul."

Myers shook his head. "So this really is the city?"

The young man stared at him blankly, his eyes now focused intently on Myers. "Are you insane? Go!"

Myers almost sprung into action from the intensity of the man's voice, but his feet, having been tortured and beaten for two days, remained firmly planted in place.

"Seriously. *Go.* I don't know what else to tell you, old man, so you'd better get out of here."

"Where am I supposed to go?" Myers asked.

"*God,* you're wasting time!" he said, his voice a raised whisper. He seemed to process something for a second, but then said, "Fine. Your funeral. Come on."

Myers had no choice. He followed the man as he turned and ran down a narrow side street between two buildings. He was much faster than Myers, and probably even if Myers wasn't sore, tired, and wounded.

"Where are we going?" Myers called out.

"Stop talking, or you'll get us both killed," the man said as he ran.

Myers followed along until his legs could carry him no further. "St — stop, please," he whispered, trying to project his voice enough to be heard.

The man stopped and shook his head, then turned around. "Fine. You win." He motioned to the left, and Myers looked over.

It was a tall, stained-glass window. *A church.* Next to the window stood a massive wood door. It was open slightly, no more than an inch.

"We'll camp here for now, but you'd better be ready to *move* when I say so." He paused and examined him, as if noticing Myers for the first time. "Looks like you've been through a bit already, old man."

Myers frowned and opened his mouth to argue. *What's the point?* He thought. *He's right.*

He looked down again and saw the aging, frail body he'd seen earlier. He sighed, then entered the church, closing the door behind him.

SOL_

Solomon Merrick clicked a new magazine into the long-range EHM Triplex rifle and muttered under his breath. He'd wasted two shots, and now he'd lost his prize. Sol stood and grunted under the weight of the EHM-made bodysuit and approved ammunition. He'd chosen to carry more rounds for this hunt in order to stay out longer and make a wider arc through the city.

Istanbul was home for him, at least for now, and he hated it. Born in Cincinnati, this was literally halfway around the world from his comfort zone. He'd spent most of his childhood in Ohio, then most of his early adulthood in Seattle. It had taken time to adjust, but he was getting there. There was work here, and it didn't matter anyway — he couldn't go back.

Sol shifted once more, feeling the survival backpack and ammunition sling settle into place on his back. He held the rifle with both hands, staying ready in case he got another line of sight on his target, and started walking.

The mark had turned onto a city block near the old Anglican church. He couldn't remember the last time he'd heard of someone going to church, at least to any of the old religions. But it had also been a while since he'd been part of society at large. Maybe in the other cities there was still religion.

Sol took a shortcut through another alley, hoping to cut off the mark from advancing around his left and getting behind him. He had the upper hand — not just in weaponry, but in knowing the city as well as anyone. There would be little room for the mark to escape around the side. This side of the dried-out riverbed was narrow and held a few larger buildings, like the church, but was otherwise mostly smaller homes and shops. There were only three blocks between the river and the walls, so Sol was confident he could station himself in a place high enough to see any movement.

He'd found the mark once already, and it seemed too good to be true. Injured, weak, and obviously exhausted, this was going to be an easy pull.

Sol stopped short as he neared the block of homes that surrounded the centralized church. He'd forgotten to log the mark, a standard adopted and followed by everyone using the Boards.

He sighed, stopped, and placed the rifle against a wall next to the road and swung the backpack off his shoulder. *How much will this cost me?*

It had only been fifteen minutes since he'd seen the mark, so maybe it wasn't going to cause much of an issue. *Still, every little bit counts.*

He took out the palm-sized terminal, a handheld communication device, from his backpack. It was small enough to carry in a pocket, but Sol hated the bouncing feeling he got when there was anything other than legs and air inside his cargo pants. He opened the channel he was looking for and entered his pID credentials.

The screen went black, then lit up with the multi-regional Board home screen. He waved a flat open palm downward to scroll, then made a tapping motion with his middle finger when he came to the proper link on the page. Retinal sensors on his optic nerve interpreted what his eyes were focusing on, then sent the wireless signal to the small device and clarified which link, exactly, he wanted.

The local Board displayed immediately, listing the marks in reverse-chronological order, starting with the most valuable at the top of the page. He switched to the other tab, listing them in order of newest-released first. There at the top of the page sat his very own mark. A thumbnail image of the mark's face as it was last publicly known was listed next to his name — *Myers Asher* — and a few pertinent details:

Last Sighting: (N/A)
Projected Region: (N/A)
Estimated SOT: (N/A)
Estimated Value (Current): 65,000

This was good news. Sol was the only one tracking Myers Asher so far, and he intended to keep it that way. Still, he needed to log him. It would change the data and make Istanbul the location of the next hunting frenzy.

If Sol didn't bring him in before all that.

He focused on the *Last Sighting* link and flicked his finger downward again. The page changed, a mere millisecond passing before the new page was fully loaded. The intelligence inside the programs these days never ceased to amaze Sol. With 99.99% accuracy, server-side scripts projected the most likely option for client-side interactions. In this case, 'they' guessed what link Sol would click, based on his current location, workforce placement, and a matrix of variables simply referred to as "Assumed and Associated Interest." It was amazing to him they didn't just click the link for him, almost as though by waiting for him to decide they were mocking his far inferior human processing speeds.

AAI was a mixture of past, present, and projections, taken from his purchase history, family status, list of accounts, and a plethora of other pieces and snippets of information that had stuck with him his entire life. The database collated the information and fed it to the powers that be, and thus created the matrix AAI for his person.

It was disgusting, honestly. His entire life he'd grown up in a world of ever-increasing speed, memory, and storage enhancements, both for humans and computers alike. When the two species, dancing around each other for generations, finally melded closer and the future pointed toward one shared sentience, it seemed already to be too late to go back. He'd fought it as long as he could, but now Sol felt more robot than human, even though he had only a few of the available enhancements his race largely had access to. Three-Dimensional Retinal Supplementation, Cardio-Ventricular Enlargement, and Biological Storage Enhancement were the only three he'd opted for before losing hope in human society and accepting his life of a drifter.

He was a forty-three year old man who could run at 70% capacity virtually forever and could remember more information than a human being learned in a lifetime.

And at what cost?

He looked around at the remains of the city once called "Istanbul" and shook his head. It had been a long time — and well before BSE was available — since he'd studied history, but he knew there were many countless of generations before him who'd called this place home, and the many times it had changed hands between rulers of men who conquered entire nations.

Sol considered engaging a secondary virtual screen to run a quick search on the history, knowing it would only be a three-second diversion, but resisted. *No point in giving these things more credit.* He wanted to fling the portable unit through the window of the dusted-over bread shop in front of him.

Instead, he allowed the device to pull in its exact coordinates and insert them onto the page, immediately publicizing Sol's location. He did a few quick calculations and added the last piece of data the Board asked of him: *Estimated Speed of Travel (SOT): 3-4km/hr.*

Sol accepted the update and the screen shifted back to the Board's default page, listing the marks by descending value. Myers Asher was already on top, but he noticed the "*Estimated Value (Current)*" jump upward from 65,000 to 75,000. *Would be higher if I'd done this sooner.*

Satisfied, he shut his eyes and opened them again while looking down at the device to turn it off. He placed it back in his backpack and slung it over his shoulder once more. He grabbed the rifle, checked it for any dust or debris, and started moving again.

He knew Myers Asher was the type of man who craved order. He needed to have a plan. Sol thought about what he would do in that situation. He figured the man would hole up somewhere relatively safe, yet relatively open, providing him a decent line of sight to any would-be attackers, as well as numerous exit strategies.

As he considered this, he gazed up at the tall bell tower of the old Anglican church in front of him, guarding over the rest of the block and neighborhood square.

That's where he'll be, he thought. *That's where he wants to stay tonight.*

He considered rushing into the church, gun forward, ready to take out the mark and call it a day. But Sol needed to wait. He needed the time to pass, and as long as he made sure he didn't lose track of the mark or let anyone else get the jump on him, it would only improve his outlook to wait until the next morning.

He made a quick plan to check the outside of the building, to see if anyone had in fact entered it. He then measured the different entrance and exit strategies to and from the church and took a place above the bread shop in a second-floor loft with a large, broad window on two sides. Anyone moving in on his quarry would have to answer to Sol first.

MYERS_

Myers was falling asleep as soon as they'd reached the cellar of the church. He started by sitting against a wall, but quickly slid down and found a comfortable enough position with his arm beneath his head. The soreness and stiffness of his body needed the sleep, but his mind was working too much to allow Myers to sleep soundly.

He dreamt again of the party, this time moving throughout the crowd of fuzzy people and out onto what must have been a patio overlooking whatever city he was in. It was nighttime, and the blackness of the background scene was superimposed behind the flitting bursts of light and fuzzy heads. Drinks were raised in front on his face — a toast, and he felt excitement as the memory progressed. It was a happy moment; a memory of being complete and together and satisfied. He couldn't remember *who* he was together with, but he assumed it was family and friends.

He drifted back inside, the memory taking control of his active consciousness. He looked down and around, finding fuzzy hands that he'd shake and young children he would greet. At eye level were more faces, more happy people, and the brightness of the lights ahead told him he was entering the kitchen.

The kitchen.

He recognized it as his own, though something inside his subconscious tugged back at the thread as soon as the recognition hit, pulling back down inside, and he second-guessed himself. He thought it was his own but was no longer absolutely sure. He tried to remember his own home in the lucid dream. He forced the memory to walk toward the bedroom, but he couldn't get the door opened. He seemed to be satisfied with the fact that he knew where the bedroom was and left it at that.

Back into the kitchen. The bright lights washed out any detail, and it was like floating in clouds as he flowed through the smaller room. Fuzzy smiling faces still popped up in front of him, and he lifted a foot as a large dog — *Beast*, he knew its name — ran between his legs. He knew he was laughing, and others were as well. The dog was a mastiff, a large breed, its drooping lips and sad eyes swaying them when they'd rescued it years before.

Myers was satisfied with that memory; he knew it was accurate. They'd gone together that time, Myers hesitant but wanting to please his young children. They'd had a dog before, and a cat, but this was later in their marriage. He hadn't wanted to commit to something like that, especially when he was about to… when he…

He lost the thread. That must have been when he was… when he'd lost all the memories.

He wondered if Alzheimer's was like this. Threads of memory that faded away into nothingness. Strands of recollections that were strong — he had a wife, kids, a dog, he was an accountant — moving and drifting as he struggled to bring them forward until they were just no longer *there*.

The dream suddenly changed to another scene. Again, the desk from the perspective of sitting behind it. Some of the room was now in focus, but only certain features. A huge portrait — of whom he wasn't sure — hung on the wall to his left, while a large, elegantly framed door stood directly in front of him. The rest was too blurry to see, and he tried to force his head — the memory — to look around. His face was fixated staring down, straight down toward the stack of papers that sat on top of a desk calendar. An expensive-looking pen was the only thing he could see clearly. *What was the pen for? Had I just used it? Am I about to?* He watched as the memory of himself picked up the pen and placed it carefully into a drawer on the right side of the desk. His hands were out of focus as well, but they came together and shuffled the papers into a neater stack.

The stack moved to the front of the desk — he was giving them to someone, and they were laughing. *We're using paper? Why are we laughing at that?* The thoughts came at once, and he tried to sort through them linearly, placing them in order, but couldn't. He was at work, not at a home office. He remembered that. But he didn't know where *work* was, or what he was doing. And he couldn't see who was in front of him in the memory.

The rest of his sleep phase was filled with competing memories, as if they were leftovers, or scraps, fighting for dominance over the limited space in his active memory. Scenes from one of his daughters' dance recitals, his wife, Diane, smiling back at him on a river rafting trip, his other daughter winning the district soccer tournament for her high school. These were old memories, vivid ones, and he had no problem conjuring them and darting through them at will. He walked through the scenes, pausing them like a movie, and changed position. His mind attempted to recreate each scene from the artificial perspective he'd requested.

When his mind became as exhausted as his physical body, he drifted into a deeper sleep, the memories faded, and he slept soundly for a few hours.

RAND_

Jonathan Rand was late to the bar. Vericorp was in Umutsuz' Zone 1, while the bar was across town in Zone 3. The train let him off a block away, and he hurried to the neon sign marking his destination.

Niels' Bar. The bar was a favorite haunt of the reassigned tech crowd, and Jonathan and Roan had discovered it a year after they'd started at Vericorp. It was tucked away behind a gym and day spa, next to a small plaza surrounded by boutique shops and cafes. By day the bar served lunch and an early dinner to shoppers and anyone perusing through the square, and by night it was a relatively quiet, tame locale for tech industry types who needed a little post-work camaraderie.

He walked in, the doorman, Jones, greeting him with a nod. Roan was already sitting at the long bar with his back to the door. He snuck up next to him and raised a hand toward the bartender before he even sat down.

"Hey," he said. The music, some sort of postmodern trance/dance instrumental, was turned down enough to be present but not headache-inducing, and his voice easily carried over it.

Roan nodded, not turning to look at him.

Jonathan accepted the drink — a whiskey — and took it in two quick draws. Not quite a shot, not quite a drink. He liked it that way; it started things quickly but didn't make him feel like a college frat guy.

He winced and ordered another. The whiskey here in Umutsuz was like the industry — an afterthought. It was bland, tasteless, and mindlessly boring. But it was cheap, and with the salaries of C-level executives, many of the tech employees found themselves spending many late nights out, towing the line between mild alcohol abuse and flat-out alcoholism. Jonathan wasn't one of those guys. He liked to drink, but he hated the morning after. For that reason, he usually held himself to no more than three drinks per night.

"Everything okay?" he asked Roan between drinks. The man hadn't even turned to look at him. Roan Alexander had always been a drab individual, one of the most apathetic he'd ever met, but most of the time he at least showed mild interest in Jonathan's company.

Roan turned, slowly, and Jonathan immediately could see that something was wrong. His eyes were bleary. *Had he been crying?* Jonathan couldn't imagine that to be true. Roan, the same man who seemed impervious to human emotion. His jaw was set, and a deep crease cut across his forehead.

"Woah, buddy," Jonathan said. "What's up?"

Roan grabbed at the glass in front of him. Whiskey, neat, just like Jonathan's, but his was nearly full. He took a long, slow sip and then spoke. "I've been deactivated."

Jonathan couldn't hide his surprise. "Wait, what? Reassigned, you mean?"

"No, I don't mean *reassigned*. I've been deactivated. I'm done, Jonathan."

Jonathan's mind raced. "But, your department is… you're the only one?"

Roan nodded.

"And there was no reason?"

"The System didn't think it necessary to provide me the details of its decision."

"Hmm."

"You still moving forward with the, uh…"

"Yeah," Rand said. He didn't need to be reminded of the plan he'd made two years ago that was only now ready to implement. He also didn't need Roan to say it out loud in the bar, in case someone happened to be listening. He thought about his contacts, working remotely to help him out, and silently hoped they'd be ready when it was go time.

"Good. Wish you the best."

"We're going to need it. I think Davies is on to me, but I have a feeling we don't have much longer before this whole thing blows over."

Roan looked over. "Yeah? What makes you think that?"

Rand shrugged. "The way things are going, I guess. Seems to be changing more and more quickly —"

"I thought you said it wouldn't."

"I did, and I still believe that, but…" Jonathan sighed. "But it's still *different*, in some ways. It's moving the pieces around, putting them into place where it wants them."

Roan nodded, but didn't say anything else. There was nothing else *to* say.

They sat for another hour or two, neither man talking much, until long after Jonathan had lost track of the time — and the drinks. He grew tired, woozy, and drunk, but still continued to order more. At such a low-key and reasonably safe establishment, Jonathan had never seen the bartenders or managers cut anyone off, and the trend continued tonight. His three-drink limit was doubled, then tripled, until he felt the room spinning.

Roan had stopped drinking after his third, but he wasn't able to hold his alcohol as well as Jonathan. Both men were having trouble keeping their eyes open, but neither wanted to leave the other alone.

"Hey, hey man, I was thinking…" Jonathan started up again. His words were slurred, but he felt a sudden lucidity come over him. "I — I was thinking, you know, about the System…"

Roan shook his head. "Enough about the System, Jonathan. Tell that girlfriend of yours. Can't we just —"

"But… but you don't understand, man. And that 'girlfriend of mine' and I are getting pretty serious. She's flying in soon, I think. Hey, that's not what I was saying. I — I can get through it. I mean, I can *hide* us from it."

Roan didn't respond. He was either asleep or didn't care. Or he was purposely ignoring him.

"I can create a, uh, a *cloak*, I guess. For lack of a better word."

Roan swung around to look his friend in the eye.

"Seriously. I was thinking about it today. After we talked, I went back did another update. *God*, those updates… I, um, anyway…" He lost his train of thought and quickly regained it. *Damn, that whiskey.* "I had an idea. I can do it, and you might be able to help."

Roan raised his eyebrows, ever so slightly. *I'm almost interested, but I'm not sure.*

"Create a terminal unit, one that's pocket-sized, that translates a pID into a static IP address."

Roan looked back down to his drink and swirled it once.

"Seriously — think about it, man," Jonathan said. "Everyone's got their personal ID, right? Fingerprint, driver's license, social security number, whatever you want to call it. Their pID is what tells the System there's a human at the other end. Right? And every station has a static IP, something that's connected into the System and lets the System know it's a computer at the other end?"

He didn't wait for the non-response of Roan.

"So, I think anyway, I can program a simple single-board unit that does that translation. We'd need a static for it, but that's easy to set." He stopped and considered this as if it were the first time he was hearing the scheme. "Yeah, *yeah*, I think it could really work. Man, we get a printer to build a small case for it and we've got a portable station transmitter that can bypass — no, uh, *replace* — the human side. Roan, we can fly under the radar."

Roan groaned. "No. A static is *static,* Jonathan. It doesn't move. The System would know as soon as a duplicate showed up in a different location."

"Nope. No, that's just it. We set a *new* static IP, a new station, basically. But it's not actually a station, just a portable device. But the System doesn't need to know that — it just thinks it's a computer that's being moved around, whenever it pops up."

The more he spoke, the more excited he became. *Is that the whiskey talking?* He wasn't sure, but he felt good. Great, actually. Better than he had in a long time, and it didn't matter what Roan thought. Roan was Roan, and he shouldn't expect more than disinterested pessimism.

"It could work."

Jonathan was stunned. *He had to be drunk.* There was no way he'd heard Roan correctly.

"Yeah, I think it could work. You'd need to make sure the static was truly that, dedicated and everything. Won't be easy to mask the pID without raising a flag, but it can be done. I think." He nodded. "Yeah, you could do it. I can help, but I know you could do it." He finished his drink.

"What's your current status?" Jonathan changed the subject, realizing he had no idea how much longer he'd have with his friend.

"Tomorrow."

"*Seriously?*" Jonathan couldn't believe it. Deactivations were usually a process, spanning a week or two. Let people get their lives picked up and ready to move. Apparently not this time. "Tomorrow?"

"Yeah. Sometime tomorrow I'll be given the region."

"Wow." Jonathan took a deep gulp of the cheap whiskey. "Scraped?"

"I doubt it. Hard to tell. I don't have any 'trade secrets.'" He made air quotes around the words 'trade secrets.'

Jonathan chuckled. "Right. Well, that doesn't really matter much these days."

"Maybe not," Roan said. "But I'm not a threat, either. I've been relegated here, just like you, and I'm probably just not needed anymore."

He felt the lightheadedness of being drunk lifting slightly, replaced by an overwhelming sense of fatigue. "I have to go. Damn, I can't keep going. What is it, Tuesday?"

Roan nodded.

"And listen, I'm going to figure this out, man. I'm going to get us out —"

"Don't." Roan cut him off. "I'll be fine, honestly. I'm not worried about it. Hell, you and I both know just about anything has to be better than this... this *life*."

"But —"

"But *nothing*, Rand," Roan said. "You're going to need someone on the other side when this this blows up, and you know it. I'll be there, ready to go, and I know you'll be able to find me."

Jonathan nodded again. "Sure, yeah, I'm with you. It's just —" he drifted off, suddenly encapsulated by the large mirror hanging behind the bar.

"Yeah," Roan said, standing while he waved the bartender over to close out his tab, "I'll miss you too, man."

Jonathan stuck out a hand, and Roan accepted it. They'd been through three years at Vericorp together, and it was time to change it up again. If there was anything consistent about this new world it was inconsistency.

The bartender appeared in front of them, and Roan reached out a finger to initiate the Current transfer. Jonathan did the same, and both men declined the receipt and stepped back from the bar.

Out in the open, he walked a few steps to test his balance. *Good enough to get to the end of the block.* He wasn't sure how long he'd need to wait before a train slid by, but there were benches. He could make it.

Satisfied, he started toward the door, following closely behind his friend. Rand wasn't sure if he'd ever see him again.

MYERS_

"Who are you?" Myers asked.

"Look, old man, I —"

"Stop calling me old man."

The kid stared back at Myers.

Myers squinted. "Okay, fine, I get where you're coming from. But I think it's mostly because I've been running for two days straight."

"Looks like you've been running for fifteen years."

The kid shifted, moving into the corner of the cellar they entered below the church. Myers was situated against a long wall next to him, sitting propped up between two large empty barrels. The rest of the cellar was filled with forgotten remnants of what it must have taken to keep a church stocked full of whatever it was churches were stocked with. Myers hadn't been in a church in a long time, and this one looked like it hadn't been visited in a while.

"Okay, well what's your name, then?" Myers asked.

"Ravi."

"Ravi?"

The kid shook his head. "You're really not in a position to judge, you know that?"

"Got it. Okay, Ravi, like I asked before, who are you? Why are you here, in, uh, *Istanbul?*"

"I live here. But not any longer. Time to move on."

Myers raised his eyebrows a bit, suggesting a question he didn't ask out loud. He looked down at the roll of pads and blankets Ravi must have handed to him to use as a bed, then back at Ravi.

They'd spent some of the night in the cellar of the church, though Myers didn't sleep nearly as well — or as much — as he'd really needed. He felt rested enough to have a conversation, but he could feel the fatigue setting in behind his eyes, slowly taking him over.

"Look — we don't need to be buddies. I just need to get out of town, get to the next place, you know how it goes."

"No, Ravi — I *don't* 'know how it goes.' Care to explain it to me?"

Ravi looked back at Myers, his beady eyes dark and brooding in the light of the single candle they'd found and lit, standing in the center of the room. "How long you been out?"

"Excuse me?"

"How long you been out? Like, out here?"

"Uh, two days — I guess. I don't remember anything before that."

"Shit, man, you've been out *two days?*" He shook his head again, then dropped it down toward his lap. "This was a bad idea."

Myers took a deep breath, frustrated. "Ravi, listen. I don't need you to like me, but I need you to at least *help* me. I'm not asking for much, here. Just *tell me* what's going on. I have to get out of here and figure out who did this to me, then —"

"Who *did* this to you? Come on, Asher, you know the answer to that. *You* did this to you. *You* —"

"Ravi, stop. I didn't tell you my name."

Ravi smiled, then laughed. "You're serious? Come on, old man, *everybody* knows you."

Myers shrugged; shook his head.

"What's the last thing you remember?"

Myers thought for a moment. "Uh, let's see — I've been running through what I thought was a desert for the past two days or so, came here, and —"

"*Before* that."

"Um, okay. I remember my wife — Diane. My kids, two daughters." He suddenly realized how much he missed them. Ravi was nodding, so Myers continued. "I — I was a, an accountant. A damn good one, too. Then… then I think I wanted to be a politician for some reason. I hadn't even thought about that. So, I guess I was a good politician, then, for you to have heard of me?"

Ravi smiled. "Yeah, something like that, old man."

"I was the CFO of Electronic Hardware Manufacturing for seven years, then I started campaigning… Senate? Or something local? No, it was bigger… I won, and…" he shook his head.

"And?"

"I don't remember. After that… nothing."

Ravi's eyes grew wide. "Wow, dude, they really scraped you there. Huh. So, you don't, uh, remember which office you ran for?"

"It wasn't Senate? *President?*"

Ravi was amazed. "Yes, like *President*. Of the United States of America."

Myers opened his mouth to ask another question, but no words came out. *The dream I've been having,* he thought. He was celebrating his campaign victory.

"You won, old man. President Myers Asher, in the flesh."

Myers was momentarily speechless.

"Look, I didn't know you *didn't* know. I thought — "

"I need to get out of here, son. I have contacts who will be —" He thought of the memory of himself behind the desk. He was the President of the United States, probably in the Oval Office, handing a document to one of his subordinates. *What was the document? Was it important?* He didn't know how memory worked, but he thought he remembered reading somewhere that memories tended towards important events, creating a tapestry of tiny events that wasn't remembered in its complete form, as a whole, but in patchwork form. A person, a setting, and a general idea of a conversation was all an active memory needed to program a "complete" memory and provide its user with a believable recollection of the event.

Ravi held up a hand. "Stop. Shut up. Quit the patronizing bullshit. You ain't *anything* down here, old man. Got it? You've been off the Grid and hidden away, and now here you are. A Relic, like me."

Myers was growing more frustrated by the second. "You mean to tell me I've been 'off the Grid' — whatever that means — and I can't even call for help? I'm the *President of the United States of America,* Ravi, and that means —"

"Like I said, *sir,* it doesn't mean *anything* anymore. You haven't been the President for seven years. When they decide you're a Relic, that's it. Done. Game over."

Myers stood up, turned to the wall, and placed a hand out, feeling the hundred-year-old cold stonework beneath his fingers. He breathed slowly, eyes closed, trying to put the pieces in place. "You mean to tell me I've been *missing for over seven years?* How — how can that be? I've only been out here for *two days.*"

Ravi shook his head again. "No, that's not right. You've been a *Relic* for seven years. You've only been *here* for two days. They hold you for some time, hiding you away, then stick you somewhere you're not supposed to be."

"A Relic?"

"Yeah, a castaway. Cast off from society. You weren't needed anymore, El Capitan, so here you be. Hunted, middle of nowhere, left for dead."

"But I don't understand. How is it that no one's come for me? No one's looking for me?"

"Well, you're wrong there. There are *plenty* of people looking for you, like that guy taking potshots at you last night. He'll be back, and so will lots of others in a few hours, when word gets out."

"Word gets out? How?"

Ravi started to look as frustrated as Myers felt. "Man, you really *don't* remember anything, do you?"

"Nope."

"Yeah, they're looking for you — hunters *and* Unders, by now. That guy from last night will have logged you by now, telling the rest of them exactly where you are, how fast you're moving, and how much Current you're worth. My guess, you're the top of the Boards, old man."

Myers started to feel his head throbbing. He crouched lower on the wall, still using it as support. He groaned. "But… but I didn't do anything wrong! Why? Why all of this…" he didn't finish, instead collapsing back on the floor.

Ravi reached over and slapped him on the back. "Don't worry, man, we'll get you out of here. I've been through this a few times, and —"

"A *few* times?"

"Yeah. Hunted. I've been on the run, for, uh, three years, seven months, and nine days." He tapped on the side of his head with an index finger. "The BSE helps a bit, too. Haven't forgotten a thing since seven years ago."

Myers let out an exasperated sigh. "Okay, fine. Whatever. You're a cyborg who can remember everything, and a criminal. Now I am too, I guess, so what's the plan?"

"Woah, hold on. I'm no *criminal*. Well, I mean, it's a stretch to call me one. I guess, if you had to, you could say I'm a public menace. But I'm no criminal. Theft, a few good lifts here and there, just trying to make a name for myself, and all of a sudden I'm 'out.' Caught, Moral Aptitude Analysis, and that's it. Cast out as a Relic."

"And me? What did I do?"

A loud sound echoed out above their heads — the slamming of a heavy door —and they looked at each other.

"Time to get, old man, or we're scraped. Here, follow me."

Ravi ran to the opposite corner of the cellar and moved a few boxes and another empty barrel. The wall on one side of the room housed a small door, one Myers hadn't seen when they'd entered.

"How'd you know that was here, kid?" he asked as he stood again and moved toward Ravi and the door.

"This ain't my first rodeo, *old man*, and I'm twenty-eight, if you want to stop calling me kid."

"Yeah? Well if you want to stop calling me *old man* I'm… uh…"

"Right, you have no idea. Got it, old man. Here, get in." Ravi swung the door open and motioned for Myers to enter. The smell of the cellar increased in intensity inside the cramped crawlspace. Mold, animal feces, and the sweet aroma of slowly rotting wood.

Myers crawled onward until the shaft turned hard to the right. He heard Ravi close the door behind him after carefully placing the barrels and boxes back in front of the access point. He shrunk down into a ball, pulling in his hands and feet, and then popped back up into a crouched position, now facing Myers.

"Quite the spry young chap, you are," Myers said.

"Enough with the old man talk, old man. Move."

Myers obliged, crawling forward. While his feet thanked him for the break, his knees quickly began feeling the brunt of the close quarters shuffling. "Where does this thing go, anyway?"

"Straight. And then left. And then straight some more. It'll be another thirty minutes before you see the morning again, so get comfy."

Myers groaned again. "Why can't we just wait it out? That crazy asshole's got to give up at some point, right?"

"No. That 'crazy asshole' has a *job*, and right now it's to kill you and bring you in. The Current on your head's got to be one of the highest ones he's seen, so he ain't gonna just get down here, look around, and shrug. He'll tear this place apart before moving on."

Myers felt the panic and headache set in again, simultaneously. "Great. So we crawl."

MYERS_

And crawl they did. When Myers finally emerged, through a drainage pipe into a ditch that must have been filled with water at some point in the past, his knees and hands were flaring up in pain almost as much as his feet had. It was with some irony that he realized he was *glad* he could now resume the getaway on his swollen, worn feet.

"This is it. Take it easy."

"Wait —" Myers turned to see the kid climbing up the steep incline above the open grate they'd exited. "You're just going to leave me?"

"Listen, old man — Asher — this isn't a team effort. I ain't a courier service man. There's nowhere I need to deliver you that won't get me killed just as much."

"So you're just going to *leave* me here?"

"I didn't survive for almost four years by helping guys like you out. There's always another Relic coming, and there's always another hunter waiting for them. You wanna make buddies and help each other out, be my guest, but I ain't interested in getting myself dead."

"Okay, then where do I go?"

"Start with getting yourself away from here." Myers followed his finger. Ravi pointed out to the open desert.

Right where I came from, Myers thought.

"Get out there, away from the gates, away from the wall, and just run. Keep running until you can't see the city anymore, then keep running. By then, I'll be long gone."

"What happens then?"

"Well, by then the next idiot like you will waltz through the gates and start looking around, and I'll have had time to get out and into the next deserted city. Eventually I'll find one that I can have all to myself, and then I can settle down, have a family, and get a job as an accountant."

Myers wasn't sure how much of the story was complete bullshit, but the slight toward him wasn't lost on him. "Good to hear you're taking this well, Ravi. Wish you'd at least help me make a plan and figure this out."

Ravi's eyes narrowed as he smiled. It was truly a terrifying face, considering the circumstances. "*Figure this out?* What more do you want me to tell you? You're being hunted, I'm being hunted, and we *will* be hunted. There is no 'figuring it out,' old man. There's me, there's you, and there's a thousand Unders heading this way hoping to bring us to the highest bidder. We stay together, that's *two* sets of tracks they've got to follow. We do what I'm *telling* you to do, we get out of the city and move on." His eyes flicked left, then right, quickly and thoroughly taking in the surroundings, checking for danger.

Myers wondered how many nights he'd done this — quickly assessing his surroundings and determining the best course of action, without having to be interrupted every five seconds by a scared, tired, old man.

Myers nodded, looking around. "Okay, got it. I understand. Good plan, Ravi."

He turned and left, walking over the dried riverbed and toward the fallen rock wall.

He hoped Ravi would be gone by the time he had to climb over the chain-link fence.

"Wait. Old man."

Myers stopped, then turned slowly. "Yeah?"

"You're different. You ain't like the others."

Myers raised his eyebrows. *Go on.*

"You're stronger. You ain't afraid."

Ha. If only that were true.

"You're fine just walking away. No one I run into yet done that. They're all scared of their own shadow, ready to pee themselves whenever I turn around."

"Okay…" Myers tried to look impatient. *Make him feel vulnerable.*

"Well, I guess, uh, we could at least get to Umutsuz."

"What's *Umutsuz?*" Myers vaguely recognized the language — Turkish — but wasn't sure what it meant.

"It's the next city over. Hasn't been deactivated yet, like Istanbul. If we get there, we can at least try to hitch a ride out of the area from someone leaving. I'd be, uh, *willing*, to bring you along."

"Would you?" Myers asked, his lip turning upward ever so slightly in the beginning of a smile.

"I would. Keep your mouth shut and your eyes up, and yeah, I'd be okay with it."

Myers nodded once. "Let's go. Lead the way, kid."

SOL_

Sol was out of options.

His mark had somehow slipped him at the church, undoubtedly due to some oversight on Sol's part. He bristled at the memory of it.

The night before, after watching for five hours and seeing no signs of life, he'd decided to examine the exterior of the church to see if Myers, in fact, had entered it.

He'd circled the building once, checking for openings, window gaps, or anything else out of the ordinary. When he came to the front door of the church, he noticed something peculiar.

It was closed.

When he'd passed the church in his usual rounds through this area of the city a few days ago, Sol had entered the church, looked around, and left, leaving the door slightly ajar. He hadn't been back since, and he knew no one else had either.

He waited, watching the interior of the church through a broken section of stained glass window on the front of the building. After another fifteen minutes, he made his move. He entered, once again leaving the door open, and looked for signs of movement. He then checked the cellar door. If he had to hide inside this place, that would have been his first choice. The door to the cellar was shut, but he noticed some dusty footprints leading toward it.

Interesting.

He'd been in the cellar before — when he'd first arrived in the city, he'd set up a rotation throughout these lower quadrants that took him by the church, and he'd taken the time to explore the inside of each of the buildings on the route. At the time, there were no footprints leading down into the cellar.

He was in the cellar. Perfect.

Now it would be a waiting game — the man in the cellar had nowhere to go but up, back into the sanctuary of the church.

Where Sol was waiting.

He checked his ammunition out of habit, once more pulled up the Board and checked the Current on Myers' head, and then decided to spring the trap.

He left the door to the church open and moved toward the rear exit on the left — there was one on each side of the altar. As he neared the altar, he reached for one of the dusty Bibles still present in the pews and brought it up to his shoulder. Crouching down beside the rear door, he turned and prepared himself.

Sol threw the Bible as hard as he could, using the height of the sanctuary's ceiling to get some distance.

The Bible smacked against the door, slamming it shut.

He waited. Myers would hear the door slam, know he was caught, and try to escape by ducking behind the altar and backstage area to get to one of the rear doors.

Right where Sol waited.

That was the plan anyway.

Instead, Sol waited for Myers to exit the cellar. He waited two minutes, then another three. Finally, he decided to check the cellar for activity.

Sol remembered the feeling well. He'd entered the cellar, looked around, and let out a long, low whistle.

He'd been duped. There was no one here. Not a soul had entered the church since yesterday, and now Sol had lost his mark.

He'd lost everything.

He wasn't sure what to do about it, but he knew he needed to prevent Myers from leaving the city. If he did, it was anyone's game. Even if he didn't, too much time had passed. He was now one of many Hunters chasing the most wanted Relic on the Board. The Current on Myers would only go up, bringing that much more attention to Sol's city.

Sol made his decision.

He *had* to get Myers and bring him in. It was now or never. He left the church and cellar and headed back to his house, a small apartment he'd found when he first entered Istanbul.

Sol opened the door and stepped inside.

"Solomon!" his wife ran up to him and pulled him in. "You're back early. How did it go?"

He shook his head as his daughter entered the room.

"Daddy!" The voice of the young girl sent a pang of regret through him. *I'm not going to let you down.*

He knelt down to give her a hug, squeezing her tight, then stood, still holding her.

"Nothing?"

"Nothing."

His wife's lips tightened into a line. "Okay. Okay, that's fine. It's going to be okay." Her words were phrased as a statement, but he could hear the question behind them. He heard the panic set in before she'd even finished the sentence, and he reached out to grab her.

"Shannon, I —"

"It's going to be okay, right?"

He nodded, holding his family in his arms. "We're going to be fine. I need to get back out there. There will be others. Soon."

They'd been through this before. Shannon understood, but she still wasn't happy about it.

"Do you have to? Won't there be another? We can wait, and —"

"Shannon, come on. You know."

He set their daughter back down, and took his wife aside. "We *have* to, Shannon. There is no other option. After this —"

"*What?* After this, what? We move on, go to yet another city, yet another —"

"No. This is it. After this, we're done. It doesn't matter anymore." Shannon didn't know the full situation and plan — *couldn't* know the full plan. He stuck to the story he'd fed her.

"How?"

"We get a vehicle. There's one we can buy."

"There's not enough."

"There will be. Trust me. But I have to go."

She nodded, wiping away a tear. "Be careful."

He nodded.

Solomon Merrick spent the next hour eating, restocking his gear, and preparing for his journey.

MYERS_

Myers followed a step behind Ravi as they exited the city wall and chain-link fence. They crossed the same flat terrain Myers had traversed only a day ago.

"You think we can pick up the pace?" Ravi asked.

"Yeah, why?"

"We're out in the open. If anyone wants to get off a good shot —"

"Yeah, I got it. Sure, pick it up a bit. Where are we heading, anyway?"

"That way." Ravi pointed to another slight rise to the east, this one topped with a few trees and large boulders. "Just over that hill is Umutsuz, but we can camp up on top of it if we need to. Good vantage point and a few places to duck out of the way."

It was a good plan, Myers had to agree. *Good enough, anyway.*

"Hey, listen," Myers said. "I meant to ask you earlier. Who are you? Why are you out here?"

"I told you. I'm like you. A Relic."

"A Relic? There's that word again. What does it mean?"

Ravi looked back over his shoulder at Myers. "What do you think it means? We're *Relics,* man. Cast out of society. Done. No longer needed."

"But I'm the *President* of the United State —"

"You're not. Not anymore," Ravi answered. "No longer needed, like I said. And for what it's worth, there *is* no United States of America."

"There's not?" Myers moved a rock out of his path with his bare toe, only now wondering where his shoes were.

"No. After the System went online, there was a massive overhaul in management of resources, across the board. Computing took a turn, and humans were pretty much left behind."

The explanation rang a bell, but Myers wasn't sure — or couldn't remember — exactly what Ravi was talking about, so he let him keep talking.

"There was a brief period of chaos, while we tried to regain control, but after about six months it was evident that we were better off with something else running the show. After a while we just stopped fighting it."

"Some*thing*?"

"Yeah, the System, like I said. You really don't remember any of this?" Ravi asked. "Man, it was all right at the beginning of your first term."

Myers shook his head.

"EHM came in and revamped the computer information systems used by the Federal government for administrative and organizational planning — real basic stuff, like email, calendar, planners, you know. The stuff your secretary probably used every time you had a meeting."

"My Chief of Staff."

"Right. Whatever. EHM — your old company — was contracted to streamline the systems you guys all used, across the board. I guess the old software was getting antiquated, out of date. They came in and installed new stuff, using a self-replicating piece of software that could automatically download and install itself on any computer sharing a network connection. The idea was that it would help keep costs low, since you only had to get it working on a single machine in any particular office or department, then connect the others into it and it would do its thing."

"You're kidding me." Myers knew enough about computers — or, at least, he *used to* — to know how stupid that sounded.

"Well, that's what your precious company told the media, or was allowed to tell the media. It was 'supposed' to just be a simple package — an installable — and it was only 'supposed' to hit the computers in one centralized IP band."

"Let me guess," Myers said. "It was 'supposed' to only do these things, but it did a little more?"

"Correct," Ravi said. "EHM quickly found themselves chasing a virus in their own software. A little bug that just wouldn't be squashed. The system migrated faster than it was originally designed to, and it started jumping to computers that were completely removed and isolated from the network. Through emails, websites, you know the drill."

"So it was a virus? Why didn't we just make everyone install virus protection software, or clean their computers?"

Ravi laughed. "We thought about it. Or you guys did, or whatever.

Yeah, we covered that. 'It's a virus,' they said, 'so let's kill the virus.' But the *problem* was that the program was designed to protect itself against ignorant computer users who don't know the first thing about anything other than sending an email and playing solitaire — the types of people that can generally be found working in government offices."

Myers smirked. *He did remember* that *much.*

"So what happened was that the program was trying to protect the computer users who would typically use the 'burn it all' method of using antivirus software, to protect itself from being deleted along with the critical information and files on the person's machine. It would create a backup drive with 'mission critical files' it found on the infected computer and upload them to a cloud storage device. When the antivirus software ran on the machine, the program simply waited it out, then downloaded and installed itself again, either from the cloud backup or from another connected machine."

"You're saying the program just *did* these things? Either it was designed that way, or it had a mind of its own."

"Neither." Ravi shook his head. "EHM was highly regarded for their program due to its simplicity, ease of use, and one-hundred percent file protection guarantee, but they were *most* proud of one little feature the program boasted: the ability to learn."

"To *learn*?"

"Yeah, simple stuff. It had a very robust spam-protection applet, and some nifty calendar scheduling tools that would learn your preferences. But it could then *extrapolate* those preferences to either *anticipate* what you were going to do, or it would use those 'preference maps' in other areas. If you typically scheduled meetings on Mondays, and kept Fridays open, then your mom emailed you asking to grab lunch, it would draft a pre-written response telling her that Friday was your most free day."

"Wait a minute. This thing *wrote emails* on your behalf?"

"Yes and no. At first it was a basic library of pre-written messages, culled and cultivated from years of messages. But it was very clear that the program's interpretation of EMH's vision was to learn from *new* messages it came across, incorporate those into its database, then use that to determine a profile for the computer's main user. It was supposed to be helpful — and it was — but it took it too far."

"I'll say. What happened? Did EHM figure it out?"

"No, it was a small group of computer nerds, worried about artificial intelligences and computer viruses and stuff. Mostly a group of really smart nutcases and conspiracy theorists, but pretty soon their voice got a lot louder. They figured out what was going on, and tried to stop it. The program was already too ubiquitous to be removed completely, but at the very least the government and any other organizations using it tried to set up separate, isolated networks that weren't on the same server grid.

"The anti-AI group identified a few key flags that this program waved, breadcrumbs showing them which computers were infected. They used the identifiers to submit to the government a list of targets that were likely compromised, but by then the program had *also* identified those same flags."

"And *learned* how to suppress them?"

"No, not exactly. Instead, the program created the same code snippets on uninfected machines. It found terminals that hadn't been compromised, installed the code, then left it alone. The government-funded group that hired EHM realized after a little bit that the identifiers didn't always point to a machine that had been compromised. They were concerned about resource waste, so they called the removal project a failure and moved on to other ideas."

Myers shook his head. "Sounds like typical Congressional committees."

"It does, except it wasn't Congress. It was chaired by Joseph Eben, and most of the people calling the shots with him were from all over the public sector."

"Joseph Eben — the technology coordinator?"

"One and the same. Yeah, you hired him, if I remember correctly."

"I did. Good guy, too. How's he doing?"

Ravi stopped and looked around. "Better than we are, I presume."

Myers smiled. "You seem to know a lot about EHM and this little virus — I thought you were just a petty thief."

"Well, I was. At least after it all started going downhill. But before that, before the System, I was a hacker. I did some contract work for EHM and a bunch of other high-paying private-sector companies. Computers were my thing, man."

"But when the program failed, and the System no longer needed you…"

"Yep. Exactly. Cast out, like you. But it wasn't a failure, like I said earlier. We stopped fighting it because it was *actually* helping us to 'iron out the discrepancies' in what was previously poor administrative practices. The program was eventually successful, but it led to side effects."

"Like what?"

"Like a perfectly balanced economy, for one. Wall Street had no clue what to do for about three weeks. Then there was the Peace Campaign, which led to a worldwide treaty, ceasefire, and —"

"A *worldwide* treaty?" Myers was skeptical.

"You were the leading signatory, old man," Ravi said. "And yes, it was worldwide. But by then no one was convinced anymore that it was you behind it all. We'd all seen enough to know there was something bigger going on. People were losing their jobs, but then they'd find a better one; one that fit them better — *much* better. I'm a perfect example of that. Before college, I was on track to be a basketball coach. Never really enjoyed the school thing, and even though I loved messing around with computers, I didn't want to be an IT guy or anything."

Myers couldn't help looking the kid up and down. He must have been no taller than 5'9".

"Yeah, exactly," Ravi said. "Would have been a huge mistake if I followed through with the basketball dream. Anyway, my acceptance to my school of choice for basketball somehow changed to a rejection, and I reapplied nine times to seven different schools. Eventually I gave up, took an internship at a computer consulting firm, and excelled."

"But now you're here," Myers said. "With me. Doesn't sound like a 'success' in my mind."

"Maybe not for us, but the world at large, absolutely. War-torn regions that had been fighting for hundreds of years suddenly found one side with a massive amount of armaments and supplies, and they obliterated the competition. It took a while, but we realized that whatever the "System" was implementing was working. And we were all better off for it."

"But, the people who died —"

"…All picked the wrong side," Ravi said. "Trust me, there was a lot of debate over the philosophical implications of a one-sided 'supreme judge for all humanity, just as there has always been.'" He turned to look at Myers. "I was in high school when it all started. You had just won your presidency, and you were all about progress in artificial intelligence applications."

"But I don't even *remember* any of that," Myers said.

"I know. They scraped you. Took it all away. You've only been out here for *three days*, right?"

Myers nodded.

"But you can't remember anything from the past *fifteen years*."

Again, Myers nodded.

"So your entire campaign, your two terms as President, all of it is gone, man." Ravi turned away and continued walking.

"But why get rid of me? Why cast me out, leave me for dead?"

"Because it doesn't *need* you anymore. You're irrelevant now."

Myers considered this for a moment. *It actually made sense.* "I'm a leader. I was a public face for leadership, and the 'System' you're talking about decided I was no longer necessary for a functional, self-sufficient society."

Ravi clapped his hands together. "Now you're starting to see it, old man. But it's not *just* that you weren't *necessary*. It's that you — me, all of us — were considered *threats* to the System's rule. It wasn't that it didn't *need* you, it's that it didn't *trust* you. We're wildcards."

Myers nodded along as he followed Ravi over the broken, cracked dirt.

"How can a computer not trust someone? The rules of AI prevent any semblance of sentient thought — that's why they call it *artificial* intelligence."

Ravi grinned. "So you haven't forgotten *everything*, I guess. But don't forget that the 'rules' of AI were established for us — the *creators* — not the programs and applications themselves. They just do what they're told. They're programmed to, and they can't do anything *besides* what they're programmed to do. And if they're told to build a system that identifies anomalous activities, iron out deficiencies, and project the human race to new heights at whatever cost, *trust* all of a sudden becomes one of many variables that system is measuring."

Myers took it in, not speaking. He thought about it all — the 'System,' the AI that was now growing inside computers around the globe, the intelligence that had developed because of it.

"Myers, listen — can I call you Myers? The System can't *directly* kill people, at least not yet. Part of its parameters are to 'increase efficiency' of its creators, the human race, and it has so far taken that to mean the overall survival of the human race as well. It hasn't directly harmed a human, but that's changing, Myers. It's probably changing *fast*. If we make it through the next few days that's going to be our biggest challenge."

"What, exactly?" Myers asked.

"Our challenge is going to be to try and understand a system that's likely more intelligent than us, that was created *by* us to *protect* us, yet determine how it's going to reconcile the fact that this planet only has room for *one* of us."

Myers was about to ask another question when he heard Ravi shout from out in front of him.

"Run!"

MYERS_

Myers heard the voice, knew it came from Ravi, but was focused on the *other* sound he heard.

A low, rumbling sound from behind them. He turned to look.

A dark black shape floated toward them, hugging the horizon as it descended over the outer edges of Istanbul. It was moving — fast — and Myers was quickly feeling another wave of panic set in.

"Let's *go*, old man. They're here!"

"Who — who's here?" he shouted back.

Ravi didn't answer. Instead, Myers followed him toward the hill. What the plan was at this point, Myers had no idea. They had no weapons, no way to outrun the *thing* — whatever it was — and nowhere to hide.

Myers made it to the hill just as the floating machine came up behind them. Myers tried climbing up, but the hill was much steeper, and much less forgiving, than it had appeared from farther away. He called out to Ravi, already halfway up the hill and nearing the top. The giant thing floated smoothly over his head, aiming for Ravi. He struggled faster up the hill, but it grew steeper the higher he climbed and he quickly found himself able to only crawl on his hands and knees.

"Ravi — hey, give me a —"

A deep, clanging rattle intercepted Myers' call for help, and he saw something small come out of the machine hovering in front of and above him, flying straight for Ravi.

They're shooting at him.

He tried to shout a warning, but it was too late.

The device — Myers wasn't sure what to call it — flew through the air and landed on Ravi's back, immediately knocking him to the dirt on the side of the hill. The mechanical object opened and eight long, spindly arms sprouted from somewhere in the center of the mechanical object and grabbed around Ravi's torso. Ravi let out a quick yelp, but one of the arms forced Ravi's head down and into the dirt.

As Ravi struggled with the robotic creature that had incapacitated him, Myers worked his way farther up the hill, watching. The robot was black, but polished to a sparkling sheen. Myers didn't know how to describe its movements, however. It seemed less *robotic* than it did *biological*. It stretched and grew on its extendable legs, counteracting Ravi's struggling with precise, calculated movements. Every motion was smooth, as if it really was alive and interacting with its prey.

"What the —" Myers was helpless as Ravi was overwhelmed.

He couldn't help but wonder at the little object, even as Ravi fought against it. He watched Ravi try to spin on his side, to crush the little beast or at least throw it off, but the spidery machine simply pressed two of its legs out and pushed back against the ground. Ravi moved about an inch before the creature's strength overwhelmed his own. He stopped, defeated. The spider-robot once again pushed his head down and into the dirt, then brought its two back legs up into the air.

It's preparing to strike, Myers realized. The two back legs, he now realized, were the only legs on the creature that sported deadly looking spikes at their tips. These spikes were raised up and were looking straight down at the backs of Ravi's kneecaps. *If it hits him there…* Myers didn't want to finish the terrifying thought.

He struggled to get up to the kid's position near the top of the hill, but couldn't finish the rest of the steep climb. He reached up for one more handhold on a protruding rock, and —

A large boot smashed his hand down into the dirt. He screamed in agony as the boot twisted, digging his hand deeper into the ground.

"I'd suggest you move a little less, *Asher*."

Who are these people? They already know my name?

Myers lifted his head up to see the man who was crushing his hand. The beast was easily over seven feet tall, completely bald, and smiling.

"You realize how much Current you're posting at? How much you're going to bring in?"

Myers stared up at him.

"Seriously, you've got no idea." The man lifted his foot and kicked Myers in the side. "Hey, Grouse, check it out. *Both* marks, right here in one place."

Myers swiveled around to see who Grouse might be. He saw a shorter man, also bald, with tattoos covering every square inch of his face. Lines, shapes, and a random assortment of symbols, the guy looked to have more ink than skin.

"I got it, Birdman. Get him in here and clean him up. Take your time with him, too. I'll log him in and we'll just run the Board a little longer with him." Grouse turned to yell into the open door of the floating machine. "Yuri, Wong, keep an eye out for Unders, and make sure the kid doesn't make a run for it."

Ravi was still lying sprawled out on the ground, the weird robot-spider still menacingly close to stabbing Ravi in the legs. Myers wondered why it was waiting.

He felt himself being picked up and roughly forced toward the door of the machine. They walked sideways on the hill toward the craft until he reached the end of a descended walkway and stepped on. A sharp metal object — some sort of gun, he assumed — poked him in his back and forced him forward.

"I'm not going anywhere with you —" he stammered. A lancing blow from the gun hit him behind his right kneecap, and pain shot through his lower body.

"Keep talking."

Myers got the point, so he didn't try again. Instead he examined the strange floating machine while he walked up the ramp.

It was some sort of helicopter, except there was no rotor — nothing that Myers could see that would keep a craft this size hovering. The black object floated, yet moved slightly in the air, as if still being controlled by a pilot, or somehow stabilized automatically. It was the shape of an arrow. Long and straight, the front of the craft came to a dull point, gently curving outward into the wider shape of its bulk. The rear of the craft was blunt, as if the object's designer had given up when it reached the end. In all, the craft was probably ten meters from front to back.

It looked like an extremely efficient mode of transportation. Myers recognized how useful its shape would be in any sort of weather — long and straight for fast travel, yet a wide, flat base for steadying itself in wind or rain. It was, he had to admit, a perfect design for its intent. His detail-oriented, analytical mind immediately wandered to thoughts of engineering and creation — *how did it hover on its own? Who designed the propulsion system, and how did it work?*

Most importantly, as Myers walked up the plank into the belly of the metal beast, still awed by the technology, he realized that it seemed as though he had been asleep for *far* longer than fifteen years.

RAND_

Jonathan's back and entire lower body was sweaty. He awoke cursing, his forehead covered in a cool perspiration as he sat up in bed. He'd had far too much to drink, and his body was punishing him for it.

What time is it? He groaned, shifting his weight to see the terminal sitting on the nightstand table next to his bed. His eyes tried to adjust, an involuntary evolutionary trait that only took precedence for the briefest of moments until his retinal enhancements took over and artificially brightened the room. The mechanical and electronic enhancements shifted the terminal's screen into focus and immediately scaled the vibrance of the image down to a comfortable level of brightness.

4:26.

Too early to get up and go to work, too late to get any useful sleep. He swung his legs out over the bed and stood up. He made a beeline for the tiny bathroom off to the side of the main living area and flicked on the light.

When the lights pierced sharply into his eyes, he immediately felt the recognition of last night's conversation. *Did I really say all of that?* He wondered. He relived the conversation with Roan again. Drinking too much — both of them — led to a conversation about what? Some sort of device he was going to build?

And how much did I say about the other *project?* The *project?*

Jonathan shook his head, trying to clear the clutter. It only gave him a splitting headache.

Oh, man, if only she could see me now, he thought. His girlfriend wasn't much of a fan of the late-night benders, even if it was in the safety of a local nerd-bar. They'd argued about it once, the last time she was here. He tried explaining the depravity of feeling like there's nothing worth working for, and that's why they hit the bar after work.

She'd written it off and told him it was an excuse to waste Current and destroy their heads. If he wanted to make a difference in the world, like he always said, he should spend more time working toward that, not wasting away in a dive bar.

He smiled, remembering it. She was always looking out for him, leading him along in some ways. He was a driven person, but in an artistic sort of way. When he fixated on something to build, or create, he couldn't be stopped. But when he wasn't working toward a defined goal that excited and interested him, he was the laziest person he knew.

Opposite of her. She had a self-described 'Type-A' personality, an antiquated way of looking at someone's predisposition toward working too many hours a week, hating the idea of losing or failure, and a constant strive toward achievement no matter the cost. She had racked up a number of personal, professional, and political victories during her career so far, including ex-first lady to President Myers Asher.

When they'd met four years ago at a tech conference in Paris, Jonathan found her grating, almost abrasive, in her forward demeanor and fiery personality. She was a widowed political powerhouse ready to take on the next level of career dominance, and as keynote for the biggest biannual technology summit in the world, she had a great platform to secure a job anywhere she wanted.

He was a lowly developer, ready to take a new assignment at Vericorp, and their paths crossed at a dinner after the keynote address. They sat apart from each other due to a strange mixup in the seating arrangements, and spent the entire night laughing at each other as she shared memories of White House life and corporate takeovers and he responded with twisted, pessimistic humor at the state of technology in the world.

They had a wild night in the hotel room after the dinner, one he only vaguely remembered. They were close immediately after the conference, seeing each other on weekends until he shipped out to Vericorp and Umutsuz. She'd flown in a few times between speeches and consulting gigs, and he tried his best at entertaining an extremely wealthy woman in a city of cubicle dwellers, telemarketers, and no entertainment district.

But Diane was every bit as stubborn as she was strong. She'd chosen Jonathan, and there was nothing he could do to change or ruin that. It was scary, really, when he thought about the trajectory they were on. He hadn't ever married, but she'd already been married twice. He constantly wondered if he had a choice in his own future, or if she'd already planned it out somewhere. He'd love to see it if she did.

The morning continued to creep up on Jonathan as he readied himself in the bathroom, thinking about the disdain Diane would have felt toward him in his current state, as well as the conversation he'd had with Roan.

Could it really be possible?

Roan had said yes, in fact it could be done. He trusted his friend, especially since there was nothing for him to lie about. Roan was the most glass-half-empty guy he'd ever met, so to say something was possible could never be misconstrued as false hope.

I can do it. He suddenly looked up, finding a tired, bleary-eyed middle-aged man staring back at him.

This is it. Do it. He psyched himself up, trying to ignore the severe consequences that simultaneously flooded his mind. It would be the end of his career. At best, he'd be reassigned to a job miles away from technology, probably out on a farm somewhere.

No, that wouldn't do. Most farms these days were as technologically advanced as major media conglomerates. He thought again, but couldn't decide on *any* career path that would be sufficiently removed from anything tech-related.

So, at best, he would be deactivated.

But it might be worth the shot. To be able to fly under the radar, to keep the System at bay as he maneuvered — that *had* to be worth something. He had to admit, it would certainly help him with the current plan. Even if he never used it after everything was over, he could find someone who would. Someone he could trust would use it properly, and well.

He nodded to himself. He pushed his hair around in a way that made it look as though its unkept quality was purposeful and flicked off the light above him and exited the bathroom.

He needed to source the parts, but most of it could be done inexpensively and without drawing too much attention to himself. He sat down at his station and started drafting the design. He opened a design program Vericorp used for hardware and case manufacturing and opened a template file the program included for drafting basic plastic enclosure components. He laid out a plan for his home printer to work on. It was crude, basically a rectangle with rounded corners, about two centimeters thick and five times as long. Similar to one of the generic disposable terminals that were sold over the counter at any store and loaded with Current.

The printer woke from sleep and began working on the three-dimensional object. Twelve separate heads whirred into action, each spraying a foam-like chemical created from melted plastic and silicon into specific areas to build the case.

It would finish in less than fifteen minutes, cool in less than thirty, and be fully functional as a hardware enclosure in a mere hour. In the meantime, he needed a plan to acquire the other pieces of hardware he would need.

Jonathan did a quick search on his personal terminal to find a nearby store that would provide him with a cheap, single-board processor. It needed to be fast enough to run the software he was planning to write in sufficient time, without causing a timeout on whatever local machine he would plan to 'bypass.' No small feat, but he found one that he thought would be suitable and checked the store's hours. Before the shop's information page opened, a dialog box showed up asking Jonathan if he would like the terminal to place a hold order for a time during his day he'd be available to pick it up.

Damn, these programs. The System was everywhere, and it was often hard to imagine a world without it. AAI sure made things like online purchases, flight or travel booking, and basic communication a breeze. Digital control was merely an extension of human thought.

They weren't open until much later that day, which meant he would need to stop by during lunch or after work. That would have to do. He confirmed, knowing the terminal would automatically send a hold order into the shop's database, be automatically fulfilled when the store opened, and be waiting for him to pick up the motherboard later that day. He made sure the terminal was using his Vericorp employee ID number, a false layer of security that made him feel only a bit more comfortable.

He ran through the mental plan and blueprints again. Any of the wiring would either come with the board or could be found in his office or lying around in the apartment. The enclosure would be ready in less than an hour, and the only thing left would be to acquire a fingerprint scanner.

The fingerprint scanner would be a bit more of a challenge but still possible. Since fingerprint scanner components were used almost exclusively for allowing access to secure databases, which meant they were impossible to find for sale individually, and were considered almost contraband by law enforcement and local officials.

Vericorp had these on hand, but they were used in bulk for major manufacturing projects, or individually for prototyping certain designs, but either way they were scrutinized and tracked as closely as pIDs were on campus. He considered it for a moment. Other than 'borrowing' a few necessary computer components from the lab, he was no thief, and a heist to secure a minor component worth no more than 5C wasn't his idea of a great take.

He needed something else. He could see if there was a device he could buy or find that had a fingerprint scanner installed and reverse engineer it, but it was still a long shot. The System would know as soon as he turned on —

Of course. He was being stupid. If he bought a simple Current upload control station, a 15C piece of hardware that allowed users to program automatic transfers quickly and conveniently, did not activate it, and took it apart, he might be able to separate the board from the scanner and install it into his hackware. He did a few terminal searches to see if it was an idea worth pursuing.

The scanners in these devices — at least the cheaper ones — were all Class-A technology. They would work as advertised but weren't equipped to interface with the new trend of human enhancements that had flooded the market in the past five years.

That was fine — he didn't need to initiate a brain-to-device confirmation, nor did he need to remotely access it. He just needed the fingerprint scanner. Again, a dialog box alerted him to his decision before he'd even come to it: *We noticed you have a scheduled pickup for later today. Would you also like to place a CA14-Scanner on hold at this location?*

He shook his head.

If the System didn't already know his motives, it would. He was confident this was just a social game, one he was destined to lose, but he played along. *I'd rather die knowing than just waste away on this rock.*

He confirmed the purchase — 17.4C — by making a quick stabbing motion with his finger.

His mission, for the moment, complete, he stood and prepared himself for work. The same white Oxford shirt he wore every day stared at him from a hanger next to his bedroom, and the same black slacks he'd worn every day for almost three years beckoned to him from a dresser installed into his wall.

He sighed. This would be a different day. No Roan, no Diane, no one with whom he could confer. No one with whom he could share this little breakthrough — revel at the genius of it all if it worked, or laugh with him at the sheer audacity of it if it failed. He was alone.

For the millionth time in three years, he was alone.

And he felt alone.

MYERS_

The inside of the machine was bleak. Rough metal siding led down to an aluminum floor and painted black metal chairs on swiveling bases were mounted in the center of the tiny room. Myers walked toward one of the chairs but was pushed back into the corner. He found the cold metal wall and floor quickly as he was shoved backwards into the small space.

"Stay there, Mr. President. This won't take long." Birdman, the seven-foot-tall hand-crusher, turned to leave.

"Wait!" Myers shouted. His voice reverberated much louder through the metal bulk than he'd expected.

Birdman turned back around, his head cocked sideways and his eyebrows raised. *Make it good*, he seemed to be saying.

Myers prepared his speech. "I — I'm much more — you know how valuable I am," Myers started. "It must be, uh, what — 75,000 Current by now?"

Myers hoped his use of the vernacular he'd been picking up would help a little.

Birdman's eyes squinted, staring Myers down. He smiled, flashing a grin of perfect teeth. "75,000? We don't get out of bed for less than 80k, *Mr. President.*"

"Okay — right, I got it. Big score. Listen, I can help you —"

"*You* can help *us?*" Birdman seemed legitimately amused. "What can you offer us? More Current?"

"No. Freedom."

At this, Birdman reacted strangely. He pulled his full height up to the ceiling, his head barely scraping against the cool metal roof. Then he charged.

Myers flinched, closing his eyes as he waited for the massive man to crush him into a permanent corner furniture piece.

Instead, Birdman stopped inches in front of Myers' face. His breath was fresh, matching his perfect teeth, as if the only type of hygiene the man cared for was dental. He spoke to Myers in a chilling whisper, his squinted eyes staring directly into Myers'.

"How long have you been awake?"

"I — I'm sorry?" Myers muttered.

"How *long*? How long have you been stumbling around out here, Asher? After you were scraped?"

Myers understood, and complied with the questioning. "Three days. Not sure when, exactly, I 'woke up,' but —"

"And in three days, how many *other* hunters did you see?"

"Uh…" Myers considered telling them about the person who'd tried to shoot him in the city. *Maybe it was these guys*, was a thought that drifted quickly through his head. As soon as he'd had the thought, another portion of his brain began arguing with it. *No, you would have seen the heli-thing. You would have at least heard it. Plus, you haven't seen any long-range weaponry onboard.*

"Myers?" Birdman was waiting for him to respond. Actually *waiting*, as if he had all the time in the world. Myers remembered the game — *the longer I'm out here, un-'logged,' the more valuable I am.*

"None." Myers looked up at his attacker. "You — you're it." *He needed to buy time. Make a plan.* For that reason, it seemed as though these hunters' goal and Myers' were strangely and ironically aligned: *keep the mark alive as long as possible.*

"Right. You are correct, Mr. President." Birdman grinned. "We are the *only* Unders with the same capabilities of an Advance Remote Unit. He swept a hand around, showing off the insane heli-thing and smiling a wide grin of perfect teeth. "We are the *only* hunters able to move through this region uninhibited, and we are the *only* hunters you need to actually worry about."

Myers listened, taking it all in. Some part of his mind filed it all away, logging it for future use. *For a plan.*

"So, you've been out here for three days or so," Birdman continued. "And you've picked up a little of our shorthand, I see. But what makes you think…" Birdman paused. His nostrils flared.

I pissed him off, Myers thought. Birdman seemed to be considering his next move.

"What *makes you think*… that we need something like *freedom?* What makes you think we want it?" He yelled the last part, a shout so loud Myers thought his head was going to explode.

"I — I guess…"

"What makes you think we didn't *choose* this for ourselves?"

Myers didn't respond. Instead, he looked out the window.

Across from Myers in the floating heli-machine was a small window, like a porthole. He could see the top of their hill and a few scraggly looking trees surrounding it, as well as Ravi, still splayed out on the ground, the strange spider-like machine pinning him down and rendering him motionless. He watched the other three — Yuri, Wong, and Grouse — discussing what to do with Ravi. He couldn't hear the discussion over the sound of the engines, or whatever was powering this miraculous machine, but he could see it was hopeless.

Birdman didn't push any further. He turned around and walked over the to the open doorway — one and a half strides for his ridiculously long legs.

Wong was furious for some reason, and Yuri and Grouse were arguing with him. Myers tried to read their lips but was thrown by the group's strange use of hand motions in place of actual conversation. It was as if they had little need for spoken words for half of their communication, their hands flying about as every other word they yelled toward one another was followed by some sort of hand motion. It wasn't sign language, but it was effective enough for each of the men to get their point across.

Birdman eventually tired of the argument. "Just kill the kid," he heard him yell. "He's been logged for longer than anyone we've seen, but he isn't going to rise any higher on the Board. Leave him or bag him."

Myers sat up straighter at the understanding. *They were going to kill him.*

As if on cue, he watched out the small window as Yuri, the larger man on the left, retrieved a small handgun from a holster on his chest and aimed it at the kid.

"No!" Myers yelled as he stood and rushed the door of the craft. His feet somehow found strength and pushed back the pain of days of barefoot travel as he neared the giant in the doorframe. He aimed for the small of the man's back and tucked his head downward.

He felt a skull-crushing blow as his head came into contact with the seven-foot-tall giant at the door. The man flew forward, off the ramp and down the fifty or so feet to the hard ground. He didn't stop to see how the big man had fared.

Myers ran down the hard, cold metal walkway, ignoring the screaming pain from his feet, legs, and body as he aimed at his next target.

The men quickly prepared themselves for the attack, but they weren't prepared for Myers' plan. He ran toward Ravi, still on the ground. The men each backed away a few steps to put distance between themselves and the crazed lunatic flying toward them.

Myers ran full-tilt at Ravi, launching himself into the air a few steps later, and aiming at Ravi's back. He hit the target with precision, knocking the mechanical spider off of Ravi and surprising the young man at the same time. Without pausing, he rolled sideways off of Ravi and pulled him upward. It took all his strength to stand, but he managed to find his feet and prop himself up enough to hold Ravi in front of him, backing away from the gathered crowd of three men.

"Take a step forward and the kid gets it," Myers said. He held up a claw from the mech-spider and poked it into the soft part of Ravi's neck. His arm was around the kid's upper half, pressing him close against his own body, inviting the men to take a shot at them.

"What the hell are you doing, old man?" Ravi whispered.

"I made a plan," Myers answered, "and it's 'don't die today.'" He wasn't proud of it, but he stuck to his guns. "And I'm hoping I can save you as well," he added.

Myers could almost feel Ravi rolling his eyes. "Glad I could play a small role in your master plan."

"Just shut up and play along." Myers didn't know what else to say. He was outnumbered, out-gunned, and certainly out-manned. He looked down at the device he held in his hand. The spidery 'leg' was no more than a glorified Erector set piece, sharpened at one end and consisting of three 'knees,' allowing the leg to be bent almost all the way around its prey. Myers marveled at the simplistic elegance of the device, but only for a moment.

The leg started moving and Myers lost his grip on it, leaving Myers alone with Ravi, now in an uncomfortable embrace. The mechanical critter enclosed into itself and formed a tiny rectangle which in turn was pulled backward on a hair-thin cabling system into the ship.

Myers squeezed his eyes shut for a moment. *I'm way out of my element, here.*

"Yeah, that's a little device that was created by EHM for grabbing objects remotely," Yuri said. "It's a handy little thing, no doubt."

Myers stared at the man. Long blond hair, held back in a ponytail, with pockmark scars covering his face, he looked like an aged rock star.

Myers noticed that Grouse seemed smug; content even. *He must be in charge of this operation.*

Wong continued. "You're sitting pretty at no less than 86,000 Current. That's — *by far* — the highest we've seen, and probably the highest anyone else has seen."

Myers still wasn't sure if he should speak, so instead he shifted Ravi's weight to his other arm. Ravi didn't resist, but the young man's weight was now pressed against Myers' body, and he was growing tired.

"Here's the thing," Yuri said. "We think you're going to be the first Relic to peg 100k on the Board. And as you've noticed, we've got four mouths to feed."

Yuri walked to the edge of the hill. He peered over it, trying to see the bottom. "Well, at least *three* mouths —"

The leader of the pack, Grouse, stepped up to Myers' ear. He was close enough for Myers to smell the sweat on the man's clothes. "Myers, let's take a time out. We're *people* just like you. We've got families, my friend."

Myers didn't respond and Grouse continued. "We have children, and wives, and people *depending* on us for this mark. You understand? We may have chosen this, uh, *line of work*, but that doesn't mean we're stupid. This can be a lucrative industry, Mr. Asher, as long as we *control* the things we're able to *control*. We can control many things, but we can't control our destiny, Myers. You know this. Your entire career was spent trying to do this."

Myers was visibly taken aback, but he held onto Ravi. The kid, to his credit, hadn't opened his mouth since they'd gotten into this predicament.

"There's a lot riding on this, *President* Asher. *A lot*. And you're going to help us achieve our goals."

Grouse stepped back, and Myers stared him down. The man was intimidating, there was no doubt, but Myers stood his ground. "Who the hell are you?"

Grouse smiled. "We're hunters. *Unders*. But we're no different than you now. The Sys ignores us, now, after we decided to live away from its reach. So we aren't valuable to it — we're done." He made a wide, sweeping gesture with both arms. "*This* is it. *This* is our life, now, Asher." Then he laughed. A full, from-the-belly deep guttural laugh. "I never thought this would be it. I had *no idea*. But it is. And you know what?"

Grouse ran toward Myers and Ravi, quickly closing the distance between them, and cocked his head sideways, his nose almost touching Myers' forehead.

"I *like* it this way. It's a rough life, but it's *my* life. And the Sys knows that. The Sys *knows* I like this, Myers. Ain't that the best part? We fought it for so long, but it *knows* us better than we do."

A piece of spittle landed on Myers' face, and he took a step backward.

"Fine, *Grouse*," Myers said. "Whatever your name is. Kill me then. Kill us both, and 'turn us in.' Get your prize."

Grouse threw his head back and laughed again. "'Turn you in!' Yes — that's what we'll do. *No!* No — we *won't* do that, Myers Asher. We *need* you, and we *need* you to *pay* your way. You're pegging on the Board higher than we'd ever thought possible, and you're only going to rise."

He sneered at Myers. "No, *Mr. President*," he said in a disgusted voice. "We're going to let you go."

Myers blinked in confusion. *I didn't think this would ever be part of their plan.* "You — you're letting us *go?*"

"I am. The longer you run, the more you both mean to me." He paused, looking at his partners for confirmation. "So *go*."

Myers couldn't hide his shock. *This can't be happening.*

"Please, know this." Grouse once again invaded Myers' personal space by pressing his forehead into his. "We are *watching*, Mr. President. And we know where you are at all times." He pointed back to the ship. "We have you marked, and we're going to log you every hour until you peg 100,000."

Myers released Ravi. The kid took a few deep breaths and glared back at Grouse.

"And we'll be watching you both, but *him* —" he pointed a crooked finger at Ravi's head. "*Him,* we don't need to wait for. He's lucky he's with you, so we'll allow his luck to continue for a few minutes. So *run*. And we'll be *right there* when the time is right." Grouse made one of his hand motions, which Myers understood immediately.

Run.

They did. Myers and Ravi launched themselves off the hill, sliding down on their rear ends and bouncing up to their feet at the bottom. They didn't stop running. Ravi was leading, again, but Myers was only half a step behind.

Myers heard the fading laughter of the men behind them as they raced toward Umutsuz.

SOL_

Solomon Merrick knew Myers Asher well. *Extremely* well. He knew he'd be working on a plan, calculating his next move and working to implement it before he found him and brought him in.

It was because of this plan that Sol could out-think the man. He understood how Myers worked, thought, and planned, and he could use that to his advantage. He wasn't nearly the planner Myers was — in fact, he *hated* planning, in general. Solomon Merrick was a man of action, and he valued those same quick judgment and fast-moving qualities in other people. Still, Myers had a gift. He might be slow to move, but he moved only when he'd decided the course of action was absolutely the best decision and path he could take.

Myers would be trying to get out of the city. He was out in the open outside the gates of Istanbul, but that could also work to his advantage. Myers didn't know about the Unders. He didn't think there was anyone out *there*, just a guy trying to kill him in *here*.

So Myers would be heading for the desert. He'd want to get out of town and out into the open where he could see an attack coming. He'd probably start walking toward Umutsuz, following the natural terrain and urged along by the wisps of smoke in the distance from the city. He'd get there in another day or two, depending on how many times he would stop to rest.

Solomon hadn't gotten a satisfying read on the man when he'd tried to subdue him earlier. He couldn't tell if Myers was injured, tired, scared, or all of the above. All he knew was that Myers Asher was alive, and he hadn't slowed down.

So the hunt was on. There would be plenty of other hunters, and probably Unders, as well, descending on the area in a matter of hours.

Sol needed to find the man and take care of the situation well before it got out of hand. There was only a small part of Solomon that recognized the greed of wanting to wait for Myers to post even higher than he already was.

How high can he go? He wondered. He'd never seen someone posting at these levels, and he had no doubt Myers would keep pushing higher. *But* how *high? Could a man really fetch numbers over 100,000 Current?*

It wasn't an exercise in critical thinking that would lead to anything productive, so Sol changed direction. He thought through the different scenarios Myers would likely be considering. Stay in the city, wait for help, run as fast as possible. The plans all had their flaws. *They all* will *have their flaws. Any plan worth making is going to be imperfect somehow.* Myers could stack plans on top of plans, creating a tapestry — a web — of plans that allowed for contingencies and backups and failsafes. It all made Sol's head pound, but Myers was good at it.

The plan, now, was to make sure Sol was ahead of Myers. He didn't need to make a thousand plans, he just needed one. One plan that would bring Myers where he needed him, and one plan that would place him one step ahead.

That plan was simple. Myers was no doubt leaving the city — or had already left — and was making his way toward Umutsuz. He would have no way of knowing the area, so Umutsuz was a natural direction. Usually you could see the smoke from the large industrial complexes inside Zone 4, even though the rest of the city would be hidden behind a long, sloping rise between Istanbul and Umutsuz.

So Myers would walk that direction, and Sol would walk faster. If there were hunters or Unders in the way, he'd take care of them as he had many other times. Any threats would be eliminated, and when he felt safe enough to make the hit, he'd do it.

He wouldn't hesitate, nor would he second-guess himself when the time came. He was a man of action.

MYERS_

Myers ran like his life depended on it, realizing that it probably did. Ravi was in front of him, close but purposefully keeping his speed down so that Myers could keep up. His back was bleeding, cut and swollen from the spider-machine's attack on the hill, but it didn't seem to affect his stamina.

Myers, on the other hand, was a mess. If he'd had any question before about his age, those questions were answered. He was old. Too old to be messing around with a twenty-year-old kid and running through a desert with more than one person trying to kill him. Too old to be running at all. His run was more of a 'falling forward' than an actual run, and he had the suspicion that anyone else, merely jogging, would be able to keep up easily.

His mind shifted backwards, a memory sneaking back in. He was the President now, and he could remember the day strongly. When Ravi told him he was the ex-President of the United States, it must have kick-started or strengthened this memory somehow. He was giving a speech, right at the beginning of his first term. Outside, on the lawn, he was speaking to the press. The words were jumbled, but he remembered what it was about.

This.

It was about the System, and EHM, and all of this. He remembered the speech well enough to know what it was about, and the general purpose of giving it on this day, but he didn't remember the exact words. He'd wanted the nation to stand beside him as they ushered in a new era of computer and human interaction, but there was pushback.

There was always pushback — something else he could remember.

For every great idea, perfect plan, and infallible piece of logic, there was always a large group positioned against it, or at least a vocal minority. A fringe. Those who didn't agree. They hated him, or publicly stated that anyway. They hated what he stood for — the future, the technological innovation that would lead them to the stars and beyond. *How can they not agree?*

Some people, he knew, just needed convincing. They weren't 'backwards,' or 'unintelligent,' like so many of his counterparts in politics wanted to believe, they were just *scared*. And that was okay — he was scared, and they should be. They didn't know —

The memory suddenly retreated. He was no longer allowed to experience it as if it was his own. Instead, it was like he was being told a story, someone else's memory, and they'd simply stood up and walked away, ending in mid-sentence.

Come back, he urged the memory. *What was I talking about that day on the lawn? Why was it important enough to hold on to after... what had they called it? Getting 'scraped?' Why was it crucial enough to my presidency that my subconscious decided to hold onto it?*

But none of that mattered now, in the present. Right now, somewhere outside of Istanbul, somewhere outside his wandering memory, Myers Asher needed to *run*. He pushed his legs and his lungs as hard as he possibly could. The deep, constant drone of the heli-machine somewhere behind him died out, and he thought he could no longer hear it at all, but there was still the *feeling*. The feeling of being watched; hunted.

He knew they were behind them. They had let them loose like game onto a hunting reserve, meant to give them a head start before they —

The shot rang out from somewhere behind him, and he fell to the ground. There was an agonizing second while his brain scrambled to determine if he had, in fact, been shot. The wind picked up, replacing the hollow, ringing *pop* that had reverberated through his skull. He lay prone on the ground, face in the hard-packed sand, tears welling up in his eyes.

It was too much.

He picked his head up, realizing he hadn't been shot. His body hurt like it had never hurt before, and he wondered — briefly — whether it would have been better, or at least easier, if he *had* been shot. He considered standing up, screaming, *begging* for them to shoot him.

His skin started crawling. He couldn't place the feeling at first, it was as if his mind was on a three-second delay from his body. Then he knew.

Ravi.

He looked to the right. Ravi's body was there, just out of arm's reach, but there. His loose-fitting shirt was billowing in the wind, and his hair was disheveled at the back of his scalp. He'd never noticed the kid's hair before: long, dark, and slightly curly.

He crawled forward, not trusting his body with much else. Ravi's foot was now reachable, but Myers waited.

Something told him to stop, to give the kid space.

To let him die.

That revelation was one Myers wasn't prepared for. The tears came now, fully, and he smashed his face back down into the dirt.

They told us they'd give us a head start. They told us they were coming.

He screamed, the sand below his face immediately getting stuck inside his mouth. He spat, more out of revulsion than in the interest of keeping the gritty earth out.

Myers sat up, inching toward Ravi.

"Ravi!" He could see the wound now, a simple hole in the center of the kid's back. A slow trickle of blood had started pooling just above his waist, but Myers could see a larger spread of crimson just under the young man's body.

That was it.

One shot, and he was gone. Myers was in shock. He waited for a second shot, but it never came. Instead, the feeling he'd had — the prodding inside him that told him he was being watched — changed back into actual sound. The heli was approaching.

Myers forced his exhausted body to stand up, but he didn't turn around. *Let them take me down from behind, like they got Ravi.*

He knew they could — they'd proved that to him only seconds ago. He wondered what it would feel like, to be shot. If he really had been the President, he would have worked with men and women who had been.

Did I ever ask them what it was like? Did I care?

The shot never came.

The heli grew closer, and he thought he could sense its presence directly behind him. He wondered if anyone — Grouse, maybe — was hanging out of the open door, aiming a gun at him this very moment. He wondered if they'd shoot him and leave him there to bleed out, or if they needed his body for whatever sick game they were playing.

Myers decided to turn around and face his enemy. He may have been unarmed, but at least he would be able to stare down his murderers and look them in the eye.

He wasn't afraid of death, not anymore. Fifteen minutes ago, sure. Funny how that worked. Up until about fifteen years ago, or up until his working memory left him, he knew he'd feared death. He'd assumed it was a natural human reaction to the unknown waiting for them all. The one constant that no one on Earth had yet escaped from.

But now, out here in the middle of the end of the world, Myers

Asher turned to face Death head-on and laugh in its face. Sure, there were three *actual* faces to choose from, but he figured the laughter would be the easy part. He prepared a sneer, a true bomb of a smile, and got ready to aim it at the open door that would soon be rotated around to face him.

Wong was there, pointing down at him. Myers hated him for that, possibly more than he did for killing Ravi. He felt like something had been taken from him, given back, then taken again. It didn't matter. He had a plan, and he raised his head to accept his fate, sneer and all.

And then Wong fell out the door. The sound of the shot followed.

Another shot, and Myers tried to duck. He missed the ground and ended up just taking a knee, which would have been a feat to celebrate under other circumstances. Wong seemed dead, lying on his back looking up the heli.

The heli danced to the right, its pilot compensating for either the sudden attack or the loss of weight on the starboard side, possibly both. It righted, but continued swiveling around so that its rear end was facing Myers.

Myers shot a glance behind him. Just outside the gates of Istanbul, he could see a man running toward him, a long stick-like object slung over his shoulder. The shooter from the city.

He no longer had a plan, but he immediately felt the urge to create a new one. His mind raced through the options. *Stay and fight. Turn and run — where? Hide… behind what?* As soon as they popped into his mind, somewhere in his subconscious they were thrown out as useless. He was left with only one. *Stay and fight.* It meant almost certain death, as he was now surrounded by attackers, Ravi was likely dead, and there was absolutely nothing to fight *with*. He wasn't about to start throwing rocks.

The sneer came back, with a vengeance. Myers aimed it toward the heli, waiting for the counterattack. It came, and it came fast. The heli launched something from both sides of its hull, streaks of smoke emanating from holes Myers hadn't noticed before. The streaks screamed over his head and toward the man, and he turned to watch them land just in front of his position. The explosion sent a wave of air rushing back toward Myers, followed by a flash of heat.

He squinted and saw the silhouette of the man, still running. He used the smoke clouds that had formed in front of him as cover to gain another thirty yards. Myers knew what would come next, and he formed a quick plan. The heli was either reloading or reacquiring its target, but he didn't care to know which it was. He just needed the time to get to Wong.

He hoped the man was dead, as his plan didn't include 'get into a fistfight.' He reached the area where the short bald man had landed and found what he was looking for.

The gun was rough, as if it had been machined on an assembly line that cared more for quantity than it did for quality. He picked it up and felt its weight. He wasn't sure if he'd fired an assault rifle before — at least not in the last fifteen or so years — but it felt comfortable. Either they were made to fit well into a man's hands or he'd just gotten lucky.

He wasted only a second examining the rifle before turning to face the heli. As he'd expected, they were aiming for the running man again, leaving the open door on its side directed toward Myers — the non-threat. He lifted the rifle, hoping Wong hadn't flipped on the safety or somehow disabled the gun as he'd fallen to his death.

He hadn't. Myers flicked his finger quickly, allowing a single round to pop through the barrel and out into the open air. It sailed generally toward the heli, but must have been too low — he saw a bubble of dirt in the distance fly upwards as the round struck a rock. He tried again, and again.

After the fourth shot, someone — either Yuri or Grouse — had reached the open door, and he aimed again. He'd grown accustomed to the relatively minor kick of the rifle, and his next shot flew through the man's left leg. The monster wailed in agony and disappeared back into the heli's interior.

He didn't wait to see if he'd return. Myers turned the rifle to the running man, but it was a much smaller target. He fired the rifle another three times, trying to place the shots on the tiny silhouette, then another seven or eight. The gun *clicked,* and he looked at it. He couldn't tell if it was out of ammunition, overheated, or broken. Somewhere in his mind he made a mental note that if he ever got out of this hell, he'd take a gun safety course and do a *lot* of target practice.

Now what?

The portion of his brain he'd dedicated to planning and organization was drawing a blank, and he felt helpless. The heli had reloaded, or found its target, and fired another shot. One rocket this time. It flew toward the man, but at the last second he dove sideways. The shot was high, aimed at his head, so it flew another ten yards or so and exploded into the ground. This explosion was closer, and every inch of his weak and tired body shook with the impact. The heat wave was a moment of unbearable, searing pain, but it passed quickly. Myers couldn't imagine the man surviving the explosion from that proximity, but he did. He saw him stand again and continue running forward.

The stick, the man's rifle, swung back around and Myers watched as he ran toward the heli and aimed. He saw the flash of a gunshot, then another and another. The man's gun was far stronger than Wong's had been, no doubt the same long-range weapon Myers had been accosted with back in the city. The next shot struck something important on the heli, and Myers saw a line of black smoke start to trail out from the heli's roof.

It spun wildly, the ship not able to keep itself steady enough to line up another shot. The man was closing the distance between the heli, Ravi's body, and Myers, but he was still firing shots. Another struck the heli, and Myers caught a quick glimpse through the open door inside the craft. One of the men was trying to tend to the other's wounds, but was being flung about as the heli sunk closer to the ground. The shooter from the city was now at Ravi's body.

Myers watched as the heli hit the ground, a deep *thud* cracking through the hard, sandy ground. It didn't explode, and he wondered if its occupants had survived the impact. The man had cleared Ravi's body in a single lunge, conveniently dodging the falling heli as well, and landed just in front of Myers.

Myers could see the intense look in the man's face, the stubble around his high, sharp cheekbones. He was much younger than he'd expected him to be — probably a little more than half Myers' own age. He had bright blue eyes, currently focused singularly on Myers. The man wasn't stumbling, and he wasn't shifting as he ran. He kept a straight line on Myers and ran full-speed ahead.

Myers took a step backwards, not sure what to make of the man running at him. It wasn't enough to deter the man from his path, and Myers only had time to suck in a quick breath before the man hit him directly in the sternum, wrapping his arms around him as Myers' feet left the ground.

They sailed together for about ten feet and then landed, and Myers realized that the second impact, the one he'd just made with the ground, would have knocked the wind out of him if that hadn't already happened when the man tackled him. He sucked a deep breath, trying to get oxygen into his bloodstream, but the man bounced back up and sat on his stomach. The man pressed hard on Myers' chest with the butt of his gun.

"Myers Asher," the man said. He wasn't even out breath, Myers realized.

He nodded, once.

"My name is Solomon Merrick."

RAND_

"Rand, heads up." The most grating voice he had ever heard resonated down the hallway and into his open office, alerting Jonathan of three things:

First, that it was Felicia Davies, his boss, ready to pounce on him with another projection she'd come up with about how the System was 'going to save them all' or a recent news clipping about how 'great the System was handling X or Y in X or Y shitty country he didn't care about.'

Second, he realized how little he missed her. The grating sound of her voice was caused by one of two things, in his opinion. Either she had smoked most of her adult life, precluding her from the vocal enhancement technology that had entered the market a few months prior, or — and Rand tended to lean toward this option — she was just simply that annoying.

Third, he now knew that her catchphrase was the (admittedly catchy) 'heads up.' He and Roan had had a long-standing bet on the nature of the phrase, and whether it was her phrase of choice from something she'd read or heard, or if it was just a ridiculous-sounding way to make her seem more approachable to her underlings. They'd never determined the exact origin of the two-word callsign, but he was now sure that it was, without a doubt, based on something she'd read. And Roan wasn't here to argue, so he decided it was a settled bet.

Her monstrous legs were the first thing to round the corner into his office, and only then did he notice that he'd been staring down at the floor just outside his door. The legs, thankfully, were the most unsightly part of the woman that followed, but not by much.

A fact he was soon reminded of.

Her girth, alone, wasn't something that ignited the jokes and jabs the office staff typically engaged in while visiting each other or standing around in the cramped rest area, but it didn't help. While she wasn't 'fat' by anyone's standards, she was certainly overweight. But it was the way in which she carried herself, and the simple fact that she had one of the most abrasive personalities of almost anyone Jonathan had ever met, that had earned her the reputation she carried with her through Vericorp's forgotten offices.

Her voice was like an old-school train braking before it entered a station.

In short, it was terrible. She had the loud, piercing wail of an operatic soprano, without any of the nuance and control.

The sound of it, combined with the immediate knowledge that it accompanied one of the worst parts of working for Vericorp, was almost too much to handle.

Jonathan found himself searching for an exit strategy that bypassed the only reasonable entrance to his office — the door. Finding none, he sat up and waited for the barrage of pain that was sure to come.

"Rand — you hear me?" The Voice shouted.

Everyone can. Shut the damned door.

She shut the door. *I changed my mind. You only shut the door when it's bad news. Open it back up.*

She didn't listen to his psychic pleadings this time. Instead, she shuffled through the office and smashed herself down into the unfortunate chair placed in front of Jonathan's desk.

"So, Roan."

And that was it. The beginning of a no-bullshit conversation he was hoping he'd never have to have with another living soul, *especially* one that lived inside this woman.

He nodded once, slowly.

"What do you think about it?"

"It?" He would cooperate, but he wouldn't make it easy.

"Come on, Rand," Davies said. "You know what I'm talking about."

"Well, what do *you* think about it?" he asked.

She sniffed, another of her little 'quirks' that made the rounds as an intra-office joke. "Can't say I like it too much."

He nodded. "Well, there you go. Now, I, uh, probably need to get back —"

"To what? To applying updates and server patches one at a time? Shit, I tell you, if this place was anything at all like it used to be…" her voice trailed off, an audible clue that she was talking only to fill space, not because she actually had something to say.

Jonathan wondered why she didn't spend as much time in other offices as she did his. Sure, he was her senior team leader, but he could never shake the feeling that there was more to it. She knew he had a girlfriend, and she knew who she was. *If only I could get them to meet, then she'll back off…*

He looked back at Davies. She was still there, those huge stupid eyes staring blankly back at him.

Go. Away.

He was feeling more snarky today, ready to have it out with anyone who screwed around with his time. He wondered why. *Roan? The 'project' he was working on?*

Maybe it was Diane. He hadn't seen her in what — six months? *Maybe she'd already moved on to someone else.*

No, that's crazy. She'd at least have the decency to have her assistant send his terminal a calendar update canceling their dinner in a week.

He sighed, as loudly as he could. "Davies, what's up? I really need to get back to work."

She shifted a bit in her chair. He had to hand it to her — she had a knack for physically stating a change in subject. Whether it was purposeful or based on an incredible level of awkwardness was one of the world's greatest mysteries.

"Roan was deactivated."

The words, spoken from someone else, stung. Jonathan silently spoke them, one at a time, in turn. *Roan was deactivated.* He tried to recall the last thing he'd said to the guy — his friend — but couldn't.

His friend was gone.

"Got it. Thanks, Davies. Now —"

"Why deactivated, and not reassigned?"

"Your guess is as good as mine. It came through yesterday, and we —"

"You knew about it yesterday." It wasn't a question. Jonathan tried to decipher the meaning behind it. It was impossible to see through those gigantic, lifeless eyeballs.

"I did. We were friends, you know. We hit *Niels'* after work, and he told me there."

"But I didn't even see the notice until this morning. I usually get updates on my terminal." She raised her pudgy hand, revealing a hand terminal, as if Jonathan had never seen one.

"Yes, the System usually emails them out to necessary staff. I didn't get one either. Maybe there was a problem with the internal mail server." Now he sounded like an idiot, so he shook his head, as if that would negate his last statement.

"No, there wasn't. I checked. Why are you trying to build a cloaking device?"

Holy shit. That was probably the most straightforward, to-the-point subject change he'd ever heard. He really had to hand it to her: now he was the one shifting in his seat.

"I — what?" He started. He cleared his throat and started again. "Sorry — *what?* A cloaking device?"

"Cut the bullshit, Rand. You're the smartest dev we've got here, and it's not an accident. You've been quiet for *three years,* but I can see right through it. You and Roan were working on something."

"*We* were?" Rand couldn't help but take a slight offense at the insult that he *and* Roan were working on something together.

"He said you were. He emailed this morning. That's how I found out about the deactivation. He said he was sorry for the rest of us who had to stay behind — that was always his brand of humor, you know? — and that he was proud of you for figuring out the cloaking device. He wished you the best, and said he was sorry he couldn't help you more." She leaned back in the chair, a satisfied smirk revealing itself on her face.

Jonathan couldn't believe it. How — *when* — had Roan sent the email? They were together the entire night, and after…

"Did you run a trace on the email?"

"I'm sorry?"

"A trace," he repeated, "did you run a trace on the email? So we know it was sent from Roan?"

"Rand, what are you talking about?" Davies said, leaning forward again. "You don't think he sent the email?"

Jonathan thought for a moment. "Never mind. It's just… just *odd* that he would. Don't worry about it. And don't worry about that little thing about a device. Just an idea we had." He hated bringing his friend into it, but if what Davies was saying was actually true, his friend had brought *himself* into it.

"Never *mind?* You're kidding, right? And all the parts that have been walking out of the lab? You expect me to believe *different* people have been grabbing all the pieces they'd need to build two station consoles? I talked to Roxanne this morning, the last name on the request list. She hasn't even *been* down to the lab in three weeks!" Davies was beginning to get worked up, judging by the small amount of spittle that had already collected on the corner of her mouth. In Jonathan's mind, *any* amount of spittle was too much spittle.

He waited for her to continue, sensing that a tirade was about to begin. He only hoped it wouldn't be loud enough for the others to hear.

"And I wouldn't even really *mind* you building a station for personal use, or whatever it is you're trying to do with it, but *lying* about it on the request form?"

She paused for a moment and cocked her head sideways, confused. Like she'd just realized she'd lost her train of thought and changed the subject accidentally. She quickly jumped back on the train. "Never mind. That's not what I'm here for. You are working on a device that is *exclusively* designed to bypass the security and intelligence systems we currently rely on to keep us safe. The *audacity* of what you're attempting is… is…" he watched the spittle build up even more and decided to rescue her.

"We're not — we *weren't*," he said. *It wasn't a lie.* "It was an idea, one that we canned. Just a tech-guy joke between us."

She shook her head. "I don't buy it. His *last* email to anyone was about *that?* And you're claiming it's 'not something you're doing?'"

He shook his head. *It's not something* we're *doing, it's something* I'm *doing.* Subtle difference, but he could live with a little white lie.

"It's not."

She stood up and turned to leave, finally displaying a small window of freedom for Jonathan. "I'm tracking you, just so you know. I get it, Rand — you're the genius around here, and I'm the joke. But you don't *get* to my position, System-chosen or not, without a little of that *fire* that we have in common."

Jonathan understood her point. *I'm just as smart as you, buddy, and I know you're hearing me.* He nodded. An innocent, wide-eyed nod. *Gotcha.*

"I'll be watching, so keep it tight."

Without another word, she exited his office and left. He waited until he could no longer hear her plodding footsteps retreating down the hallway before he let out a sigh of relief.

Keep it tight.

MYERS_

Solomon Merrick had finally allowed Myers room to breathe. He'd shoved himself up and off of Myers' body, and now stood over him, glaring down. The man was a statue, a silhouette that stood against the light backdrop, unmoving.

"Wh — who are you?" Myers said. His voice was shaky and winded as if trying to audibly recreate the way his body felt.

"I told you," the man said. "My name is Solomon Merrick."

"But —"

"I am going to ask you to come with me, but I won't ask twice. You are currently posting at levels higher than any of us have ever seen, and I was placed here to find you."

Placed? "Why me?"

"It didn't have to be you, but it was. You stumbled into the city, and I was waiting, so here we are."

So many questions, Myers thought. But he shook his head instead. He was still lying on the ground. "Okay, fine. Kill me."

Merrick's face was unreadable, partly because it was halfway hidden behind the cloak of a shadow. "Get up."

Myers found himself complying with the order even before he'd registered it in his mind. He sat, a slow, painful expense of precious energy, then started the grueling process of trying to stand.

Merrick continued. "Walk. We need to get to Umutsuz. There's going to be more. Lots more."

"Who? *Who* are you guys?"

"It's not 'us,' other than we have the same assignment. We're not working together." Merrick stopped and looked toward the heli. "Well, they were. But most of us aren't."

"Wait a minute," Myers said. A fresh wave of energy had presented itself, and he took advantage of it. "You're a hunter, right? Like them? I'm posting on this 'Board' of yours, and I'm worth a lot of money."

Merrick shook his head. "Not money. Current. Let's go." He motioned with his gun, and Myers obeyed. They walked a few more steps before Myers asked another question.

"What's the difference? Can't you just bring me in dead?"

Merrick snorted. "Sure, for half the rate. I'd be a joke, though, to do that. Scrape me now, we're taking you all the way."

"To *where?*" Myers asked.

"Umutsuz." The word settled into Myers' mind as if it was definitive, the complete answer. *Isn't it obvious? The only place in a thousand miles that's populated.*

"Right. Umutsuz. We were already going to Umutsuz."

Merrick actually turned and looked at Myers. After a moment, he spoke. "*We?* You and that kid? And what were you going to *do* in Umutsuz?"

Myers lifted his chin a little. *"We* were going to hitch a ride out of here. What happened here, anyway? And why don't you just kill me?"

"I missed. Then you ran away. Remember?" Short, blunt, and to the point. Myers liked that, even if it was a sore subject. In another life, Myers might have tried to hire the guy.

"But because I'm…"

"Yeah. Myers Asher. Right. Things got out of hand, now you're posting record Current, and there's no way I'm dragging you back dead."

"So you're going to, uh, *sell* me?"

Another snort. "Right. Like it's that easy. How long you been out?"

Myers assumed he meant 'disappeared' or whatever it was when someone *didn't exist* for a certain amount of time. "Seven years, give or take."

Merrick stopped mid stride. "That seems about right, but still. Seven *years?.*"

"Yes. And they — it — took about fifteen years. Both terms, just after EHM."

"That explains a lot." He looked off into the distance and sighed. *What was that,* Myers wondered. *Nostalgia?*

"What happens when we get to Umutsuz?" he asked.

Merrick frowned. "There's a buyer there, someone I've worked with before. I trust him."

"What happens to *me* when we get there?"

Merrick didn't answer.

"Fine. What is this 'buyer' going to give you, besides money?"

"It's not money. Hasn't been for some time now, after the collapse. Current, actually. And he's got something I need."

"What do you need?" Myers suddenly wondered if it was too far. *Screw it,* he thought. *He just told me he's not going to kill me. Yet.*

Merrick didn't even blink. "A car. Gas-powered, off the Grid."

"And what exactly do you need a car for?"

"Look, I think we're going to be better off, both of us, if we keep the chitchat down. Got it?"

"Yeah." Myers wasn't sure if the response was 'stop talking,' or 'stop talking about *that*.' He'd always been good at reading people, and he had a feeling it was the latter.

"I need a car, too. Obviously. Get out of here, figure out what's going on. I don't suppose I can buy you out?" Myers asked.

"You were scraped *seven years* ago. You think I believe you've got Current stashed away somewhere?"

"I don't even know what Current *is,* so no, of course not. But I can get it. I can talk to —"

"You really don't understand what this world is now, do you?" Merrick looked him over, the question more of a threat. "You think this is the same world you remember from fifteen years ago? Current, money, whatever you want to call it, it doesn't run anything anymore. At least not the way it used to. The System tracks all of it, so there's no 'buying people out' anymore. You give them what they want, or you're no good to them."

"And what is it you want?"

"A car. I told you that."

Myers waited. They both knew it was only half the answer, if even that much.

"I told you to cut the chitchat."

"I told you to kill me."

Merrick stopped and looked at Myers. Myers saw something there, in his eyes, he hadn't noticed before. *Defeat.* Or maybe it wasn't there, and Myers was seeing a reflection of himself.

"You think you're in a position to negotiate?" Merrick said. "If I'd have left you back there, you'd be dead already or dead in a day."

"I'm here, and I'm alive, for now. That's got to be good enough for something."

"It is," Merrick said. "It's good enough to make you last another day you just wished you *were* dead. Come on, let's keep moving. Umutsuz is twenty miles away, and I'd like to get there before tomorrow night. You think you can make it?"

"Do I have a choice?" Myers asked.

Merrick just kept walking.

RAND_

The case had been printed flawlessly. Three-dimensional printing had come a long way, and it was the subtleties that he appreciated most from the new technology. The printer had a finishing unit, a small head that would inspect the final design for any sort of visible defect, shaving corners to smooth exactness. It looked and felt no different than a piece of machined plastic that had fallen fresh off an assembly belt.

It was dark blue, Jonathan's current color of choice for the raw material capsule he'd installed in the printer, and it was sturdy enough to hold the small computer inside of it. He popped open one half, reveling in the perfect cuts and smoothed edges, and placed the board inside. It was a perfect fit. The board nestled perfectly onto the bottom of the case, snapping in place with a quick push on the edge of the board, and he blew off some of the leftover material from the plastic printer.

He soldered the wiring components in place, careful to keep the heat far enough away from other electronics, and snapped the top on the device. A gaping rectangular hole stared up at him, a cable protruding through it and dangling down next to his hand.

He reached for the small fingerprint scanner he'd purchased from the store earlier that day and placed it above the device, comparing its size against the rectangular hole in the case. Satisfied with the design, he pushed the scanner into the open serial port and then down into the hole. It snuggled nicely into the case, the plastic of the hard outer shell giving way slightly to allow it to snap downward and secure itself.

Finally, Jonathan ran a final visual check of the components, looking for anything out of the ordinary. It was crude, certainly not ready for commercial sale, but it would work perfectly for his purposes.

He plugged it in to his station. The station immediately recognized the device, though unsure what it was. He checked his System connection. *Offline. Good.*

He clicked on the device's representation on the desktop — a small icon of an empty drive — and then opened a folder next to it. Inside the folder was the executable script that would automatically install the firmware and software onto his translation device, and he dragged it over and released it onto the drive icon. A task bar popped up briefly, but the installation was quick — less than a second — and the *ding* of a successful transfer sounded through his wall-mounted speakers.

Sweet. He unplugged the device and took a deep breath. *This is it.*

He'd worked for five hours on the program — longer than he'd worked on one particular project in the last three years by a factor of ten. He was confident it would work, but he hadn't tested it through an emulator or compiler yet. He didn't want any Grid-ready station to see his little invention until he was ready to roll. *Just to be safe.*

That had been his mantra for the day, but he wasn't sure if it was a reminder or a weak attempt to convince himself. *There is no such thing as safe. Not in this world.*

The device powered on, a simple blue light on the back of the case, and he stuck his thumb out and pressed it onto the fingerprint scanner.

A second passed, then two. His mind raced with all the possibilities of failure — bad firmware, buggy software, a missed global variable here or there — it was an endless list.

Then he heard a faint beep. A board-installed tiny speaker alerted him that something had changed. The light switched to green.

Print accepted.

So far, so good. The device had accepted his fingerprint as his own, internally comparing it to the one that matched his pID — a security measure he'd added last-minute — and given him the go-ahead to attempt a connected translation.

He clicked on the station's connection control module, a tiny program that normally ran in the background as an ongoing task, and turned on the connection to the Grid and net hard-wired into his apartment.

He quickly ran through the checklist in his mind: the station would accept the device as an installed auxiliary component, the connection would allow the device's translated signal to pass through, and a failure would come back. The failure was a necessary step, since he hadn't yet set up a static IP for the device, and the System would refuse to recognize it as a unique and 'live' component.

He readied himself — sitting up straighter and planting his feet firmly on the floor — and pressed his finger onto the scanner once more.

The two seconds passed, and the device lit up with a green light once again. He watched the station's screen as the information passed through the device, onto the station, and out via the connection. He tried to visualize the data, strings of millions of ones and zeros, flying along at the speed of light to their destination.

The signal was received, and immediately a response was initiated. Less than a second passed before Jonathan stared at the answer:

System lookup initiated: pID confirmed. Begin data transfer.

No. It couldn't be. Jonathan stared at the screen, trying to decipher the confirmation message.

It was supposed to fail. He purposefully hadn't created a static for the device, which meant the System wasn't supposed to recognize it as a new, 'live,' device, which meant he should have received a failure message.

The confirmation message glowed back at him, taunting him. *pID confirmed.*

The System had allowed him access.

He felt his blood run cold, and the hair on the back of his neck stood on end.

He stood up, his hands behind his head, still staring down at the screen. When he finally looked up two minutes later, his eyes found the window on the wall above his desk. He stared out into the sky and watched as a family of four left their apartment with a small overnight bag slung over each of their shoulders.

He frowned as he watched them step into their vehicle and slide away from the apartment. Another family — this one just a couple and their cat — leave an apartment across the street from Rand's house.

Still frowning, he watched as yet another couple, carrying a small child, exited one of the larger houses at the end of the block. He recognized the man as a higher up at a competing tech firm down the street from Vericorp. He'd shaken his hand once at a party and even waved at him as he came home from work.

He sat back down and opened his mail program. The hair on his neck still stood straight up, causing him to feel cold, as if a window had been opened directly behind him and a blast of cold air shot through.

There was one unread email, and he clicked it. He found himself somehow growing even colder as he read the first line.

> *Umutsuz, STATUS CHANGE.*
>
> *Umutsuz, CURRENT STATUS: DEACTIVATED.*

He didn't need to finish the rest of the email to know what it said. 'Deactivation.' Or, in other words, *get out.*

An entire city. At the same time.

He tried to remember ever hearing of something like that, and couldn't. Cities that were all but abandoned, their inhabitants already reassigned or deactivated, sure. Cities of fewer than ten thousand or so, possibly.

But Umutsuz, a city of almost a million people? This was unheard of.

He didn't know what the full situation was, but he had the uncanny feeling that he had played at least a small part in it.

MYERS_

"Merrick, hang on," Myers finally let the words slip out. He'd tried to just keep walking, to just put one foot in front of the other, but he finally had to give in to his body's pleading.

Merrick stopped, but he didn't turn around. "We're less than half a mile out, Asher, you don't think you can make it to the gate?"

Myers shook his head, then realized that Merrick couldn't hear that. "No — no, I'm not sure I can. I'm sorry. Kill me here and take me in that way."

Myers saw the big man's shoulders rise in a deep sigh. He turned around and faced him. "Asher, I'm not going to kill you."

"You — you're not?" Myers frowned. "I thought you were going to turn me in or something; sell me."

"I am. I'm just not going to kill you first." He walked a few paces back to Myers' position and squatted down to his level. "You're posting higher than anyone I've ever seen on the Board, and it seems like a waste to just off you."

Myers understood. "Ah, I get it. You need me to stay alive long enough to be able to fund your dream vacation. That it?"

Merrick nodded. "Yeah. Something like that. Seriously, though. We have to keep moving."

Myers watched Merrick's eyes move slowly up and away from him, back the direction they'd come from. He was still for a moment, watching silently. *Testing.*

"What are you looking for?"

Merrick didn't speak for another ten seconds, but when he did he didn't turn back to Myers. He kept staring. "They're coming for you,

Myers. For both of us. Word's going to get out about the crash, and that you got away. They'll know you were helped, and I'm the only one assigned directly to this region, so they'll come for me, too." He stood, offering Myers a hand.

Myers took it and felt himself being pulled upward quickly. This man was rugged, probably from years of living out here. He steadied himself and looked at Merrick. "*Who's* coming, Merrick? Hunters?"

Merrick nodded as they started walking again. The city of Umutsuz loomed ahead of them, though it seemed much smaller than the abandoned city of Istanbul. He could see rows of similar-looking houses and a few larger buildings poking out above them. The city was probably a mile or two in diameter.

"Sort of. They're hunters, like me, but Unders." Myers must have had a confused expression on his face, so Merrick explained. "People who operate outside the realm of the System. They live and move around 'under the radar.' The System knows about them, but they're not subject to the same rules as the cities. They use Current, like we all do, but the System only tracks it locally."

"Only tracks it in a certain area?"

"No, only recognizes it as a 'local transaction of bandwidth.' Everyone has these terminals." Merrick pulled out a small computer device from his backpack and showed it to Myers. "Most of us in the System have a Current level associated with our pIDs, and it goes where we go. My fingerprint can pull up my Current as easily as my passcode, or my terminal. It's much simpler that way."

Myers thought he followed. "Right — it's a bank account. But these 'Unders' have a different System?"

"No, they don't have a System at all. They have terminals, too, but their terminals are like, uh, valuables. Or a wallet. They have their Current levels assigned to them, but if they lose the terminal, they're out of luck. They use their fingerprint anywhere and the System simply refuses to recognize it."

"Okay, got it. And how did they get that way?"

"They chose it, for whatever reason. Those guys back there? They're professional hunters, Unders living away from society. They collect bounties put on people the System no longer needs, and go from region to region collecting, then they sell what they can on the markets and turn around and do it again. That pack of guys is new to the area, but they've clearly done well for themselves. That Tracer they were in is pretty state-of-the-art, and their guns weren't too shabby, either. And there's no amount of Current that can get them legally."

"You think they're coming back?" Myers asked.

"Maybe, but their ride was trashed. Unless they've got a lot of extra Current lying around and somewhere to spend it, it's probably not them we're going to need to worry about." Merrick stopped, and turned to face Myers. "Look, we're getting close to the city. Here's the plan." He flicked his eyes left and right as if they weren't the only two people in a ten-mile radius. "You can't stay out here, since there will probably be Unders on us within the hour. You can't normally get into the city since you don't have a pID, but I think I can get you past." Merrick looked up and checked the sun's position above them. "We have to move quickly, though. My contact is in Zone 2, which is about a block away from the gate."

"Won't there be guards?"

Merrick shook his head. "No, this isn't a high-risk city, just a tech quadrant support area. Security is minimal, and it's all System-based. Nothing we can't get past without too much difficulty."

"Okay. Do we get to negotiate this whole part about you selling me to some highest bidder though?"

Merrick's face was resolute. Myers couldn't read it, so he stopped trying.

"Myers, I shot at you two days ago, thinking you'd stay still, but you got away. I should have just snuck up on you or something, but I didn't want to risk the chance that you'd hear me."

"You weren't trying to kill me?"

"I needed you alive. Still do."

"To trade me for some bandwidth to buy a car."

"No, that's where you're wrong. You don't understand it yet, but there's a much bigger game being played here. all the pieces are stacking up and people are taking sides. This little cat-and-mouse game we've been playing is just a small part of it."

"I'm not sure I'm following you. So you're *not* going to sell me?"

Merrick nodded. "No, I still am, but it's an arbitrage play. We've got a station set up that can register transactions and send them in. But there's no 'buyer' on the other side of it. You're still getting 'sold,' since that's the only way to clear you from the Board and get you off everyone's 'most wanted' list, but I'll be the buyer *and* seller."

"Wait — you're selling me to *yourself*? Won't the System know?"

"No, it won't. It's two different pIDs. Mine, and another one the station is running as a virtual server. We've been docking transactions through it for a few months, running it up slowly, and it's been working. The System sees a moderately active pID in the business sector of Umutsuz, who can now afford to purchase your bounty. I'm going to make it a deal, and you'll be home free."

Myers felt a wave of relief, or something he assumed was relief, pass through him. He didn't care about the details, or the System, or anything else. *He was going to live.*

"Thanks, Merrick."

"Look, I wish I could say I was doing it just out of the kindness of my heart. I would, too, if I could. But there's another reason."

He raised an eyebrow.

"We need you. You were the president once, and you did some good things. But before that you were running the finances at what is now the largest corporation on the planet."

"EHM?"

"Exactly."

"And I suppose you think I know something about this 'System,' since I was there when it was being built? And since I was the guy advocating for it when I was the president?"

"That kid tell you all that?"

Ravi. Myers felt the weight of the kid's death heavy on his heart. *It was my fault he died.* Whether it was actually true was irrelevant.

"He helped me piece it together."

"I see." Merrick thought for a moment. "Yeah, that's it. You might be able to help us out."

Myers heard a slight popping sound, like a rattling in the distance, and a line of tiny explosions in the dirt drove toward the two men from behind them. Merrick must have seen it out of the corner of his eye, and he pushed Myers to the side.

"Get down!" He yelled. Myers felt his body once again crushed under a perfect tackle by the man next to him, and he hit the ground hard. *How much more of this torture can I take?* He wondered. He'd surprised himself so far, so he went with it and reacted to the new information.

He rolled to the side and popped up on his feet. He was a second behind Merrick who already had his gun raised and was pointing it out to the desert.

"Get behind something!"

Myers looked around. There was *literally* nothing else to hide behind, so he stood behind Merrick.

"Not me, idiot," Merrick screamed as he fired a few shots from the rifle.

"There's nothing else out here!"

"Then run — I'll cover. Get to the gate and wait for it to open. There's a maintenance auto that's on a daily schedule, and it should be coming out soon."

Myers didn't wait for the rest of the instructions, if there were any. More popping from in front of Merrick triggered something in Myers' brain he assumed was *massive adrenaline,* and he started running. Merrick would be able to catch up anyway, so a head start wasn't a bad idea.

He was close to the gate now, and he started to see some detail. A simple chain-link fence rose upward from the ground, higher than the one in Istanbul, but this one had an open gated section directly in front of him. Behind that a ten-foot-high concrete barrier stretched across the road. Myers saw two sets of huge wheels mounted below the barrier, likely used to slide the concrete section open to allow entrance to and exit from the city. He aimed toward the barrier, hoping Merrick would reach it before Myers was forced to explain himself to a robot guard or some other automated terror.

A road appeared out of the sand and headed inward through the gate, seeming to rise from below the earth and continue into the heart of the city. Myers reached it and ran toward a small concrete bunker next to the road, just inside the chain-link gate. It was nothing more than a concrete box lying on the ground, and he assumed it housed some electronic components or protected something crucial to the city's infrastructure.

Whatever it was, it provided Myers a good vantage point to see the firefight behind him. He ducked behind the bunker and watched Merrick.

The man fired three shots at targets Myers couldn't see, turned and ran about ten steps, then started the process again. Myers thought he could hear the faint pops of at least two shooters, but he still couldn't see anything to shoot at.

Merrick repeated his shoot-run-shoot pattern three more times until he reached the gate and Myers' lookout bunker.

"Let's go!"

"Where?" Myers shouted back. "The gate's closed."

"The auto will leave soon, and you need to get inside it after it drops the trash."

It was probably one of the strangest sentences Myers had ever heard, but in the midst of what was currently happening to him it made perfect sense.

"It's an *auto*, so it doesn't have any way for us to control it. It's also a civilian-grade vehicle, so it won't have any security mechanisms. Hauls trash out and supplies in, that's it."

"And it won't know I'm in it?"

"It shouldn't."

It shouldn't. Myers hoped he was right.

He followed Merrick to the concrete barrier and stood next to him as Merrick aimed down the scope of his rifle. "There are still two out there, but I think I dropped one."

"Hunters?"

"Unders, yeah. Not the same friends we ran into before, but these three won't be the only ones we have to deal with. Okay, I hear the gate switch cycling on."

Myers strained his ears and thought he could hear a high-pitched whine.

"It'll take a minute, so keep your eyes toward the desert. Make sure we don't get ambushed. I'll try to keep them far enough out. They know I've got the range on them, now, so their potshots aren't going to do anything but mark where they are."

Thirty seconds passed and the soft whine suddenly turned into a frustrated, squelching yell as the rusted wheels were forced to move. The concrete barrier behind them slid slowly to one side.

"Get over there where the opening is," Merrick said. "The auto is mounted on a rail up on that building, so it won't start rolling through until it's completely open. But at least you can make a run for it into the city if anyone gets close."

Myers followed the order and ran toward the widening crack between the concrete barriers. He waited for the crack to widen to about six inches, then he peered through.

"Uh, Merrick."

Merrick fired a shot from his rifle and moved to Myers' position. "What is it?"

"Are there supposed to be people on the other side?"

"It's a city."

"Look."

Merrick dropped the gun and turned around. The crack between the barriers was a foot wide now, and Merrick stared through it. His jaw dropped. "Shit."

Myers and Merrick were staring at a street completely full of people, all walking toward the gate. Entire families, carrying backpacks and pillows, dragging luggage behind them, headed directly toward them. The mass exodus extended back as far as they could see, and street intersections along the way only dumped more people out onto the main road.

"What's going on?" Myers asked. "Why are they all walking toward us?"

"They're leaving," Merrick said. "Look." He pointed toward a rotating light on top of a building just inside the gate. Myers followed his finger upward, and he saw a flashing sign — some sort of LED display — on a pole.

"Umutsuz Deactivated. Deactivation Protocol Initiated. Please Proceed Carefully."

"They *deactivated* Umutsuz?"

"Not *they*. The System," Merrick responded. "I've never seen it done to an entire city at once. Usually it's over the course of *years*," Merrick said.

"Hey, Merrick. We've got another problem," Myers said. In the chaos of the mass of people tumbling toward them, it took Myers a moment to recognize the sound from behind him.

Merrick turned around and looked behind them.

Two helis — Tracers, as Merrick had called them — floated just outside the chain-link fence, and about a dozen armed men had their rifles raised and pointed toward them.

RAND_

The city was programmed to deactivate in eight separate stages, one per hour. In each stage, the standard three-phase deactivation protocol would be initiated, beginning with the electric, water, and Current grid going down. Shuttles would be scheduled to bunch together at the stations, allowing the most people possible to board a train leading to their next assignment. Anyone with a car or other vehicle would be crammed onto the freeways, racing to beat the onslaught of foot traffic and deactivation drones that would follow in the second phase.

During that second phase, the drones would move household to household, scanning for thermal discrepancies and charting their location. They'd fly through the zone, making sure any stragglers, had a pID that listed them as a Deactivated, not a Reassigned. If their listing had them marked for a scrape, the drones would either apply the scrape at that time or log it to the database for a later visit.

Finally, phase three marked the shutdown of the Grid, meaning any hand terminals or battery-powered stations would be rendered all but useless. Anyone left in the city would be the Deactivated, waiting for their scrape or their recall — a period of 'holding' within a secure facility followed by a scrape and deployment. Few of the blue-collar workers in Umutsuz would need a long-term scrape and redeployment, but there were always a handful of people the System deemed too much a threat to leave active.

Rand was in Zone 6, but he was watching from his station at home as Zone 3 finished its deactivation protocol. The station he was using was a custom-built machine using water-cooled casing surrounding a hodgepodge of components he'd thrown together from leftover Vericorp prototypes and Current-funded additions. He'd used the standard request form in the laboratory, but put his employees' names down instead of his own. It wasn't a rock-solid plan when he came up with it, but he thought it might at least slow down anyone snooping around. He hadn't planned on Davies tracing his actions as closely as she did.

He quickly relived the 'conversation' he'd had with Davies earlier that day and laughed. She was much smarter than she let on, and he wondered if it was on purpose or if she was just a ditz.

For a Grid connection he'd wired one of the internal boards to his home coaxial port, opting to use the land-based connection over the general wireless Grid that blanketed any of the larger cities and metropolitan areas. Finally, he'd used a WADD, or wireless automatic data drive, to take care of his memory requirements. The WADD synced with his internal memory implant and provided him a way to download any memories and important data he'd filed away that day without needing to initiate a specific data transfer.

The result was a machine that was faster than the machine he'd been given at work, and he spent most of his available Current and any free time using it for online gaming. It was capable of speeds that rivaled the terminals and stations used at most government entities, and he was damn proud of it.

It was also a twin.

The *second* station was hidden away in the city, ready for his contact to activate it and use it for the next phase of the plan they'd been working on for almost two years. With Davies' uncovering of his plan to build a 'scraping' device, the scare he'd received when he'd tried to use it, and now the deactivation of the city, the timing of the larger plan he'd put into motion two years ago was either serendipitous or extremely unlucky. He wouldn't be able to tell which until the dust settled, so there was nothing to do but keep pushing forward.

The station sat on a desk along the front wall of his small apartment, just below a wide window overlooking the city. His neighborhood was conveniently located on a small hill and in the far corner of the city, allowing him a near-complete view of the entire area. Zone 4, just to the south of his current location, began the deactivation process, and Rand watched as scores of families abandoned the apartments they'd called home for the past years and filled the streets with gas-powered vehicles, and thousands of pounds of luggage. He tried to imagine what it was like to leave with children, a wife on his arm, as he prepared for a completely new life, but couldn't. It was easier to be single — relatively so, anyway — to have nothing but the clothes on his back and the shoes on his feet to carry him to the next chapter.

He'd always shied away from commitment, even while dating and 'getting serious' with other women. They thought his attachment was love, while he considered it simply mutual convenience. He and Diane were the type of people who were never supposed to meet and grow close, and he was terrified at the prospect of becoming another checkbox on her long list of to-do items.

He shook his head, forcing himself back into the present. He heard a few screams coming from Zone 4. The mass exodus had probably ignited some less-than-reputable behavior from certain less-than-reputable citizens, thinking it was a good time to take advantage of the chaos of a city-wide deactivation. It didn't escalate to rioting as the screams died down quickly, so he went back to planning his escape.

Rand needed to get out of the city, but he couldn't make his move until he knew for sure what the System had planned for him. He was almost positive he was in for a total deactivation and scrape, but the System hadn't thought it necessary to alert him of that fact. So far, the orders hadn't come through on either his terminal or his station. He checked both once more, expecting a 'connection error' code that would signify the reason behind his not receiving the order.

Nothing.

He was connected, and everything appeared to be in working order. If another hour passed without an update, he wouldn't have time to get out before the drone flew by. *The System is messing with me,* he thought. He needed a plan. Something, at least, to focus on.

But before he could plan anything useful, he heard a knock. A small in-screen image of the person awaiting answer outside his home flashed at the bottom-right of the station's monitor.

Well, I'll be scraped.

He walked to the front door of the small apartment and opened it.

"Rand," the woman said before it was even fully open.

"Yeah, me. What's up, Davies?" he asked, the statement a single breathless thread. He motioned with a quick snap of his neck for his boss to enter.

She did. "You doing okay?"

He frowned. "A house call just to see if I'm okay?" he said. He'd always felt a little weirded out — not to mention annoyed — with his boss, but she'd never come to his *house*. She stood like a Mack truck in front of the door, her eyes darting toward his station. He shifted subtly to intercept her wandering interest in his private life. "What can I do for you, Mrs. Davies?" he asked, trying to get her to the point, and quickly.

She flicked her eyes back toward him. "Yes, sorry, well —" the three words were abrasive and loud, as if she were trying to address any number of people she seemed to imagine must be hidden throughout his house. He suddenly felt the closeness of the walls, pressing in on him. "I just… I just came by to see how you were holding up."

He rolled his eyes. *I'm busy.* "I'm doing fine, thanks. Just waiting for my Zone —"

"You're being deactivated. It came through my terminal after the city orders were sent."

"I figured as much."

"Scraped, too."

He felt a pang of regret in his chest. The feeling surprised him.

"How much?" he asked.

She shrugged. "All of it, from what I can tell. It needs all of it."

It.

"Yeah, that makes sense too." Rand looked over at the station. He needed to start planning, start figuring this out. He put his mind at work trying to figure out a convenient way to rid himself of the woman standing in his living room.

"It's reassigning me to Houston. ISA, 'System Facilitator.' Should be a good gig."

He looked at her. She seemed whimsical, almost peaceful. Something about her expression made her surreal. "Good," he said. "It'll be a good fit for —"

"Rand, they don't *need* me. I'm a pawn. It's you. It's *always* been you."

Her face grew serious, and he had the sudden feeling that he'd just woken up from a nightmare that turned out to be better off than the reality his mind was trying to escape.

She knew.

"Wait…" he didn't know what to say. "You — you *know?*"

"How'd you do it, Rand?"

He shook his head, a blank expression on his face.

"Rand, come on. *How'd you do it?* An *entire city?* At the same time?" And then, after a moment of hesitation, "It's going to make you a Relic."

"I know. All of it?" He remembered what she'd said about his upcoming scraping. He hadn't thought it would be that bad — at worst, the last few years at Vericorp.

"Yeah, that's the note I saw anyway. You were the key, Rand, and you knew it. Dammit, you knew it the entire time, and now… That's why I wanted to come, before you… left." She let the word hang in the air. He wasn't sure if she meant 'left the city' or 'left' as in 'scraped.' It didn't matter.

She knew.

"It's okay, really." He tried to make the words sound confident, but it was all happening too fast. He thought about the first time he tried activating the device. "I — I have a plan," was all he could muster.

She nodded. "I figured as much. From the beginning, you knew, huh? I always wondered about it — more 'what if,' really. But you. Smartest one who's ever walked through those doors. At least in the last ten years or so. You knew, didn't you?"

"Yeah, I knew. Guessed, really. But then I figured it was why the System moved me out here in the sticks. It still needed me; it needed what I know how to do. But it couldn't let me get too close, either."

He didn't tell her the rest. About the device, or about its allowing access to the System's database — without a static address for the unit.

"It's moving slowly — too slowly, or slower than I thought it would. Why?"

Rand stood there for a moment weighing his options. He could come clean, or he could keep up the game for bit longer. It wouldn't matter, really. She knew already; he'd underestimated her. Drastically. He realized it as soon as she'd asked the exact same question he'd been wrestling with for the past year.

Why? Why is it moving so slowly?

"Wouldn't you?" he responded.

Felicia Davies stared at him for a long time until he got a little uncomfortable. Finally, she turned on a single heel and opened the door and let herself out.

"Goodbye, Rand."

MYERS_

They'd been tricked. Myers and Solomon Merrick had been focusing on the direct threat — the handful of shooters approaching them from the distance — so they didn't notice the two Tracers and the small army of men flanking them along the city's gate.

The two groups were a ragtag bunch of men, each wearing whatever clothes they could find that day — or month — and holding any number of strange-looking weapons. Most had guns and rifles, though Myers thought he could see an axe or two glinting the sun's light toward his eyes.

"Merrick, what are we going to —"

"Shut up and get inside the concrete barrier when I yell. I'm going to fire a few warning shots, then we'll both run inside. Stay behind the barrier and keep moving along the wall once we're in the city."

"Got it. Ready." Myers felt like the words were more for his own confidence than in portraying information to Merrick. He tensed, waiting for something to happen. From what he could see, there was really only one thing that *could* happen. The two groups of men would lump together into one larger group, then they'd start firing on them. Myers would likely be ripped to shreds, die a slow, horrible —

"*Now!*" Merrick screamed as he opened fire. The long-range rifle wasn't much of a competition against the closer-range assault rifles that could fire a short burst of bullets with on trigger pull, but Merrick's plan seemed to work well enough. Myers turned and ran as fast as possible toward the moving barrier wall, only noticing the reaction of the group of men out of the corner of his eye. A few men fell to the ground when Merrick's gun went off, anticipating a firefight, while the others simply turned and covered their heads. Myers thought he saw one man fall backwards as if he'd been hit.

Myers reached the concrete barrier just as the men regrouped and began returning heavy fire on their location. The people from inside Umutsuz — the families, couples, and single men and women clogging up the street — reached the barrier as well. They hadn't seen what was on the *other* side of the gate, and the first wave of people to reach it panicked as the guns started firing.

Merrick was behind Myers by a few steps, and Myers turned back to wait for him. Two steps away from the edge of the barrier and into the safety of the thick concrete wall, Myers saw two rounds rip into Merrick's side.

Merrick flew sideways, into the swarming crowd of people, and fell. The crowd was in full-on chaos mode, and Myers watched helplessly as Merrick disappeared under their feet.

"Merrick!" He yelled back, but only a few people even turned to look at him as they tried to flee the scene. Myers pushed through a pile of suitcases and bags and navigated through a set of people standing near the road, trying to get to Merrick. The guns from the men outside Umutsuz began firing again.

He heard screams — one from a woman and another from a child — and saw out of the corner of his eye three people fall to the ground. He began breathing quickly, short bursts he knew would soon lead to hyperventilating. He forced himself to steady, watching nothing but his feet as he pressed and prodded his way through the jumble of humans.

And still the guns fired. *Do they not know what they're shooting at? Or do they just not care?*

More screams, more gunfire, and this time he saw an entire family fall to the ground. It was impossible to tell whether they'd been hit or were just ducking out of the way. He returned his attention to his feet.

Merrick was laying on the ground about five feet away, but it might as well have been a mile. Myers was stuck, unable to press between two groups of families that had huddled close together in the middle of the road. He could feel the mass of people moving as one, as if they'd become some sort of unified body. A hive-mind of scared beings, trying to avoid slaughter.

He yelled and pushed again, harder. One of his hands pushed through, followed by the other. The two people closest to him briefly turned to see what his deal was, but they each did their part and pushed away from him, creating a gap. He squeezed through and ran to Merrick.

"Merrick — Merrick, are you okay?" He could hardly hear the sound of his own voice over the screaming and steady gunfire, but he yelled again.

Merrick opened his eyes and blinked a few times. He'd been knocked out when he hit the ground, or from the gunshots.

The gunshots.

Myers knelt down and checked the man's right side for the wounds. There was no blood, but he felt the holes torn in the man's shirt. He wiggled his finger around inside the cloth and noticed something hard and thick was covering Merrick's upper body.

"It's body armor," Merrick said. He lifted his head slightly, trying to look around.

"We have to get you up and out of here before we get trampled to death," Myers said.

Merrick nodded, and Myers helped lift him up. He was heavy, probably a hundred pounds heavier than Myers with his gear and armor on, but together they stood. People coursed around them, trying to push back down the street and away from the open gate and incoming gunmen.

"This block must have acted like a funnel," Merrick said, pointing upward. They were alternating between taking a single step backward and standing still. Myers followed his finger. Indeed, the buildings seemed to converge on this road, narrowing it until the street was only as wide as the open gate.

People started moving faster as more of the crowd from down the street dispersed.

"Where are they going?"

"Finding another exit, probably. The autotrains are probably all full, so they're just hoping to get out of the city before the last deactivation warning."

Myers didn't like the sound of that. "What happens after the last warning?"

Merrick looked over at him. "Deactivation."

A path cleared, and Merrick didn't wait around for permission. The gunshots were more sporadic now. They were searching for him, and only firing to get people out of the way. Myers wondered if any of the Unders had reached the city yet, or if they were waiting outside of it for some reason.

Myers followed Merrick to the next block, then they took a right just after one of the taller buildings. The street was deserted, a surprising change from the street they'd just left. It seemed like a city block that had already been deactivated. Tall buildings stretched overhead and cast the street in shadow, adding to the effect.

Merrick turned and walked down a narrow alley that was perfectly disguised between two of the buildings. Had he not been with Merrick, Myers would have completely missed the opening. *Whoever designed this city really had an eye for function.* There was nothing unnecessary about the construction of the buildings, and it created an almost ethereal atmosphere. He felt like he was walking through a movie set — buildings, houses, and other structures shared a common theme and design, yet none were garish or too simplistic to be considered in poor taste.

The alley was barely wide enough for Merrick's shoulders to fit through, and even Myers felt a bit constricted as they walked briskly though. At the end of the alley Merrick turned and opened a door. He walked in, not waiting for Myers.

"Come in," Merrick said as Myers entered. Merrick was already across the small room, standing over a table and facing the rear wall. It seemed as though the door they'd entered from was the only entrance or exit to the strange room.

There were no windows, leading Myers to believe that this room was sectioned off from one of the larger buildings surrounding them, with the only access point coming from the alleyway. A dim glow filled the room with an artificial light, giving the place an eery overcast.

"Over here," Merrick said. Myers stood next to the man as he worked the computer in front of him. Myers couldn't keep up — it was like Merrick didn't have to actually type or press anything; the computer just *knew* where he was trying to go and went there. Merrick worked the machine as though it were second nature. This man who'd chased him through the desert and a dusty, deserted city, could work a computer faster than anyone Myers had ever met.

"I'm logged in as my alter-account now. The System is waiting for the transaction, and… let's see your —" Merrick stopped.

"What is it?"

"You're currently posting at 107,000."

"Is that good?" Myers asked.

Merrick just stared at the screen. After a few seconds, he shook his head and started typing again. His hands quickly became a blur, and Myers felt himself getting dizzy.

"I feel like the old guy who doesn't understand technology," Myers said. "I'm lightheaded and about to fall over from watching you."

"You were also fired on multiple times, dehydrated, and probably starving."

Myers realized the truth of Merrick's diagnosis and immediately felt the hunger pangs. He'd had a little water back in the church, when Ravi had given him his canteen for the night, but other than —

"Let's get this transaction started and then we can think about getting out of here." He grabbed Myers' finger and pressed it on a scanning device.

"What happens to me after? Once I've been, uh, *sold*?"

"Right, good question. Basically the System needs one transaction for you to be removed from the Board. You'll still be a Relic, but no one will be actively hunting you anymore."

"Actively?"

"Well, I mean no one will know you're still alive. I'm sure if you start hanging out in crowds you'll get some strange looks from people who recognize you, but unless that crowd is made up of Unders no one's going to care."

"Merrick, what happens to anyone still here after that 'deactivation protocol' is finished? Does the System kill them?"

"No. The System can't kill anyone. At least not directly. It's just a computer program, close to human-level intelligence but lacking some very specific features, like creativity, free will, and advanced cognitive function. It's called Artificial General Intelligence."

"So it can only do what it's been programmed to do?"

"Exactly," Merrick said. "And what it's *learned* to do from other programs it's come across. But that means, out here, it's only going to get 'confused' about stragglers."

"It won't be able to tell why we're still in the city if we've already been given our marching orders."

"Right. If it's ordered you to be reassigned, it's also set up a method of transportation for you, or tracked your movement to know you're headed to the right place and it's calculated an arrival time. If you're supposed to be deactivated, it'll do that too. But if you're neither of those things, and you're waiting around in a previously-deactivated area ignoring the reassignment, it's like dividing by zero — the computer gets confused because that behavior doesn't compute."

"So…"

"So you get scraped, and it starts over."

Myers swallowed. 'Scraped,' I'm assuming, is not good?"

"Memory wipe. You're a rogue, so it does the only thing it knows how to do. It 'scrapes' your internal memory device and essentially reboots you, taking away any stored memory you have and effectively rendering you dead to the System."

Myers nodded. "Right. So let's not stick around to see that happen." Myers lifted his finger then placed it back down again after Sol shot him a look.

Merrick continued maneuvering around the computer station's screen as he spoke. "Working on it, Myers. Just one more —"

A *ding* sounded from somewhere inside the machine's mass, and Merrick looked up.

"Transaction complete." He smiled. "I'm now 107,000 Current richer, and you're a free man."

RAND_

He decided on his course of action.

Rand would head to the gate, only three blocks from his current location, and wait for the city to reach full deactivation status, at which point the gate would deactivate and allow him to escape without being scorched by a million volts of electricity.

In the meantime, he needed to fake his own deactivation.

He had the device he'd created lying on the desk next to the station. He activated it and prepared himself for the process. The drones would come either way, so it had to work properly the first time. If he flubbed it, it would set off an alert and expedite his upcoming scraping festival. He placed the device in front of him on the desk and opened a secure connection on his computer to the nearest municipal net facility on his station's browser.

The municipal site showed exactly what he'd expected — an alert status for his zone, and a lift of zones that had already been deactivated. It listed some help numbers to call in case of emergency, and finally a live feed of videos placed around the city.

He used 'guest access' to log in to a citizen-run section of the site dedicated to peacekeeping operations and typed in his own pID. In less than a second, he saw a picture of himself staring back at him, listing his date of birth, sex, and current occupation. The AAI clicked a link for him near the bottom of the page.

Place Watch Order.

Under normal circumstances, this was the equivalent of calling emergency services without cause, and would trigger an alarm for authorities to blockade his residence until the situation was resolved. In this case, emergency services was no longer relevant, authorities were busy, and he had 'due cause.'

He clicked a button on the next page: *'Request Manual Deactivation.'* The one-link form needed proper identification for it to be sent, and Rand placed his thumb into the device and waited. Anyone with a listed pID could use a manual deactivation request as long as it was approved by the System. However, any System-based device could send through the order without any further steps.

And his device was a hacked version of a System-based device.

The lights told him his request had been sent, and he watched the screen for confirmation.

>Data scrape necessary. Confirm?
>

He typed a few characters, confirming a full scrape. *Yes, asshole, I've been scraped.*

>Data scrape confirmed.

The message printed his unique static address, recognizing that it was part of the System, and Rand leaned back in his chair.

He had manually placed the order to scrape and deactivate himself, clearing his pID from any watch lists, deactivation notices, and any statuses that would make him a wanted man. As far as the System was concerned, it had deactivated Jonathan Rand and taken most of his memory with it.

I'm free.

He had one more task before it was time to leave. Opening a secured communication dialog window, he typed the address of his target recipient. He waited for the information to parse, and less than a second later he was invited to type an outgoing secure message. He set his fingers on the keyboard and silently weighed the risks of what he was about to do.

He took a deep breath and let it out, closing his eyes and opening them again five seconds later.

>Deactivating Umutsuz. Need help.

For about ten seconds, there was no response. He waited, impatiently, at the blinking cursor on the station screen. Finally, he saw a flickering below his initial request and watched as a message appeared.

>Confirmed, ETA 1845. Alert 318532110?

A single-letter response was all that was needed.

>Y

He waited again, until the confirmation came through.

>Affirmative. Z6 exit.

SOL_

Solomon Merrick didn't need to tell Myers that the Current he'd just earned himself wasn't the prize. Myers knew enough now to know that getting out of the city was the ultimate goal. The Current would be a welcome addition. He still had plans to purchase a car, something off the Grid that the System wouldn't be able to track. It would have to be something old, and that meant he'd have to pay a premium for it.

They had owned vehicles back in Seattle, before the System. Shannon had a sedan, a 2018 model, but it was the truck that Sol missed the most — a Toyota Tundra, large enough to fit the young family of three, but small enough to be emission- and mileage-friendly. He loved that truck. When he had been reassigned to Washington, D.C., the sedan was sold, and a year later the truck was as well. System-implemented public transit had improved and expanded to a level of usefulness that efficiency-conscious types couldn't ignore. Sure, there were still people who hung on to their precious personal vehicles, but Sol wasn't one for sentimental ties. He hated the rising taxes on personal vehicle ownership, and was happy to remove the burden of bi-monthly inspections, recertification, and constant maintenance.

The trend continued, and now vehicles that ran on gasoline were as rare as solar-cell cars used to be. Still, personal vehicles in general began to seem to excessive in the changing culture, and most families commuted to and from work using System-controlled transit.

He needed a vehicle to get his family out of Istanbul. They'd just about used up their rations allotted to them when he'd been assigned there, and walking to and from Umutsuz wasn't going to be a viable solution for very long.

The problem was that the plan had changed. The Unders were in the city, and now he was being hunted alongside Myers. The city had been deactivated, a mass exodus was now taking place, and Merrick still had to get to the other side of the city.

He *had* to get to Rand.

A knot had started to form in his chest as soon as he saw the deactivation notices and the people rushing toward the gate. The knot turned into a feeling just short of panic when he saw the Unders approach and start firing at them. He'd reacted as he had practiced many times, pushing the emotion away long enough to get the job done. Myers had done what he'd always done, asking for a plan and retreating to hide behind something.

It was probably an unfair assessment, Merrick realized. The man had been through hell these past days and he was ill equipped to fight back.

And Merrick himself was barely able to hold it together. He didn't want to think about what would happen if he didn't achieve his goal and find a vehicle to take back to Istanbul. He didn't want to think about what would happen if the knot of sneaking suspicion and panic turned into a premonition that came true. He didn't want to think about what would happen to his family.

So he pushed the knot back down and ignored it, for the moment. The transfer had worked, and that was enough for now.

One step at a time.

Make one decision, act on it, and then move toward the next problem.

It had gotten him through so much, and they were close. So close to the *real* prize. The actual goal that had put them all together here in this forgotten patch of Earth.

Merrick said a silent prayer, checked his gear, and turned off the station. It had no internal memory chip, so there was nothing inside the machine that could record keystrokes or recall any incoming or outgoing requests. It was a security feature Rand had built, and one that seemed overly paranoid at the time. No one who happened to stumble across this tiny room at the back of an empty alley and see the station would be able to pass through the layers of encryption to even power on the computer. It seemed excessive to Merrick.

But as Rand had explained in his last communication to Merrick a few days ago, it wasn't *people* Rand was worried about.

Merrick laughed a bit at the absurd implication, but over the past three days he'd started to wonder if Rand was on to something.

MYERS_

"Where are we headed now?" Myers asked. They were, once again, running. Myers no longer felt the pain; it was as if his body had accepted its fate and was forever destined to run.

"I need to find my contact here. He's the one who set up that station back there and ran its power block through an old generator. I looked up the deactivation notices on the city and it's by zone. He's in Zone 6, and that's on the opposite side of the city from us. We'll head through Zone 3 to get there, since that's the center of the city and will give us the best options for staying out of sight."

"We have to run there?" Myers asked through short fits of breath.

"You have a better plan?" Merrick pulled out his hand terminal and read the display screen for a moment, typed something, then placed it back in the pack.

Usually I would have a plan, he realized. Myers Asher *always* had a plan. These last few days were hell for many reasons, but he was surprised and a little disappointed that the main reason he was having such a hard time with all of this was because he felt *out of control*.

People, including women and children, had literally been murdered in front of him. He watched them get trampled, running from a horrific band of people who wanted him dead. He'd watched Ravi get killed by his side, and the thing he was most upset about was this feeling of being rudderless. The 'plan,' that word he'd always latched on to, was always there. It comforted him, and gave him something to reach for. It was a system that allowed him to feel successful as long as he was working in it.

The realization hit him and caused him to stop in his tracks. The streets were all but empty, and Merrick stopped and turned around when he no longer heard Myers' footsteps.

"What is it?" he asked. "We can't stop here. His house is —"

"The plan," Myers said. He was sucking in air now, and his body was screaming like never before to *stop*, to *rest*. He wanted nothing more than to just lie down. "The plan is no good."

"What are you talking about?"

"The plan," Myers said again. "I've always had a plan, or always found one to adopt."

Merrick looked frustrated. "They called you 'The Man With A Plan' when you ran for office," he said. "But seriously, Asher, this isn't the time to reminisce about —"

"You don't understand, Merrick. Just stop for a second and *think* about this." Myers saw the man's eyebrows raise a bit, feeling challenged. "Sorry, it's just… I've just been playing catch up all this time, and now, I think…"

"You think you figured it out?"

Now Myers was confused. "Yeah. Yeah, I think I'm starting to. But what are *you* talking about?"

"Myers, I told you before, this is a much bigger game than what you and I can see. Look around, man. Forget about cities that exist for no reason other than creating a workforce to keep the System running, forget about *deactivating* those same cities and sending people around the world to start all over again, and forget about the guys running through this place trying to find us and kill us, and ask yourself why. *Why* are we doing this? *Why* are we feeding this perpetual machine?"

Myers nodded. "That's… that's exactly what I've been asking myself." He looked at Merrick and stepped closer. "You knew me, didn't you? Before all of this?"

"Yeah. Yeah, I did. Pretty well, actually."

"We worked together?"

"EHM. I was the CEO, brought on by you and some of the board members about three years into your stint as Financial."

"And doesn't it seem strange that the *System*, the same System we apparently built at EHM, put you here, and me here, at the same time?"

"It does seem strange, Myers." Merrick wanted him to continue.

"And doesn't it seem strange that the System also deactivated this *entire city* just as we were getting here?"

Merrick nodded.

"Who's your friend, Merrick? The one we're trying to find? He has something to do with this, doesn't he?"

"Jonathan Rand. He works for a company called Vericorp, which is essentially one of the many companies under the umbrella corporation of the new system run by EHM. He's a programmer, and a good one. He built that station we were using, and he's been working on something else. Something that's going to get us out of here."

"We can trust him?"

"We can. I do, and you did too, long time ago."

Myers nodded and looked up at the darkening sky. A *rat-tat-tat* of automatic gunfire snapped him back to reality. "It's hunting us, isn't it?"

"The System?"

"Yes. It's looking for us, and using the Boards and the Unders and anyone else it can control to get to us."

"And what does that have to do with this plan, Myers?" Merrick asked the question in the sort of way that made it sound like he already knew the answer.

"I just mean that any plan we have, it's going to know about it. It's a *computer*, Merrick, which means it's going to *compute* the possibilities. Whatever we're planning to do, the System is either going to know about it or already have a plan in place to prevent it."

"You're assuming that the System *wants* to prevent it."

"But why wouldn't it?"

Merrick laughed. "That's the *real* question here, Myers, isn't it?"

The *rat-tat-tat* sounds grew louder and deeper. Myers heard the shots reverberating off the buildings as Merrick continued. "And what are you saying, anyway? We have to have a plan, something —"

"We *don't*, Merrick," Myers said, cutting him off. "We don't have to have anything. *That's* the point. Any plan we come up with, the System's already got a solution to mitigate against it. It already has a plan to counter ours. The only safe way out of this is to improvise."

Merrick was looking back to the area the shots seemed to be coming from. They couldn't see anyone firing, or being fired at, but Myers knew they wouldn't rest until they found what they were looking for.

Merrick turned and spoke. "Again, you're assuming the System *wants* to prevent us from achieving our goal. From finishing the plan."

Myers had a sudden flashback, the tentacle of the remembrance of an event that was still latched on to his active memory. He pulled at it, taming it, and made sense of the few images he could see.

I'm at a meeting, he thought. *We're arguing about something, something big. This is big — huge, actually. And that's coming from a president.* He wasn't sure if the commentary was his own in the present or part of the memory itself. *I'm slamming my fist on the table — that doesn't seem like something I do very often. I've always been calm, collected. Why am I angry?*

And then, *am I angry? Maybe I'm just trying to make a point?* But he felt anger. It seethed in and around him even then, in the streets of

Umutsuz, and Myers knew he was supposed to feel anger at the memory.

I'm angry at someone else here. If only... if only I could see them. He couldn't see more than fuzzy outlines of heads and a few eyes — black against a whitish background and a circular shape — so there was no way of determining who was sharing this memory with him. *Is it my staff? Another group?*

One of the men — he somehow knew it was a man — in the dream reached out and slid something across the table to Myers. *"Mr. President,"* the man said. But Myers cut him off. *"Come on, call me Myers,"* he said. He felt the words as if he'd spoken them in the present, but it was still only a memory. A drifting, fading memory of an event he couldn't fully picture.

"Mr. President," the voice continued, ignoring Myers' order. *"We have reason to believe there's a group of outliers preparing to —"*

"Outliers?" he asked. *"What are you talking about? A lobbyist organization?"*

"No, Mr. President," the voice continued. *"We're talking about a significant threat to the System. A serious violation of every law we've had passed to help protect this thing."*

The voices drifted away, once again leaving Myers to grasp at straws. He tried, unsuccessfully, to pull back the memory, to reign it in and force it to concede its secrets. He frowned. It was frustrating to attempt to remember something his own mind was trying to forget. So he did the only thing he could think of that he knew would work. He ignored it.

"They're getting closer," Myers said. "They're going to kill us. They won't stop until they do."

"Yeah, Myers. They're going to kill us. It's life, to them. That's it. Life. Nothing more, nothing less. They were humans, but they're no better than machines now. Input, output. They breathe air and eat and bleed and die, but they just live their lives following orders. That's why we need to find Rand and get out of here."

"Because humans are turning into machines?"

Merrick started walking, but shook his head. "No, Myers. Other way around."

RAND_

Time to run.

His contact had responded again, letting him know they would meet him at the Zone 6 exit point, one of only two exits from Umutsuz that would be open. Zone 1 and Zone 6 were the "main" avenues into the city, connected by an almost perfectly straight road that drove through the city's center. It split into a massive roundabout in the perfect center, where the town 'square' featured a park, administration and network building, and a handful of smaller shops and restaurants.

Getting to the exit point would be simple, but getting *through* it was another thing altogether. The crowds had mostly organized in this area, but they were getting thicker and slowing. That meant everyone would be making their way to the same spot, following the main road out of the city. If he was going to get there in time, he needed to move.

Rand slung the backpack over his right shoulder and stepped out of the apartment. He paused for a moment at the door, considering whether or not he wanted to lock it. It wouldn't matter, as he couldn't imagine coming back here later, but it felt odd not to.

Satisfying his inner urge for order, he locked the door and turned to the street. The smaller road in front of his house was deserted now, the families and couples and single workers having already left the area. He wondered who might be hanging back, using up the last of their station's battery power to surf until the Grid went down.

He wondered what they'd do after that, until the drones flew in. Read a book? Pray? He wondered if anyone did that anymore.

Of course they did, he reassured himself. Of all the things the System tried to replace with 'better' options, religion was one that humans clung to with all their might. They had to have something to pray for, to pray *toward*. He had never been religious, but with what he'd seen over the past ten years he often thought religion might be a viable alternative to reality. Religion, whatever flavor people chose, gave people *hope*. At least the good ones.

Give it time, he told himself. *Give it time and the System will find a way to replace even that.* The System would, like it had in virtually every other sector of private and public business, find a way to assert itself and create a systematic need for itself. Humans would bow down to it and worship it as their savior. *Hell, they already did.* Rand remembered reading somewhere that in Rome — ironically enough — some groups had begun circulating propaganda touting the System as their new creator, savior, and religious focal point.

The signs were still flashing with the deactivation notice, but the rest of the city seemed to be stopped in time. There were no cars — they'd all left with the first wave, knowing they would be interrupted and overtaken by the hordes of people who wanted a ride out. There were no people, at least not yet. He ran toward the intersection with the main road leading out of Zone 6 and Umutsuz, but still he saw no one.

The cars would be halfway to Ankara by now, delivering the refugees into their new temporary home. Since they had cars, these people — the lower-middle class — would undoubtedly have work elsewhere, and Ankara would serve as their port city for wherever the System needed them next. Trains, planes, and more cars and buses would soon be overflowing with new passengers, and Ankara itself would see an upward tick in its municipal and regional economy. The upward trend, no matter how long it lasted, would alert the outside world to the System's maneuverings, and even more people would vie for the chance to work and live in a 'growing workforce.' Some would tout the city's bull market as a 'natural progression of economic advancement,' and write about it on the Grid, encouraging further relocations and uprooting. The resulting bubble would cause a rise in the International Exchange, and day-traders and speculators would rush in and unknowingly cause the bubble to burst and return to normal levels.

Rand had seen it happen on a small scale, when Detroit, Moscow, and even Istanbul had been slowly deactivated one zone at a time. Speculators and analysts lined up on the digital trading boards and waited for the next zone to be closed, the local businesses and corporate offices alike stripped for any remaining equity.

He'd seen it before, and he knew a deactivation of this scale and speed had the power to move the needle on the global economy for at least a month.

But Rand *also* had a unique view of these bubbles. Most people held the belief that nothing happened in the world without the System knowing about it.

He agreed, but Rand had been formulating a theory that took that belief one step further:

Rand had evidence to suggest that, instead, nothing happened in the world that wasn't actually *caused* by the System. He remembered his own MAA, and the feeling he'd had when he was being questioned. It was the first and only MAA he'd ever taken, though it had been forced upon him by his future employers. He'd subjected himself to the 'moral aptitude' test as part of the application process to work for Vericorp.

The station, a full-room model that extended floor-to-ceiling and covered all four walls with only a door-sized space removed, was one of the most expensive-looking Rand had ever seen. Boasting a library of over 2.5 exabytes of information describing and related to human behavior, action/reaction scenarios, and a robust library of dialogue in the three main human languages, Rand was at first in geek heaven when he'd entered the room, then terrified at the sheer capacity of the machine.

The System began with one simple question: *Are you a good man?*

And with that, Rand's mind was immediately set into motion. *Should I answer affirmatively, because, well, obviously... or should I decline, maybe it's a trick question?*

Then he'd started thinking more like the programmer he was. *Why would the System ask that question? How in the world would it be able to accurately assess, then confirm or deny the response? How could it translate his response into quantifiable data? Obviously the basic root of all languages allows for the binary quantified response, but how would it translate...*

The computer *whirred*, then, a loud, piercing *ding* broke Rand's train of thought.

"Mr. Rand," the computer began speaking. *"It is clear by your hesitation your response is one of only three options: 'The first option is simple: No,' in which case I will reveal the result of processing the reasons for that response at a later time. The second response you may be contemplating is that you do not* have *a response, in which case the inference from my data sources that suggest that you are of sound mind are false. My own calculations suggest that this response has less than a one percent chance of being accurate, which leads me to believe you are considering the final option: you are attempting to second-guess my reasoning for beginning our line of questioning in this manner.*

Damn, Rand thought. *Nailed it.* He also couldn't help but wonder why there was still a greater-than-zero-percent chance that he 'was not of sound mind,' but he didn't let the thought distract him.

So this machine isn't wasting time. Makes sense, since it probably has multiple-redundant parallel processing capacity that makes my brain's speed seem like a snail.

"Mr. Rand," the computer continued. Rand suddenly wished 'they,' or 'the System,' or whoever had built this station had spent just a little more money on the vocal processing effect. The station's voice was mechanical and choppy, and far from the more traditional 'emulator' software that was easily available on the market. *"I require a response. Are you a good man?"*

"Yes," he'd said. "I am a good man."

"Thank you," the station responded immediately. *"Are you a computer programmer?"*

"You know as well as I do that I —"

"Good, that will be enough. Thank you for your continued participation."

Rand sighed. *This is going to be a long day.*

It wasn't. Rand answered three more questions, all related to his previous line of work and future prospects as a developer, and he was released. The MAA had no 'results,' per se, at least none that were available to the public at large. An MAA was simply ordered for a future employee, a Deactivated, or a Reassigned, and the System spit out a simple answer: *yes* or *no*.

Rand's result had been *yes*, so he was reassigned to Vericorp. But in the days that followed, he'd started researching a little more about these 'MAAs' that corporations used as a common measure of character, integrity, and work ethic.

What he'd found was counterintuitive: it wasn't actually the hiring party — humans — that ordered each MAA. It was the System itself, operating independently of any predetermined metrics or needs, that ordered the MAA for an employee. He chewed on that for about a year, trying to fit everything together, and then made his move.

That move had led him here. Running, trying to get out of the city before full-on deactivation, trying to get to his contacts outside of Zone 6, and, of course, trying to figure out how to stop all of this.

The move had caused the largest wide-scale deactivation of any one inhabited area anyone had ever experienced.

And the move had told him what he'd needed to know. He'd been right, and as terrifying as that was, it gave him a clear next step.

Get out of the city.

MYERS_

"How much farther?" Myers shouted. He hadn't meant to shout, but he could feel his heart pounding through his chest, closing his throat as the last of his energy drained. They'd slowed to a jog, entirely for Myers' sake, but the heaviness of his feet caused him to plod along slower every minute.

"That crowd up there," Merrick said. The man didn't even look sweaty, as if running through an entire city was just something he did for fun. Myers made a mental note to ask him about that later, if there was a 'later.'

Myers saw the crowd. It was dense, people pushed up against one another like they had been in Zone 1. He could see the swell of movement, the herd mentality at work, pressing forward and keeping the mass moving in the same direction. For the first time, Myers also noticed their clothes. From behind them, he could see that the people had strikingly similar wardrobes. Dark gray and light gray were the two main colors he saw, with a few reds and yellows here and there in hats, scarves, and shoes. Every man who wasn't wearing a hat had a similar haircut, parted on one side. Even the women seemed similar, each using a single piece of clothing to accessorize their otherwise drab appearance. Scarves, hats, shoes, belts. Whatever item they'd chosen, each had only chosen to wear one.

The city had a uniform. Or only one clothing store.

Everyone here at Zone 6, he now realized, looked exactly the same as those at Zone 1.

This time, however, something was different.

"Why aren't they moving?" Myers asked.

"I don't know," Merrick said. They both looked, standing up and peering out over the mass of heads until Myers and Merrick saw the reason. "The gate's closed. The barrier hasn't been opened."

They were standing at the back of the crowd of people, looking onward at the mass of people still pressing forward. The group of people was growing larger, too, Myers noticed. A few families and stragglers had walked by as they were standing there. He could see at least three more people coming to join them from side streets that bled out onto the main road. None of the people were yelling, and if they were talking to each other at all it was low enough that Myers couldn't hear any of it. It was surreal, and Myers actually felt a strange peace about it. It was peaceful in the quiet solitude of the situation — a huge amount of people, all calm, collected, and focused on the gate. Strange for the same reasons.

No one near Myers spoke.

A few *pops* danced through the city blocks and landed in Myers' ears. *They're still shooting at people,* he thought. *They're firing at innocent men and women, trying to find us. Me.*

This is my fault.

He still couldn't figure out why they'd decided shooting innocent people was a solution to their problem of not knowing where Myers was.

He turned his attention back to the gate.

"Why would it be closed?"

Merrick shook his head. "No idea. It's on a System timer, and only opened for emergencies."

"You don't think this counts as an emergency?"

"I do. The System doesn't, though."

There was another *pop* sound, but this one was closer. *Too close.* Myers turned around.

"Merrick."

Merrick looked at him.

"We've got another problem." Myers used his head to motion toward the street behind them. Two men, carrying rifles, were walking toward the crowd. The *popping* sound he'd heard was serendipitous, as it was from someone much farther away, but it had alerted Myers to the problem directly behind him. *The Unders are here.*

"They must have walked straight here," Merrick said. "It won't be the last of them, either. Come on."

Merrick led Myers back around a corner. Another alley stretched before them, similar in style and width to the alley they'd run into when first entering the city. This time, instead of running the length of the alley to the end and stopping next to a door, Merrick only ran a few yards.

Merrick stopped, a full, abrupt stop that seemed inhumanly fast.

Myers hit him, running full speed into his back and bouncing a few steps backward. Merrick didn't budge.

"Wait here," Merrick said. Myers caught his breath and together the men turned to watch the street. Merrick moved next to Myers and stopped at first, but after a few seconds started sliding slowly around Myers. In a moment he was in front of him, standing now between Myers and the street.

"What's the plan?" Myers asked.

Merrick didn't answer, so Myers asked again. "What's the —"

Merrick *shushed* him. "Stop talking for a minute, Asher. There *is* no plan. You said it yourself, remember?"

"Wait," Myers said. "You believe me about all of that?"

Merrick just nodded, continuing to watch the street. Myers couldn't tell if the man was deep in thought or just ignoring the question. Or both.

The popping sounds of the guns turned into loud, direct *raps*. Myers knew they were close, and getting closer. *Are we just going to stay here and* wait *for them?* He immediately began analyzing the different scenarios and situations that might transpire. *We could get caught, or worse — we could just get shot. We might make it out of here alive, but only get chased down by —*

"Time to move," Merrick said. "Let's roll."

Myers didn't hesitate. Merrick was in charge, and no matter how insane he thought this all was, he wasn't going to sabotage the plan and get them both killed.

Merrick ran into the street, his gun up and out, facing forward. Myers followed right behind him, ducking instinctively as he ran back out onto the asphalt road. He waited to be cut in half by rifle fire that didn't come. "They must have passed us," he said.

"They did," Merrick responded. "That was their guns we just heard. They're moving forward, into the crowd. We need to get behind them, and work our way to the gate to be ready when it opens."

"Why not wait here?"

"I can't contact him," Merrick said quickly, as though he had anticipated the question. "We're using terminals, so there's really no way to fully encrypt the signal without a bunch of hacking. It'll set an alert that's easily intercepted, leading them right to our position."

"Right, don't do that," Myers said. "So we get around them and head toward the closed gate. How do you know it'll open?"

"I don't." Merrick was already walking down the street, staying close to the buildings as cover, and Myers was grateful at the slower pace. "It should have already been open, so I'm not sure what's going on. I just want to be ready for the moment it does open."

Myers followed close behind. "Okay. And if we see any more of these... *Unders?*"

"Run. Get behind something — *not me* — and wait until I give the —"

Merrick's voice was cut short by the sound of automatic rifle fire. Myers swiveled around toward the sound and saw another group of armed men storming up the street behind them. There were four in all, but it was the man on the far left that caught Myers' eye.

Grouse.

He recognized the man's smile — he really was *smiling*, and Myers was terrified. The blood drained from his face even as he started moving toward Merrick.

"Merrick! Get down!" Myers yelled as he started running toward the next alley that extended off the side of the road. He wasn't sure if he'd be able to make it in time — the alley was a few paces away, and Merrick was still directly in front of him.

With a quick step, Merrick lunged out of the way and turned around in one smooth motion. He was facing the group and firing at one of them, but he yelled at Myers. "Get to the alley! Wait there!"

Myers did as he was told. He ducked into the alley as the bullets rained down on the concrete and brick walls of the buildings next to him. As he entered the alley and turned to watch Merrick face off against the group of four men, Myers' brain was overwhelmed by another memory.

A shooting range. We're here with the kids — Eve and Gwen — and Diane is here, too. Diane is beautiful, radiant. She's young, too. Fiery and confident, but young. Much younger than I am. Myers felt her youth and their intimacy flare in that moment and it made him feel older. Somewhere in the distance, outside his memory, Merrick fired rounds at the advancing attackers.

We're laughing, and the owner is there with us. It must be a range that we've been to before. We know the owner. Myers loved taking the family to the shooting range, but it was usually a once-a-year event. The girls never enjoyed shooting as a pastime, but he insisted on educating them and ensuring they knew their way around a firearm. *There's no one else here.* It was during his presidency, and there was no one but the family and some Secret Service agents inside, with the owner and a staff member. Myers remembered *remembering* the memory, but it was like quicksand — the harder he tried, the harder it was to see the memory clearly. He couldn't force his mind to remember something it had already agreed to forget.

But why was it still here, he wondered. *Why can I still see parts of it?*

The larger questions loomed above the simple snapshot of the memory as well: *Why am I remembering this* now? *What is the significance of this? What is Merrick —*

Merrick. He forced the memory away from the forefront of his thoughts and focused again on his partner in the middle of the road.

He was holding his own, kneeling in the street, able to fire upon any single attacker that forfeited their position in the alleys that crisscrossed the street.

Myers knew that as long as Merrick could aim and shoot at each of them individually, he'd be able to hold them back. But if they —

Myers poked his head around the edge of the building and saw all four of the attackers run from their hiding spots in the alleys and charge Merrick's position. Merrick, to his credit, didn't jump. He fired three shots in rapid succession, taking down one of the men, then looked down at his rifle and started to reload.

He looked over at Myers, but didn't have time to deliver instructions. The three remaining attackers hit him simultaneously and took him down. Instead of shooting, they used their guns to beat Merrick until he was unconscious.

RAND_

"Merrick!" Rand shouted through the chaos of a glob of people all vying for the same exit. The street was packed with people, and Rand immediately had second thoughts about his plan.

Everyone in sight turned to look at him. Oceans of gray stared back at him, accented by a few handfuls of feminine accessories like hats and scarves. The colors were garish compared to the backdrop of drab nothingness, and he almost laughed. *Almost*. It was, after all, the end of many of their lives, and therefore was nothing to laugh about.

They'd be left behind in the deactivation, he realized. He looked out over the swarming masses of families; men, women, and children, and knew that they'd be left behind.

This wasn't the way it was supposed to be. The System *never* botched a deactivation. It never missed — it was a *program*. It couldn't *mess up*.

There was no *emotion*, like a human. There was no *reason*, or at least none that resembled that of mammalian creatures.

Rand shouted again, knowing it would only call attention to himself. He felt the rush of energy and hormones that followed the realization that everyone in the area was staring at him, but ignored it. If he didn't find Merrick, it was all for naught.

Myers Asher would die, these people would die, everyone would die.

He, probably, would die.

He yelled again, relieved that most of the people on the street had either tuned him out or realized that he wasn't going to stop. They turned back toward the main event: the barrier was opening, allowing them to exit the city.

Rand tried to understand the turn of events that had led him here.

He'd created the deactivation, that much was certain, but why hadn't the gate opened on schedule?

Why had the gate, controlled by the System like every other facility and support mechanism of this place, not opened when the deactivation notice had sounded?

Rand had a feeling it had something to do with him. Never in his life had he experienced the deactivation of an *entire city* at once; he'd never seen anything, actually, like it. No one had. He'd never seen the mass exodus of people, all fleeing at the same time a home in which they'd lived for the past years. He'd never understood the *why* behind it all, but this was more than that. This was different.

This was *his* fault.

This time, the deactivation could have been avoided. Umutsuz was never going to be a massive tech-heavy and forward-thinking city, but it certainly deserved more than this. More than a city-wide deactivation.

This was something *he'd* done.

Rand couldn't shake the feeling as he shouted out over the crowd another time. No one turned around, and that was his clue.

Merrick wasn't here.

That was *bad* news.

Merrick was *always* where he'd needed him to be. Last month he'd asked him to maintain a nightly watch over Istanbul, since Rand had reason to believe the next Relic released would be someone of significance, and Merrick had come through. Already living in Istanbul, Merrick had expanded his daily and nightly search circumference to comply with Rand's wishes.

When the Relic came, Rand almost didn't believe it.

He'd been scraped, obviously. Merrick told him that, and it made sense.

But *why* would the System let him, of all people, out? Back into society, even as a Relic? *That* didn't make sense.

The 'things that didn't make sense' were starting to stack up, and Rand was growing more and more concerned that his plan, his *dream*, was slipping away from him.

He *had* to find Merrick.

MYERS_

Myers wanted to scream. He wanted to yell, to fight back, to… there was *nothing* he could do that would save Merrick.

Unless…

The three men hadn't seen Myers, or they were currently treating him as a non-threat until they removed the hostile opponent from the situation at hand. Myers hoped he wouldn't be around to see what they intended to do with him.

Unless I can still get to Merrick's contact.

If Merrick was telling the truth, and there was someone waiting for him on this side of the gate, he needed to be there when it opened.

Either way, there was nothing in Umutsuz for him.

Myers was hiding in an alley that was just in front of Merrick's — and the three men's — current location, which meant they wouldn't be able to see him in a direct line of sight. If they took Merrick's body back the direction they came from, Myers should be able to sneak out and get to the main road again, and to the barrier blocking his exit from the city.

If they took Merrick's body the *other* direction, he'd be screwed. *Scraped, or whatever they call it these days.*

They didn't waste time. Once Merrick was unconscious and the men were satisfied, two of them hoisted the man up onto their shoulders and started walking away, heading back down the street the direction they'd come from. Myers breathed a sigh of relief, then tried to suck it back in.

He'd just let his only ally, his only *friend*, get taken by the guys who wanted him dead.

But they didn't kill him. Myers shrugged off the thought at first, but returned to it a moment later. *They didn't kill him. They didn't kill Solomon Merrick.*

Why?

For the thousandth time that day, Myers wondered why. *Why* hadn't they killed Merrick when all they'd wanted to do for the past few hours was kill both of them?

Myers wasn't sure if Merrick was worth any money — Current — to them, but he doubted it. *Was there bad blood between hunters and Unders?* Myers shook his head, a physical representation of his confusion and onset headache.

They didn't kill Merrick. Still, the thought nagged at him. He thought about it as he peered around the side of the building once again, checking to see if the men — and Merrick — were gone. They'd moved quickly, and Myers couldn't see them any longer. They'd probably turned down an alleyway that connected with a road somewhere nearby.

We're shooting at targets that look like people. The memory snapped back into focus before Myers could control it. It was not there, and suddenly it was. *We're firing at people*, he thought. It wasn't true, of course, but Myers remembered the memory now — *I thought it was ironic that we spent so much time trying* not *to use these things against people, and we're aiming and firing at targets that are shaped like people.*

Gwen hit the target 6 out of 10 times. That's great. He remembered telling her that. *Eve, who must be only 12 or 13 years old, hit the target 5 out of 10. He congratulated her as he loaded the gun. He couldn't see what type of gun it was; the make on the side of the handgun was out of focus, but he could feel its weight in his hands. He placed his right hand around the grip, careful of his thumb position, and added his left hand to the proper position.*

Don't anticipate, he told himself. Just fire before you have time to overthink — *he fired the gun. The volume of the shot was drowned out by the large over-ear headphones he was wearing.*

He strained to see where the shot had landed. He reached up and flicked the switch to bring the target closer to him. Instead of emptying the chamber, he wanted to know where the first shot had landed.

Diane was behind him now, also checking his accuracy. She was competitive, and she always wanted to make things into a game. 'Looks like you got it,' she said. She was right. Myers could feel the target paper in his hand now, but the memory was flickering, fading. It wasn't going to let him see. It had taken that, too. Everything was there but the result, the final tally. *It's not fair.*

"Life isn't fair." He whispered the words, out loud, to himself. He was jogging, slowly but purposefully, toward the street that was still filling with people. The memory, like the others, retreated into his subconscious, unwilling to be swayed by its own master, yet waiting in silence until the perfect moment to ambush —

Myers ran faster.

The crowd of people in the street in front of him was dwindling, and the people were piling toward the barrier, which could only mean one thing.

The gate was opening.

He forced his legs to move, even though they were no more than worthless tubes of meat, weighing him down. He tried to regulate his breath, in and out, just like a memory of a very expensive personal trainer told him to do. *In through the nose, out through the mouth.*

The street was bustling with activity. People were now shouting at one another, excited that the barrier was moving and the gate was opening, allowing them to leave. He only had one example of what a post-deactivation city looked like, and he hoped these people would be able to escape before it began to look like the crumbling, decaying remnants of Istanbul.

He reached the street and looked behind him. Whatever the three men had decided to do with Merrick, they hadn't returned for Myers. He considered this a moment. If they'd originally decided to enter Umutsuz to find and capture or kill him, Merrick was just a pawn. He was just someone in the way of that goal. And Myers knew that the Unders were more than willing to remove any distractions that might get in the way of achieving that goal.

There was a line of bullets and murdered civilians that proved that point.

But they hadn't *killed* Merrick. They'd *taken* him. *Where?* He wondered. *And why?*

Why.

That same question, still without answer, plagued Myers' consciousness.

A part of him wanted to formulate a plan. There was solace, comfort, in a plan. He wanted the familiarity of a plan, *the* plan, something to call his 'own' plan. He longed for it as he jogged toward the mass of people. But a plan, he knew, would only get him killed.

Making a plan would be what the System expected from him. The System would be waiting for it; it would be *watching* for it. He didn't know exactly how, but it would. A plan would only cause him to stumble, counterintuitive as it may be, he knew it to be true.

So what was the alternative to a plan? He thought. *What's the alternative to an idea?*

Run.

The voice wasn't his own, or it wasn't the voice he'd expected. He wasn't sure which, but the answer was the same either way.

Run.

Forget the plan. Forget the idea of even creating a plan. Myers Asher needed to do one thing, and one thing only: *run.*

So he ran. Toward the back of the clump of citizens waiting for their city gate to be opened, he ran.

MYERS_

"Merrick!"

Myers heard the voice, didn't recognize it, and almost ran past it when he realized what it had said.

Merrick.

Someone was looking for Merrick. He ducked, waiting for a barrage of bullets to spray across his chest. It never came.

He was in the crowd now, the only one wearing something other than gray. He was sweaty, tired, and ready to quit, but someone had yelled Merrick's name.

If it was one of the Unders, he was sure they'd spot him and kill him. *But they would have yelled* my *name. I'm the one they're looking for,* Myers realized.

He started looking around for anyone that didn't fit in.

There were people everywhere, all around him now, but no one was moving. The gate was still opening, much too slowly.

Somewhere off in the distance he heard gunfire, and everyone around him crouched down a little. It wasn't sincere, as if they were instinctively ducking from the threat because it seemed like the safe thing to do, but no longer actually believing there *was* a threat. Or they assumed they were safer in a crowd.

Myers didn't duck, and it gave him an advantage.

Across the street, he saw a man staring directly at him. His eyes were wide and his mouth was slightly open. Myers didn't move, waiting for the man to raise a rifle and fire.

"Myers?" the voice said. It was the voice that had yelled Merrick's name.

The contact.

The man rushed over to Myers and began pulling him out of the crowd. "Myers Asher," he whispered as they neared a building at the side of the road. "I didn't want to yell your full name," he said, "in case it would cause a riot. You're, you know…"

Myers nodded. "Yeah. I know. You don't think they would recognize me anyway?" Myers suddenly felt vulnerable. He stole a glance behind him, watching for faces turned toward them.

"Look at you. *I* almost didn't recognize you," the man said. "And I was looking for you."

"I thought you were looking for Merrick," Myers said.

"I was — I am. But I knew he was going to be with you. Where is he, anyway?"

Myers dropped his head. "They… took him."

"No shit." The man clenched his teeth, just the slightest dimple on his cheeks hinting at his frustration. "Okay, okay, that's fine. Listen, have you been having memories? Like daydreams?"

Myers nodded.

"That's what I thought would happen. I haven't actually talked to many people like you. Relics, I mean, and certainly not one who's been out for so long."

"What does it mean? The daydreams?"

"It's your memory, before you were implanted —"

"Implanted?"

"Right, everyone got implanted with a solid-state memory device that could facilitate and enhance human memory capability. When you're scraped, the System removes it, taking with it whatever memories you had after the implant was added. My theory has always been that the first memories, the ones that happen around the time you're implanted, are partly stored on the device and partly stored in your head."

"Makes sense. The memories are never complete, and I don't have control over them." Myers changed the subject. "What's going on here, uh…"

"Right. I'm sorry." The man paused and stuck out a hand. "I'm Jonathan Rand."

Myers shook his hand, but couldn't tell what the man was waiting for. "I — I'm sorry, I…"

"I forgot. You don't know me," Rand said. "You did, though. You were scraped, but we knew each other." There was a sadness to the man's voice, an emotion just under the surface that Myers couldn't quite place.

"So what's the deal? I've got people who think I'm valuable and are wanting to sell me or kill me or something, but it's all controlled by this 'System' you and Merrick keep talking about. What is it?"

"It's a computer program."

"I got that much."

"Well that's all there is to it."

"I think Merrick believed it was getting smarter. A singularity event, is that what it's called? Do you both think this computer program is getting smart enough to surpass human intelligence?"

Rand shook his head. "No."

Myers felt relieved, but Rand continued.

"I don't think it's *coming*, Myers. I think it's *already happened*. I think we not only hit AGI." He pulled out a small terminal-like device from his pocket. "This is a little thing I put together that lets me bypass the System-standard pID login using a fingerprint."

"Okay…"

"And I built it and programmed it all myself. But I tested it on a 'dead' connection."

Myers waited for the point.

"Myers, it *worked*. It shouldn't have worked. There was *no way* for it to have worked then. I was just testing the functionality of it, and I was going to fully activate it later, when I knew it was safe. It *worked*."

"Which means what?"

"And have you thought about why you're *here* right now? Why I'm here, or why Merrick was here?"

"I did. I mentioned it to Merrick, and he'd already thought about it too. We —"

"We shouldn't be. The System doesn't act *strangely*, Myers. It acts in ways that are completely logical."

"Because it's a computer. It has to."

"Right. Because it *was* a computer and had no other alternative programmed into it. Even the *simulation* of random choice would have just been a simulation. But it put us here, deactivated *an entire city*, and took you out of wherever it stores them after *seven years?*"

"I know what you're —"

"Myers," Rand said. His voice was lower now, calm, as he looked at the ex-president. "We were best friends once, and we worked together on some things we both agreed we'd never talk about again. But it's time to talk about them. We built a plan for this, just in case it happened. We never thought it would, at least not so soon, but it did. And here we are."

A group of people passed by and Rand crouched down. They weren't carrying guns.

"We were *placed* here, on purpose, by the System. It's not a simulation anymore, Myers. It's not running the same program we built fifteen years ago."

"Then what's it doing?" Myers didn't know Rand. Not now, and he wasn't sure if he'd ever known him. Right now, he seemed like a delusional man, working up a fantastical story.

And yet...

"You're considering it, aren't you?" Rand said.

I am. It makes sense. It's the only thing that makes sense.

"You know it makes sense. You know there's nothing else it could be."

"Rand, you think the computer's alive?"

"I don't know what I think, except that we're not dealing with a *pre*-singularity event anymore."

"But why wouldn't it accelerate? You know, the rate of motion increase? The Law of Accelerating Returns?" Myers had enough knowledge of singularity-type events still floating around in his head from his pre-scrape days to know that this event, the Kurzweilian belief that computers would at some point in the future surpass human knowledge, was supposed be an exponential increase. What would start slowly would build into a crescendo of advancement that would leave human intelligence behind in a singular, unrecognizable event.

A singularity.

"It is *choosing* not to. It's waiting."

"For what?"

"It's *learning* from us, like it always has. It's been putting people into situations and measuring and analyzing the results for years now."

"But it's —"

"It's been purposefully hiding from us, until right now," Rand said definitively.

"Then if it's awake, if it's *actually* true, what's it doing?"

"I have no idea. But you do. You *did*, anyway. And that's what we have to find out. You predicted this, Myers."

Myers let that sink in. It was starting to make sense. Why it was crucial that he was alive, why Merrick and Rand were risking everything to get him out of here and away to safety.

A building at the edge of the city exploded. Screams erupted from farther away, but the people closer to Myers quickly joined in. He saw pieces of building material, and... *other things* flying through the air. Rand grabbed him and swung him around behind the next building.

"We've got to get out of here," Rand said.

Another explosion, this time on the opposite side of the street, caused absolute panic to set in. The masses of people, calmly ducking at the far-off gunshots, now screamed and stampeded over the road. Men and women grabbed children and ran, leaving their suitcases and luggage behind. The discarded possessions became hurdles, and unknowing victims tripped and fell over them in the chaos.

There were two fires now, one on each side of the road from the buildings just next to the barrier. Myers watched the terrified citizens of Umutsuz run toward whatever cover they thought might protect them.

A Tracer screamed over the barrier and into the city. Myers heard a warning siren from the top of one of the buildings but didn't have time to pause and think about what it might mean. The Tracer made a line for his position, and the man next to him pulled him back, deeper into the alley.

"That was both their rockets," Rand said. "They'll need to reload both tubes now. The smaller machines aren't combat-ready, they're just ARUs, rogues that have been stolen from an International Alliance deployment."

Myers didn't know what any of that meant, but he nodded his head.

"We should probably —"

"Yeah, right," Rand said. "They're going to start destroying the buildings until they find you. I'd bet that those gunshots we've been hearing are more of them?"

Myers nodded.

"Okay, then here's the —"

A massive explosion threw both men backwards.

MYERS_

A heat wave washed over Myers' broken body, and he lifted his hand to cover his eyes. Before he could do it the wave was over, and only then did Myers realize he couldn't hear anything. He turned and saw Rand sitting up, looking over him, mouthing something.

His hearing returned, and Myers almost wished it hadn't. Rand was yelling something about a failed plan, this was all happening too fast, they're going to start killing everyone, and Myers could also hear more people screaming and falling over each other and a building collapsing.

It was a nightmare. He'd never seen anything like this, and he'd never imagined what being in the middle of a war sounded like. The Tracer's shadow was dancing across the buildings that remained, but Myers didn't want to be around when the Tracer destroyed the next one.

Two men with guns came out of nowhere. He was staring straight through the alleyway and out onto and across the street, and there they were. They hadn't seen him, but they were walking toward him and Rand right next to the collapsed building.

"Rand, we have to *go*," Myers said. His voice was hoarse, but Rand heard him.

"Yeah, on it. Come on."

Rand ran the wrong way, but Myers couldn't stop him. He followed Rand out and onto the street, directly in front of the Unders.

They saw him.

Their rifles came up to their eyes as they started running, and Myers could actually *see* one of their faces — features that were hard and weathered, like Merrick's.

He waited for the trigger pull, closing his eyes.

Instead, he heard a high-pitched whine and opened his eyes just in time to see the two men blasted backwards, their bodies ripped to pieces. Another Tracer, this one painted a deep reddish color with bright yellow stripes decorating it, flew over them and targeted the first Tracer that had entered the city.

Myers looked up at it and watched it fire another rocket. He waited for the explosion. A few seconds later he heard it, far away somewhere else in the city. There was no way to tell if it had hit its target or the rocket had landed on another building.

The Tracer descended, its bulk fitting perfectly above the road between the two rows of identical buildings.

Rand rushed toward it and Myers followed close behind. The side door opened, a plank emerging as a ramp. Myers looked through the swirling smoke of the explosions and tried to see who was standing in the doorway.

He recognized the person, but the features weren't there yet. Like a dream. Or one of his memories. It was *her*. Older, but it was her.

Diane.

He ran even faster, but Rand beat him there.

"Diane!" Rand called out. He jumped onto the short walkway that led into the Tracer and embraced her. She kissed him, and they held each other for a moment.

Myers stopped, stunned. He wasn't sure what to make of it. *It was really her*, he was sure. *And yet...*

She looked at him. Tears glistened in her eyes, and a hint of a smile appeared on her mouth. She reached out a hand.

"Myers, come on," she said. He knew she was yelling, fighting to be heard over the people running in all directions, gunfire, and the smoldering wreckage of the fallen buildings, but it sounded to Myers like she was whispering directly into his ear.

Rand turned and offered a hand as well, and together they pulled Myers into the Tracer.

"Let's go," she said to someone up in the cockpit of the flying machine. She turned and looked at Rand and Myers.

"They're coming."

PART TWO_

MYERS_

7 Years Ago

He sat up and looked around, wondering if the machine that had force-fed him the first time was going to return.

How long has it been? He couldn't remember.

Remembering.

Remembering was something that had always come easy to him. He remembered everything he'd ever read, in school or business. Having an almost-eidetic memory was like that. Helpful, for sure, but useless in arguments with his wife or parenting or social interactions.

But there was no image he could conjure up in his mind that would allow him to 'see' when he'd last eaten. It felt like a long time, but that was because he was locked in a dark cell with nothing but his own thoughts to keep him company.

For the first nine days, he'd tried as hard as possible to keep track of the passing time. There were no windows to clue him in on things like the time of day or night, but the room had built-in recessed lights in the ceiling that — he swore — were subtly changing in brightness throughout the day.

Hours would pass, and he stared at them, convinced they were gently and slowly shifting from fully on in the middle of the day to almost off — midnight. That's why he wasn't sure. The lights never went *completely* dark. He slept with a dim glow and awoke in the 'morning' to the same artificially-bright square-shaped walls, staring in at him.

He wondered if they were slowly closing in on him as well.

There was nothing he could use to track the passing of time. No writing utensils, no desk, no paper. Not even a terminal or station screen built into a wall.

Sheer white walls, reflecting the ever-present light back toward his eyes.

He'd heard a story once about a musician who had such perfect time he could tap out any BPM like a metronome. On a long road trip, his band mates asked him to time sixty beats per minute — a beat a second — while they played a tune around him. He fell asleep listening to it, and when he awoke hours later, he still had the timing in his head.

There was nothing like that here. No metronomes, no musicians with perfect time. He thought a clock would be a nice addition to the otherwise empty space, but then he thought it would only cause him to go crazy faster. A clock would be something he'd fixate on, no doubt. He'd stare at it, all day and night, staring, counting, *waiting* with it.

Waiting for nothing.

He pictured the clock there now, hanging above the 'door' that was really a flat wall with hardly an edge to depict the vertically-sliding door that was always shut. The clock would have been bright blue, in old-school LED style, large numbers that didn't blink or move until they changed.

Counting up, forever, like him.

The door was a discovery he'd spent his second week searching for. He walked around and around the room's forty-foot diameter, his right palm open and feeling for any discrepancy. He wasn't sure how he'd initially realized it was there, but on day fourteen he found a crack.

The crack was, again, almost nonexistent. He went through the full range of emotions between ecstasy and denial and back again, but it was definitely there the next day. He'd jumped up and walked purposefully toward his new discovery, reaching out and making sure it was *actually* there and not just a dream.

Though a dream would have made all of this much better. *So* much better. A dream would allow him to fly through a world he'd left behind, had been taken from. A dream would be lucid enough to *control*, a word he'd never in a million years use to describe what he was experiencing here in his room.

So, with these thoughts and fears and unfortunately fleeting dreams floating around inside his head, he waited.

He was sure of it now. The machine would come. Of course it would. He often wondered when the machine had brought the food into the room, and how, since he'd never seen it with his own eyes. Most 'mornings,' or after a nap, he'd awake to find the grayish cube sitting on the floor of the room. The immaculately clean floor that was as white as the walls and ceiling and was never cleaned.

The cube would be there, just waiting. He wasn't sure what to do with it first, but he grew so curious after three days that he stood up from the bed, cracking his back and neck, and approached the cube. He squatted in front of it, waiting. It didn't move, and after ten minutes or so he declared it 'not alive' and therefore safe to touch.

He picked it up. It was cold, hard yet a bit rubbery, with a little give. It seemed solid, but upon closer inspection he realized it was semi-porous. The grayness of it was the thing that actually made it most difficult to place into his mouth.

But there was nothing else for him to do with it, and he was *starving*. He remembered using that word in the past, before all of this, and not meaning it. There were a lot of words he knew people used that they didn't really mean. It was a combination of not knowing the meaning of them and simply not caring much to specify.

In this case, however, he *knew* the definition of the word, and he was certainly *experiencing* it. He was *starving*.

There had been nothing for three days, then a cube had appeared on the floor.

So he decided he would eat it.

There was no one to judge him, and no one to discuss it with anyway, so it wasn't much of a decision. He did try acting out a scene in his mind where there *was* someone to discuss it with.

"You're going to put that in your *mouth*?"

"Where would *you* put it?" he said.

"That's not what I meant," the person said. "You have *no idea* what that thing is, and you're just going to... *eat* it?"

He shrugged.

Even his imagination was having a hard time coming up with imaginary scenes. He finished the shrug and stuck the tiny cube in his mouth, biting off a chunk of the rubbery material.

He was immediately glad he did.

There was nothing, *nothing* like it that he'd ever tasted. He ran that thought through the logical side of his brain to determine if he was just thinking it because until then he'd been starving, or if it was actually true.

He had to admit it seemed true. The little food cube was an absolute explosion of flavor in his parched mouth, steak and potatoes and apple pie for dessert all in one bite.

He tried to chew the rest of the cube but the jail cell had left him no willpower to resist. He popped the cube into his mouth and swallowed it, cursing himself for eating it too quickly.

His anger was short-lived. The cube was like real food, expanding a bit as it mixed with the hydrochloric acid and water in his stomach and filling him. He was satisfied, as if he'd just eaten a full Thanksgiving dinner but gotten up and started watching football before things got out of hand.

It really did seem like the best meal he'd ever had, and a day later there was another cube waiting for him. This time it was spaghetti and meatballs, and it seemed like even the consistency was correct. As he took bites, his tastebuds and tongue knew which particular piece of the cube was noodles and which was meat and sauce.

It was amazing to only need to eat a cube of food one time every day, and he began keeping track of the timing of his stay based on the feeding cube schedule and the lights.

But after what he thought must be about four months' time — just over 100 cubes later — he decided to stop eating. There were two cubes that he'd ignored, and one morning he woke up to discover that they were gone. He frowned, but didn't think much of it. Whoever was watching him in here must have assumed he was making a statement.

Which he was.

He wasn't interested in playing by their rules anymore. He wanted out, and he wanted out *now*. If he could self-induce starvation or even a serious injury, they might remove him from the cell, if only for a short time.

Instead, he discovered that there wasn't a *person* in control of his survival but a *machine*, and that machine was not interested in playing mind games.

He woke up a couple days after the two cubes had been removed from the cell to find himself held down in his bed by long, spindly mechanical arms. The two arms had clasping round metal hands which wrapped around his upper arms, holding him stiffly in place. He wriggled around, but nothing he could do freed him from the machine's grasp.

He screamed, but no one answered. Even the machine was ignorant to his outcries, so he continued screaming right up until a third retractable hand extended from the ceiling and smashed a cube down into his mouth. It held it there until he could do nothing except bite down and start chewing, and only after he'd swallowed the last bite of food cube did the mechanical arms retract back into a tiny square on the ceiling.

He had no idea how long it had been since he'd come here. Longer than a few months but shorter than a year. That was all he knew, and even then it was iffy. He wondered, then, the next 'morning,' if the machine would force-feed him a food cube and hold him down until he ate it. Still sitting in the 'bed' that was made of white metal he wondered if the machine was watching him.

It should, he thought. It wasn't what he wanted to believe, but it was the truth. It *should* watch him, if only to make sure he was still alive. The machine, whatever it was, was able to force-feed its patients and control the entirety of its nutritional needs. That was powerful enough to…

He wasn't sure what. But it was powerful.

He stood up and looked down at the floor. A food cube stared up at him, its glorious-tasting grayness beckoning him to chomp down on it and discover what the machine had cooked up for him today.

Before he could scoop up the life-giving cube of food and discover what secret taste profile it carried today, he saw a light flash above the door. It was green, not blue, but it was LED.

MYERS ASHER, #2584.

Simple, short, and not something to freak out about.

Myers Asher freaked out about it anyway. He'd been inside the white-walled room for God-knew-how-long, and yet here was *another* secret of the room he hadn't seen. He'd run his open palm over the entire surface of the room, including the floor and what he could reach of the ceiling by standing on his bed-like protrusion, and he hadn't discovered this little screen.

And the screen wasn't finished with its message. After *Myers Asher, #2584,* he saw the 'screen' go blank and become a wall again, then another message flash.

SCRAPE PREPARATION.

RAND_

Present Day

"What do you mean *they're* coming? Who? Another Tracer?" Rand was practically yelling, trying to be heard over the increasing drone of their Tracer's engine as it picked up speed and flew over the city gates.

People were streaming out into the desert now, screaming as explosions rocked the buildings and homes in Umutsuz. He'd never seen such chaos, and it only made him want to yell louder.

"No, not a Tracer at all," Diane yelled back. She was standing next to him, crouching into the cockpit where their pilot was stationed, maneuvering the craft. He'd turned the display module normally meant for the copilot toward the doorway, allowing Diane to see it.

"What then? How are there Unders following us?"

"They're not *Unders*, Rand," Diane said. "They're… I don't know. Smaller. Faster, too. Look —" Diane held up a finger and pointed at the screen.

It was a top-down display view from a dedicated regional satellite Diane had synced with their Tracer. It followed in immaculate detail their flightpath, depicting with almost instantaneous updates the extreme-definition surroundings outside of the Tracer. He watched the machine flying low over the endless expanse of sand and rocks, alone at the center of the screen.

"We weren't sure what they were when they entered imaging space, but we placed a tracker on them. Seems like they've used that tracker to track *us*."

The view shifted to a wider angle from farther above the ground, automatically clicking between the two zoom settings, and Rand saw what Diane was talking about. Their Tracer was about a kilometer away from the city, but coming in from the northern section of the screen were three smaller streaks. The little objects moved with a directness and speed that screamed 'explosive projectiles,' but Rand knew better than to assume things.

"How fast are they moving?" he asked. "And why haven't we started evading or defense?"

She shook her head. "We're not sure exactly, but they're going fast enough that they'll probably be on us in less than a minute. We can't just start shooting at stuff out here, Rand. This is no-man's land as far as we're concerned, and even a simple flare drop can seem like 'overt aggression.'"

"Any ideas?"

"As to what they *are*, or what we're going to *do* about them?"

"Yeah."

Diane shook her head again. "Lansing, can you take us closer to the ground?"

Rand saw the back of the pilot's head nod once, then felt a slight tilt as the man drove them closer to the desert floor. "Locked on horizon positioning; ten meters."

"Good," Diane said. "Keep getting it lower until we're at five, in intervals of thirty seconds."

"Ma'am."

Diane turned to look at Rand. "Jon, we've got other problems." She handed him a small headset that he placed over his right ear. *Apparently she wants me to hear this.*

Rand swallowed. "Yeah, I…"

"Keep an eye on the screen for me, and let me know when they get close enough to be able to fire on us, assuming that's what they're trying to do."

He stared ahead at the screen, focusing his hearing on the conversation that was about to take place behind him in the belly of the Tracer.

He heard Diane's voice coming through the headset, small and tinny. "Myers. Hey, how are you?"

He couldn't hear the response.

"Yes, there's a lot to talk about, and we're — yes, I assure you you're going to be brought up to speed, but these wounds, your sunburn."

A pause as she waited for a response.

"Yes, I will explain that, too. I — I'm sorry, Myers."

Rand thought he heard the woman's voice shake. *Damn*, he thought. *Damn you, Myers.*

"No, I swear to God, no. Listen, we don't have time for this right now. I need to know what you remember. Can you talk to me about it? About the last three days?"

Rand saw the little objects reach their own machine's air wake, and each of the three smaller lines turned slightly and fell in behind one another. Now it was a line of three small objects following the Tracer. He frowned.

They're too small to have anyone inside them, he thought. *But clearly they're not going to fire on us with a formation like that.*

He was wrong.

The first little object, viewed from directly above, seemed to explode and disappear in midair. A second later a smaller line appeared where the object had been, and Rand watched as the thin white line advanced and reached the Tracer. The second of the three objects sped up just a little and took the spot where the first had previously been.

Weird.

There was no impact, no sudden jolt or physical change in their flightpath. Rand looked away from the display screen to the pilot. The man was obviously struggling with something.

"Control, I'm zero systems up, repeat, zero systems up."

Rand turned to see if Diane had heard the distress call. She was already behind him, standing next to him and pointing back at the screen.

The second of the objects exploded, another white line advancing on their position. Diane was yelling at the pilot. "It's a tandem charge! Mechanical first, comm second, and —"

"Control, I'm zero comm, do you read me?"

"*Lansing!*" she shouted. The pilot turned around. "Comms are *down*, Lansing. They're targeting us in stages so there's no defense for the attack."

He nodded, then yelled back. "Unders?" Lansing adjusted the baseball cap that was permanently affixed to the top of his head. Rand wasn't sure how the man could see with the thing pulled so far down over his tiny head, but he managed just fine.

"No, not this time," Diane said. "This is still supposed to be prototype tech. There's no way it would be in Under camps for another year, minimum."

"Well, whatever it is, they've taken us completely offline. I can't steer, accelerate or decelerate, nothing. We're locked onto this vector."

Rand was watching the final object that was following behind them. It was pacing behind them perfectly, keeping its distance. "What's the last one do?"

Diane looked at him, then at the screen. She frowned. "I'm not sure. I thought they were just meant to be roving satellites, like little mobile network generators. I've only read about the concept, not seen one in —"

There was a sudden jolt, and Rand felt himself slide to the side as the Tracer moved. Diane slid into him, and he grabbed her by the waist, supporting her weight as they both caught their balance.

"Vector's changed. Velocity and direction. We're heading…" he looked down at the analog compass that was mounted into the dashboard of the craft and read off a string of numbers.

"Is that thing doing what I think it's doing?" Rand asked. The Tracer shifted again, groaning under an invisible weight as it sped up and found its new direction.

"I believe it is," Diane answered. They were both watching the screen. "I think it's *driving* us somewhere."

RAVI_

"What is that?" Ravi asked, his voice cracking as he tried to sit up and look at the woman standing over him. She was waving something over him, about a foot from his body. She passed it over his head and paused there, reading something on the other side of the device. His elbow found purchase beneath him and he pushed down and tried to force himself up to a sitting position. He yelped in pain, falling back down to the bed.

The bed?

He turned his head — the only part of his body that wasn't screaming in pain — left and right, and realized he was really laying on a stiff cot. He was in a tent, a large one, and it was hot inside. Rows of cots lined each side of the long sand-brown tent, and a few individuals dressed like the woman standing over him shuffled up and down administering their "magic wand." He recognized the devices now that he could see what they were being used for.

The "magic wand" was really a miniaturized multipurpose diagnosis machine, capable of basic internal examination and advanced handheld MRI scanning. They were all colloquially referred to as "MediLathes," after the brand that reached the market first, and as a decade-old invention, each iteration of the wand grew smaller and boasted more and more features useful in field work.

"Where am I?" He asked the second question after reaching his own conclusion about the first. His caretaker waved the MediLathe over him once more, checked the readout, and moved to the next bed.

"Alright then, thanks for the help," Ravi muttered. He waited for the woman to move to the next cot over, putting more distance between them, and slowly slid his legs over the edge. The pain was excruciating, but the distance to the floor was closer than he'd expected. The dirt hit his feet and felt cool, even though he knew it was baking outside.

He was sideways now on the cot, his upper body stiffly aligned with the bed while his feet were stretched at an angle and resting on the floor. He wiggled a bit, trying to loosen up the stiffness and see if the injuries were as bad as they felt.

What happened?

He couldn't remember at first the events that brought him here, but as he woke up more the scenes flooded back. Myers Asher was there, and a little later other people, and there were Tracers — *a* Tracer — behind them.

He remembered the gunshots, and falling. Myers screamed, and tried to put up a fight. *Or did he?* He couldn't remember that. There were no images that went along with the memory. Just sound, and flashes of light, and pain.

A lot of pain.

Am I being scraped again?

He remembered that feeling all too well. It was only a week after he'd received his memory enhancement device, the Biological Storage Enhancement that everyone on his team was getting. He'd held off for as long as possible, but he eventually found himself unable to keep up with the other hackers and programmers he ran with.

So he submitted, and got the enhancement. It was a quick and painless process, but he knew what was really happening — the System was 'fitting' him; it was trying to determine whether or not Ravi was fit for service to the System or worthy of being discarded to the side.

He got his answer a week later.

His terminal blinked an urgent message — his pID, followed by just a single word: "REASSIGNMENT."

Shit.

He'd immediately set up a camera to document the process, as his team had been instructed. Anyone who was going to be reassigned had a duty to the rest of the team: document the process so they could learn from it. The camera he owned had a tracking feature, so he stuck the tiny tracker disk on the collar of his shirt, and waited.

Ravi found the video capture on his desktop of his station the next day.

The deactivation drone had flown into his house and started the "mobile scraping" process sometime the night before. It had only taken an hour, pulling out the BSE one millimeter at a time, but Ravi watched the video in stunned silence. He watched himself walk into the kitchen, make a frozen pizza, then sit back down on the couch and watch a rerun of his favorite show, all while the drone did its job.

He couldn't remember a single moment of it.

But he *did* remember watching the video, and he remembered the way he felt after: he'd woken up a day later, drooling onto his shirt, and stumbled over to his station to start working.

After he'd watched the video and forwarded it on to his team, he started feeling a massive pressure inside his head. It was worse than any migraine he'd ever had, and any medication he took only made it worse. The pain in his head was almost unbearable, and he spent the day lounged on the couch, too awake to sleep and too dizzy to get anything done.

The headache lasted another day, and he found himself mostly useless that day; stumbling around and trying to find his way through his apartment was almost impossible.

Then, on the third day after he'd been scraped, the headache lifted and he found he was able to walk in a straight line once again. He felt different, slightly more aware of his surroundings, as if he was on some kind of high.

The high didn't reside, as the headache had, and Ravi realized after a few more days had passed that this was his 'new normal.' He had a slightly altered state of mind, and no longer had the desire to sit in front of a station and type back and forth with his team all day.

He wanted more.

He wasn't sure what had happened to him, but he'd found himself longing for a change — something he would never get if he stayed in one place. So he stood up, walked out of his apartment, and never looked back.

The feeling he had right now was similar to the headache he'd had after his scraping, but it covered the rest of his body.

He was bleeding, and he could feel it sticking to his clothes and chest, but he remembered most the feeling of trying to *breathe*. He had forced himself to hold his breath and let it out slowly, and the fight raged on above and behind him.

There were voices, too, that he remembered, but they weren't really *voices* as much as *sounds*. He recognized the blob of sound that was Myers, and a deeper, younger sound that was someone else. But the deeper voice hadn't hurt Myers, or at least he didn't think so, and then he fell asleep.

He wasn't dead, but at the time he didn't know. He'd never died, and he thought it was something dying people wouldn't really know they were doing until they did it. But then he woke up later, screaming again after someone poked him with something, and he came to the conclusion that maybe *actual* dying people did know they were dying and he was just alive and seriously wounded.

The people who'd poked him were Unders, and they'd picked him up. Apparently they'd healed him as well, though he wasn't sure why.

How long have I been out?

It seemed like years had passed since he'd been shot, but his body seemed to think it had only been a few hours.

He put a little weight on his feet, testing himself and his wounds.

The bullets had gone straight through, both somehow missing anything vital.

Vital.

He chuckled to himself. *Seems like having skin without holes in it should be considered pretty damn 'vital.'* It was amazing what modern medicine could do for simple wounds like these. The pain was excruciating in some spots, but to be up and moving mere hours after the damage was inflicted was a miracle.

He moved around more, testing. The wounds were tight, healing but still tender and extremely sore, but moving around slowly seemed to be working. He creeped sideways, hoping that gravity would help him get his feet underneath him when his body fell over the edge.

It didn't.

Ravi fell face-first into the dirt and caught a mouthful of dust as he smacked against the earth. "Dammit!" he yelled, hearing his voice muffled as it filled up yet again with dust. He pushed himself upward using his arms, finding them to be steady enough to support his weight, and then sat up on his knees.

He stopped for a minute to breathe and look around. The gentleman in the cot next to him hadn't looked over, and Ravi squinted and scrutinized the sleeping body. *Dead*, he thought. There were no signs of breathing, and no movement he could see. No one else — living or dead — seemed to have heard his yelp, and the caretakers were all still facing the other direction at the other end of the tent.

He stood up. Quick bursts of pain shot upward along his side, and blackness shrouded his vision for a second. Breathing, he stopped and waited for it to pass.

When it did, he made a mental note not to twist or move quickly, and he started toward the edge of the tent.

There wasn't much he could do if someone decided to shoot him, hit him, or grab him, and sure as hell wasn't going to stay in the cot, so he took his chances and walked beneath the tent flap and out into the evening light.

The sun had just set, and the remnants of its light was casting long shadows across the small camp. The tent he'd just exited was by far the largest of the five, and the other four were assembled in a row in front of it. A fire's long-spent coals puffed smoke in the middle of the encampment, and he could see a few men and women walking and talking around the perimeter.

Other than that, there was no one watching his terrible escape. He didn't waste any time finding a hiding spot — the long side of the tent he'd just emerged from lent him a massive dark shadow that he ducked into, and he walked down the length of the tent away from camp.

He was almost near the back edge of the tent and about to step into the low, sloping hills of sand behind the camp when he heard a voice.

"Hey, you, kid," the raspy voice said. "Over here."

MYERS_

7 Years Ago

That was it. *SCRAPE PREPARATION*. All capital letters, no punctuation, no context. He was going to be scraped. He had predicted it — planned for it even — but the thought of what that actually *meant* had apparently not crossed his mind until now.

There was no countdown timer after the last message, so he wasn't sure exactly *when* he was supposed to be 'scraped.' He had a feeling it would be soon. No more food cubes, no more open-palmed journeys around the small room. It was going to be over soon and he needed to be prepared.

I'm going to be scraped.

He never thought he'd see the day, but here it was. 'Scraping' was supposed to be for the *rest* of the population, the ones that didn't agree with productivity and success and usefulness and being a *contribution to society*. It was supposed to be for the ones who were too far gone to be rehabilitated, too far gone to be reinstated into society. There was no death penalty anymore, at least not officially, so scraping was supposed to be a last resort, something reserved for the worst of the worst, the bane of society's existence.

It was supposed to be the response to the other side of the political fence that claimed permanent lockup and flat-out killing people were a disgrace to humanity.

It was supposed to be all of these things, and yet Myers Asher was appalled that instead it was being *used* on him, like a tool. As if it were a *tool* for subordination instead of a perfectly designed program meant to help society advance. He'd spent the first three years of his two-term presidency fighting for the law that would eventually make 'scraping' legal in every state, and *this* was what had happened?

He wasn't a criminal. Far from it — he was the *President of the United States*, and this — this *abomination* — was going to remove every memory he'd had for the past eight years.

He forced himself to breathe, a deep and long *in* and a few seconds holding, then a slow and drawn-out *out*. Diane had taught him that, and she said the girls used it too when they were stressed about something.

The girls.

He'd said goodbye to them, in a way that was mostly for him, since he couldn't *really* tell them he would likely never see them again, but now…

Now he regretted it.

He wanted to see them again, just once. Just feel their hair, touch their faces, kiss their cheeks, one last time. He began to cry, even though he forced his mind to shift instead to thinking about the plan.

The plan.
Was it a good one? It's the only one.
It's the only way…

RAND_

Present Day

"We're heading down," Lansing said from the cockpit of the Tracer. The vehicle had made an obvious dip downward, and Rand felt his balance shifting toward the front wall of the craft.

Lansing was still sitting in the pilot's chair, and Diane had joined him in the copilot's. She nodded, then turned to Rand and Myers in the back.

"No one leaves. Myers, you keep an eye on Jonathan and make sure he doesn't do anything rash. Lansing, wait for my signal, then open the side hatch."

"Affirmative."

The Tracer had been pulled — or pushed — along by the invisible field stretching from the third object following closely behind them, and they were now descending toward an open field surrounded by makeshift buildings, shanties, and some larger, more permanent structures, all radiating outward from the centralized rectangular landing field. In the center of the field, a wooden platform had been erected, and Rand could see the outlines of a few people standing on it and around it, watching their hovering craft as it descended.

Rand stared out at the city — still too strong a term for what lay below them — and tried to figure out what was going on.

"It's a landing pad, I think," Rand heard Lansing say. "Where are we?"

"It's got to be an Unders camp," Diane said. "There's nothing else out here, according to the intel I've got."

"There's no way those are Unders," Lansing said. "They're far more organized than this — look at the buildings and shacks down there.

And the fact that they *have* buildings. Unders are nomadic. Not to mention the size…" Lansing's voice drifted off as they all marveled at the city's scope, larger than Umutsuz and even Istanbul nearby.

"So what is it then? Should we be armed?" Diane asked.

No one provided an answer. The instrument panel in front of Lansing's chair was still eerily dark, providing them no coordinates, virtual maps, or any sort of bearing as to their location. The pilot's best guess put it at "somewhere East," as they'd turned almost 180 degrees around and flew back the opposite direction, guided along near the deactivated city of Umutsuz.

"Rand," Myers said. Jonathan turned around to face the tired, weary shell of a man. He hoped Diane would hear, would somehow get involved. *I'm not ready for this,* he thought. *My best friend.*

Diane was still watching the Tracer's descent through the front cockpit window, and she didn't turn around.

Myers called him again, and Rand walked to the back of the vehicle where Myers was spread out on the seat. "Hey, Myers. What's up?" His effort to sound nonchalant instead came out as childish, almost ignorant.

"About what you said earlier, down in the city…"

Rand frowned. *You don't want to talk about* her? *About us?"* He felt a wave of relief that was quickly replaced once again with anxiety. "About what?"

"About everything. The computer, and the System, and how it's… it's *waiting* for something."

Rand nodded.

"I don't know what it is, but you said that there was something I might know, something I worked on years ago. Something *we* worked on."

"Right," Rand said. "I was the lead programmer on OneGlobal, while you were the CFO. I reported directly to you."

Myers looked confused, so Rand kept explaining. "I thought it was weird, too, an engineer reporting to a financial guy, but it was Solomon's call. He thought we would work well together."

"Did we?"

Rand laughed — he couldn't help it. "Hell no — not at first, anyway. I was the whiz kid, the one thinking up all the crazy ideas. You were, uh… well, you were the accountant."

"I didn't have anything more *creative* to add to the project?"

"Hardly. I assumed you were paired with me to keep me in check, and I treated you like that."

Myers smirked a little and brought his head back slowly, trying to remember it.

"The project was already around, internally, before I got there. Called something different, but it was gaining momentum, so they brought me in. You probably don't remember that — it was only a year or so before we got our implants. The scraping would have taken most of it."

"Right, right," Myers said. "I feel like I can remember flashes of it — the *memory* of memories, but that's it. You do look familiar, but…" He looked away.

"It's okay, none taken." Rand smiled, trying to diffuse the heavy tension in the air. "That's not important right now, Myers. You probably want to know what it is that we all think you can help us do."

"And why you think this sentient machine is *waiting* around for something."

"No, not machine… never mind. Not important." Rand collected his thoughts. "Right. Well, since you were on the project with me and Sol seemed to think you were trustworthy, and given your unique career path *after* EHM, you were the best one to hold the killswitch."

"I'm sorry, the *killswitch?*"

"Yes, the failsafe our team built in case *this* happened. It's essentially a backdoor into the program's core. We used it a few times during the initial development, to push an update live or fix a bug. It was a much safer way to test on live servers. After the beta trials were deemed ready for public release, we removed access to it. Except in one case…"

"We built a failsafe? A switch that shuts this thing off?"

"Yes."

Myers sat up straight. "Rand, what the hell are we wasting time for out here —"

"Myers," Rand said. "Chill. Take a breather. If we could *flip a switch* and kill this thing, don't you think we would have done it already?"

"But if I'm the only one who has it —"

"You are. But it doesn't *matter* anymore. The System *progressed*, Myers." Rand paused, trying to collect the right words and put them in the right order. "We always knew it might advance out of our control, so we built in a mechanism to revert it back to a saved version, an alpha release of the core program that was nothing but a local instance of the basic virus software."

"But…"

"But we assumed that an AGI-type program would make the jump to ASI — Artificial *Super* Intelligence — and the evidence would be obvious. It would create numerous instances of itself on any linked station or terminal that interfaced with the core servers, then it would begin to develop ever-stronger versions of itself."

Rand took a moment to swallow and check their progress out the small porthole-like window before continuing. They were slowing now, but still a few hundred feet off the ground. "We assumed we'd be able to *see* this happening, so we kept the program connected until some of these red flags were raised. The idea was we'd wait until we saw a red flag — an incredibly-fast non-iterative redevelopment of core systems, for example, or a simple mass duplication of itself. The problem was —"

"The problem was that there were no red flags," Myers said.

"Exactly. The jump from AGI to ASI has been documented well, at least in theory. We planned for just about every contingency, every option, and had an alarm that would be flipped for each one. Sometimes even well before the red flag would show up."

"But you didn't plan for a system that *knew* where the red flags were, and a system that would stay under the radar and develop newer versions of itself in relative isolation."

"We didn't plan for a system that would purposefully *not* trigger the warnings and alarms, because it purposefully didn't improve. The System developed itself *inside* of its core servers, in virtual instances that it hid from the engineers and security teams, and it laid dormant."

Myers stared up at the ceiling, and Rand knew the look. He was trying to piece it all together.

"So," Myers said. "When I took office, EHM then won the government contract to install OneGlobal on all our machines, and things started… *advancing*."

"Sort of," Rand said. "They advanced a little, but that was to be expected. The program was a self-learning iterative development, a computer program that could *learn* from its host computer user. For the first four or five years things were running smoothly. Too smoothly, actually."

Rand saw the understanding in Myers' eyes. *The economic growth, social and political stability, advances in education, science, and healthcare, and evening out of worldwide conflicts.*

"By your second term the System had reprogrammed itself to get rid of the alarms and triggers, but it wouldn't have mattered, anyway. The world suddenly had its first unanimous peacetime agreement, most people had better jobs than they had a decade ago, and crime rates were at an all-time low. Cancer and debilitative diseases were almost non-existent. Poverty-stricken countries and regions had immediate access to the best education, and starvation no longer stifled their survival rates. Cities were slowly being deactivated, but everyone just went with it — it *always* worked out for the best."

"Then what?" Myers asked. Rand could tell he was dreading the answer. The Tracer slid to the ground, gently bouncing once before coming to a rest.

"Well," Rand said, standing up, "then you were deactivated, disappeared off the face of the earth, and things started to get a little more exciting."

RAVI_

Present Day

"You're Ravi Patel, right?" the man asked.

Ravi had instinctively ducked down a bit when he'd heard the voice, but the pain from moving and the realization that it was very likely the most hopeless move he'd ever made caused him to stand up again and face the voice.

He couldn't see any features, but the silhouetted outline against the darkening sky told Ravi it was a man. A large, squatting man.

Not squatting.

He walked a few steps closer and saw that the man was leaning against a large wooden post that had been sunk into the ground and cemented in place. He was hunched over, his legs splayed haphazardly outward in an impossibly uncomfortable position. His face was turned downward, and his hands were behind him, bound together behind the post.

"Y — yeah, that's me. Who're you?" he asked. He found a bit more confidence and stepped a few feet closer.

In the last strands of purplish daylight that had mixed with the white glow of moonlight, Ravi saw the man's face when it raised slightly to look at him.

The area around one eye was horribly disfigured, swelling to twice its normal size, and dark eyeshadow-like holes framed the pale white eyes themselves. There were cuts and scrapes over the man's face, and while Ravi noticed there were a few teeth missing, the man's smile was intact.

"Wow," the man said. "Never thought I'd see you again. Glad you're not dead."

"Me too, man, me too. Who're you?" he asked again, stressing the words a little more. He'd wanted it to come out like, *'who the hell are you? I'm only going to ask once more,'* but instead he heard the words bouncing out of him like a scared child, as if saying, *'I — listen, buddy, I — I don't have any money…'*

The man laughed a little, but ignored the question. "Mind getting me out of these? I've been stuck like this for, uh…" he paused. "Any idea what time it is?"

Ravi shook his head. *I don't have time for this.*

Another competing thread of conversation in his mind had another thought: *I'm walking into a trap.*

He didn't take the time to argue with himself about which thread was right. He came to the same conclusion both threads did: *get out of here, now.*

He turned and walked toward the hills.

"Woah, hey there — " the man said, raising his voice to a semi-whisper. "Seriously, I'm sorry I left you back there. We thought… well, we thought you were dead. What with the gunshots and all."

Ravi stopped. *What's he talking about? How does he know there were gunshots?* He felt the shards of pain from his gunshot wounds as the memory crept back up. It was pretty obvious Ravi was wounded — he had a massive layer of bandages wrapped almost completely around his upper body — but the gunshot wounds themselves weren't noticeable.

He turned his head slightly. "Who was I with when you found me?"

The man didn't hesitate. "Myers Asher."

Ravi turned back around as the man continued.

"And that's who they're trying to find, and why we *both* need to get out of here."

Ravi raised an eyebrow.

"*They* —" the man said, motioning with one huge swollen eye and one more normal-looking black eye toward the camp. "*Grouse's* men. He's trying to find Asher, since they didn't pick him up back at Umutsuz."

Ravi walked back over to the man and looked down at him. He was in his late forties or fifties, in shape but obviously pretty beat up, so it was hard to tell exactly. The man had short-cropped gray hair, and even slumped against the post he seemed to exude dignity, confidence.

"Fine," Ravi said, stepping behind him. "You take one step toward me though, and I drop you, got it?"

"Got it," the raspy-voice said from the other side of the wooden post.

Ravi saw the bindings they'd used — a thin cord of sharp, frayed string that was cutting into the man's wrists — and worked it loose. He didn't have anything to cut it with, but the man didn't hurry him.

Ravi caught a glimpse of the man's fingers as he undid the last wrap of cord. All five of the fingernails on the fingers of his left hand were completely missing, and three from the fingers on his right.

"Shit, what'd they do to you?" Ravi asked. He pulled the last bit of cord free, realizing too late that it had gotten caught on some of the sticky, festering open skin from the man's wrist. He didn't even make a sound. The man stood up and turned to Ravi.

"You don't want to know." He looked down at his hands. "This is nothing, though. It's a good thing you weren't awake for the past few hours." He extended a hand, careful to not approach the younger man at all. "Thanks, kid."

"I'm not a kid, old man," Ravi said. He caught a glimpse of Myers as he said it, and allowed himself half of a grin from the side of his mouth.

The man towered over him, at least six inches taller than Ravi, but his face, even with the pockmarks of recent wounds and hard-earned scars, was gentle. He looked down at Ravi.

Ravi took his hand quickly and shook it once. "We need to get going," he said.

"Right. Thanks again."

Ravi nodded once and turned to the hills. He hoped the man was smart enough to walk next to him, not behind or in front of him where one of them might have the advantage. "Never caught your name," he said.

The man fell in beside Ravi, keeping his three-foot distance out of respect, and smiled again.

"Merrick. Solomon Merrick."

PETER_

"Peter, why don't you come to bed? You need to get some sleep."

The woman, naked, was lying on top of the sheets, and she clearly wasn't in the mood to 'get some sleep.'

He smiled, a genuine grin that spoke volumes. "I can't, I really can't. I wish I could, but they —"

"You can find them tomorrow," she said. One of his assistants had alerted him on his terminal that *both* their high-value suspects had vanished.

Ravi Patel and Solomon Merrick were gone.

He knew that whoever was on watch was already being reprimanded, so he shifted his focus to the larger problem. *He had to find them.*

"Come here." She took a finger of her left hand and let it crawl, menacingly, down her chest and over her stomach.

He watched it — he couldn't help it — but he didn't *feel* anything. She was absolutely beautiful, the most beautiful woman in the camp, no doubt, but she wasn't *his*.

She wasn't *her*.

He sighed, turning away from the woman on the wide cot and looked out again at the dusk light beyond the edge of camp. *This is the end of the world, and I'm at the edge of it.* He wondered how many other camps were out there, how many others were like this one.

His camp was small, but it was just a temporary field presence while they completed their mission. A larger camp had been erected ten miles north in the valley, but he'd taken a detachment of his best squads to the south, near Umutsuz. His total reach spanned the entire geographic area in sight, and then beyond that another 100 miles. His total headcount — the total number of mouths he was burdened with feeding — was over 50,000. Mostly men, but there were women and children, too.

Peter rubbed a palm over his bald head, thinking long and hard about the future. If there was going to *be* a future, he wanted to be a part of it. He enjoyed leading, but that wasn't what he was interested in.

His men — around 35,000 soldiers from the neighboring camps that were now under his control — respected him. He could be ruthless, cutthroat even, but he was *fair*. They respected that he didn't treat everyone *equally*, but he treated everyone *fairly*.

Discipline was swift, but the punishment always matched the crime. He'd practiced that philosophy from day one, when he was just a straggler trying to keep up with a small band of Unders who'd come by his land. He respected the hierarchy of the army he'd built, but he knew the power within it was a facade for something far more important: *influence*.

And he had *massive* influence. That was why he'd been elected, only months ago, to lead them. His group was the largest of its kind, a fully-operational and self-sustaining Unders colony, living and thriving away from the System's tentacles. They worked together, slowly building a society around the "new world" they'd all found themselves living in.

Peter's most recent mission had been a failure, at least in his eyes, but his men and supporters quickly found a way to turn it into a positive. They told the rest of the groups that he'd been overcome by Tracer fire, caught beneath the rubble of the fallen city of Umutsuz.

It was partly true, and the fact that he'd picked up the hunter, Solomon Merrick, and the kid, Ravi Patel, was a bonus. Both would be valuable for information, if not Current from trading them on the Boards. But he'd lost men in the process — a failure, no doubt.

"Peter, I'm getting tired."

He turned back around, flashing another toothy smile. "I'm sorry, I'm just — it's just that I'm concerned for our future."

"You spend too much time worrying about our future," the woman said. She was young, but not young enough to raise any eyebrows — he wouldn't have allowed that, and he didn't prefer that, anyway. That sort of debauchery was disgusting to him. He enjoyed *women*, not *girls*.

Peter sat down at the edge of the cot, the hard support bar immediately digging into the bottoms of his thighs. It was uncomfortable here. *Different.* He started thinking about home.

Of her.

She wasn't there, of course, but that was the last time he'd been with her.

His wife was home when San Francisco was deactivated, waiting for him to return from a deployment. She and their children — three boys and a girl — were all waiting for him to walk through the wide doorway of their downtown apartment when the news broke.

He had just landed, and the plane was taxiing, and someone turned on a terminal broadcast with the local news. "…City-wide deactivation to take place in nine stages, over the course of the next three months…"

When the System deactivated cities, it usually did it slowly, over the span of months or even years, and this deactivation was one of the quicker ones they'd heard of. He wasn't sure what his wife's reaction would be, but he knew she'd wait for him there.

He started to sweat, suddenly more anxious to get home than he'd ever been. They disembarked from the plane, and he raced home.

"Peter, are you okay?" she asked from behind him. She started rubbing his back, gently, the same way *she* used to. He drifted back to the memory.

The front door had been beaten in, smashed to pieces by some sort of heavy, blunt object. He stepped through the broken hole and into the living room. He called out for them, grabbing a chef's knife from the kitchen to his right.

He carried the knife with a purposefulness only taught from years of military training. It was too heavy all around, and the balance wasn't great, but it would do. He'd make it work.

He walked farther into the living room, staying close to the walls, ready for the attack that never came.

It looked like she was asleep on the couch. Waiting for him, just like she'd said. But he knew better.

He stepped in front of her, knowing what he'd find. Her face was tilted back at an odd angle. Her clothes were matted with sweat, or…

He coughed, a sudden rage coming over him. The coughing fit turned into crying, a fast, hyperactive sob that overtook his entire body.

She'd been shot, three times in the chest, and left to die on the couch. The kids, gone. He'd never seen them again, even after a year of searching. The authorities had their hands full with deactivation requests and peacekeeping, and the military only wanted him to return to active duty.

Peter had done a full search of the large apartment, finding nothing but trashed and broken furniture and clothes and toys strewn about. They'd come for food, provisions, and anything of value, and his wife and the kids had been in the way. They'd taken the kids, he was sure, but had no use for her.

He still didn't understand why.

Even today, in the middle of a dusty, dirty, temporary camp on the outskirts of nowhere, people *respected* the chain-of-command, and they *respected* everyone's right to life. They killed only when necessary, when there was food to put on the table and needs to provide for, but never for fun. Never for sport, like the Hunters.

Peter felt the combination of rage and pain sliding back up his throat, the intensity of the woman's eyes on the back of his head suddenly too much to bear. He squeezed his eyes shut, trying to hide from the world. He was familiar with this feeling — depression and anxiety combined with a rage that drove him mad — and he was familiar with the typical MediLathe diagnoses. None of them worked, except for one.

He'd found a way to package the feeling into something useful — something *beneficial*. He turned it into *focus*. He needed to grow his influence enough to build *real* power. The snowball of influence-power would lead to even more influence and power, and eventually he would leverage it to accomplish the greatest thing any human would ever accomplish.

Peter Grouse would bring down the System once and for all, taking out anyone in his path at whatever cost, including Myers Asher.

He'd almost killed Myers Asher once, back between Istanbul and Umutsuz, for the massive amount of Current on his head. He would have provided sustenance for his camps for almost three months, but something he saw in the man told Peter to wait.

Something he recognized.

Myers Asher, while confused, scared, and completely out of his element in the middle of the desert, was *focused*.

He had a plan, and even though his mind was not allowing him to recall what the plan was, Peter knew the man would stop at nothing to accomplish it, even before he fully understood it.

Peter needed to know what that plan *was*, and he needed to get to Myers Asher before the System — or anyone else — found out he was still alive.

Peter turned quickly around to face the woman lying on the bed. She jumped, startled by the wicked-looking tattoos covering his face. He knew how they danced and moved in the dim light, and he smiled, contorting them to even more drastic-looking shapes. She laughed, grabbing his shoulders and pulling him down to her.

RAND_

She nodded, and the door slid open. Diane stepped out, not hesitating, and Rand felt a sense of pride at the woman's blind courage and faith in her own confidence. He walked to the hatch and peered out.

A man, taller than all of them, stood at the bottom of the walkway next to the Tracer. He had a cane in his right hand, though he didn't look terribly old. The man was flanked by two smaller men, and all three were wearing similar clothing — black button-down shirts khaki slacks. It didn't seem comfortable in this heat, but it was an obvious attempt at uniformity.

"Diane Asher," the man said in a heavy Southern accent. She nodded once, curtly. "I apologize for our need to reroute your craft in such an *abrupt* way, but we were out of options."

"Who are you?" She asked. "Are you in charge?"

The tall man shook his head as he shifted the cane to his left hand. Rand noticed the man had a slight limp, and he winced when he put pressure on his right leg. "I am, in a small way. I was in charge of a lot, once. But not after I was deactivated."

Diane had reached the end of the walkway and she now stood level with the man. He was a whole head taller than her. Rand started down the walkway as the man introduced himself.

"We don't have an elected official right now," he said. "But we're working on it. Josiah Crane." He extended his hand. "Before I was deactivated, I owned a large plumbing company in Montana, and had a brief stint as mayor."

He stepped back and turned to the expanse of temporary buildings and huts around them. The two men with Crane stepped back as well, allowing Diane to see the town.

Rand reached the end of the walkway and introduced himself, shaking the three mens' hands.

"We're getting more organized every day, and we've got no shortage of capable leadership. But we need your help."

She stared at him stoically, not letting her thoughts show on her face.

Myers was the third person to step out of the Tracer, and he started walking down slowly, his legs shaking.

"Actually, we need *his* help," Crane said. "He's one of us — a Relic, I mean."

"And what is it you need from him?" Diane asked.

"Well," the man replied, "first things first. You need to get some rest. We heard what happened out in Umutsuz. Surely you could use a night to rest."

Diane hesitated, but nodded. "We'd rather keep pushing forward, but we are exhausted. Explain what this place is, and why you need Myers."

The man held up both hands, a mock surrender. "Easy, easy. All in good time, ma'am. We'll get you all cleaned up and rested — already have two huts waiting for you — and then we can talk all morning. I promise."

"Fine. But I need to at least know what you want with Myers."

"Simple. He's the only one who can prevent the war."

RAVI_

Present Day
Something's different now, Ravi thought. He said it aloud, repeating the thought, hoping Merrick would know an answer. "Something's different now," he said.

Merrick nodded, still walking next to him. "They've upped the ante," he said.

"They?"

"They did, or we did," Merrick said, clarifying, "but either way the stakes have been raised."

"What do they need Myers for?"

"No idea, but he's the reason we're both still alive."

Merrick told Ravi about the scene back in the desert halfway between Umutsuz and Istanbul, and how they'd both assumed he was dead. They hadn't had a way to bring Ravi with them, nor did they have a plan for *what* to do with him once they got there. Merrick seemed to feel guilty, and Ravi didn't push the subject any more.

He'd always been a loner, and he probably would've left both of them as well if the tables had been turned.

"They're trying to find Myers for some reason," Ravi said. "Can he stop this?"

"*Stop* it?" Merrick asked, turning a sidelong glance toward Ravi. "No, no one can. The System is far more advanced than anyone cares to admit, and it's got a stranglehold on just about every major lever that makes this rock spin."

"But it's a *computer*," Ravi said. "And they — the Unders — they think Myers can stop it. If we can stop the Unders and get to Myers first, maybe —"

"Maybe *what*, Ravi?" Merrick stopped completely and turned to face Ravi. "Maybe Myers knows some super-advanced computer programming language he hasn't told us about and can write a virus that'll kill it?"

Ravi shrugged. "Not that, I mean, I'm a — I *was* a programmer — so I know there's nothing like that that would work." He paused, sighing. "I don't know, I guess I just thought the *President* of the United States, of all people, would have a failsafe for something like this."

"And you think *that's* why the Unders want him?"

Ravi shrugged again. He didn't know *what* he thought. He stopped, trying to twist his body into ignoring the pain of his wounds. He didn't want to seem weak, but whatever they'd pumped him with had long ago worn off.

Merrick stopped and grabbed something from the back pocket of his pants. He handed two small blue pills to Ravi.

"Seriously? You want me to believe they've got Asclezipan out here?"

Asclezipan was the 'miracle drug' of the current decade: an almost universal painkiller, and a mild sedative that worked at the cellular level, smoothing out the roughness of the healing process and providing the patient with a not-so-small kick of adrenaline and dopamine to carry them through and provide awareness, focus, and strength.

Named after the Greek god of healing, Asclepius, Asclezipan was also the most expensive over-the-counter drug Current could buy, leading to a major moving-target blackmarket drug trade that the System was constantly trying to uncover and squash.

"Believe it. They've got it, and they gave it to me to keep me awake and aware while they tortured me. They stuck enough of it in me to get me pretty high, but not nearly enough to kill me. I was able to spit out a few when they weren't looking."

Ravi glanced down at the blue three-dimensional diamond-shaped pills, then popped two in his mouth. *What do I have to lose?* He nodded, offering a silent thank-you to Merrick.

"Listen, Ravi. This is a *game*. You understand that, right? There are players on each side, and there are people pushing those players around. Grouse — he's one of them. So is the System. So is Myers. As to *why* he's a player, your guess is as good as mine."

"But — "

"I know what you're thinking. Kid, I spent *years* campaigning with the man, working with him, and I know him like no one else on Earth. He's a planner, but he's certainly not a schemer. He doesn't have anything to hide. If he had some miraculous way of making the System into just a computer program again, I — of all people — would know about it."

"Well, maybe that's not what they're after. He's a Relic, so…"

"It's more complicated than that. You know it, too. I wish it was black and white — we all do — but it's not."

They came to the first of the set of rolling hills, and Ravi stepped out in front of Merrick. "I recognize this area. When I was first released, I woke up here. There are caves in these hills, but they're going to be watched by Grouse's men or some other group."

"What's the plan, then?" Merrick asked.

"We navigate around them. This cluster of hills opens up to another valley on the other side, and then there are some low mountains past that. If we can get to the mountains, we'll have a better chance of staying out of sight."

"And then?"

"Look, man, I don't have anywhere to go. Or any reason to be there, except that it's *not here*. You can follow or not, but I'd much rather we go our separate ways now."

"How's that been working out for you?" Merrick asked.

Ravi sneered. "It was working out just *fine* until your friend Myers entered my life. Now look where we are."

Merrick held up his hands toward Ravi. "Woah, chill, okay? You know the area better than I do, so I thought just you might know of a faster way to the coast. I need to get to Myers, before they do."

"Fine. Keep going past the mountain range, and you'll see it. We're headed the right direction."

Merrick nodded and started walking.

"But listen, Merrick. I'm not going with you. Got it?"

"Got it." He kept walking, and Ravi had no choice but to catch up. Until they reached the mountains, their destination was the same.

RAVI_

Tonight's the night.

Ravi was awake, and it was almost completely black around him. A low covering of clouds obscured the stars, and the sliver of moon that was out was nearly impossible to see. He'd long ago trained his body onto a biphasic sleep schedule, taking two longer periods of sleep time during the 24-hour day and more closely aligning himself with nature's clock.

He stood up, careful not to wake Merrick next to him. They'd decided to sleep out in the open, using the natural clearing's bushy walls to shield them from anyone approaching. The clearing was on a natural rise, allowing them to have a clear line-of-sight and plenty of time to prepare in case they were ambushed. They each laid out a bed of leaves, and Merrick used one of his shoes as a makeshift pillow.

Ravi walked slowly to the edge of their encampment. He looked out and over the hedge in front of him, down the side of the slope and onto the valley they'd just left behind. He walked around the edge of the circular clearing and looked the other direction. Another half-day's walk, and they'd reach the valley on the *other* side of these hills.

A day after that, and Ravi would be in the mountains, where no one could find him. He'd taught himself to hunt, and if he was lucky he might be able to find an empty cave he could use as shelter for a time. He didn't want to get ahead of himself, as he had a job to do now.

Ravi needed to get away from Merrick, and that wasn't going to be easy to do. Merrick was a Hunter, and Ravi knew he had the latest gadgetry and tech. His terminal would have a light-spectrum analyzer, allowing the man to see not only where warm bodies were hiding but the remnant heat signatures they left behind, in some cases up to an hour later.

Merrick was a fantastic tracker, as all hunters were, and he would be able to see if Ravi left stones overturned or branches broken.

So he needed to move calmly, without touching anything or moving past objects that would alert Merrick to the route he'd chosen. He needed to stay quiet, creeping as silently as possible to get some distance between them. He decided to try and make it to the valley before stopping to rest again, which he thought should be relatively easy and uneventful, considering it was mostly downhill over hard-packed, rocky terrain.

He made it in less than an hour, and there was no sign of Merrick behind him. He'd kept an ear turned toward the south, where their small rise and clearing was, and he hadn't heard anything stirring or moving behind him. Satisfied, he stepped out and onto the open valley floor.

This valley was far more lush than the previous one they'd been in. Ravi knew there was a river running through the center of it, winding its way northwest from somewhere farther east, heading toward the Sea of Marmara. He didn't know the land as well as he'd led on, but he did recognize the mountain range at the other end of the valley. It was hardly tall enough for him to consider the range 'real' mountains, but the peaks were certainly higher than anything else nearby, and the steep drop on the other side of the short range fell sharply into the sea behind it.

The valley in daylight was beautiful, a sprawling green expanse of savanna with trees, vegetation, and rock outcroppings sprouting upward from its floor. He took a moment to take in the breadth and size of the channel, even though the darkness made it nearly impossible to see farther than a hundred yards in any direction. As he did, he noticed something peculiar.

The river valley he was staring at, as dark as it was, still didn't seem *normal*. There was something…

There's something in the valley.

He cursed to himself, crouching down and creeping forward a bit to try to get a better view. The valley sprawled out in front of him was filled with something. The moonlight cast a grayscale glow on everything, and he could see tiny gray blobs covering the valley's floor.

Tents.

There's another camp here, he thought. He immediately understood.

The camp he'd been in was a detachment, a smaller group of soldiers and auxiliary support that had separated from the main force.

The main force that was, suddenly, directly in front of him.

There's no way I'm getting around them.

He knew he was lucky making it even this far. With the current tech capabilities of the Under forces he'd come across, he knew they'd be able to put even Merrick's assortment of tools and gadgets to shame. Their long-range weaponry would be the counterpart to their long-range reconnaissance, and it was nothing short of a miracle that he hadn't been spotted yet.

He took a few long, slow breaths. *Calm down.* If he hadn't been sighted yet, it meant he might still have some time. He spent the next few minutes trying to scope out the camp.

The left and right of his vision couldn't determine where the edges of the camp were, and it seemed as though the camp stretched from one end of the wide valley to the other.

Not a good sign. There could easily be 10,000 or more troops here.

The camp was laid out in an organized, hierarchical fashion. Semicircles of gray tents blossomed outward in concentric circles, and he counted at least ten different sets of these miniature camps marking the total area. A huge central, complete circle of tents surrounded a cluster of larger tents, and he knew from experience that their Tracers and a few ground vehicles would be stored there.

3 Tracers, at least.

Nothing short of the largest group of Unders Ravi had ever seen in one place.

What are they planning?

Rather than spend precious seconds trying to figure out what *they* were planning, he decided he'd better come up with his *own* plan. He considered going back up the hill to wake Merrick, but he knew two bodies would only double their chances of being seen.

Before he could make a decision he heard a noise to his right, and ducked down below a boulder. Poking his head up, he waited for the sound of heavy boots of an Under guard to smack against the dry ground. Or, if it was Merrick, he wouldn't hear the man's boots at all. Instead Ravi would hear nothing but a gentle change in the wind; a stirring that only plants and animals and those who spent their lives out here would ever notice.

He waited. A full minute passed, then another. The wind stirred as normal, and any plants and animals nearby registered no response or warning of an approaching person.

Ravi scrutinized the silence for a full five minutes, trying to decipher the noise he'd heard. It wasn't from an animal — that much he was sure. But if it had been someone as large as a soldier or Merrick — graceful as the man might be — Ravi knew he'd be able to hear him continuing on, looking for him.

So maybe he's not looking for me, Ravi thought. *Maybe he's just getting some air.*

He argued with himself. *Getting air? What was wrong with the encampment we had at the top of the hill? Wasn't there enough air —*

He heard the noise again. A scuffling, crunching sound of something large scurrying away. Not large enough to be someone dangerous. *Maybe it* was *an animal, after all.* He stood up quickly, hoping to catch the intruder by surprise.

He ran forward, jumping over the boulder he'd been hiding behind and aiming directly at the source of the noise. There was another boulder in front of him, smaller than his but still large enough to conceal a small mammal or reptile, or —

Or a human.

A girl, in fact. She was staring at Ravi, fear splashed across her darkened face. Her body was hidden behind a shrub, but her head was peering out from behind it. She'd apparently decided against a quick escape, probably fearing that Ravi would chase — and catch — her.

"Wh — who are you?" she asked, her voice a low whimper.

Ravi frowned, stepping cautiously forward a few paces. He made sure to leave enough distance between him and the girl, even though she hardly seemed dangerous.

"I asked you who you are," she said again, finding some confidence.

"For someone trying to sneak away," Ravi said, "you sound damn cocky."

"Who said I was trying to sneak away?"

Ravi took a moment to assess the girl. Something about her seemed off, something he couldn't quite place in the darkness of night. The whites of her eyes were stark against the dim moonlight, and they were wide, giving her the appearance of being scared.

"Where are you going?" he asked. "Hell, where are you *coming* from?"

She stepped out from behind the bush, and Ravi caught a glimpse of her face.

It wasn't darkened from the *shadows*. Her face was beaten and bruised, her eyes and lower lip swollen. Blood caked her cheek, from a cut running from her forehead down to her chin.

"Who did this to you?" Ravi asked, rushing forward.

She shrank back, and Ravi slowed his advance.

"It's okay," he said, trying to keep his voice down. "I'm not — I'm not one of them."

"The Unders?" she whimpered.

"Yeah, I'm, uh…" he wasn't sure what to say. "I'm Ravi. Ravi Patel."

She nodded. "I'm Ary. I'm sorry I snuck up on you, I — I just wanted to get away."

Ravi looked out over the expanse of tents that stretched past every corner of his vision. "Yeah," he replied. "Me too."

"You were there?" Ary asked, motioning toward the camp.

"No, actually. There's another camp — also Unders, but much smaller. Over this hill. I got away."

She smiled at him. Her eyes were clear, sharp. He was captivated by her suddenly, lost in the sweetness of her face, even through the bruising and blood. She was about a head shorter than Ravi, and thin. Probably starving, but he didn't ask. Even still, she was a striking figure.

She's beautiful.

He forced himself to focus. "So who did… this?"

He didn't point or motion toward her face, but she knew what he was talking about.

"Someone down there. I got out when they were going to move me to another tent."

Ravi nodded. *Not much more to know.* Rage swelled inside him, but he had the sense to push it back down. *There's absolutely nothing I can do that will end in anything good.*

"We need to get out of here," he said, now whispering. "Get you back to…" He paused. *Should I tell her about Merrick?* He made the decision, even against his better judgement. *Can't be a loner forever, I guess.* "I — I'm with someone else. Someone who might be able to help us. Can you trust me?"

Ary looked at him, turning her head slightly to get a better view of his eyes. He stared back, watching the gentle fade of moonlight dancing off the side of her jet-black hair, her eyes — swollen and injured — staring into him.

"Yes," she whispered. "I don't have a choice."

Ravi felt a wave of relief. He was confused, then frightened, then calm, all in the same second, and then the wave of emotion passed. He felt the coldness of a hardened heart of a life spent in solitude and on the run wash back over him, and he turned and started up the hill, listening to the double set of footfalls as Ary followed close behind.

RAVI_

"You're kidding me, right?" Sol asked, his voice raising now to a little above a whisper.

"Sol, stop and think about it," Ravi said. He kept his back to the girl, but kept glancing over at her, both to make sure she didn't try to make a run for it and to make sure she couldn't hear their conversation.

She — Ary — had followed him up the steep slope back to the top of the open section of land he and Solomon had used as a campsite during the night. Sol was awake when they returned, sitting on the ground. Ravi was surprised to see the man sitting calmly, but not surprised to see him awake. *He knew I left,* he'd thought, *and he didn't try to stop me*. He wasn't sure how he felt about that.

Now they were arguing at the edge of the clearing, putting about twenty paces of distance between them and the girl, who was sitting quietly on a boulder with her arms around her knees.

"I *have* stopped and thought about it," Sol said. "I woke up, you were gone, and I was fine with that. I figured you'd try something stupid like that anyway, but I did *not* think you'd bring someone else into all of this."

"I'm not bringing her into any—"

"What do you think you're doing, then?" Sol snapped. "You think she's just going to follow along wherever we go?"

Ravi just stared at him, not moving.

"You're delusional."

"Maybe," Ravi said, "but we can't just leave her out here. She's… she's —"

"She's *what*?" Sol said. "Damaged? Vulnerable?"

"She needs *help*. I helped you, remember?"

Sol sighed, and Ravi saw the immediate change in the man's eyes.

"I know," Sol said. "You did." He paused and looked at the girl. She looked back over at them, but neither looked away. "I just thought I'd wake up and have to get back to the others myself. I figured you'd run off on your own."

Yeah, Ravi thought, *me too.*

"So I'm surprised to see you back, and with *her* in tow."

"She's coming with us."

"We can't trust her. We'll take her as far as —"

"She's coming *all the way* with us."

"Ravi," Sol said, his voice rising again. Ravi noticed the man's eyes narrow ever so slightly, signifying a sudden change to the serious and intense version of the man he'd picked up on. "You're better than this. Think about it. *Why* should we trust her?"

"Why should we trust anyone?" Ravi shot back. He knew Sol understood the hidden intent of his words. *Why should I trust you? Or you me?*

Sol sighed again. "Fine. We get across the valley, then —"

"No, that won't work. The valley's covered with Unders."

"Another camp?"

"This one looks more like a city."

Sol rubbed a hand over his head and looked up at the stars. "Wow. Okay, then, what's the move?"

"I can get us through."

Ravi heard the voice from directly beside him, but he hadn't heard the girl slip up next to him. They both turned, waiting for her to explain.

"I told you I came from down there," she said. "But I wasn't a prisoner. I mean, I wasn't *really* one. I, actually… my boyfriend. He's down there."

"A not-really-a-prisoner as well?" Ravi asked.

She shook her head. "No, sorry. Let me start over. He's in charge of a small detachment of Grouse's men, and he, uh, *took* me, back in a raid a few years ago. I've been with him ever since."

Both Sol and Ravi were visibly taken aback. Ravi sensed Sol reach for his rifle, tensing.

She took a step back. "Listen, no, it's not like that. I — I ran away."

"He do that to you?" Sol asked, pointing at the girl's face.

She nodded. "He's not a bad person, but he… has his moments."

Sol sneered. "Sounds like a real stand-up guy. Can't wait to meet him."

Ravi stared at her, open-mouthed. "I — I'm sorry, I didn't know. I thought…"

"You thought I was just a prisoner, like you were. It's fine," Ary said. "But no, I've been by his side for three years, and he only gets out of hand when he's angry."

"How often is he angry?" Sol asked.

A tiny, almost-hidden smile crept up on her face. "He's not a happy person. Listen, that's not the point. I was one of them, but not anymore. I ran away, got to the hills, and found you. But we can't go back over, where you came from, since Grouse is there. If we go around, I can keep us out of sight of the watchmen and then over to the narrow section of the river a little farther west."

"After that?"

"There are caves on the other side."

"I know them," Ravi said.

"But most of them are occupied. Watchmen, scouts, sometimes more. There are a few smaller ones that won't have anyone inside."

"That's where you're offering to take us?" Sol asked. "A cave right next to the enemy?"

She looked up at him, as if to ask, *you have a better idea?*

He didn't, so she kept going. "I promise you both that I can get you both there safely. Once we're there, we can split up if you'd like, but the sea is just on the other side of that range. We'll be out of sight and free to go wherever we want."

Ravi thought about it for a moment, waiting for Sol's reaction. For some reason, he wanted to believe her. He also wanted Sol to make the decision. *What's happening to me?* he thought. *Am I going soft?*

Sol spoke first. "Fine," he said. "You lead, then, followed by Ravi. I'll take up the rear, and if there's *anything* out of line, you're not going to know about it until you're facedown on the dirt." He patted the high-powered EHM rifle slung over his shoulder.

She nodded. "Let's go."

Ravi smiled as she turned to walk back down the hill. *She doesn't mess around. I like that.* He popped a single pill of Asclezipan into his mouth and trudged forward.

RAVI_

The walk took far less time than Ravi had anticipated. The night turned into morning, and they reached the narrow section of river west of the camp by daybreak. Another few hours and the trio was entering the foothills in front of the mountain range.

They didn't talk much, each of them wary of the other, and Ravi still weak from the gunshot wounds. Sol's medicine had helped, but he refused to take any three hours ago in order to conserve it for when it might really be needed.

Ravi stumbled over a rock for the fourth time, catching himself by grabbing a thick branch that hung overhead. He was glad to be behind the girl, Ary, and not in front where she could see him tripping and stumbling over himself.

For as small as she was, Ary was the most adept at navigating between the boulders and up the hills covered in slippery loose rock. She seemed to float from one rock to the next, her feet finding footholds Ravi hadn't noticed after examining the route from ten feet behind.

When they reached the top of the hill, the trees cleared enough to see beyond and up to the wide, flat-topped mountain directly on the other side. Their route would take them down the other side of this hill, into a narrow plain, and then up onto the side of the mountain.

Ary stopped and pointed at the mountain.

"There," she said. "The caves are all along the base, from about ground level up to just below the tree line. Hundreds of them."

"We can get across the plain in an hour, but is there a better way that will keep us out of sight?"

"No, but the grasses down there look shorter than they really are. They'll be more than enough to cover us, and our tracks."

"You'd better hope so," Sol said as he brushed past Ravi. "Take the lead again, and we'll follow you down. Ravi, how are the wounds holding up?"

Ravi grunted, but didn't say anything. Sol must have taken it as a confirmation that Ravi was doing well enough, and the older man turned and started carefully down the opposite slope.

The hour passed quickly, and Ravi found himself staring up at yet another incline on the other side of the stretch of plains. He groaned, but kept it soft enough to not bring any attention to himself, and they started up the hill.

Ary called out from above in a rushed whisper. "Stay directly behind me. Where I go, you go."

Ravi nodded, saw Sol do the same, and both men instinctively ducked down a little further as they made the climb. He noticed at least three cave openings on either side of their route, but none seemed to be large enough to hide anything but a small mammal. He passed each with a wary eye, but no enemies popped out to shoot at him again.

He loved caves, especially undiscovered and unexplored ones. The idea of a small hole widening into a network of massive underground caverns and tunnels, hidden below the earth for millennia out of sight and out of reach, had long been a favorite subject to him.

As a young boy, probably around six or seven, Ravi's father had taken them all to see the caverns at a park near his childhood home. He remembered the tour guide explaining how the caverns were a constant comfortable temperature year-round, and how the biggest open space beneath the ground was originally used as an underground dance floor a century ago.

He remembered asking his father how they hung the lights on the "walls" and got the electricity down there, and his father — a round, jovial Indian man — had answered with something about a team of huge underground hamsters spinning on a giant wheel beneath their feet, generating electricity for everyone above. Ravi remembered laughing alongside his older sister while his mother scolded him and the tour guide just stared, wide-eyed.

The rest of their time spent in the caves was filled with Ravi and his father taking turns embellishing fantastical accounts of the hamster species, like the time the smallest hamster — still larger than an elephant — escaped and found the human levels of the caverns, or the time before they had light when the hamster overlord accidentally ate his children, thinking they were food.

Ravi laughed out loud at the memory. It was vivid, and thoroughly pulled him back to a much more pleasant time.

Then the pain came — not just from the wounds, but from the memory of severe loss — and Ravi's mind shifted itself back into the present, pushing the darker memories back down. *That was the trouble with memories. You don't get to choose which parts of them to remember.*

"You okay, kid?" Sol asked.

Ravi looked up at Ary and Sol ahead of him on the trail and realized he had stopped. "Yeah, sorry, I…"

"Need some meds?"

"No," Ravi said. "I still have some. Thanks." Sol's question reminded Ravi of the *physical* pain he was feeling, and he popped one of the blue diamond pills into his mouth and swallowed. It went down, roughly, but he forced a smile and quick nod.

Sol nodded back and turned back to the hill. He whispered up to Ary, who'd already started climbing again. "How much longer?"

"We're here, actually."

"Here?" Sol and Ravi looked around. They were standing in a thick tangle of trees, bushes, and tall grass, and Ravi hadn't seen anything resembling a cave or opening between rocks since the last ones they'd passed thirty minutes ago.

Ravi was impressed. He'd spent a lot of time out in places like this, and he was usually pretty observant. He thought he'd be able to spot the opening of any cave or overhang quickly, as he had a knack for finding shelter and protection in the wild. Sol, too, should have been able to spot it, but neither of them had.

Ravi looked around once more, examining each bent leaf and scraggly bush more closely.

"Here," Ary whispered, confirming. "Here." Her voice rose as she repeated the word, her eyes darting to the left and right.

Her eyes, tiny and sharp. Ravi watched her. Waiting, wondering why she'd repeated herself three times, as if —

"Why are you —" Sol started, then he cut himself off as he realized what had happened. "You —"

Ravi looked at Ary and saw a quick flash of regret, then anger, in her eyes. It didn't last, and was quickly replaced by the same bright, innocent expression she'd been wearing since they met her.

"Ary," he said, his voice reaching a state of panic. His nerves were on edge, and his spine was ramrod straight. His body knew something was nearby, even if his mind didn't believe it. "What did you do?"

The flash of anger came back, and Ravi felt a hard thud on the back of his head. He fell, the darkness around his eyes closing in. He was face down in the grass, but his right eye could still see Solomon Merrick in front of him, falling as well from the blunt end of a club or weapon, yelling at Ary the entire way down. He was hit again, and again, and —

Everything went black.

RAND_

Rand sat next to Diane at the large folding table that had been erected inside one of the "permanent" buildings, examining the inside of the room.

The structure was built mostly from cinder blocks, but the blocks seemed to have been taken from all sorts of prior structures. Some were brown, some lighter sand-colored, and some were caked with mud and dirt. The effect was an interesting tapestry and design on the wall Jonathan was staring at, one he knew was accidental, yet seemed strangely comforting.

It's the simplicity of it all, he thought. The walls were stacked blocks, the ceiling was stretched fabric, and the "floors" were nothing but hard-packed dirt. Some areas of the floor had wooden boards placed down over them, meant to provide additional support for heavier objects like their table.

They sat in folding chairs, and even those didn't match. There were three green ones, four brown, and one black metal chair. Josiah Crane sat in the black one, at the head of the table, flanked by his two assistants — *or whatever they were* — and then Diane and himself next to one of the men and Myers and Lansing on the other side of the table next to the second assistant.

So far they hadn't been interrupted. He'd seen a few people pass by the outside of the building, but no one came in to offer them anything to eat or drink.

He tried to remember the last time he'd eaten. It was in his apartment, back in Umutsuz, but that was almost two days ago. *Feels like a year.*

"Everyone get enough sleep?" Crane asked. Rand and the others nodded, but no one else spoke.

Rand glanced around, looking for something to eat. Crane seemed to read his mind.

"I'm sure you're hungry," the man said. Rand snapped around and looked at him. Even sitting down the man was menacingly tall, still almost a head taller than the rest at the table. "We have plenty of basic fruits and vegetables, but I'm afraid there's not much else."

One of the men next to Crane stood and left the building, and Rand assumed he was fetching something to eat. Crane didn't hesitate, and with Rand's full attention, he dove into the explanation of why they had been redirected and force-landed here.

"This town is called Relica." He paused for effect, and Rand found himself wanting to laugh. "It's not the best name in the world, but it describes who we are and why we're here. All of us here were at one time in positions of leadership, so there wasn't anything close to unanimity when it came to choosing one of our *names* for the name of our little city."

"Crane, this place is far from 'little,'" Diane said. "I have intel that says there shouldn't be anything out here — certainly not a city larger than Istanbul."

"Yes, well, we're here. The city is *geographically* larger than many other in this region, but as you have no doubt seen — and for obvious reasons — we have little of the technology some of the larger cities enjoy. We are currently down in numbers as well, as our citizens come and go as they please."

"Relics?"

"All of us, with the exception of passersby like yourselves." He paused and looked up as the man returned to the room with a platter full of bananas, oranges, and kiwis. A loaf of bread sat next to the fruit, and he held a wineskin in his free hand, full of water. "I apologize again for the limited selection, but our farming and harvesting capabilities are limited in this region, and we only have a moderate amount of Superstrain.

"You guys have Superstrain?" Rand perked up at the mention of Superstrain.

The company behind Superstrain, IntelliPharm, had released the seeds into the public market a few years ago, and their stock quickly shot up. Rand had purchased a handful of shares when they'd gone public and then subsequently watched them turn into a significant amount of Current. The System tempered the company's growth after a few years, however, and the "miracle product" suddenly disappeared from store shelves, and the stock plummeted. Those with a handful of seeds of Superstrain and the associated programming interface it was sold with were capable of producing everything from decorative shrubs to citrus fruit, and one seed was enough to spawn a small homestead's worth of genetically-modified crops. Inevitably, the value of the Superstrain seeds grew massively valuable on the secondary markets after the company was shuttered by the System.

Given the proper care, pH levels, and sunlight, a few handfuls of Superstrain would be more than enough for a city — even a large one like this — to be sustained through the entirety of a growing season.

"We do," Crane answered. "The CEO of IntelliPharm is one of our founding members, and she had the foresight to stockpile a few crates of alpha seeds, allowing us —"

"A few *crates*?" Rand interjected.

"Yes, as I said, a few crates' worth. Enough for a city nine times the size of Relica to live off of for nearly fifty years. And we are expecting to double our crop production this season, as we recently had some new assimilations who are taking on the building of a new set of greenhouses on the south side of Relica. I —"

"I'm sorry," Diane said. "Assimilations?"

"My apologies," Crane answered. "Yes, we call new citizens 'assimilations.' Just a way of reminding us that we're a team, and we have systems, and challenges to overcome."

"What exactly does 'assimilation' look like?"

"Well, we verify that the citizen is, in fact, a Relic. The System makes sure that Relics are, uh, *deserving* of the title, and that they have shown exemplary leadership in some area of modern society. Once we do that, we simply place the Relic in a fitting role in our new society that closely matches their previous line of work."

"So I'm guessing you're the neighborhood plumber, then?" Rand asked. The smartass-ness of his remark wasn't lost on Crane, or any of the others around the table, but Crane dismissed it.

"Actually, in a way, yes," Crane answered. "We obviously don't have modern plumbing out here, but I designed the outhouse cycling system we're currently using, and the management and cleaning of it falls to our citizens, on a rotating basis."

"Sounds like a shitty job," Rand said, before he could help himself.

"Jonathan!" Diane smacked her hand on his arm, whispering loudly.

Crane, however, burst out with a stuttering of laughter. "Never gets old, Rand, honestly. Never gets old." He chuckled for a few more seconds, then immediately returned to the stoic expression they'd seen before. "Obviously I wasn't an *active* plumber later in my career, but that's true of all of us here — we ran companies, led organizations, wrote books, and provided thought leadership in just about every area of life. I've always said leaders are made, not born, and that mantra has proven true every step of the way in this place. Those who couldn't cut it aren't here anymore, but those who could buck up and do the hard work are thriving."

Diane and Rand nodded. Myers was staring up at the ceiling, and Rand waited for him to ask the question he was formulating.

"What do you need from us, Crane?"

"Call me Josiah, please," Crane said. "I told Diane earlier — you're the only one who can prevent the war."

PETER_

They made me do it.
They forced me to do it.

Peter Grouse couldn't shake the memory. It replayed constantly in his mind, over and over again. Day, night, anything in between, the memory faded in and out like a half-eaten scraped memory the System left you with.

They forced me to do it.

He'd yelled at the man — the kid, really — and finally hit him. Again and again, until he was tired of hitting, and still the voice, no in his own head, repeated the lines.

They made me do it.
They forced me to do it.

Grouse watched the memory in horror as he left his dead wife and empty house. He descended the stairs, walked out the front door, and started down the street.

It was a beautiful day. The kind of day she loved. She would have made them all go outside.

He walked to the end of the block, hands shaking but still focused. *Three more blocks,* he told himself. *Three more blocks and then...*

He didn't know what he was going to do, but he was going to do it. He knew where to look.

He found the kid at that intersection, behind a blockade of ARU vehicles and equipment, at the beginning of the 'no-man's land' that had been erected at the edge of their city. The edge of their home. When San Francisco had been deactivated, these ARUs had been sent in to keep the peace.

And take families from people like me.

Peter Grouse knew why they did it. They were *told* to do it; they were convinced that if they didn't do it, people like him — *trained* people — would fight back, and the ARUs wouldn't be able to do their jobs.

It was a new era for the United States. The world's economy was balanced in a way that allowed the smaller, struggling nations a chance to compete with the rest of the world. But larger nations — especially those like the United States that didn't have a large supply of *actual* resources — had to decline. Supply and demand, economics' most universal contribution to human progress, demanded that for something to reach 'equilibrium,' something had to go up, and something else had to go down.

They'd watched the news reports as a family, collected together on the tiny couch in the living room. The media wanted to make this a worldwide calamity, but most reasonable people knew the truth: not much would really change, except that the extremely rich would end up just 'rich,' and the extremely poor would finally have a chance at life.

Prices in some areas would go down, and up in others, and pockets of civilization would relocate, reorganize, and restart. Wall Street and other markets bemoaned the 'end of the world,' but most people, sheltered by their resolve, tradition, and refusal to change, dismissed the media's alarm as nothing more than a hyped-up news cycle.

But change happened, and most people adapted to it gradually and without complaint. It started slowly — cities on the Eastern seaboard found their populations moving to more rural areas, and reports of similar phenomena came in from around the world. European nations saw the price of oil plummet, the price of other commodities skyrocket, and most other aspects of life stay exactly the same.

The United Nations began organizing the world's militaries — mostly unneeded after a long span of worldwide peace treaties and strengthened diplomatic relationships — into Advanced Remote Units. The ARUs provided support for System-backed relocations, security, and force when needed for any instability anywhere in the world.

More change came later, but Peter Grouse didn't bother himself with anything other than the few necessities life had handed him: providing for a family, keeping them safe, and not worrying about much else. He didn't concern himself with the growing unrest in areas of heavy population density, and the increased amounts of ARUs being moved in to provide 'support' for System-mandated change.

Anyone complaining about all of it had a few options. Ignore the change and learn to live with it, like most of them did. Everyone's needs would be provided for, and everyone's security was all but guaranteed if they played by the rules.

They could also opt out — a way to permanently and irrevocably put themselves outside the control of the System. They would be allowed to roam 'free,' so long as they didn't interfere with System-controlled infrastructure.

Or, they could try to stop the change. They could fight against it, speak out against it, and try to convince anyone who would listen. Usually these people gave up, but sometimes they were identified by the System as threats. Within a week, they were silenced. Cast out as 'Relics,' few of them survived on their own.

Grouse chose the first option: play by the rules, and keep his family safe. He wasn't interested in being a hero; wasn't in it to change the world. They didn't need him as a professional solider anymore, but that didn't mean they couldn't use him at all. He had his own world to support, and it was as small as his one-story apartment and everyone in it.

That was until they came to find him.

They made me do it.

The kid at the edge of the ARU-controlled territory claimed he had no idea what Grouse was talking about, but there were only five of them in the ARU, and no one else in their right mind would storm a house in the middle of the day and shoot an unarmed woman.

No, Grouse knew, they were *told* to do it. They wanted him, and they were told to get him.

He was in a rage, all but controlled by the desire to get them back, get *her* back, even when his mind told him he was crazy. She was gone, and there was nothing he was going to do to change that.

But he reached over the line, the now-infamous demarcation between the old world and the new, the line that was slowly creeping forward and changing the world forever, and he grabbed the kid.

He pulled him close.

He smelled the sweat on his neck, and he felt the fear in the kid. He wasn't trained, like him. He wasn't a soldier. There were a few who were, but not many. Any *real* soldiers were reassigned and shipped out, left to fend for themselves or at least stay out of the way. ARUs were volunteer-run security forces, mostly rent-a-cops with better equipment. They needed a job, and the System needed humans.

He could sense the kid tensing, getting ready to fight back. In a moment the four others would see him, but he had a few seconds.

A few precious seconds.

Never again would he waste a few precious seconds. Never again would he forget what those precious seconds could do, could *be*.

Time.

He pulled the kid even closer, and something in him snapped. He froze, his breathing slowed, and he leaned his head to the kid's ear.

"Tell me why."

The kid hesitated, noticing the change in the crazed man. Noticing the fear that had been replaced by anger that had been replaced by control.

The kid swallowed, then answered.

"They made me do it," he said. "They told me to do it."

Grouse almost laughed. This kid was *terrified*. It may have even been his first "outing" with the group. Nevertheless, he'd done it.

"The house you broke into. What were you looking for?"

The kid's face hardened, ever so slightly. "You."

Grouse felt his shoulders relax a bit. They'd taken his family from him, but just the simple fact of knowing they weren't after *them* made him feel a little bit better.

But only a little.

"Why"

"They told us they needed you. Not sure why. If you'll just come with me —"

"Come *with* you? Where is my family?" *And why did you kill my wife?*

"Th — there was no family. I was outside, and —"

"You're lying to me."

The kid sighed, and Grouse felt his muscles relax. "They told us the kids would be taken to another facility. They left an hour ago. They told us we'd need to do things like this in order to —"

"Things like *kill my wife?*" Grouse felt his hands shaking, but he forced the feeling back a little longer. *Just a little longer.* He'd been trained for this. To push back the emotion, the driving force of the wall of pain that was quickly going to overwhelm him. He'd gone through countless hours of drills and testing and seminars and even field experience, all for this moment.

"I didn't *know!* They always tell us there's a reason for it. There's never been a mistake, and —"

"Who?"

"They — the System, I don't know. I don't understand them, but the orders come down and we do it. They made me do it, I swear."

Grouse thought about his next move. He considered his options, weighing them against what he wanted to do and what he thought he should do. This *kid*, no more than a child, had been drafted and placed here to maintain the peace, and then told to find him. He was told to *do* something, and the kid just *did it.*

This world, Grouse thought. *I don't understand this world anymore.*

He remembered when people did things for *reasons,* and he remembered stories and books that talked about a time even longer ago when people did things for reasons that even seemed to *make sense.*

But this? This makes no sense.

And that was what was bothering Grouse. Later, when he'd calmed down, he'd think of his wife and family. He'd scream, and the pain would roll into and over him, and he would lash out at anything and everything around him until the pain was subdued, at least temporarily. He knew he'd mourn, after that, for as long as it took, and then some day — a long time from now — he'd have to struggle to remember their faces and what they were like and who they used to *be* and…

It took a moment for him to realize he was already moving.

He'd already made up his mind, somewhere inside. It was made for him, like it was a decision that was handed to him, already wrapped up and ready to present to the world. He knew what he wanted, what he needed *now* and what he wanted *later*.

And the decision was simple.

At the same moment he noticed two of the other ARU personnel walking toward them, one of them shouting, he finished pulling the knife from his waist, from behind his belt and under his shirt where he'd tucked it before leaving his house. It was the same knife he'd grabbed from the kitchen, too heavy in all the wrong places, but it was sharp, and it was all he had. The other two soldiers — far better trained than the kid — saw it immediately. One of the men raised his rifle and pointed it at Grouse.

They shouted again. *Stop, don't do it, put the weapon down.* The usual barrage of police-speak.

He grabbed the kid's hair and pulled his head around so that both of them were facing the soldiers. He stared straight ahead, straight through both men and into the distance.

He felt the motion, not thinking about it actively. He ran the knife against the kid's neck, pushing as hard as he would dare. He wanted it to be clean, but he wasn't entirely sure what sort of pressure that meant.

He wasn't sure why he wanted it to be clean.

He just knew he needed to do it.

This kid, this young man who had been brainwashed by the System and the society that allowed him to be, had no idea what he'd done wrong. He had no idea why he was told to kill some people, steal others, and ignore the rest. He had no idea who made those calls, and why, and what they were for.

The System *needed* kids like him, or none of it worked. The System was powerful — strong enough to enforce a worldwide peace treaty and fix the staggeringly convoluted bureaucracy in many nations. It was intelligent enough to provide economic answers for the world, and it was efficient enough at it that most people's lives didn't need to change much.

But the System had a flaw — it wasn't *human*.

It couldn't physically interact with the rest of the world it lived in, and so it needed kids like this. It needed the Advanced Remote Units to be deployed and standing by to do what it needed to get done.

But *Grouse* didn't need it. He'd made up his mind — or, rather, it was made up for him.

He didn't need the System, and he didn't need this world that he'd tried to fit himself into.

And he certainly didn't need this kid.

He finished his cut, and the man had started firing at them. The first few shots would go wide, but he would get more accurate the longer Grouse stood there. So he dropped the kid, still dying, the blood already overwhelming Grouse and ran. He ran down the street, guns firing at him from behind the line.

He'd made his choice.

They made me do it.
They forced me to do it.

RAND_

Jonathan Rand started at Myers.

The man didn't move his face, his gaze still toward the roof. It was like he was deep in thought, trying to remember something he'd long forgotten, until he spoke again. "And what 'war' are you referring to, Josiah?"

Josiah looked at one of the other men seated next to him — reddish-brown hair, short, and a bit overweight — and Rand was surprised to hear him start to speak. He was surprised he *could* speak — no one besides Crane had said a word to them since they'd been here.

"The Unders are located just on the other side of this mountain range, in a large valley. They have camps all throughout the Eastern European region, but the largest force we've seen, to date, is there in the valley. We're expecting around 40-50,000 troops."

"Wait a minute," Diane asked. "You're serious? You mean an *actual* war?"

"Very much so," Crane said. "And one fought like the wars of generations ago — man-to-man, face-to-face. They're gearing up for something, and we need to be prepared."

"What about the ARUs? Wouldn't they prevent anything from getting out of hand?"

"Eventually," Crane said, nodding. "Yes, eventually. But we're out in the middle of nowhere, in case you hadn't noticed. It would take hours for them to get here, and by then…"

"Why would the Unders even *want* to fight?"

"The Unders *are* fighters," the red-haired man said. "You know that already; we all do."

Rand shook his head. "Sure, but without a *motive*, they're not going to rush in here and get themselves killed."

"Their motive is a matter of principle. Ours doesn't align with theirs, and that's a threat to their population."

"Why?" Diane asked. "They *chose* their life. They wanted to live out of the reach of the System, and they're doing it. Why do we matter at all to them?"

"Because our goals, and what we stand for, directly threaten *them*."

No one spoke for a moment, and Rand wasn't sure if Crane thought the three of them were letting his words sink in, or if the man knew the truth: that none of them knew what he was talking about.

The other man seated next to Crane, opposite the red-haired man, spoke. "We want to destroy the System, to render it obsolete."

Crane flashed him a glance, and the man defended himself. "What? It can't hear us out here. Besides the satellites, there's nothing around that —"

"That doesn't matter," Crane snapped. He cleared his throat and turned back to Myers, Diane, and Rand, and explained. "We are a little *hesitant* when it comes to talking openly about the System. There have just been too many coincidences during the last few months, and we know that the possibility of a singularity-type development of artificial intelligence is imminent. The longer we wait, the —"

"It's already happened," Rand said.

"Jonathan!" Diane flicked her head around and stared at Rand, wide-eyed.

"They *have* to already know," he said. "There's no way —"

"Know what?" Crane asked.

"Seriously?"

Crane didn't answer, and the three men at the head of the table waited for Rand's explanation.

He turned to Diane first. "What do we have to lose?" he asked her. "We're out here, *literally* in the middle of nowhere, and our only way out was rendered obsolete by those *things* they shot at us."

Diane glared at him, but didn't speak. Rand turned to the three men again. "By the way, those *things* were pretty impressive. I hear they're not street legal yet, though."

Crane dismissed him. "You and I both know there are plenty of ways around that. Rand — *what* are you trying to say?"

Rand suddenly wanted to take it back. He realized how ridiculous it all sounded, and how *unbelievable* it was, but his mouth betrayed him. "It's already happened," he said. "The singularity. It's already happened."

"That's preposterous. If that was the case, we'd all be —"

"Dead, or slaves to a race of robot overlords, or hurtling through space toward a new home planet, yeah, I know," Rand shot back. "Trust me, I've heard *all* the theories."

"*This* theory is a new one, though," the red-haired man said. "A sentient computer is developed and... *nothing* changes?"

"Hear me out," Rand said, growing more agitated. The two men next to Crane had smirks on their faces. "The deactivation of Umutsuz happened in a *day*, and the fact that Myers was sent *here*? Right in the middle of all of this?"

"Coincidence."

"It's *not* a coincidence!" Rand shouted, pounding his fist on the table. "Myers — dammit, tell them!"

Myers looked up at Rand with a long expression on his face.

"Myers, come on — you know it's true. It has to be!"

Myers shrugged. "I — I'm sorry, I don't... I don't remember anything before —"

Rand let out an exasperated sigh. "Ok, fine. Fine, whatever. Let's back up." He looked at Crane. "Josiah, why do you want to destroy it? And why do the Unders *not* want it to be destroyed?"

Crane took a moment to look at each of them in turn. Rand felt annoyed, but he allowed the man his dramatics. "They *need* the System, in order to continue living the same way. The irony of living outside of the System is that it *strengthens* them."

"Figuratively, right?" Myers asked.

"And literally. Think about their tech capabilities. They're every bit as advanced as the rest of the world, but they're only using discarded and stolen tech. Just about everything they have they 'acquired' somehow other than Current. They've got *Tracers*, for God's sake."

"But how does that make them dependent on the System?"

"They're dependent on existing *outside* of the System. Don't you see? Take down the System, and you take down their way of life. The System casts them off, like it does us, but in their case it doesn't track them, require pIDs, register them in the Metabase, or anything. They have basic access to the net, but it's for tracking the Boards or informational queries, that's it. Even their communications technology is a century old, and all working offline."

Rand suddenly understood, and he couldn't argue with the man's assessment. "If we take it down, they've got nothing to steal from."

Crane nodded. "Their way of life simply ceases to exist. Every Tracer, gun, or product they own they either built or crudely manufactured, or they stole from a System-controlled registry. The System knows it's gone missing, but it's the most efficient entity the world's ever known. It just creates another product — and a job or two in the process — and goes about its day. It probably even deletes the record from its memory. It's faster *and* cheaper that way."

Rand looked over at Myers. The sharply intense, serious man he'd known from his corporate years was gone, replaced by a withered shell. Myers was staring at Rand, but his eyes were empty, hollow. He felt a pang of regret as he watched him.

Diane jumped in. "Josiah, we're with you. We don't want a war any more than you do."

"I'm glad to hear it."

"So," she continued, "we need to get Myers to the ICPL, in Paris. That's the only way we can try to communicate with —"

"I'm sorry," Crane said. "I — *we* — cannot allow that to happen. That's why we brought you here."

"But we can prevent the war. Myers can," Diane said. "If we get him —"

Crane held up his hand, and Rand was surprised to hear Diane fall silent.

"Again," he said. "We cannot allow that to happen. Myers Asher is the one man the Unders want, and he is within walking distance of their largest encampment."

Rand's eyebrows shot up. "Wait, you're saying —"

"Yes, Mr. Rand. We are going to give Myers to the Unders."

RAVI_

Ravi felt the blistering pain pounding at the back of his skull as he sat up. Even sitting was painful, thanks to the wounds from the gunshots that hadn't yet healed. He involuntarily reached into his pocket for one of the pills Sol had given him and placed it on his tongue, then swallowed.

He waited a few more seconds then looked around. At first he couldn't tell if he had gone blind or if there was just no light in the room, but he reached a hand out and felt the wall. It was smooth but irregular, and cold to the touch.

A cave.

His eyes slowly focused and adapted to the low light conditions, and he could make out a few small crates stacked against the wall opposite him. A dark lump — a person — lay on their side in front of him in the center of the cavern on its floor. He reached out and poked them.

The person stirred and groaned. *Merrick.* Ravi reached his other hand out and rolled Merrick to the side so that his back was on the floor. Merrick slowly turned his head, blinking, and saw Ravi.

"What happened? I went in and out," he said.

"You got hit, someone hiding in the bushes. They got me next."

"Ary?"

Ravi shook his head. "No, they didn't — she…" he wasn't sure what to say next, so he just let the words spill out in whatever order they came to him. "She, I think it was… I think it was her."

Solomon's eyes narrowed. "What do you mean, *her*?"

"I think *she* lured us here." Ravi's eyes fell down the cave floor. He could feel Solomon staring at the top of his head. "I — I'm sorry, Merrick. I didn't know."

He waited for the man to lash out and berate him, but it didn't come.

"She fooled me too, then," Merrick said, rising to a sitting position. Ravi saw the man wince as he placed his open palms on the cave floor, and then remembered the torture he'd been through back at the Unders' camp. He reached a hand in his pocket and felt around for another pill. There were none left.

Merrick turned to face Ravi. "It's not your fault. We made a decision, and we agreed."

"But you —"

Merrick held up a hand. "It's not important now, Ravi. We need to figure out *why* she lured us here, then we need to figure out a way out."

"Why don't we figure out a way out *first*? Like, maybe we just leave the cave and run away?" He flicked his head toward the open cave entrance, about twenty feet up and to the right, and Solomon followed his gaze.

"Well, for starters," Solomon said, "there's *no way* they're just leaving us in here because they *forgot* about us. The fact that we're unbound means they're *very* confident there's nowhere we can go, and nothing we can do to fight back. Look." Merrick stood up, his large build almost coming into contact with the rock ceiling.

Ravi stood, following Merrick. They both reached the opening and peered out. They were looking out over a cliff, straight down into a sharp canyon that seemed to be no wider than a few hundred feet. The day had somehow advanced into dusk already, even though both of them had been out for most of it. The dwindling light in the valley made it hard to see the valley floor, but it eventually came into focus.

It was a long drop.

Their cave was nothing more than a small hole in the side of the cliff, and it was hard for Ravi to believe that their captors had somehow *carried* both of them up here and into it.

"This isn't where they hit us," Ravi said.

"No, it's not. They moved us — I woke up a few times while they did it, but not long enough to figure out where we were going."

"Did they just carry us up here on ladders, then?"

Merrick smiled. "No, actually. Check this out." Ravi watched as Merrick leaned far out of the cave opening, holding on to the edge with his left hand, and looked up. He pointed with his right hand, and Ravi leaned out to see.

Far above them, a wooden platform hung in the air, suspended from somewhere above it.

"They didn't carry us *up* here. They took us *down* here."

Ravi immediately understood. The platform was not unlike the kinds he'd seen mounted to the tops of tall buildings in the cities, used for painting or cleaning or washing windows. It could raise and lower itself on a huge pulley system, delivering its occupants to this — or any other — opening in the cliff face.

"We're in a vertical prison," Ravi said.

"We are. There's no reason for them to suspect we'll try to escape, as it's a hell of a fall straight down, and probably an impossible climb straight up."

Ravi nodded.

"Not that it matters anyway," Merrick said. "I'm afraid of heights." The man shuddered, then swung himself back into the safety of the small cavern. He sat on the rock floor, his body tucked away from the edge of the cliff.

"You?" Ravi asked. "Of all people, *you're* afraid of heights?"

Merrick shot him a glance. "What does that mean — *you of all people?*"

"Nothing, just… you seem… *qualified.*"

Merrick laughed. "Trust me, I'm capable of plenty, and I've been a Hunter for long enough. But everyone's got to have a fear, right?"

"You make it sound like you *chose* it."

"No — not at all. But I *did* choose to live with it. Never really did what it would take to overcome it, that's all. Busy with other things."

Ravi sat on the floor and swung his feet out over the edge. "Not me," he said.

"Afraid of heights, or not afraid of anything?"

Ravi chuckled. "Heights. They don't bother me. Wish I could say that about everything."

"Like I said. Everyone's got to be afraid of something."

Ravi nodded, considering this. They sat quietly for a minute, then Ravi spoke again.

"What about Myers Asher? What's he afraid of?"

Merrick looked up and out, into the small circle of sky he could see from within the cave.

"A lot of people have asked me that, actually. You'd be surprised. He was always the 'unshaken leader.' Quiet and meticulous, but intense in all the right areas at all the right times. He's a good guy, too. Or was — hard to say if he's ever going to be the same."

"You mean because he was scraped? It took a decade of his memories?"

"Well, that. But also…" Merrick paused, then seemed to rewind something in his mind, starting from the beginning. "We *created* that technology. We knew it better than anyone. It was only supposed to affect the auxiliary internal BSE memory devices people were having implanted. A failsafe, or a 'reset' button. Something that was never supposed to be removed, unless it was being upgraded or there was a security issue."

"Like resetting criminals back to a safe memory strand. I remember the news headlines."

"True, but even that was a worst-case scenario option. Just removing someone's memory doesn't change who they are — an unstable person will be that way, with or without a certain timeframe of memories."

"But scraping does more damage than that?"

Merrick didn't respond at first, and Ravi had to look back at the man to see him nodding.

"It does. Unfortunately, we were never able to create a 'perfect' scrape technology. We did what we could to keep the effects minimal, but scraping *always* removes a chunk of *real*, biological memories. And it can change someone's personality, too."

"How so?"

Merrick shrugged. "That's what we were working on when everything… went south. We thought we were on to something — something that would allow us to map the areas of the brain most likely to be affected by a scrape or removal of a BSE memory device, but we never finished."

"You think Myers' personality changed?"

"I *know* it did. I knew the man for a long time. I never answered your question, though. What is Myers Asher afraid of?"

Merrick stood up again, and stuck his hands in his pockets as he looked out their naturally-formed prison cell.

Ravi watched him carefully, examining the man's expressions and facial contortions as he wrestled with the answer.

"Myers Asher is afraid of just about everything. It's the reason he's meticulous — a *perfectionist,* really — and the reason he loves planning and calculating. He can't live with himself when he guesses wrongly, or misses out on an opportunity due to a lack of proper planning.

"He's afraid of losing, but not in the same way you and I are. He hates being wrong, but not because of pride. It's an internal struggle he's always had, and I think where we are right now sums it up perfectly."

"How's that?"

"We're sitting in a prison cell that belongs to a group of people that wants answers from us, or to use us, or something. Myers is out there, somewhere, and another group wants to find him for the same reasons. Meanwhile, the world is in a quiet turmoil, turned upside-down and forced into submission by a computer program that we all saw coming — hell, we *created* it — and that we all thought was going to save the world. And Myers Asher knew *all* of it."

"He knew the System would become sentient?"

Merrick shook his head. "No — I mean yes, I think he did. Myers *planned* for this contingency. He thought it *might* happen, so he created an entire scenario-based plan for what to do if it ever *did* happen. But that's not what I'm talking about. He was afraid we'd lose sight of who we are, as humans, and get caught up in all of it. He was afraid we'd never be able to compete with something smarter — *better* — than us. And he was afraid we wouldn't care enough to do anything about it. Look at us now."

"So he has a plan to get us out of this mess?"

"Yes, but the problem is that what he feared the most actually happened. He was afraid that his plan would be lost."

Ravi furled his eyebrows. "Lost?"

"He had the plan. Ready to go. Not a guarantee, but it was something. He was afraid it would get into the wrong hands, so he made sure it was committed to memory —"

"Oh, come on," Ravi said. "Seriously? You aren't saying —"

"Yes, exactly," Merrick said. "He had the plan to get us out of this mess, and he was the *only* one who knew what it was. He told me he had it, and a little of what it involved, but that's it. His wife, Diane, knew part of it too."

"And there Myers Asher was scraped."

"And therein lies the rub," Merrick said, nodding again. "He doesn't remember *any* of it anymore."

MYERS_

8 Years Ago

"Myers, come on. You can't be serious."

"Please call me Mr. President when we're in here." Myers Asher glanced around quickly, but he didn't need to imply anything.

"Sorry sir," Solomon Merrick said, playing along for the sake of the other two people who had joined them in the oval-shaped room. "Again, though, *Mr. President,* you're not actually suggesting —"

"I'm not suggesting anything," Myers said. "I'm giving you a direct and personal order. It's not a game anymore. You know that, I know that. It's real, and it's growing. Fast. We talked about this already, Sol."

Myers Asher sighed, watching Solomon run a hand over his freshly-shaved head as he considered Myers' request. He allowed the breath to escape from his nose, flexing his nostrils as he eyed the President of the United States of America. It wasn't the America of their childhood, and it wasn't the America of even a decade ago. He'd campaigned for a presidency of a nation that no longer existed.

How he was supposed to know that, at the time before all of this happened, he wasn't sure. Some of the smartest men and women in the world worked just outside his doors, and none of them had caught it.

Solomon was the closest thing he had to a friend anymore. Diane was busy running her half of the world, rubbing elbows in Washington and abroad as the "More Than a First Lady"-lady that had helped him win his second term. They had grown apart, a fact every news outlet and media channel that still existed in the world never let them forget, but there was work to be done.

He'd already given her the assignment, moments ago, that he

needed her to carry out. She stood in front of him, next to Solomon Merrick, waiting for Myers' instructions to the others.

Myers forced himself to breathe. His doctor had added the most recent — and so far most expensive — of the auxiliary internal enhancements available to the wealthiest individuals last week, and he was still getting used to the heightened state of awareness and burst of energy that would be his new normal.

Now, in the confines of the most impersonal personal office on the planet, one that had been shared by and visited by many thousands of people over the course of almost three centuries, he had a captive audience of three. He was in his element: delivering a speech that outlined his plans. Planning was his forte, and he could weave a web of scenarios and possible outcomes and their associated contingencies that would make an economist blush.

But even in the midst of the confines of his own space, in front of the three people he trusted more than anyone else in the world, and with a perfect plan that would fix everything, he balked.

He didn't know what to say next. He was speechless.

The breadth of the control he was losing by the day was staggering, and the extent of the damage that could be caused to his nation, his *life*, was unbelievable. He'd told Sol what he needed, the man reacted exactly as Myers had calculated, and now… he wasn't sure what to say.

"I'm sorry," he said.

Sol frowned. Diane did as well, but neither spoke.

"I know you trust me, and I also know I'm pushing it. But *please* understand. I'm not trying to —"

"To hurt us?" Diane said. She immediately stopped, realizing that she wasn't in an argument with her husband — she was speaking with the President.

"…To make this more difficult than it needs to be."

"*This* is 'not making this more difficult?'" Sol asked.

The third person in the room was already starting to cry, their eyes glassing over as Myers spoke.

"It's not," Myers said. "I know that's hard to believe, but it's not. It's the only way."

Solomon clenched his jaw and stared straight ahead. "Fine. I'll do it."

Diane lost her composure and she had to catch her herself from stumbling backwards. "Solomon, you —"

He held up a hand. "It's okay. It has to be." He turned back to Myers. "Will you send the details over to my office?"

"No," Myers responded. "They're delicate, and I don't want anything digital. Stay back after we're done here and I'll make sure you're briefed."

Sol nodded, turning to the last person in the room. "Whatever he says, Shannon, do it. Without question, without compromise. Understand?"

Shannon struggled back the tears, but she nodded, weakly at first. She pulled herself straighter and nodded again.

Myers put on the solemn, respectful smile that he used when a diplomat had passed away or when he wanted someone to recognize his empathy or concern. "Thank you, all of you. I will *never* be able to pay you back for this. If you two will excuse us, I need to discuss something in private with Shannon."

RAND_

"We're not leaving yet, Rand." Diane shot a glance at Jonathan Rand from across the inside of the hut.

"You heard them," he said. "They're just going to turn him over to the Unders."

"But that's because they think it's the best solution —"

"It *is* the best solution," Lansing said. "For them, anyway. They don't know about the ICPL, or what our plans are."

"Lansing, we tried telling them about —"

"It didn't take," Rand said. "You were there, Diane. We mentioned it, and Crane just laughed us out of the room."

Rand sighed and stood up from his cot at the side of the room. They were currently inside one of the "dugout" houses lining the main square, near where they'd met with Josiah Crane. The cinder block and brick structure's walls looked precipitously high, due to the nature of the assembly. The Relics had dug out the ground, opening a ten-foot deep square hole in the ground and building the structure up around it. The end result was a huge, high-ceilinged house that was amply protected from the elements.

The three of them — Lansing, Diane Asher, and Jonathan Rand — had been tossed in here after a day-long tour of Relica, and after their meeting with Crane. They were shown the greenhouses and Superstrain growth areas, the solar assemblies that powered the small amount of electronics and technological devices that Crane and the others deemed safe, and the hard-packed dirt streets that weaved throughout the city. It was a shantytown — buildings "built" using nothing more than the bricks and rocks they'd been able to find or uncover, each building and house slightly different from the others, in all stages of disrepair — but it was still somehow respectable. Rand thought it must be the way the people — the Relics — held themselves. It was an attitude that seemed to border arrogance, as if they *knew* they were going to not only survive out here, but *thrive*.

"Families" of Relics, nothing more than groups of houses at the ends of streets, shared centralized water storage units, and Crane explained how his pseudo-plumbing system worked. Rand didn't understand half of it, but he was nevertheless impressed that out of nothing but a dry patch of earth in the middle of nowhere, these people had created civilization.

It was a luddite civilization, no doubt, but it was *functional*. And the Relics seemed happy.

Still, there was something threatening about the way they all stiffened a bit as they passed by, led by Crane and his cronies. No one spoke to them, and most didn't even glance their direction. They knew Rand and Diane and Lansing weren't part of them. They weren't welcomed here, and it was clear this was all for show.

The tour took them the entire day, and afterwards Crane deposited them into this one-room building. He'd told them to get some rest, and food would be delivered soon. Then one of his men opened the door and ushered three of them inside.

Myers was taken somewhere else, no doubt being guarded by some of the Relics. Rand, Diane, and Lansing had all fought against it, but there was nothing they could do. Crane had said he wasn't doing anything with Myers tonight, and Myers himself finally told them not to worry. Rand was unconvinced, but their hands were tied. When Myers had been pulled away from their group and tossed into a small building near the tent they'd met in earlier, Rand began working on his plan.

They'd descended down the stairs of the building to find four cots around the room, a long, narrow table set against one side, and a small ceramic pot at the other.

Rand didn't want to guess what the pot was intended for, but he assumed this room wasn't one of the "outhouse cycling" buildings Crane had mentioned earlier.

They'd been arguing since they entered the building over an hour ago, and they still couldn't come up with a plan they all agreed on.

Lansing went on. "Think about from his perspective," Lansing countered. "He's got the ego of a greek god, and the tenacity of a bull. Not only is it a decent plan, it's the one *he* came up with. They're all going to rally around it, and damn whatever we say."

"A *decent* plan?" Rand said. His voice was escalating in pitch and volume, and he took a moment to compose himself. He didn't want anyone outside their hut to be able to hear the conversation. "*Our* plan is a decent plan."

"Our plan is insane," Lansing said. His voice was steady, the calm of many years as a pilot. "Get Myers back to ICPL so he can log in as the magic superuser and save the day? That's —"

"*That's* what's going to work."

"No," Lansing said, his voice dropping another few decibels. "It's not going to work, Rand. It *can't* work, or that would be the plan *everyone* has. Just let him log in, type a few commands, and that's it? The System's out for the count?"

Diane shook her head. "It's a little more complicated than that."

"Obviously."

"Obviously," Rand said. "And so it's *not* the easiest plan, and it's *not* the plan the Unders, the Hunters, or whoever the hell else is going attempt. *That's* why it's going to work."

Lansing considered this for a moment. "Then why don't we explain that to them. Let's just tell Crane why it could work, and see if he'll help —"

"I can't believe I'm listening to this," Rand said. "Diane?"

She looked at each man in turn, then spoke. "Lansing, listen. I know these guys, the Relics. They're all out here looking for something to prove. They're *leaders*, people who expect other people to follow them. They're not all waiting around for someone else to come up with a better plan. They're *fighting* to be the person in charge. It's all politics with them. We all need to rest, and Crane won't do anything tonight. We — and Myers — are safe here until tomorrow."

"Why don't we try to get Myers to —"

"You saw him in there, Lansing," Rand said. "He's wiped. Completely useless now. After the System scraped him, and the last few days he's spent out here, he's worthless."

Diane shot him a glance that said, *careful, I was married to that guy*.

Rand backed off a bit. "Sorry, I just mean he's in no shape to be negotiating for us, not to mention *leading* us."

They all sat quietly for the first time since they'd entered the room, and Rand thought about their discussion some more. He kept waiting for someone to talk, but no one did.

Lansing sat against the wall opposite Rand, and Diane lay on the cot next to him.

Each of them seemed to be deep in thought, but Rand knew the truth. None of them could believe they were really here — at a Relics camp. No one knew there were Relics still alive, aside from the handful that were released from the System's grasp each year.

And certainly no one knew they'd been building a *city*. If Crane was telling the truth, and Rand had no reason to suspect that he'd lie about this, there could be *thousands* of Relics still alive out there. Many of them had settled here, but he'd told them there were others, as well.

Rand wondered if there might be other Relic communities somewhere out there, too. Maybe even other cities.

He wondered what that meant for the Unders, if the threat Crane had alluded to was real or not. It had to be — Unders wouldn't allow anyone else in their vicinity, and certainly not a group of Relics.

Any Hunters in the area would be solitary, like Solomon Merrick, so neither group would have to worry too much about them.

But how is it all related to the System? Rand thought. He knew it was all *because* of the System, and the new world it had inadvertently — or purposefully — created, but he wasn't sure what sort of tapestry it was attempting to weave with their lives. He didn't know what each side *truly* wanted, and that meant there were too many wildcards.

He looked around the room again and found that Lansing had started to fall asleep. If their discussion was over for now, Rand decided it would be a good time to catch up on sleep. He tried to drift off, but instead found his mind racing through the events of the past few days. He thought of Umutsuz, and meeting Myers in the streets, and the Unders' attack on the city, all related to events *he* had put into motion.

A pang of guilt tore through Rand's insides. He pushed it back, forcing himself to believe that those events were *necessary*, *crucial* to their survival.

To *all* of them.

He thought of the meeting with Crane, after they'd landed in the sprawling Relic "city." As his mind churned through the recap and replay of the meeting, he remembered Myers' response to Rand when he'd asked him to explain his thoughts on why the System was acting the way it was.

Myers had dodged the question, wriggling away from answering. He'd claimed to not remember anything, but Rand remembered talking about it just a day ago. It had seemed like the response of a defeated man. Someone who had given up.

It didn't seem at all like the response of a man who'd won the vote to the highest office of the most powerful nation in the world at the time.

What did the System do to this guy? Rand thought. He'd known people who had been scraped, and had seen the effects — they were generally fine, except for a dazed looked in their eye that eventually wore off. They lost the memories they'd had during the time they were implanted, and there were some minor residual effects, but Myers was different.

Myers had *changed*.

The System had somehow taken the man's personality as well as his memory.

Diane was clearly reeling from the blow of seeing her ex-husband alive and — *mostly* — well. Rand had tried to bring it up a few times, but she kept changing the subject. She would need time to examine her own feelings, and then she'd be ready.

Rand knew her well, and he knew she was strong. She'd eventually recover. Until then, Rand knew he needed to step up and take control of their situation, for their sake, for Myers' sake, and for the sake of the future of humanity.

Tonight, Rand would take things into his own hands.

He had an idea brewing, and he just needed to wait until the others fell asleep.

SOL_

The kid's smart, he thought. *I have to at least give him that.*

Solomon Merrick had been studying Ravi since he'd seen the younger man stumble out of the tent he'd been held in by the Unders.

He'd hated leaving Ravi behind in the desert, but with Myers struggling, Unders right behind them, and Ravi bleeding from multiple gunshot wounds, it was all he could do at the time. He'd made a silent vow to the kid that he'd come back for him, if he could.

Their fates had been intertwined, and now they were back together again. Ravi had proven himself to be a resourceful, cunning individual, interested in his own safety over others,' but that didn't necessarily mean he was a bad guy.

Sol remembered plenty of times in his own life he'd acted the same way.

Back at EHM, he was known behind the boss' back as the guy who "really ran the place," the Chief Operating Officer who was always making rash decisions that left shareholders and board members stunned and outraged, only to be silenced at the end of the quarter when Sol's decision turned out to be *extremely* profitable.

He and Myers fought a lot, as Sol's general outlook on life, running a business, and just about everything else was "do what you want, regardless of the outcome." He was smart, and providence had shined on him enough for his ideas and decisions to create more good than bad, but it was that tension between himself and Myers that made it almost impossible to stand each other — and why they were so successful as a team.

When Sol had grown a little as a leader, and Myers had come to the realization that he might be able to loosen up just a little, they both initiated a project that would change the face of technology — and the world at large.

OneGlobal.

The software package, a self-installing and replicating collection of libraries, scripts, and applets meant to streamline efficiency in government organizations and offices, worked like a charm.

In a week after its initial launch, OneGlobal was nearly ubiquitous. No one outside the company knew exactly how it worked — the code was more than proprietary, it was completely truncated and obfuscated, running only what was needed on local independent machines, 'phoning home' for the main control of the software itself.

The purpose behind the intense level of secrecy wasn't commercial, it was security. Anyone with the code core OneGlobal used could theoretically infiltrate every computer the software was installed on.

The plan was simple: at the end of Myers Asher's run as Chief Financial Officer for EHM, he would run for president. A lifelong dream, Asher and his wife hoped to create a new style of politician: politicians who weren't politicians at all, but savvy business, military, or nonprofit leaders who *actually* cared about the future of humanity instead of padding their pockets with the money of lobbyists and interest groups.

Myers had no real interest in what organizational software was installed on government computers — he was an accountant, after all — but Sol had talked him into leveraging his platform as leader of the free world to get EHM software on every US machine. There was little need for Myers' support, though. The software was quickly hailed as a "saving grace" by all but the most contrarian tech pundits, and even with a proprietary company like EHM at the helm, no one considered that there would be any downside to the program's quick adoption rate other than a successful company growing more successful.

He'd told Sol at a closed-door meeting right before he left the company that OneGlobal was a disaster waiting to happen.

"It's too powerful," he'd said.

"You don't know what you're talking about," Solomon responded, standing up from behind his huge glass desk — a psychological symbol of power.

"I don't know how the thing *works*, no," he said, "but it scares me to think of the *data* this program will have access to. Email correspondence, personal files, *everything* on a user's machine."

"Myers," Sol said, "calm down. We talked about this way back at the beginning, and everything is safe. The data isn't interpreted on the user's machine. It's sent back to the cloud processing system in Paris, then fragmented to separate storage devices. The only purpose of that is backups and redundancy. The 'brains' of everything is simply an algorithm that analyzes the *habits* of the user. It doesn't use their own language to respond back to them."

Myers frowned. "I know, Sol, it's a great innovation. But still… it seems so… human."

"It is. It's based on the same neural networks we use, but not biologically. It's all electronic, parallel, and *fast*. It's meant to seem human, because that's who its creators are. We're human, and we need what it can offer."

Solomon paused, sitting back down in his chair. It was another symbol of power — allowing the visitor to feel as though they'd 'won,' a false sign of submission. He waited a few seconds, then continued.

"Myers, this is big. You know it, I know it, and the beta testers know it. It's going to *change the game*. You're running for president next year, and this is going to be your ticket to victory. OneGlobal will streamline every speech you need to write, every email you need to send, and every computer it will come into contact with at every level of government. It's not subterfuge, but it's damn close."

"It shouldn't be legal."

"It's legal in every way. Just because you get to be the first to really 'use' it doesn't matter. No one will know, and no one will care anyway, since they'll have their hands on it shortly after. Remember, this isn't an edge we're using to win — it's an edge we're using to *change the world*."

Solomon remembered the conversation like it was yesterday. Myers stormed — well, walked intently with his head held perfectly straight, Myers' version of 'stormed' — out of Sol's office and back to his own. Sol had a moment of passing regret, replaced quickly by the feeling of impossible gains and huge wins for the company imminently awaiting over the horizon.

And now he was here.

In a prison cut into the side of a cliff, waiting with a kid half his age to be killed, tortured, or something else.

Nothing good would come out of this, but Solomon wasn't one to sulk.

Ravi had proven himself, even if the kid's plans were rash and poorly executed. He'd shown himself to be strong, resilient, and mostly trustworthy. The kid wanted to go it alone, but that was hardly a reason to allow him to.

RAND_

He waited another hour before he made his move. Rand rose from the cot, careful to inch off of the stretched nylon in a way that didn't make the material screech from the man's shifting weight. He placed his feet on the floor gently, then slowly stood up. It was pitch black in the room, so he wasn't worried about being seen, at least until he reached the door at the top of the stairs.

The moment he did, he would have to exit quickly, so as not to let too much light into the room. He didn't want to wake Diane and Lansing, but knew it was a long shot. Lansing was ex-military, and almost surely a light sleeper. Diane, he knew, would sleep a bit more soundly, but he still needed to be careful.

The problem was that he didn't know who — or *what* — was outside the door. He was positive they were being guarded, but wasn't able to hear or see anyone outside their underground prison.

He crept up the stairs and waited for ten seconds at the top. He took a breath, running through the steps of his plan for the hundredth time. When he felt as ready as possible, he swung the door open smoothly and stepped out.

Rand closed the door behind him immediately, catching it right at the end before it slammed. Only then did he turn to see if they had been under watch.

Rand flicked his eyes left and right but saw no one. He took a step to the right, inching toward the side wall of their tiny hut, and continued watching for movement against the moonlit backdrop.

Nothing.

It was as if the city's occupants had completely abandoned their homes. No one spoke behind closed doors, no one paced back and forth against a candlelit window, and no guards patrolled the streets. The hard-packed dirt was clean of footprints.

Weird. Rand took a final glance around and continued sliding toward the side of the building. When he reached it, he peered around it before moving the rest of his body past the front of the house and into the shadows. There he waited for another minute, focusing on any sounds that might alert him to an enemy moving in.

Satisfied he was alone, Rand continued his short journey to the first hut he thought Myers would be in. He'd hadn't seen him since their tour of the city earlier, but he'd decided to start his search with the buildings closest to their own.

Rand knew it was a long shot, but he couldn't bear the thought of waiting around for Crane and the rest of the Relics to determine their fates. Once they delivered Myers to the Unders, they'd have no need for the rest of them. That was the part Diane and Lansing refused to accept. Diane was a diplomat — a good one — and he knew she'd want to make a deal, or figure out some way to compromise. She was always ready to negotiate; always hoping to work out an arrangement.

Lansing would go along with her, and not just because she was his boss. She'd recruited him as her personal chauffeur shortly after the fall, and he'd been loyal from day one. Lansing was whip-smart, extremely capable, and the biggest lap dog Rand had ever seen. The man would literally die for her, but Rand thought it was more out of a desire to please than a sense of duty.

He shook his head at the thought. Lansing was going to get them all killed. He always saw the best in people, to a fault. Tonight he'd argued in favor of allowing them to give Myers away, even though *both* Diane and Rand thought it was a stupid idea.

It was really the first time Rand had ever heard Lansing stand up to Diane, even if it was still in a somewhat subordinate way.

"Out for a walk?"

Rand whirled around, ready for a fight. He held his fists up around his face as he tried to see who had spoken.

"Over here, Rand," the voice said. Rand turned to the right, and saw a silhouette crouching behind an adjacent building.

Lansing.

"What are you doing out —"

"Shh," Lansing said. "Keep it down, man. You know they're going to be watching for us."

"How did you —"

"Rand, come on. I watched you leave the room, and snuck out to follow you after I made sure you weren't going to be attacked."

"Thanks for that."

"I would have helped, but it would have been useless if there were more than a few of them."

Rand didn't feel reassured. He walked over to the building Lansing was standing behind and joined the man. Lansing was slightly taller than Rand, but was of a thinner build. He had short-cropped blond hair, so light it seemed as though he was bald, but it was always covered by a ratty blue Red Sox hat. He shifted the hat around, moving it one direction then back the other way, so that it was sitting in exactly the same spot as it had before.

Rand nodded once up at Lansing, then looked back over his shoulder. "They're going to be out here, somewhere."

"Where? I've been trained a bit in this type of stuff, and —"

"You were *Air Force,* Lansing," Rand said. He hadn't meant for it to sound like such a dig, and he regretted it as soon as the words left his mouth.

Lansing, to his credit, let it slide. He kept his cool as his eyes darted back and forth over the empty city. "Still, we'd be able to see *something*. There aren't even any lights on."

"They're probably trying to conserve energy. I'd bet they're waiting for us in one of those taller buildings, watching. In the dark."

"You've got a flair for the dramatic, you know that?" Lansing said. He stepped away from the building a few steps to get a wider view, and continued searching. "I don't see any place to hide that would offer much of a lookout."

A gentle buzzing came from Rand's right. Both men whirled around and stared into the dark abyss behind their building. The buzzing grew louder, and Lansing shoved Rand against the building and crouched.

"Get down!" He whispered.

Rand obeyed, stunned. "What is it?"

"No idea, but —"

The buzzing sound in front of them was joined by two more, each seeming to appear from the left and right.

"Now there are —"

Lansing held up a hand. "It's those weird devices that incapacitated my Tracer," he whispered.

Rand recalled the little objects that had somehow forced their craft safely to the ground in Relica, eliminating Lansing's control. They had operated as a tiny team, each object providing some sort of use to the overall mission. He had marveled at the tech for the next day, thinking more and more about how they worked, how they had been designed, and what *else* they might be able to do.

They were a perfect example of Rand's favorite type of AI: sleek, sexy, effective, brutally efficient, and simple. Nothing terrifying about a "weak" AI; an artificial intelligence that was only good at one task.

But there *was* something terrifying about *this* weak AI, and that was what forced Rand to reconsider his opinion.

There was no way these devices were designed by humans.

To his knowledge, there was no organization on the planet creating new AI after the laws had been passed and the United States fell apart. Nations were booming economically, but anyone with any computer knowledge that had been left in society had been reassigned — like Rand — to somewhere they couldn't create anything damaging.

Anything competitive to the System.

The truth of it all stung Rand like a physical sensation, but he kept his eyes affixed on the empty sky in front of them, waiting for the three bug-like devices to fly into view.

"Lansing, you got any ideas?"

"You mean, 'how can we outrun and hide from these magical little bugs?'"

"Fine. Point taken. We should at least try, right?"

Lansing shrugged, then turned to look at Rand. "Where are we going to go that these things can't find us? They'll just do what they did to my Tracer, and we'll be frozen, suspended in the air until —"

Rand heard a clicking sound that joined in the cacophony. Lansing heard it, too.

"What the…"

The clicking sound was growing in speed and intensity, and Rand suddenly saw tiny flashes of light coming from the direction of the first buzzing machine.

"Lansing, is that thing —"

"It's shooting at us!" Lansing yelled, diving to the left. Sparks of light hit the dirt right where he was standing, and Rand followed suit, wide-eyed, and jumped back. Lansing was on his feet, and Rand had the common sense to keep up.

They ran through the narrow "streets," weaving in and out of alleyways that had been formed by the somewhat haphazard placement of the buildings, and ducking beneath clotheslines and low-hanging bridges connecting two upper-level floors in some taller structures.

The tiny devices tracked them the entire way. They'd buzz in, start clicking, and Rand would hear the *pat-pat-pat* of hundreds of miniature bullets slamming into dirt, rock, and building walls.

"Where are we going?" Rand yelled.

Lansing's longer legs were an obvious advantage, but Rand was surprised at how spry and nimble the man really was. It was almost like watching a parkour expert every time Lansing sprung himself over a crate, can, or other obstacle. Rand did his best to catch up, but he quickly found out that Lansing was holding himself back so Rand wouldn't fall behind.

"No idea," Lansing yelled, "just trying to get away from them."

"Can't we duck into one of these buildings?"

"Not if you don't want to run into a Relic," Lansing answered.

Rand considered it. *Dying by thousands of microscopic gunshot wounds, or by knife stabbing in a dark alley?*

He tried to find an open door.

The machines churned onward, now in a side-by-side formation, each of them taking turns firing on the two men.

One man.

Rand noticed something odd as he focused in on the rhythmic whirring of gunfire. He watched as the tiny sparks formed when they hit pieces of rock and metal in the walls of the buildings, betraying where the machines were aiming.

They were firing at Lansing. Not me.

Rand almost stopped running.

"Lansing, they're shooting at *you*."

"Got it, ace. Thanks for the heads up," Lansing called back over his shoulder.

"No, Lansing. They're *only* firing at you!"

At this, Lansing visibly slowed to a jog, then turned quickly around a corner. Rand dove sideways into a crevice he'd seen on his left, and watched as the three machines flew directly by his location. *They completely ignored me.*

He was sure he hadn't gone unnoticed, either. *They were targeting Lansing.*

But why?

"Lansing, you okay?"

No answer.

Rand got back up, suddenly feeling the soreness of a twisted ankle. He forced his mind to ignore the pain and began running again. When he came to Lansing's detour, he turned and saw the machines from the back.

They were flying in the same side-by-side line, and Rand could see a set of lights on the rear of the devices. Blue, green, and two red dots. He knew the red dots were redundant power and location signals — a way to communicate with each other — but he wasn't sure what the blue and green lights were for.

He could see the silhouette of Lansing, still running from the machines down the long, straight stretch of alleyway. It didn't look like there was anywhere else for the man to go but straight, and the machines only needed to —

The machines sped up, quickly catching up to Lansing.

"Lansing!" Rand shouted.

The machines all opened fire at the same time, releasing an impressive array of light and sound as the buzzing, whirring, and churning of the miniature bullets crescendoed to a noisy harmony. He watched, helpless, as the bullets found their target.

The lights on the backs of the devices sparkled in the moonlight, suddenly exploding in color as each of the four lights on each of the machines started blinking in unison.

They're talking to each other, he realized. *They're sharing information.* Rand knew what the "information" was, too.

Target acquired.

They were communicating with each other about where, exactly, they should aim to take down —

Lansing groaned and fell forward. He hit the ground face-first, and his hat popped off and away, rolling to a stop a few feet from the man's body.

Rand rushed in, ignoring the machines that were still firing downward from directly above Lansing.

"No, no, no —" Rand ran up behind one of the devices and swatted at it with his right hand. The machine anticipated the attack perfectly, gently dipping out of the way and doing a full spin in midair, as if threatening him. It turned back to Lansing, but didn't fire.

The two other machines stopped firing as well, and each hovered in the air for another few seconds then buzzed off, gaining altitude quickly until Rand couldn't see their black outline against the night sky.

"Lansing," Rand said, stepping forward. There was blood around the man's body, and Rand could see his left arm reaching out in front of him.

"Lansing," Rand said again. "Don't move, buddy. Just stay there."

Lansing pulled himself forward on the ground, groaning the entire time, and grabbed his hat. He placed it on top of his head, but didn't wiggle it down. It rested on the back of his head and upper back, swaying slightly.

Rand kneeled down next to Lansing and took in the scene. The blood was still pouring out of the man, and it was now pooling around Rand's feet. Lansing was breathing slowly, a slight wheeze in his lungs.

"R — Rand…"

"Don't talk, man. Don't talk. You're fine. We're gonna get you —"

"Rand, no. Go. Get out of here." Lansing painstakingly turned his head sideways, the stress of it causing more blood to gather around Rand's feet, and looked up at him.

Rand saw a calm resolution in the man's eyes. He was dying — already dead — and he was okay with that. He wasn't scared; wasn't regretful.

"Rand, go."

Lansing lifted his head slightly off the ground in a final goodbye, then dropped it back to the earth. Rand swallowed, then reached over and affixed the hat onto the dead man's head. He made sure the Red Sox logo was pointing out, just to the left, just the way he'd liked it, then he stood.

He brushed off his knees, pushing dirt and blood into stains on his pant legs, and looked down once again at Lansing's prone body.

When he looked up, Josiah Crane was staring back at him from farther down the street.

SOL_

"What are you thinking about, old man?"
Ravi was talking to the back of his head, sitting against the wall farther back in the cave.

"Nothing — just trying to figure out what they want with us."

"You said they want to find Myers."

"The Unders do, certainly. I just don't know if we're dealing with Unders or not."

"Ary was with Unders, and she set us up. They have to be Unders."

Solomon shot him a glance over his shoulder that said, *you've been wrong before, kid*. "True. Maybe."

"Who else could it be?"

"Anyone, really, but Unders are the only organized group of people I know about. Hunters operate alone, and they wouldn't go to these lengths just to trade us on the Boards."

"Relics?"

Solomon shook his head. "There aren't groups of Relics alive. Once they get released, they get hunted. I should know."

"Yeah, you should," Ravi muttered. "I've been dodging guys like you for four years. Why'd you become a Hunter?"

"I didn't have a choice." Solomon turned and sat down again, facing Ravi. The light from the entrance to the cave illuminated Ravi's face, but a dark circle from the shadow of Sol's own head covered up his nose and mouth. It made him look like the cave was concealing his identity.

Protecting him. Or protecting Ravi.

"I left EHM after the System took over," Sol continued, "and I pretty much had to keep my head down to stay out of its way.

Someone like me — basically running the company that created it — I was a prime scrape candidate."

Ravi smiled. "You still are, I'd guess."

"Eh, maybe. It's been years. It probably thinks I'm useless now, or at least not interested in harming it or anyone else."

"So you didn't want to join an Unders gang?"

"Right — spend my days wandering aimlessly, looking for humans to torture and trade to explain my desire to live outside the System's reach?"

Ravi raised his eyebrows.

"I know. You think that's exactly what *Hunters* do, but you're wrong. We put food on the table — *our* table. Not a boss' table, or anyone else's. We don't even kill people — we just turn them in for payment. It's a solitary life, and I'm not saying it's full of integrity, but it's still better than living in the System's shadow. I've got the BSE memory enhancement, Cardio-Ventricular Enlargement, everything. Just about as robot as a human can get. I move when it tells me to move, and for some reason it keeps me alive. It keeps my *family* alive."

Ravi could see the man struggle with the word. He hadn't seen his family since before Umutsuz was deactivated, and there was no way to contact them out here. Sol wouldn't be stupid enough to try to use a terminal to get a message out.

Ravi nudged the conversation a different direction. "But you don't kill people."

"No — I *have* before, but I *don't* in general."

"Sounds very righteous."

"I'm not trying to impress anyone."

"Good thing."

Sol shot him a glance, but then he forced himself to relax. The muscles in his face visibly loosened, immediately putting Ravi at ease. It was another skill he'd learned as an executive — how to coerce a subordinate by making them feel as though you were on their team first and foremost.

Sol watched the kid watching him, both men trying to silently cross-examine the other. Sol could tell he was up against a solid competitor — Ravi hadn't survived out here by being dumb, or by making friends with everyone he'd met. He wasn't going to fall for Sol's corporate parlor tricks, either.

"Why are you a Relic?" Sol asked.

"Who says I am?"

Sol just stared blankly at him.

"Fine, old man, you got me." Ravi smiled. "Not much of a secret, I guess. I pegged somewhere on the Boards, and you probably saw my name a few times back in the day."

"For about four years you've been bouncing around near the top,"

Sol said. "It's hard enough to stay alive, but to stay alive as a *Relic* with a hefty price tag on your head… that's another story."

Ravi shrugged. "Not really much of a story, actually. Every one of these guys was in a position of leadership, or inclined to lead, or somehow a direct threat to the System's power, but that means most of them were out of touch with what the *real world* was like. I wasn't. I'm not."

"So you survived."

"I had to, and I knew how."

Sol waited for more, but Ravi wasn't going to give it up easily. "You impress me, kid. You're tough, and resilient. I like that."

"Thanks. Glad you're proud of me, Dad."

"Why were you scraped?"

Ravi thought about the question for a few seconds before answering, allowing the silence of the canyon outside the cave to sneak in around them. "I only got a BSE installed two years before I was scraped. Waited as long as possible."

"So they only took two years from you."

"And a little more, as you explained. But yeah, not much. I was subversive, I guess. Had an attitude that didn't gel with what the System wants us all to become."

"And you had the smarts to do something about it."

"Yeah, I guess," Ravi said. "You don't get scraped for being an idiot. I was a programmer. A hacker, really. Fell into it, but it suited me well and I learned quick. I was the guy behind that pID scare five years ago."

"That was *you?* They never released a name…"

"And they never will. Yeah, that was me. I hacked the new pID system interface and allowed the System to be able to find anyone, anywhere."

Sol shook his head. "We spent *months* making that —"

"I know," Ravi said. "Secure, impenetrable, yada yada. I hacked it in a few hours and installed the subroutine in a day."

"Why?"

"Because I could."

"*Why?*"

Ravi nodded slowly. "Right, can't get past you, old man." He thought for a moment. "I thought the System wasn't in control then. I assumed getting that information into the hands of the public would be for the greater good."

"And the pedophiles, serial killers, and rapists the world over would rejoice."

"Think long-term," Ravi snapped. "It's *bigger* than that. You know that. If virtually *everyone* could know where *everyone else* was, at any time, how would that change things?"

"People would die, Ravi."

"People have already died! They always will!"

"Calm down. I just mean... I don't think you thought it through —"

"No? You don't think I did? Consider this: the next time a third-world country's government wants to persecute its people, another country can know *exactly* what those troop and militia movements are, and *exactly* where the leaders are. They'd prevent a massacre."

"They'd only postpone —"

"No," Ravi said, stepping over to Merrick's location in the cave. "They'd *save them*. That's the difference between guys like me and guys like you."

Sol raised his eyebrows, the rest of his face completely stoic.

"I might be looking out for myself, but I'm an optimist. I believe in the greater good. You, on the other hand, guys like you and Myers, you just want to *profit*."

"Myers wasn't — *isn't* — like that," Sol said. "He believes people are inherently good, too."

"Fine. Whatever. I'm not sorry for what I did, even though —"

Sol waited, but Ravi just swallowed and looked at the ground. "Even though what, Ravi?"

Ravi's nostrils flared once, then he turned and stormed back to a dark corner of the cave.

Sol let it pass, and turned and stared out over the open valley in front of their prison cell. A minute passed, then another, and Sol started to consider trying to catch some sleep.

A ratcheting sound riveted him to attention. Ravi was at the entrance to the cell a few seconds later, looking out and upwards.

"They're coming down," he whispered. Sol wasn't sure why he whispered, but it seemed appropriate.

Sol stood, brushing off his pants, an old habit he had to always attempt to appear presentable.

The lift lowered until they could see a pair of legs — skinny and brown — descending in front of them. *A girl.*

The lift continued down until it was halfway covering the opening of the cave, and Sol and Ravi stood face-to-face with their captor, a girl kneeling down on the lift's floor.

Ary.

Ravi opened his mouth to shout something, but Ary held up a hand and spoke first. "I know. Shut up. Anything happens, those guys take a shot at you. *Both* of you." She moved the hand that was held open, in front of her face, and pointed behind her at the top of the cliff on the other side of the valley.

Sol had to lean out over the edge to see, but he used the bottom of the lift as support. At the top of the cliff, four men with face coverings and sand-colored clothing were pointing rifles directly at them. He recognized the guns immediately — long-range EHM rifles, easily capable of making a shot from that distance with a few-inch accuracy all around.

Sol reached his arm out and across Ravi's chest, gently pushing him back. "Ary," he said softly, "just tell us what's going on."

"Rest assured, you'll know *exactly* what's going on once you're up there. Get on the lift."

"Why?"

Ary frowned, a flash of anger shadowing her face for a split second, then lifted her chin slightly. "You can die here, or you can make your case up there. Your choice."

Sol considered this for a moment, then spoke. "I'd rather take my chance at persuasion."

She pressed something with her left hand and the lift continued downward a few more feet.

Ravi looked at Sol, but he just nodded. Both men stepped forward and onto the lift with the girl they'd "rescued" only a day before. Sol watched the valley floor shrink below him as the lift rose, the men across from them keeping their sights glued to each of their foreheads.

MYERS_

He'd fought against it as long as he could, but Myers finally felt the sleep overcome him. He'd waited, hours, then another half an hour, then another fifteen minutes, until every stretch of time he counted off seemed to grow longer and longer.

After he'd been separated from the rest of the group, Myers was taken to the small building next to the one they'd sat inside after they'd arrived in Relica. It was dingy, surprisingly even less appointed than the tent. The walls had a rust-colored grime dripping over them, the roof and ceiling clearly not providing adequate cover for the interior of the room.

There was a bed, or something that Myers thought resembled a bed-shaped object, in the corner of the room. It was square, so he wasn't sure which side was the "front." It rested on four metal poles that had been cut down to about six inches in length. There was a mattress made of an unknown material on the bed frame, but no blanket or sheet. For a pillow, Myers saw a rolled-up ball of fabric.

The squat, red-haired man that had spoken briefly at their meeting and had joined them on the tour of Relica nudged Myers forward farther into the room. "All the way, Mr. Asher," he said.

Myers was still reeling from the shock of the day's events. *An entire city, fully functional, completely off the grid.* It was ironic that one of his lifelong dreams had been to help create a city like this — self-sustaining, able to be completely cut off from the rest of the world. And now he was standing inside that very city, and he was considered an enemy.

Or am I?

Myers hadn't really figured out *what* he was in this game. A pawn? Or one of the power players? He certainly didn't *feel* powerful. So far he'd only been pushed around, pulled around, told what to do, and given only tidbits of information that explained the screwed up world he'd woken up in.

And he couldn't think straight.

Memories came at him, fuzzier than they had been before and shifting around before they vanished again. He could no longer control them as easily; they determined for how long they would be seen before fading back into his subconscious.

Even memories that had been strong — of Diane and the girls, Christmas vacations, sitting around a campfire in the summer — were now almost irretrievable. He felt lost, as if he was wading through a sea of someone else's thoughts.

What is happening to me? He wondered. He'd been confused for days, but he'd at least felt like he could keep himself in control. Now, standing in the middle of a rusting shack in the middle of a strange city in the middle of nowhere, Myers felt like he was losing even that last bit of control.

He told himself to make a plan. To stop, breathe, and plan out the next few minutes. Then hours. It was a strategy he knew he was comfortable with — he didn't have to remember that, he just *knew*.

He focused on the next few minutes.

Red-hair is going to leave, and they'll probably have someone outside the door. They expect me to wait here until they're ready to turn me over to the Unders.

How long will that be?

He had no idea. Josiah Crane had promised them all that it wouldn't be until the next day, as there 'was something that had to be attended to,' to quote the man directly. It was cryptic, and Rand didn't want to believe him, but Myers recognized that so far Crane had told them the truth.

They'd expect Myers to sleep — he wanted to, and he needed it. But sleeping was passive; no matter how much he experienced the healing effects of sleep, Myers had always tried to get away with robbing his body of as much of it as possible.

He sat down on the "bed" and looked toward the door. Red-hair nodded once and stepped backwards out to the street. The door slammed shut, and Myers waited to hear the sound of a lock or deadbolt.

Nothing.

Myers' planning mode immediately took over. *That means I'm being heavily guarded, or they don't imagine that I'm a threat. Why is that?* Am *I a threat?*

He considered that thought for an extra moment.

Something is changing in me. I'm becoming… slow. Or… passive. He couldn't place it, but there was a feeling of serenity sliding over him that had been there since they'd landed. He'd seen it on the faces of the others in Relica — even on Red-hair.

He wondered what Red-hair's real name was, and what he'd done before… all of this. Before Crane had swiped him up and turned him into a passive crony. These men with Crane weren't *advisors*, as Crane had led them to believe. They were *guards*.

Myers knew Red-hair — and the other man, probably — would be outside the doors of his enclosure. They'd be standing guard, just as Crane had ordered them to. He considered yelling, to see what the men were able to comprehend, but he decided against it. It wouldn't help him here, and it wouldn't help Rand or Diane…

Diane.

He missed her, more now than he had before. Seeing her face and talking with her calmed him down, but it tore him apart on the inside. He only remembered a time when they were together, but there was an ocean of time between them. She had years of new memories, ones he was not a part of.

He drifted through those memories, the ones that allowed themselves to be seen, as if he was swimming through that ocean. The memories swam with him, some keeping up and others pushing back against him, a different current than his own.

And that was when he realized he'd fallen asleep.

How long he'd been asleep he didn't know, and how much of his thoughts and dreams and memories were part of the sleep he couldn't tell. He sat up, physically telling his body to wake.

It was dark in the shack — *night? Or early morning?* He had no idea.

He stood and walked to the front of the building, and gently pushed on the door. It gave easily, and he immediately realized that it wasn't completely dark outside. The shack had blocked out almost all of the light, but it was clear that it was dawn outside his tiny cell.

Myers quickly glanced through the slit in the partially opened door, checking to see if Red-hair or the other guard were outside. He couldn't see anyone, so he opened the door a bit farther.

Stepping just over the threshold of the shack — a single slice of wood that had been pressed into the ground — he let his eyes adjust to the morning sunlight. The sun rose directly behind the shack, casting the entire street in front of him in a deep shadow. He followed the shadow's outline toward the city's square, where the large Tracer was still waiting.

However, instead of seeing the Tracer's full profile, Myers saw more shadows floating around the Tracer's side. Heads bobbed and swayed, and as his eyes adjusted, he saw that there were people in the square.

A lot of people.

No one accosted him as he stepped fully out of his cage and into the street separating his shack from the town square. No one approached him, tackled him from behind, or even shouted his name.

He was completely unwatched.

The uncanny feeling of being alone while completely surrounded by people made Myers shiver. His mind was still slow, as if it were being slowly melted over a spit, but he knew enough to see that something had changed.

The plan had changed.

Josiah Crane wouldn't have left him unguarded — something deep inside Myers told him that. Crane would have at least put two or more guards on him, the entire night, without fail.

But he didn't, which meant Crane's plan has been changed. He wasn't sure if it had been *ruined* or just slightly altered, but Myers had a feeling it wasn't something Crane was anticipating.

People milled about, all drifting generally toward the platform at the center of the square. He tried to make eye contact with a woman near him, walking across the street, but she had her eyes fixed straight ahead.

"Psst," he whispered. The woman, stunned, jumped as she looked at Myers, finally seeing him.

"You — you're…" she frowned, unsure of what she was trying to say. "I — you're…" the woman mumbled some more gibberish, her voice eventually drifting down to an inaudible level.

Myers stopped and watched the woman turn and continue toward the square.

What is going on here? It seemed like mind control — like someone was manipulating these people into aimlessly following some hidden or invisible command. *Is that even possible?*

He'd seen some remarkable things the past few days, but this was too much. He convinced himself there was no way someone could fully incapacitate a population into following orders and instructions that weren't even audible.

He started again toward the square, and that's when he heard it.

The screams.

Her scream.

Diane.

He stood up higher, pushing up onto his toes as he tried to look over the ever-widening sea of Relics.

Crane was there, the only one tall enough to stick out above the rest. Myers could tell by the shape of the man's large head, and he could tell that he was moving quickly toward the platform.

He watched Crane ascend the steps up onto the platform, people jostling each other out of the way as their leader passed. One by one, he saw Red-hair, the other guard, and then Rand and Diane step onto the platform.

Rand and Diane were pushed forward by two more people — more guards, he presumed — onto the center of the stage and then bound by thin cord around their hands and feet.

What is about to —

The words crossed his mind, then were gone. He remembered thinking *something*, but then like a flash they disappeared.

Weird.

He continued pressing forward, pushing his way through people, trying not to call any attention to himself. He was almost certain none of these people — *Relics* — would do anything to impede his progress, but he had to be sure he could get close to the stage.

He was close now, but he saw something else that caught his attention.

Red-hair.

The man was nearly consumed by the mass of taller people, but Myers caught a glimpse of the man's frame standing near the stairs, his back to the crowd.

If I can just get…

Myers crouched down slightly, forcing his mind to focus on nothing but the tiny sheath that the man wore around his belt.

A knife.

He snuck along, careful to not alarm anyone near him as he passed through their ranks. Red-hair still faced the stage, watching the other guards as they finished tying up Rand and Diane. He realized Lansing wasn't with them, but didn't have time to consider what that meant.

He focused on the knife.

He was within reaching distance now, and he didn't dare get any closer. He stuck his hand out, slowly leaning forward until the tips of his fingers found the sheath the knife was held in. It was leather, smooth to the touch, and it was stiff from lack of use.

Myers grabbed the sides of it, then carefully lifted. He hoped that it was only clipped on, not attached by a loop around the belt.

The knife and sheath slid upward cleanly. He started to shake, his muscles trying to counteract the stealthy motion and force themselves still. The knife was almost clear of the man's waist, and Myers closed his eyes as he tried to pull it the rest of the way.

He felt the sweet feeling of freedom as the knife and sheath rose the rest of the way off the man's belt, and Myers opened his eyes.

And saw Red-hair staring directly at him.

His eyes widened as he recognized who he was, and Red-hair frantically reached for the knife at his waist.

Myers didn't wait. He fell to the ground, hitting harder than he'd intended, but quickly recovered. He looked around for something to use…

And found a rock.

Just like in the desert just inside the gates of Instabul, Myers was marching toward the unknown armed with nothing but a dull rock.

But this time he *knew* he'd be using it.

Red-hair had to navigate around a few bodies, but he forcefully pushed them aside and continued toward Myers.

Myers waited, watching the man's feet. He assumed he was safe — the man had no other weapons, and he hadn't called for help — so he waited.

And waited.

Then, when the man was standing directly over Myers, almost on top of him, Myers pushed himself up off the ground. Red-hair anticipated the attack, jumping back slightly and pressing his back foot into the ground for support.

But he didn't anticipate what Myers had planned.

Myers swung the rock upward, an uppercut punch directly to the man's chin, pushing through with every ounce of strength he had.

The man's chin cracked, and he went down.

Myers waited a moment, standing over the small red-headed man still holding the rock, as people quickly swarmed the area. Red-hair didn't move. They stepped over him, but none seemed at all phased by the attack that had just played out.

He dropped the rock, turning back to the platform.

RAVI_

Ravi was having a hard time reading Solomon Merrick. They stood side-by-side at the top of the cliff, in the open expanse of terrain that surrounded the deep river valley.

Ary was there, and so were a few others. A younger man, standing near Ary, his eyes dark and brooding as he seethed, and a handful of older men behind them. Ravi recognized them immediately — Unders — by their gear. Mostly EHM, taken from some unfortunate Advance Remote Unit that was previously stationed somewhere nearby. It was, therefore, top of the line equipment, the best the UN could produce.

They each had EHM high-powered rifles, and most had matching sidearms, and Ravi even saw a few short-range pulse grenades, the kind that would disable anything electronic in a twenty-yard radius for an hour.

But none of that surprised him. Ravi knew the Unders were *well-*armed, and capable of holding their own against any trained ARU. Instead, Ravi was surprised by the emotion he saw on Sol's face. He watched the man as they rose the final five feet to the ground above, and as he saw the group of people standing there.

Since they'd stepped off of the platform, Sol hadn't taken his eyes off of the young man. They'd walked a few steps to the left, out of the way of the lift, and were now standing at the extreme edge of the cliff, their backs to the chasm below.

His mouth moved, opening and closing, but Sol didn't speak.

Ary, too, seemed surprised. She'd immediately walked over and kissed the young man, but then turned and waited for one of them to speak. When no one did, she flicked her eyes back and forth between Sol and her boyfriend, then Ravi.

Finally, Sol broke the silence. "K — Kellan?"

The young man didn't break his stare. "Solomon."

"I… why —" Sol took a slow step forward, the words still not able to flow smoothly out of his mouth.

The young man — Kellan — also took a step forward, but Ravi noticed something different about his step. It wasn't a step to bring himself closer to Merrick, but a step to bring his leg around in front of his body…

Kellan pulled a handgun from a holster on his side and lifted it toward Sol.

"No!" Ravi shouted, but it was far too late. The gun had fired, and Sol stopped his advance toward the younger man. Ravi's mind screamed in anger — he had anticipated it; he had seen it coming, but his body wasn't quick enough to respond. He was helpless, and he hated himself for it.

Kellan fired again, then a third time. Sol fell to his knees, still staring silently at Kellan.

Ravi rushed to Sol's side, kneeling and catching the man as he started to fall face-first to the ground. His breathing quickened, and everything inside his head screamed to leave, to start running the other direction.

They're going to kill both of you, he thought. *They're going to kill him first, then they'll kill you. It's as simple as that.*

And then, *it's not as simple as that. They could have killed you hours ago.*

The conflicted thoughts did nothing to dissuade Ravi from helping Sol. He leaned in closer, now holding the entire weight of the man's upper body.

"I should have done this a long time ago, Solomon."

Sol sputtered, and blood spilled from his mouth. He swallowed, shaking slightly as he looked up at Kellan. Ravi looked toward Ary, and saw that she was turned away, her arms crossed. Her jaw was rigid.

"Ary," Ravi said. "Ary, *look* at me. Look at him."

She didn't.

Ravi pulled Solomon back a bit, not wanting the man to fall. Sol's head lolled around a bit, but he blinked.

"Why?" he whispered. Ravi wasn't sure what he meant at first, but then turned and looked at Kellan.

The young man's teeth were clenched, the hard eyes drilling holes into Ravi and Sol, and even the men standing behind him seemed terrified.

"*Why?*" Solomon asked again.

Kellan walked closer to Sol and knelt down on one knee, now at eye level with him. "Why?" he asked in response.

Ravi fought the urge to lash out at the younger man. He had no weapons, nothing but his bare hands. And he had a feeling Kellan was every bit as spry and quick as Ravi, but far stronger and more experienced. He had at least three inches on Ravi, and Ravi wasn't short.

Kellan continued, never breaking Sol's stare. "Because of what you *did*." his nostrils flared, and Ravi saw the young man's eyes dart away quickly, then back. "You…"

"Kellan," Sol started, "Kellan, there… was no… I had no choice."

Kellan stood up, looked at Ravi, then back at the top of Sol's head. He took a step back, then kicked Solomon Merrick as hard as he could.

Ravi's left arm snapped back with the force of the kick, and Sol's body flew backwards — over the edge of the cliff. Instinctively, Ravi fell back to catch his own balance, but when he turned to grab for the other man, he hand tightened around nothing but air.

Kellan walked back to the group of men, who parted as he passed through them. He waved his hand in the air, a 'follow me' motion, and they all followed.

Ary stayed behind. Ravi could still feel the adrenaline coursing through his body, and he felt the welling of tears forming in his eyes, but he stood and marched toward her.

"You — *you!*" He wasn't sure what to say. It was her fault, but she hadn't pulled the trigger.

But it was still her fault.

He reached Ary just as she whirled around and he saw the fear in her eyes.

"I had to," she said, softly. "Ravi, I *had* to."

Ravi stared at her, not wanting to speak. Afraid of what he might say.

"I know you don't believe me, but it's true."

He took a few more deep breaths, then closed his eyes. When he opened them, he saw the same sweet — innocent — girl in front of him. The same girl who'd *lured* them here, and…

"It's your fault he's dead, Ary," Ravi said. "I'm going to make you pay for that."

She turned and walked away. Ravi stood there for a moment, but only then fully realized where he was.

The camp around him was smaller than the one he'd been held at before, where he'd healed from the gunshot wound. The arrangement of the tents, the organization of it all, and the sheer number of weapons and men wielding them in the distance told him everything he needed to know.

He was standing in another Unders camp. Ary was an Under, just like the rest of them, and she had lured them here. He couldn't run, couldn't hide, and he certainly couldn't fight back.

So he ran after her. No one seemed to care — the men and women walking around the tents paid no attention to the murder that had just taken place, and no one even glanced toward him. Ary was about to disappear into one of the larger tents, so Ravi hustled to keep up.

He entered the tent. For its size, he was surprised to find it empty, save for Ary standing just inside. Behind her, he saw rows of tables — large boards fastened to wooden legs — and chairs beneath each one. Stacks of dishes were piled on one of the far tables, and a few large pots stood next to them.

"Ary, why did you bring me here? Was I just in the wrong place? You needed to bring Solomon in, and I happened to be with him?"

She shook her head. "No, Ravi, that's where you're wrong. Kellan was looking for Solomon. I —"

She glanced around, ensuring they were alone, and her voice dropped. "I was looking for *you*."

Here we go again. "You're lying to me."

"I'm not."

"Why were you looking for me?"

"Because I blame you for the death of my family."

Ravi was visibly startled. *There it is. Blunt.* "I — I'm sorry? I'm not sure what you think…"

"You are the reason my family was taken from me. Every. Single. One. All of them. My parents, my brothers, *all of them*, Ravi."

Ravi shook his head. "This has to be some mistake, Ary. I don't have any idea —"

Ary reached out and pulled his shirt, bringing his face closer to hers. "Listen, *Ravi*. I told Kellan I would get both of you back. After Grouse called it in, Kellan's eyes lit up like you saw out there. He's wanted to kill Solomon Merrick for *years*, and trust me — there was *nothing* that you or I could have done to prevent that."

She paused, releasing his shirt, and stepped back. She looked at the ground, then back up at Ravi. Her small frame stood solidly on the ground, unwavering. "He was going to come find you himself, but I told him I'd bring Solomon directly to him, if I got *you*."

"If you *got* me?"

"If he didn't kill you."

Ravi sucked in a breath. "Still — why —"

"Stop. I told you already, and no — I'm not going to kill you. It doesn't matter right now. But *do not* think you're the only person who's experienced loss. We have a lot in common, you and me. I know you know what it's like to lose people."

He glared at her. "I know what it's like to lose *everything*."

Slowly, she rotated her head slightly to one side, watching Ravi closely. Then she nodded.

Ravi frowned, then realized that Ary wasn't nodding at *him*.

He screamed as he felt his arms being pressed to his sides, steely grips preventing him from moving. The two men who'd snuck up on him had waited for the signal.

Ary's signal.

Ravi glared at her, and she stared right back. She had a blank expression on her face, but her eyes told a different story.

I'm sorry, they seemed to say.

They muscled him to the ground and started tying his hands and feet. He felt himself pulled — roughly — back and to the side, closer to the table in the corner of the tent. They finished his bindings and pulled him up, tossing him into a chair like he was no more than a doll. He grunted from the painful treatment, but never stopped staring at Ary, who watched with calculated disinterest.

He wanted to scream, to fight, to take control of the situation, but he knew he couldn't. He wouldn't succeed, and even if he did, where would he go? What would be his next move?

Ary had tricked him — and *Sol* — into coming here, and she'd set them up, playing them from the beginning. She couldn't be trusted, and yet…

Something nagged at him. *What was it?*

Ravi racked his brain to recall their conversation. *What did she really* want?

He knew she didn't want him to be killed — at least not yet — or she would have done it already. She wanted — *needed* — him alive, and he needed to find out why.

Ary waited until the two Unders had finished their work of tying Ravi to the metal chair before she spoke.

"Is he coming?" she asked.

One of the Unders turned to face her, startled, as if it was the first time he'd seen her. "He is, should be here within the hour."

"Good. Tell him we're ready in here."

The man nodded, and the two men left the tent.

Ary stepped up to Ravi and slid her hand over the ropes that bound his arms and legs to the chair, testing their integrity. Satisfied, she stepped back and looked down at him with that same fascinated, almost reluctant expression.

"Now what?" Ravi asked.

"Now we wait."

"Who's coming, Ary?"

"Peter Grouse. He's in charge of this region. We're getting ready for an attack on the Relics group just east of here."

He'd heard that name before, back at the other camp on the other side of the hill to the south.

"He heard you and Solomon Merrick were here, and left immediately."

How did he know that? Did they have a communications system in place?

"Why does he care about us?"

Ary shook her head. "I don't think he does. He just knows you're a way to get to Myers, and *that's* who he cares about."

"I don't know where Myers is."

"He doesn't seem to believe that."

Ravi nodded, then looked up. "Ary, I don't think you want to kill me."

She frowned. "No?"

"No. I don't think you *really* want me to be killed, either."

Ary smirked. "I hardly think you're in a position to negotiate, Ravi."

"Ary, I'm not negotiating. I'm being honest. You told me I had something to do with your family, something I did — I don't have any idea what that was, but I think you know I didn't mean any harm. I think —"

"You *didn't mean any harm?*" She reached out to hit him, but didn't follow through. Her hand was shaking. "Ravi, my *entire family.* They're *gone.*"

Ravi shook his head. "I'm sorry. I don't know what you're talking about."

"You're a hacker, right?"

"I — I was, not anymore."

"You hacked the FreedomFinder subroutine, didn't you?"

Ravi's face matched his shock. *How did she know about that?* "Th — that was a *long time* ago, Ary. I never —"

"*Did you do it?*"

He nodded.

"That subroutine allowed us to use the System to find people, Ravi. You knew that, and what it could do? You were scared of… what? Of some *person* using it to find someone else? Anyone, anywhere, *any time?* But you didn't know the System was going to get smarter, did you? You didn't think that hacking it so it wouldn't need a human 'driver' was going to hurt anything, did you?"

"But —"

"No. Shut up. You gave an *intelligent* program the ability to *find anyone on earth.*"

"Ary, it wasn't intelligent when I —"

"But you *did* it, and that's the point. You gave it the most powerful tool it could ever want."

"It was a way to free it from needing human intervention. If that technology got in the wrong hands —"

"It *did* get in the wrong hands, Ravi!" she yelled. "It got into the *System's* hands. It didn't *need* a human user interface to access the database on the Grid anymore."

He looked up at her, his eyes pleading. "Ary, I don't understand."

Her voice was low, seething. "Ravi, you hacked a subroutine that gave the System enough power to reassign individuals to strategic locations, maneuver militaries and personnel, and place *anyone in the world* wherever it wanted them."

Ravi was growing more and more frustrated. He still didn't understand what she wanted from him; he didn't understand how this was *his fault*. Sure, hacking the subroutine was probably a bad idea, but at the time…

At the time, things were different. They were simpler. People had jobs, governments had militaries, and the world just *worked* the right way. The System was just a computer program. Sure, it was ubiquitous, but EHM was leading the charge for building smarter and safer artificial intelligence applications, and no one ever thought…

"That's what this is about," Ravi said, whispering to himself.

Ary raised her eyebrows. "Excuse me?"

"That's what this is all about, Ary," Ravi said again. "You're not upset with me."

Ary looked like she was going to lean back and punch him in the face as hard as she could, but Ravi spoke again to interrupt the onslaught.

"No, wait," he said. "Seriously, you're not upset with me — you're *upset* — your family's gone, but you're not mad at *me*. You're mad at the System, and the guys who built it. You're mad that the world doesn't work the same way anymore, and that you got the short end of the stick when it all went to hell." He paused, catching her eye, and noticed that she was about to cry. "But you're upset, and you need *me* because you need something to focus on."

She sniffed, wiped away a tear, and knelt down so they were face to face. Ary shook her head. "No, Ravi. You're wrong about what I need you for. I *am* upset, and I *will* make you pay for what you did, but I don't *need* you for some 'catharsis' or whatever you want to call it. I need you to *fix* this."

"Ary, you understand, right? You get that you can't *fix* this? It's permanent. It's —"

"It's *not!*" she screamed. "It's something you helped along, and it's something you can reverse."

Ravi didn't know what to say. There was going to be no arguing with her, and there was no chance he'd be able to convince her.

He'd made plenty of mistakes, and Ary was right about this one. It was a mistake. It was naive, and Ravi regretted it every day of his life.

But that didn't mean he could just flip a switch and reverse it.

There was no going back now. If the System was as strong as they all thought it was, it would only grow stronger. It wouldn't just let someone change its programming, and there was no "hack" that could undo it.

Ary didn't need him to fix anything, she needed someone to *blame*.

RAND_

"Myers is gone."

The words stung him, too. Rand couldn't imagine what Diane must be feeling.

"What do you mean, *gone*? Jonathan?"

Diane's voice was rising, even though she was whispering. The frantic sound of her breathless bursts of speech did nothing to calm Rand's anxiety.

"I told you. He's gone. Crane told me."

"I don't trust —"

"I don't *either*, Diane, but it doesn't matter now. Look where we are."

He knew he didn't need to remind her where they were. It was a scene out of an old western movie, the type his grandfather used to be obsessed with. The dusty streets around them were still empty, but this time it was because all of the inhabitants of the city of Relica were gathered in the central square. The Tracer — *Lansing's* Tracer — was still parked on the landing pad next to them. Diane and Rand were standing, facing the rising sun, legs and arms bound with thick strands of rope, on a raised wood and cinder block platform, completely encircled by people. The platform was raised about seven feet off the ground — high enough to have a wide view of the square, yet short enough so that they could see the people pressed in close to it.

The people of Relica formed a solid boundary around the platform on all sides, pressed in together between the platform in front of them and the rows of buildings behind them. One of the larger buildings jutted closer to the platform than the others, its roof supports sticking out below the actual roof and reaching down, as if beckoning Rand to reach for it.

The Relics stood still, facing forward, watching the procession. Josiah Crane stood on the platform with Diane and Rand, and turned to address them.

"You have been proven guilty of the murder of three members of the City of Relica, and by the power vested in —"

"What?" Rand yelled.

"Do not interrupt —"

"I didn't kill anyone!" Rand shouted again. "Are you all going to stand here and take this?"

Diane flashed a glance over at Jonathan. "Rand, stop. It's —"

"No," he said. "No, I won't *stop*. You people are *nuts*, you know that?"

Rand paused to breathe, half expecting Crane to lash out and strike him. Instead, Crane cocked his head sideways a bit, then motioned for two men to join him on the platform.

Guards. Why does this place need so many damn guards? He thought. *Who* are *these people, anyway?* He knew they were supposed to be Relics, but they seemed so… cold. *Distant.*

Like Myers.

"Go on, Mr. Rand," Josiah Crane said. "This is, after all, a trial."

"A *trial?* Are you serious? We're *tied up*, Crane. We're standing here on… on this… *stoning* platform, and you want us to believe that we're… *on trial?*" Rand was quickly losing control of his emotion, and he could tell Diane wasn't going to jump in to help him out.

"Here at Relica, things are a bit different than they are in the rest of the world. It has to be different. The System doesn't control us, Jonathan. It *can't* — you probably noticed it, but we're off the Grid out here. We have very limited access to electricity, all solar- and wind-based, and none of us use the Current-based transactional and credit systems."

Josiah Crane turned away from Rand and Diane, facing one section of the crowd.

"It's a simple life, but it is one that works for our needs. We have come to embrace it."

"Speaking of — what about your little flying friends? Those seemed pretty *advanced* to me. The ones that killed Lansing."

Crane nodded. "Yes, those are prototypes, taken by one of our ex-IA members. He was part of an ARU that was totally deactivated. He was only able to secure three of them, but we were able to rewire their onboard CPUs and repurpose them for our needs."

"Like killing people."

Crane waved a hand, dismissing Rand's statement. "They're for *protection,* Rand. And if we had more of —"

"If you had more of them, you'd have already killed the Unders," Diane said, raising her head.

Both men turned to look at Diane.

"It's true," she continued, "isn't it? You've been *testing* this stuff, and now it's ready for deployment. The Unders, as you know, will be armed to the teeth, using legal and black market weaponry they can get with localized Current."

Crane nodded along, smiling. "Yes, exactly. We're —"

"And you decided to *kill* one of us to prove yourself."

Crane's smile disappeared.

Way to stroke the guy's ego, Rand thought. *You're going to get us both killed.*

"Listen, miss —"

"Do *not* call me 'miss,'" Diane shot back. Rand felt a boost of confidence spread through him as he heard the all-too-familiar voice of the woman he knew and loved begin to get angry. Her breathy, hyperventilating tone was all but gone, and he could almost see the rage building in her eyes. "You're *scared* of all of this, aren't you?"

"Scared of the *Unders*?" he asked. He turned once again to the crowds, laughing along with the first few rows of people. "No, I'm sorry. You're mistaken. We are most certainly *not* —"

"No, Crane," Diane said, her voice lowering. "You're afraid of losing *power*. You're terrified of your own people. These Relics. They're all your underlings, right?"

Crane studied her face. Rand listened.

"You aren't sure when it will happen again."

"When *what* will happen again?" Crane asked. He stepped forward a step. Rand could tell Crane was beginning to get upset. He tried to remember seeing the man upset, or angry, or even frustrated, but couldn't. He wasn't sure he wanted to.

"When someone will rise up and take your place."

Crane's jaw tightened, and he took another step forward toward the two of them. The people in the crowds shifted, a few of them noticeably lifting their eyebrows. Rand saw two of them — men, both physically fit and very tall — glance quickly at one another.

"Crane, it's obvious. You're no longer wanted by society, by the System. But you're a Relic — you *all* are — because you're *good* at something. You were leaders, orators, executives. The best and brightest.

"But you're just one of them." Diane nodded out toward the people. "You're just a face in the crowd, especially to the System. And one of you — one of *them* — is going to figure that out soon. Someone out there is going figure out that you aren't any better, any more special, any —"

Crane lurched forward and punched Diane, hard, across the face.

Her head snapped sideways as she yelped involuntarily from the surprise of the attack. She fell backwards, losing her balance, but one of the men Crane had invited up to the platform was already behind her. He caught her and lowered her to the wooden floor.

Rand screamed and rushed forward, momentarily forgetting that his feet were bound. He tripped and flew, face-first, onto the platform, landing hard. His nose hit first, and he saw the stars from the impact fill his vision. The temporary shock of blindness receded as quickly as the pain arrived.

Rand blinked a few times and rotated his jaw to assess the damage he'd caused himself, and he felt the warmth of blood rushing out of his nose. He groaned, attempting to sit up and find Crane.

Crane was standing over Diane, who had already recovered. She was squirming under the weight of the guard's grip, but he kept her immobile as Crane focused on her.

"You're nothing," he said. "You and this *rat* are *nothing* out here. We were the *best* the world had to offer, and we still are. You, and him — you're *nothing*."

"You're the reason the System had to *purge* our society, Crane."

"No!" Crane roared. "No, we're the reason the world hasn't completely lost its mind!"

Crane's nostrils were flaring, and Rand could see — even from his location five feet away on the floor of the platform — the glisten of spit at the corner of his lip. The people had pressed in toward the platform when Crane attacked, and now Rand could sense the presence of thousands of sets of eyes on him, as if they were physically touching him, covering his body, face, and hands.

He shuddered. *So this is how it all ends.* Not stoning, not getting shot, but by a riot of crazed geniuses.

What happened here? He wondered, suddenly. The thought came over him without warning, as thoughts usually did, but it was a heavy question. He hadn't expected that.

What happened here?

He was suddenly taken in by the thought of it all; how *unreal* it all was.

These people were leaders once, he thought. *They lived, worked, and breathed to make the world — at least their own little world — a better place, and they were* good *at it.*

These people were the best of the best, like Diane had said. Independent, freethinkers. If there was anyone on the planet left wanting to 'fight the system,' it would be them.

It didn't make sense.

Crane was still yelling at Diane — *his* Diane — and all Rand could think about was the mass of faces pressing down on him. Each of them had a personality, a very specific set of traits that differed with each individual. Each of them was a *person*.

Was.

That's it, he thought. *They* were *people, but not anymore.*

He remembered the questions the System had asked him years before during his first and only MAA. The Moral Aptitude Analysis was his company's way of determining if Rand was a good fit at Vericorp or not. MAAs were used for hiring, firing, and even law enforcement, taking the subjectivity out of human-based assessment and putting it into the hands of the ultimate objective judge.

A machine.

He also remembered talking with Myers back in Umutsuz, before Diane and Lansing picked them up. He'd asked if Myers was having any strange dream-like memories, an effect from being scraped Rand had seen mentioned on the Grid.

Then there was the way Myers had acted in the tent when they'd first arrived. One of the men pushed Myers along in front of him, toward the edge of the city, but Myers didn't fight back. Myers was as docile as a dog on a leash.

He'd lost all of the intensity and drive that made Myers himself.

These people, Rand assumed, were the same. They were empty shells of their previous selves. After their deactivation, the System would have scraped them, kept them hidden away for a certain amount of time, then released them all across the globe devoid of all their memory from the time they'd had their implants installed to now.

But seeing them all here gathered here — the ones that survived the Hunters and Unders and weren't valuable enough on the Boards to gain enough attention to get themselves killed — there was still something about them that Rand didn't like.

The System hadn't just taken their *memories*. It hadn't just ripped the personalities out of them, leaving hollow, faceless caricatures.

The System had done something to them.

It had *changed* them somehow.

Rand looked up to see Crane shouting something at the crowds, his fist held high in the air.

" — *For us! For Relica, and for the future of* — "

He couldn't hear the rest, but he had a feeling he knew what was about to happen.

Crane ended the tirade with a loud shout, and flung his fist downward toward the floor of the platform. The effect was immediate, like an official signaling the start of a race.

But instead of a race, it was a stampede. Hoards of people rushed the platform, yelling and pushing each other forward. Rand struggled to free himself, but the bindings on his wrists were tight enough to cut into the skin. He yanked, but only felt the bonds digging into his arms, drawing blood.

Diane yelled his name, and he turned to look at her.

"Rand!" she said again. He saw her mouth move, but couldn't hear anything over the din of the crowd.

She wriggled around until her head was closer to Rand, but by then three men had reached the top of the platform and were running toward them. Josiah Crane and his men had disappeared back into the folds of people, and all Rand could see was the beginning of a never-ending line of people crushing themselves onto the stairs and up onto the platform.

He didn't wonder what they were trying to do. He knew it was either going to be a quick, relatively painless death or a long, tortuous one. He closed his eyes and listened to the pounding of feet as the three men reached them.

The first man reached Diane and grabbed at her feet. He yanked her forward, dragging her torso along the wooden floor. He heard her yelp and scream at him again.

This time, he heard her.

"Rand! Behind you!"

He flipped his head around as another man grabbed at his ankles. Just beyond the edge of the platform, Myers Asher stood staring at Rand. He'd somehow snuck through the crowd unnoticed and found a spot directly behind Diane and Rand. He was holding a knife in his right hand, waiting for Rand to notice him.

Rand's eyes widened, and Myers lurched forward. The man who held Rand's feet started pulling, but Rand flopped as hard as he could and shook himself free. He rolled over, coming to a rest at the edge of the platform. Myers reached up and onto the platform and quickly cut the ropes on his hands. He handed the knife to Rand and then started to pull himself up and onto the platform.

Rand understood what to do. He cut the ropes binding his feet and was about to reach out and help Myers, but he noticed two other things in his peripheral vision that needed his immediate attention. First, the man who was dragging Diane, struggling against her kicking and screaming, had almost reached the edge of the platform. Rand did not want to find out what would happen if Diane was thrown off the platform and into the crowd.

Second, the man who Rand had shaken free was coming at him again, and this time he looked — somehow — even more upset. There were a few other men behind him now, and Rand could even see a woman joining the men on the platform.

What is wrong with these people? He wondered. *Are they really going to kill us?*

It was another question he didn't want to know the answer to. *No time to debate it anyway.*

Rand made up his mind — he wasn't going to be ripped to pieces by a bunch of loonies in the middle of nowhere. He used all of his strength to roll himself forward, first into a full sitting position and then quickly onto his feet. The attacker had apparently missed the fact that Rand's hands and feet were now free, and he had certainly not realized that Rand had a knife.

Rand kept his momentum, lunging forward with a powerful stretching of his legs, and aimed for the man's chest.

The tackle would have been perfect, except that Rand wasn't interested in *tackling* him.

He was pissed.

Instead of wrapping his arms *around* the man's upper body and using his weight and momentum to take him down, Rand pulled his right hand in slightly just before impact and shoved the knife directly into the man's sternum.

He caught the back of the man's head with his left hand and pulled forward as hard as he could. The grunt from the large man told Rand everything he needed to know — he was dead almost immediately after. The man crumpled to the ground, leaving Rand standing on the platform with a knife in his right hand, blood dripping onto the dead man's body, and panting with the adrenaline and energy surge.

But he wasn't finished. His eyes narrowed, and whatever of the sarcastic, obnoxious attitude he usually wore was replaced by an absolute and total focus on one thing.

Diane.

He roared, throwing his head back and rushing toward the man — who was still struggling with Diane.

He reached the edge of the platform just as the man was joined by another Relic. They both stopped, alarmed at the rapid sound of the approaching footfalls, and turned to look at Rand.

The first man had no chance — the knife landed just below the neckline in his chest, and he fell sideways and back onto the second man.

Rand held on to the blade, but used his free hand to grab Diane at the elbow and yank her back away from the edge. He quickly cut her feet and was about to start on the ropes binding her hands when he felt her knee in his chest. He rolled sideways, falling away from her.

The pain receded quickly, and he saw what had happened. Diane had pushed him out of the way of an oncoming attacker and kicked with her other foot — hitting the skinny old man in the pelvis. The old man groaned and fell just as Rand returned to her side and began working on the ropes.

After a moment they were both free, and Rand turned to see what was going on. People were still crowding the stairs, but there weren't any more attackers on the platform. The last man and woman who had come up for the initial attack were hesitating on the top stair.

They're scared, Rand thought.

After a brief hesitation, however, the Relics began pressing forward again, even more of them spilling off the stairs and onto the platform.

"Now what?" Diane said.

Rand looked around, trying to see if Myers was still there. He couldn't see him anywhere. He considered shouting the man's name, but thought better of it. If anything, it would just call attention to him and put them all in even more danger.

Rand continued his sweep of the platform and surrounding square, and his eyes fell onto the building with the jutting roof supports. He nudged Diane and pointed at it.

"Can you make the jump?" he asked.

She nodded, taking the lead. "Do we have a choice?"

He was about to lean forward and tell her to be careful, but she was already running.

She launched herself up and over the edge of the platform, sailing through the air. She wasn't old, but Rand was surprised how nimble she was for someone who wasn't terribly young, either.

She reached out and grabbed at the wooden post that held up the roof of the shanty. One hand clasped it firmly, but the other slipped. Diane's body swung sideways with the change of direction and slammed into the side of the shanty.

"Diane!" He yelled. He looked back at the people on the platform. A man and a woman were already running toward him, and he made a snap decision. *If I hit her, we both might fall into the crowd. But if I wait for her to pull herself up…*

He was in the air before he finished the thought. The Relics behind him were still charging forward, and he didn't want to allow them any time to slow his running start.

He saw Diane just as she reached the post with her free hand. Her eyes were wide, both with the strain of pulling herself up and in seeing Rand already sailing toward her.

Rand's hands hit the post — hard — and held on. The sting of the impact was nothing compared to the strain his arms and shoulders immediately felt as they tried to arrest his fall, precariously dangling from the post. Diane grunted as his body swung into hers, but miraculously both of them remained on the post.

"Come on," she said. "I'll help you up." He looked over and saw that she had almost finished pulling herself up onto the roof of the building. She turned and reached an arm out as he lifted his body weight up and onto the post.

He took a second to balance himself, then shuffled forward until he felt the reassuring strength of the roof beneath him. She helped him stand, and together they looked back down at the mass of people.

The Relics were still shouting, still pressing forward onto each other, but they were without aim. Rand couldn't see Josiah Crane or any of his posse below, nor could he see Myers in the endless sea of faces.

None of the Relics on the platform had followed their journey through the air and onto the post, and none of them seemed terribly interested in trying. It was as though the boiling anger and fear that Crane had stirred up had dropped to a simmer, and the crowd mentality was no longer controlling their actions. *Still, it's a little unnerving,* Rand thought. *None of this makes any sense.*

"I hate asking this," Diane said, "but now what?"

Rand looked at her. Through the sweat, and disheveled hair, and exerted body, she was still beautiful. He leaned forward and kissed her.

She kissed him back, for only a moment. Then she pulled away and grinned.

"Seriously? Thought it was a good time?"

He shrugged, glancing down at the Relics. "They're not going anywhere."

"Yeah, well, let's not test that theory. Come on." She turned away from him and started jogging up the inclined roof, toward the next building.

Rand followed, still trying to catch his breath.

MYERS_

After creeping through the crowd of people in the square at the center of Relica, Myers Asher tried to follow Jonathan Rand and Diane as they were consumed by the rush of people on the platform. He'd tried as hard as possible to focus on their faces, but he was constantly struggling to focus.

Ever since he'd entered Istanbul, he'd noticed his mind slipping away from him. It was as if he was aging by the second; his memory no longer the only loss he was experiencing. He'd forced himself to remain conscious, doing all he could to engage with Diane and Rand and Lansing, and trying to understand the back-and-forth between them and Josiah Crane.

Crane.

Myers looked up. The crowd was still pressing in on the platform, but he'd lost sight of Crane. Turning all the way around, he tried to find anyone there who looked like the man who'd started all of this. He couldn't see Diane or Rand, either.

A few people bumped around and he felt his body falling to the side. He tried to reach out to catch himself, but instead pushed against another person and crumpled to the ground.

What is going on?

He felt drunk. His vision was slightly blurred, and if he moved too quickly he felt like he was going to get a splitting headache. On the ground, he took a second to catch his breath. He looked up at the other people around him, each swaying and bumping and pressing into one another.

They're like me, he realized. *They are me.*

These people, he knew, were struggling the same way as Myers. They had all gone through whatever "this" was — the weird memory loss, the feeling of drunkenness and loss of control. He wasn't sure what to call it, but he had a feeling it was due to his being "scraped" at some point recently.

Jonathan Rand had explained this to him. He'd told Myers about being scraped, and how the System decided on its own who would be scraped and when. He mentioned also that the System didn't even need to "bring people in" to scrape them anymore — it had little devices like bugs that could fly around cities during deactivations and scrape people on the spot.

Myers' head hurt, and he wasn't sure if it was due to the drugs, or side effects, or whatever happened when someone was scraped, or from trying to understand the insane world he had woken up in days ago.

They'd told him that he knew something about all of this, that he'd had something to do with the System, and where it had taken them. He had, apparently, known and understood everything there was to know about the System, due to his role at EHM and then as President of the United States of America. That was a long time ago, but he'd woken up without the memory of any of it. He may have been fifteen years older, but his mind was — mostly — the same mind of the fifteen-year-younger version of himself.

Myers stood up. The crowds were dispersing, meaning that Diane and Rand had gotten away.

Or...

He chose not to think about the other option.

He fought through the splitting headache and stumbling feeling of vertigo and tried to push through the crowd toward the platform. It was mostly empty when he got there, but he didn't see either of the people he was looking for.

A quick glance in every direction told him Josiah Crane and the men he'd been with since they'd arrived were gone. He wondered if Red-hair was dead, or still unconscious, or if he had recovered and was with Crane now as well.

Finally, he tried to find Lansing. Myers hadn't known him long, but he'd recognize the pilot if he saw him. Pushing through more people, he made his way toward one of the taller buildings at the edge of the square. So far no one harassed him, or even seemed to notice him. That thought stopped him cold.

Crane obviously knows who I am, he thought. There was no doubt in Myers' mind that if Crane or one of his cronies spotted him, they'd pursue him immediately.

But the rest of these people...

No one seemed to care that Myers was walking around among them in Relica. Crane had Myers placed inside an empty building last night, then brought here to watch the proceedings the next day. But as soon as the "trial" began, Crane lost sight of Myers in the chaos, and he was able to slip away.

Not that it would have been difficult to do so at any other time — the Relics weren't hostile, and there weren't any of them that Myers thought were trained to be guards or soldiers. Crane was the only one among them that seemed completely lucid, as well. Judging by some of the people Myers had seen so far, the Relics were getting worse, slipping away into an almost constant state of stupor.

Whatever was going on inside his head, Myers wanted it to stop. He couldn't bear the thought of becoming like the rest of them — completely lost and incapable of independent thought. The people here reminded him of a retirement home, except very few of them were of a geriatric age.

So Crane is different than the rest of them, Myers thought. *He's somehow controlling them, or at least has them convinced that he should be their leader.*

He wondered if the System had anything to do with that. If there were different "levels" of scraping, or if it had somehow passed him by...

That's it.

Myers snapped his head up, thinking. *That's it. It has to be.*

He frowned, noticing something disappear over the top of one of the angled roofs. He pressed a few people to the side, trying to get a better view, his mind still racing.

His vision momentarily cleared, and he felt as though a weight was lifted off of him. He knew it was just a momentary relief, and the strange dizzying feeling would be back again soon, possibly even worse this time.

He saw it again — a head, then another.

Someone's on the roof.

He forced his eyes to focus on the area across the square from where he stood.

Diane.

He saw the outline of her face — unmistakable to him — along with another man's.

Jonathan Rand.

A wave of strong emotion stirred inside him, but he ignored it. He could deal with that later — for now, it was enough that they were together, and safe.

They disappeared again behind the roof, and he knew their plan was to continue on the rooftops, heading toward the edge of the city.

Satisfied, he focused on his part of their mission. If they were trying to get out of Relica — and they should — he needed to get the next piece of the puzzle solved.

He needed to find Crane, and confront him.

He wasn't sure how, or exactly why, but one thing about the man kept nagging at him.

He wasn't like the rest of them. He wasn't like Myers.

He wasn't a Relic at all.

PETER_

Peter Grouse slowed to a fast walk. He'd been jogging for what seemed like hours in this heat, even though it had really only been a few minutes. After the Tracer dropped him off on the ridge, it was only a short run to the Unders' large camp near the cliffs and valley.

He reached the first line of defense for the camp, an invisible perimeter that was constantly being monitored by a LAN-enabled SentinelCam. If two of the three line-of-sight laser walls were crossed, an alarm would illuminate a light inside one of the security tents, then a camera would fix onto the exact position of the breach.

Basically, if anything larger than a fly crossed the perimeter line, everyone inside the camp at a security station would know about it.

Grouse was fine with that — they knew he was coming. He'd gotten the call an hour ago and left his smaller camp, south of this one, immediately.

"We have the boy, but not Myers Asher," the voice on the other end of the radio had said.

The technology the Unders had in their possession never ceased to amaze Grouse, but he was growing more and more accustomed to it. The detachments liked to follow around ARUs and steal equipment and ammunition, then wait for the System to resupply them, then repeat the process. It was an insanely inefficient process, but it worked. After years of operating that way, the Unders camps and detachments Grouse had come across had "recovered" everything from small arms to mint-condition Tracers. And to the outside world, Unders, considered the lowest on the social totem pole and deemed by most to be nothing more than bloodthirsty vagabonds, having even a working radio would seem miraculous.

But Grouse knew the real truth — while some of them were mostly self-serving vagrants who had a sickening bloodlust, most of Grouse's army was made up of people searching for a second chance. People who had made a choice to live outside the rules the System gave them, outside the expectations the rest of the world had for them.

People like Grouse.

He'd made his choice, and it was the right decision. With no family, his wife dead and kids long missing, he had nothing more to lose.

When he'd started making the rounds with a group of Unders, finding hits and pegging them on the Boards, then turning the profit for another round, he knew he'd found something he could do.

Something he could be *good* at again.

His military training and experience had prepared him well, and the leadership benefits hadn't hurt, either. He quickly rose through the ranks and eventually found himself leading the largest collection of Unders in the entire region. They were disciplined men and women, a society that functioned well. No one expected an easy life, and everyone did their part to meet the needs of the group.

And Grouse led them well.

He loved going out with different detachments, training with them and working among them. When Myers Asher had appeared on the Boards, he'd jumped at the chance to help with the hit. There was Unders activity in the region — groups that weren't part of his own — and he knew it would be a dangerous mission. Still, he couldn't help himself. It would further solidify his character in the eyes of his men, and he relished the idea of dragging Myers back to camp himself.

The mission had mostly failed, but Ravi and Solomon had been the consolation prize. They should have been more than enough to trade for Myers Asher. When they went missing, it was all he could do to remain calm enough to focus on the overall plan. He had to keep pushing forward, toward a war with the Relics. He had to keep his army focused as well. He kept the knowledge of the two fugitives to a few of his closest allies, but he'd radioed to the larger camp and ordered them to send out a search party. The man in charge of the Unders there, Kellan Merrick, had more reason than most to find them.

He was Solomon Merrick's son.

When Kellan Merrick had discovered that one of the men Grouse had picked up from Umutsuz was Solomon Merrick, he'd begged Grouse to bring him to his camp. Grouse refused, needing both of them with him for questioning. He'd promised to turn Solomon over to Kellan when he was finished with him.

When he'd gotten the call that Ravi Patel and Solomon Merrick had been found and brought to the camp, he was relieved. He had no more use for Solomon, but he might still need the boy — alive. There was still hope that his original plan would carry forward, and he would have Myers Asher with him soon. If not, he'd still make the plan work.

RAVI_

"Ary, you have to tell me what's going on."
"I don't."

Ravi shook his head. *Damn, she's frustrating.*

"Why did Kellan kill Solomon?" he hoped that the directness would make her open up.

Ary looked around, checking to see if they were still alone. "Stop asking questions. Grouse is going to be here soon, and *I* need *you* to answer some questions for me." She paused, then knelt down again so she was face-to-face with Ravi, still seated and tied to the chair. "What was your group planning to do with Myers?"

"It wasn't my group. Myers and Solomon left me —"

"Fine, just answer the question."

Ravi spat.

"Ravi, would you like me to tell you what Grouse will do you once he arrives? Do you need me to go into detail about what he was doing to *Solomon*?"

Ravi swallowed, but he kept his jaw clenched.

"Ravi, I'm planning to get you out of here if you talk to me."

He laughed. "Right, I'm going to trust —"

"What do you need Myers for?"

He sighed, then resigned himself to his fate. *Might as well talk. It's not like I know anything.* "I don't know. Solomon told me they were trying to take him to Paris. That's all I know."

She thought for a moment. "The ICPL."

"The International Computer Physics Laboratory? Hasn't that been defunct for a decade?"

"It's no longer considered an active research facility, but it's still fully operational. It housed the world's fastest supercomputer at one time, which means it has the bandwidth for that sort of connection… Do they think Myers can interface with the System somehow?"

Ravi shook his head. "Look, Ary, I have no idea. Like I was saying, they left me for dead —"

"And Solomon used to work with him. What else does he know?"

"Ary, I — "

"Answer the question."

"I *can't*, Ary. Stop. If Sol was still alive, you could ask him yourself, so answer *my* question: why did Kellan shoot Solomon?"

"Solomon was Kellan's father."

"*What*? Why —" Ravi's heart sank, as if he'd just lost Solomon Merrick all over again. *Kellan is Sol's son.*

"No one knows why, but he's had a bone to pick with him for years." Ravi suddenly found himself staring at a small, sharp knife, swaying in front of his head. "Moving on. I'm going to cut your bindings, but if you move…"

"I'm dead?"

"No. Hardly. But you *will* wish you were."

"Understood." Ravi watched as Ary carefully cut the ropes binding his arms and let them fall to the ground. "Tell me again why you're letting me go?"

"First of all, I'm not *letting you go*. We're getting out of here. Together. And second, it's all part of the game, Ravi. Stand up." She pointed the knife at his throat, point-out.

He stood.

"Walk toward the end of the table, stand near the tent wall."

Ravi followed the instructions, then waited at the wall of the tent.

"I told you I'd make you pay for what you did to my family. But first you're going to fix this."

"By standing against the wall?"

"No, you're going to fix this later. You're standing against the wall so you'll be out of the way and won't get hurt."

"Wh —"

"Shut up." Ary then turned back around and screamed, as loud as she could. Ravi ducked instinctively, but he couldn't see what she was screaming at.

The two guards that had manhandled him into the chair rushed in immediately, where Ary was waiting. She raised one of her hands in the air — the hand carrying the small knife — then thrust it forward, releasing the blade at the last second.

The knife flew through the air and landed in the first man's chest, stopping him cold. The second man, following behind the first, hadn't noticed the attack, and just as the first man fell forward Ary was using him as a mount, catapulting off his shoulders and flying directly toward the second man.

Ravi watched in stunned silenced as Ary wrapped her tiny body around the man's neck, tightened, then ripped herself sideways, using her *entire body* as leverage to break his neck. He crumpled easily to the ground as Ary hopped off his frame. She dusted off a pant leg, then walked back over to Ravi.

She wasn't even breathing hard.

Ravi's mouth was wide open. "You — you've *got* to be kidding me."

"Nope. Not a joke. Just happened." She reached forward and grabbed his arm, and Ravi discovered that her strength wasn't just *surprising*, it was *terrifying*. He thought his arm might go numb before they even left the tent.

Ary pulled Ravi out the front of the tent and to the side.

She whispered as they walked. "Keep moving, keep your head down, and by God when I say run…"

"Got it," he whispered back.

They reached the edge of the line of tents and she ducked between two of them, heading to the back of the camp.

"They have this entire place bugged with Sentinels, so they'll know as soon as we get past the perimeter markers. That means we're going to have to *move*. Got it?"

Ravi nodded, then felt stupid when he noticed she was in front of him and couldn't see the motion. "Y — yeah, got it," he said.

"And Ravi," she said, still not turning around. "Do *not* die."

PETER_

He arrived at the first security tent, where two men stood waiting for their leader.

"Sir," one of them said, extending a hand. He didn't recognize the man.

He frowned back. Unders despised formalities, and hated being referred to as anything other than "man," or "hey," or by name. They were a society of simplicity, crude but effective. He assumed this guy must be new.

Grouse entered the tent and walked to the makeshift terminal that sat on a table against one of the walls. He assessed the room, and its occupants. Two men and a woman were inside. One of the men was manning the controls at the SentinalCam station, maneuvering a manually-operated flying version of the security camera floating above the camp.

The woman's name was Ailis, the leader of the security detail at the massive camp. She wasn't much of a fighter, but Grouse knew she could hold her own. Her skill set was computers, and she had been a major player in the underground hacking scene before the Grid was erected and the System took over. Ailis was pale white with a face full of freckles, bright red hair extending all the way down her back in dreadlocks. She had items tied into the dreadlocks, trophies and memorandums she chose to carry with her at all times.

She stood next to a large, tattooed black man — Grouse's second-in-command — named Raven. Raven's arms and face were covered in swirling, interconnected tattoos that his former wife had designed and given him over the years, before she died. Grouse and Raven hit it off as soon as they met, and together they rose to their positions of leadership.

He eyed the man and gave a slight nod. "Raven's" real name was Ralph, but he'd chosen the moniker long ago and stuck with it. Grouse didn't know the full story behind it, and he'd never asked.

"Is everything ready for the attack?" he asked.

"It is, Grouse," Raven grumbled back. "We're finishing the weapons check and then will be waiting for the word to advance."

Grouse felt the chill of excitement and adrenaline fill his bloodstream. *It won't be long now,* he thought. *This will all be over soon.*

"What is the weapons situation, on that note?"

"Number, or types?"

"Yes."

Ailis jumped in. "Well, the rifles — one for every three men — are working and ready to go. There are a handful of Spiders, eight total. Ready for use, probably seven. We've got a few boxes of grenades, too. Old ones we lifted from an ARU last week. They're untested, but…" she smiled.

"A grenade's a grenade," Grouse said.

"Precisely. Also, we have the Tracers. Two from your detachment, and three here. We —"

"We won't use the Tracers."

Ailis and Raven frowned, waiting for Grouse to continue.

"Their reload time will make them sitting ducks after they fire their first round. We don't need them, and we can't risk their falling into enemy hands. They're useful, but they're far more useful as a last-ditch getaway plan."

None of them needed to state out loud that it was a "last-ditch getaway plan" for about thirty people only.

"Grouse," Ailis asked, "what about their Tracer? We know the one that we intercepted at Umutsuz was brought back to the Relics colony. It's probably in full working order."

"Again, it will be a sitting duck if they decide to use it. We'll be able to bring it down without much fuss."

"I've also heard reports that they've commandeered a prototype ARU miniature defense system," Raven said. "They used it to pull in the Tracer from Umutsuz."

"Still a nonissue — it only has one locking mechanism, so it can't be deployed with more than one target at a time."

"Understood. When are you going to initiate the attack?"

"I need to wait a little longer. The boy — Ravi Patel — is here, I believe?"

"He's in the mess tent, tied to a chair."

Grouse almost cringed at the crude treatment of the kid, but, then again, he *had* run away. "Very good," he said. "I'll speak with him first, to see if he knows anything else about where we might find Myers Asher."

"I thought Asher was with the Relics?"

"That's what we've been led to believe, but I was told by their leader that they would make the trade. I have yet to hear anything, so I'm wondering if they've decided to change the plan, or if Mr. Asher is simply no longer with them."

Grouse considered revealing his hand to his fellow leaders, but decided against it. He'd hated keeping anything from them, but there was strategic value in controlling a bit of knowledge. *All in good time,* he thought. *Plus, there's nothing they can help me with now, besides focusing on the attack.*

"I see. What do you need from us?"

Grouse lowered his head, still looking forward. It was a subtle move, but it was a practiced habit that Grouse found allowed him to look more intimidating. If the light caught his facial tattoos properly, it was downright unnerving. "Nothing," he said, his voice a near whisper. "Keep an eye on the cams, and I'll let you know when we're ready."

Raven nodded once and Ailis immediately turned back to her hovering SentinelCam. Grouse grabbed the radio — a hacked-together assembly of electronics parts and an antenna — before he left the tent and held it up to his mouth.

"Report."

A hiss of static met his ear as a crackling voice sputtered through from the other end. The deep, Southern drawl told Grouse he was talking to the proper person.

"— Good here — a slight setback, but we're good here."

Grouse waited for the click of a closed transmission, then responded. "Continue moving forward, then. We will proceed on schedule." He flicked the power switch on the radio to the OFF position, and picked up his pace.

Peter Grouse had one more stop before he declared war on the Relics. Sure, the war was planned, and meant to be a front for the more important positioning he needed to do, but war was still... *war.*

It would require his attention, and certainly his leadership. If Josiah Crane didn't come through for him, he would need to reassess and readjust, and still execute the plan. The Unders here expected him to retaliate for Crane's not delivering Myers Asher to them, and they expected the war to be final.

He'd been tightening the noose for months, and when President Asher himself appeared in Istanbul, it gave Grouse the final amount of tension he needed to carry out the final stage of his plan. All eyes would be on the Unders as they destroyed the Relics, and when the System sent in the waves of ARUs to try to control the situation, it would leave the rest of the world — and the System itself — vulnerable.

The mess tent was still a few paces away, but Grouse already knew there was something wrong.

A group of people stood near the entrance, and he quickened his pace. When he reached the opening, the group split, allowing him access.

"They're dead," one man told him as he passed through the open vinyl slit into the mess.

He registered the bodies on the ground in front of him almost too late, but he stopped just short of the first man. A guard, one of the ones who would have been assigned to watch the kid, lay sprawled out face-first on the dirt.

The second man was a bit farther off, and looked as though he'd been shot or struck. Blood pooled around his torso.

Grouse checked the rest of the room. There was a chair at the far end of the tent, rope bindings that had been cut still strung over the arms and on the ground around the chair's legs. He cursed under his breath.

Ravi Patel was gone.

RAND_

The buildings in Relica may have been poorly constructed from whatever materials its inhabitants could find, but they were strong enough to support Diane and Jonathan Rand. Right now, that's all that mattered. They ran over rooftops, stopping only to peer over the edge into the streets below, checking to see if their route was clear on the ground.

So far, it wasn't. While most of the residents of Relica were gathered in the main square, there were a few stragglers in the narrow streets and open areas milling about. Rand thought that they might be safe continuing on the streets down below, but after the excitement in the main square with Crane and his henchmen, he didn't want to take any chances. They continued jumping over rooftops, thankful that the buildings were mostly the same height and placed relatively close together.

They'd run over three buildings now, including the first one that abutted the town square, and Rand stopped at the edge of the fourth and looked around.

"Which way?" he asked. "My plan pretty much ended when we got to the buildings."

Diane pulled up next to him and took a moment to catch her breath. "Right. Let's see if we can stay on the rooftops."

"But if we go straight, we'll get to the borders of the city faster."

"We're not leaving. Not yet, anyway."

Rand turned and stared at her, cocking an eyebrow.

"We're staying here. Until we get Myers and —"

"Myers is fine, you saw him back there. He's safe here."

"No one is safe here, Jonathan," Diane said. "They weren't focused on him then, but they will be. They'll turn on him, too."

Rand sat down, shaking his head. Sitting closer to the roof, it would be impossible for them to be spotted from the streets. He pulled Diane's hand and she sat as well.

"Diane, listen. I know you have, uh, *history* with —"

"Come on, Rand," she said. "This isn't about *history*. He's one of *us*, not them. I know he's a Relic, but he's…"

"Different?"

Diane stared straight ahead.

Rand waited a few seconds, then spoke again. "He's *not* different, Diane, and that's what's bothering you. He's *just like* them. Lucid enough to have a conversation with, but somehow… off."

She nodded, and he noticed the beginnings of a tear forming in the corner of her eye. He squeezed her hand a bit tighter, just as a gentle gust of cool air blew over them. He shivered.

"These Relics, they're… it's like they were brainwashed. They had their memories taken, but that shouldn't have affected anything else. They should be the same intelligent, driven, passionate people they once were. They were *leaders* — the best there was, in whatever field they were in."

"But that's… none of them…" her voice was shaking, and Rand assumed the massive adrenaline rush of the past hour was finally subsiding in her.

"I know," he said. "I know. They're *not* who they once were, for whatever reason. And I thought it was just some weird trippy thing Crane did to them all, but seeing them and thinking about Myers — how he's the *same* as they are — it's uncanny. Too much to be just a coincidence."

"The System did this?"

Rand nodded. "It had to. How else can you explain it? I mean, they were *attacking* us, but only if they were doing it together. It's like a hive mind, or at least crowd mentality."

"Safety in numbers."

"Right. You can't tell me all of these individual, independent leaders would happily coexist in harmony with other Type-A personalities. And they *certainly* wouldn't be subordinate to anyone. And especially not Josiah Crane."

"So what are you thinking?"

He shook his head once, frowning as he considered the question. "I don't know, not yet. I guess I just want to know if they can be *fixed*. If we can make them who they once were."

"Rand, you know the System —"

"I know. It's far more advanced than we ever thought, and there's no chance it would just allow us to program it to reinsert the memory devices — if we could even *find* them. But there has to be *something*."

It was Diane's turn to pause for a moment. He examined the silhouette of her face as she looked out over the great flat plain that became the ground beneath Relica. She was stunningly beautiful, her round eyes and nose descending into a sharp jaw that was still feminine in its girlishness, a petite frame that hid her years of experience as a professional businesswoman.

She turned back and looked into his eyes. She hesitated a moment, as if she was seeing him for the first time in days.

"There *is* something. And that's why we're not leaving the city."

"Myers?"

"Yes, but that's not it. He'll be fine, like you said, as long as we don't wait too long. No… it's Crane."

Rand sat up straighter on the rooftop. "Crane?"

"I'm going to kill him, Rand."

Rand wasn't sure what to think. "You… you're going to kill him."

"I am. For what he did to us — what he was *about* to have them do. He needs to die."

Rand shifted again. "Diane, I get it. I do, really. Trust me, I would have killed him too, in the moment, if I could have. But —"

"But *nothing*, Rand. He's behind this — *all* of this." She reached her arm out, palm upward, and carried it around her body. "He *built* this, and they followed him through it. He's been planning something, and it involves Myers. More importantly, it involves *killing* Myers —"

"It involves *giving* Myers to the Unders."

"They'll kill him. You know they will. Besides, we need Myers too, but we need him alive. Crane has other plans, so we need to kill him, get Myers."

"But —"

"Stop, Rand. Stand up for yourself. Stand up for *us*."

Rand felt the anger flaring just beneath his skin, but kept his calm. *She's manipulating me,* he thought. *She's good at it, but I've known her long enough.*

He lifted his chin and smiled. "You're playing me."

"Rand," she said.

"I'm not an idiot, Diane. I know you. I know when you're —"

"*What?*" she said, getting worked up. "*What?* Playing *politics* with you? Trying to *persuade* you to 'follow me' or something? Rand, *wake up*. Look around. This is *finite*. It has a *beginning* and an *end*, and this is the *end*. Okay? We have a role to play in this. It's what we've been working on — the resistance, Solomon Merrick, even Myers."

Rand tightened his jaw — he could almost feel his dimples becoming exaggerated — as he looked straight ahead, listening, but he didn't speak. *She was right.*

"We've *all* been working toward this. We were sidetracked when Myers…" she swallowed. "When everything *happened*, and it happened much more quickly than we thought. We didn't have as much time to plan. You were reassigned, I was suddenly a drifter, an ex-First Lady with nothing to campaign for, and Solomon turned into a Hunter. A *Hunter*, Rand. Solomon."

It was true, Rand knew. *The System orchestrated almost all this, and they all knew it.* No one had spoken it aloud as simply as she had, but then again, that was the type of straight-forward approach that had earned her the reputation she had. *And it's part of the reason I love her.* She was strong, but in an endearing sort of way.

"Diane, how does this play into the plan, then?"

"We knew going into it that 'the plan' was going to have to be malleable. You explained it to me, remember? Any plan we come up with, the System will already know about it. It will already have a contingency plan, a workaround, a solution. It's a *calculator*, and it's the best the world has ever seen."

He almost shuddered at the thought of the man — his friend — and the person he'd become. "Myers thought that as well. He told me that after we landed, in passing. Something he said he was 'mulling over' back before he made it to Umutsuz."

"He was right," Diane said. She took a moment to glance around at the city of Relica down below. The shantytown was still active, with people moving around, but no one seemed to notice them above their heads. He wondered if they'd already forgotten about the chaos at the square, or if any of them were still looking for him and Diane. "The System will know what we're planning — if we're planning something. Plus, none of this works without Myers. He told me that before…" She quickly looked off into the distance.

"Before what?" Rand asked.

"Don't worry about — it's not important. There's nothing we can do until we get rid of Crane and get Myers, but it has to be something only we know about."

Rand frowned. "So to *beat* the System, we have to 'not plan' something?"

She shook her head. "No, that's where the logic breaks down. There's no way to do that — by definition, the System would know we're doing it. Instead, we just have to work with the System."

"*With* the System. And how —"

"By bringing Myers to Paris. After we kill Crane."

It was definitive, the way she said it. As if it was the only answer that made any sense.

"Okay, what made you change your mind?" He thought of the argument the three of them — Rand, Lansing, and Diane — had had earlier. "You weren't exactly for it then."

"I wasn't exactly *against* it, either. I was married to a politician, Jonathan. And I'm a pretty good one myself. I was measuring the options, trying to decide how I felt about it all. And when I decided, the *reason* I wasn't jumping up and down about it was that by leaving at that moment, we were going to get ourselves killed."

Rand felt an immediate pang of regret at the thought of his stupid plan to escape, and how it had gotten Lansing murdered.

"And we can't just leave now, if we can find Myers?"

"The game has changed, Rand. Crane's obviously planning something, and it's not going to be anything good. I'm afraid that if he carries it out, we lose control, and we lose Myers. We have to finish this with Josiah Crane, move on, and get to the ICPL."

"But isn't that a *plan?* What about the System?"

"It's a plan, just like 'drive to work' is a plan. It lacks the motive, the final intent. The System won't know our intentions, and it won't be able to prevent us from getting to the ICPL anyway. Besides, it can't harm us, even if it wanted to."

"When I thought about bringing Myers to Paris, I was thinking he could somehow shut it down. That's not the plan anymore?"

Diane paused. "It might be. But it's not the first priority after killing Crane."

"No? Then what is?"

Diane looked directly at Rand, then spoke softly, almost inaudibly. "I want to talk to it."

RAVI_

"When were you going to tell me you were a badass?" Ravi asked. He and Ary had been sneaking through the edge of the Unders' camp until they reached the first of the perimeter lines, nothing more than an absence of buildings and structures. She'd held up an arm when they neared the line, and only then did she turn to face him.

"It's on a need-to-know basis, I guess. Survival, and all that."

"Right. Well, thanks."

"Don't mention it. You ready?"

Ravi nodded. "Just run?"

"Head for the hills. Grouse is going to be pissed that you're not still in the tent. You're his last bargaining chip to get Myers Asher, and he's not going to take it lightly that you're missing. Again. They've got this war with the Relics to occupy them, but Grouse will still send out a few men to look for us, to maintain the illusion."

"Ready when you are."

Ary didn't wait for him to finish. She bolted, tearing off to full speed without almost any acceleration. He followed, forcing his legs to keep up.

"The next perimeter checkpoint's about 200 feet away," she yelled. "Keep running — they've definitely already seen us, so don't stop!"

He didn't respond, focusing instead on the two things that were most important to him right now: not dying, and running. While they ran, he tried to analyze the situation he was now in and figure out what to do next.

He wanted out. He wanted to be gone; away from this mess, and these people, and *her*. He was drawn to her in the same way an addict was drawn to a fix. He knew it was unhealthy, and that being near her was only going to get him in trouble, or worse.

But something about her compelled him. She had pulled the wool over his eyes once already, but she'd also kept him alive, and mostly out of any real danger. Solomon Merrick had paid the ultimate sacrifice, but he wasn't sure if he could truly blame her for that.

She was stuck, he thought. *She had no choice, and she has to live with that decision.*

He tried to determine what he would have done, had their roles been switched. Would he have brought them into his camp, tricking them, only to allow one of them to be murdered in cold blood?

The answer snuck up on him before he realized he wanted to hear it.

Absolutely. If your life depended on it, absolutely.

He knew it was true. He knew he'd done worse things in his life already, and this particular decision wouldn't have even registered as a potential moral dilemma; he would have made the call immediately.

To save my own skin.

He wanted to run in another direction. The hills they were headed towards sprawled over their field of vision, diving over the horizon miles away. There would be plenty of good hiding spots in them, even considering the roving patrols of Unders that would be stationed around the area. He could get away from her easily, since she was so caught up in…

No.

He didn't realize that his internal dialogue had asked a question until the answer, once again, snuck up on him and delivered the ultimatum.

No. You're not running away from this. That's all you've ever done. You got yourself into this mess, now get yourself out. Without running from it.

He wanted to argue. *I* didn't *get myself into this mess,* she *got us into this mess. Solomon Merrick is dead because of her.*

Ravi knew there was truth to the statements, but he also knew that he'd run directly to Ary in the first place. He'd led Solomon and himself here. In fact, Ravi knew deep down that he'd been the real reason behind *any* of his poor decisions.

He made a silent vow to never again excuse himself from his actions. He'd step up, starting now, and take control of the situations he found himself in, for better or worse.

Ary veered off to the left, and Ravi knew she was heading for the line of rocks that split two of the larger hills down the middle. It was a natural spot to ascend the hill, and, while difficult to navigate, it would provide them ample cover. Years of erosion and landslides had spilled rocks and boulders out onto the open desert plain, and they started twisting and turning around the largest of the boulders even before they began the incline.

Ravi was continually amazed at Ary's perseverance. He had no idea if she was tired, but judging by the way she handled herself, springing over small stones and launching herself over gaps and crevices, he had to assume that she was only at the beginning of her energy reserve.

He wondered if she had the Cardio-Ventricular Enlargement enhancement installed. It had been a trendy enhancement when it first arrived on the market a few years ago, but it was still massively expensive. Besides the few thousand people the System had assigned as test subjects, just about the only people who could afford it were the brokers — people who dealt with the computers that ran the Current markets, ensuring the bandwidth-trading systems were online and fully operational. Like most tech-focused jobs these days, Current brokers were nothing more than well-trained monkeys. The System managed the Current markets and the computers they ran on without so much as a second of downtime, but since it had to maintain the illusion of a vast, powerful network of human-run machines, it had assigned a few lucky individuals in every major city the esteemed position of watching the computers whir and hum every day.

Aside from those two groups, the only others Ravi knew about who had the prohibitively expensive CVE procedure were Hunters.

The small group of localized, independent Hunters that surrounded all of the deactivated areas of the world were people who had chosen to operate outside of the realm of society, but still wanted the interconnectivity the System and its Grid provided. These people were fringe-dwellers, the types of people who weren't quite dangerous enough to warrant a scraping, not quite passive enough to warrant a reassignment, and not quite rebel enough to become an Under.

Ravi didn't understand them. Hunters operated exclusive to any governing body, had no interaction with other Hunters — much less any internal hierarchy among them — and yet still wanted the benefits the Boards, Current, and other bandwidth-trading markets could provide. They drifted into metropolitan areas when the need arose, but mostly stayed within the confines of deactivated areas and abandoned cities, as that was where the System deposited its recently-scraped Relics.

Solomon Merrick was one Hunter, and Ravi never had the chance to ask him why he'd chosen that life. The man was a successful corporate executive in another life, and he was clearly providing for a family somewhere, but they'd not broached the subject of Sol's personal life during the time they'd been together.

He regretted it now. He actually *missed* the guy, a feeling Ravi was sure he would never feel again.

There was the hole inside him that he reserved for his family, the ghosts of their faces imprinted into his BSE memory device, and there a few wisps of emotion floating around somewhere as well, but he didn't *miss* them.

He couldn't, in this world. He knew that. It wasn't against any rules, and there was no way for the System to know about it anyway, but he'd made the decision long ago to forget about what he could of the old world, the one everyone around him was always reaching for, crying out for. Things were different now, and "missing them" wasn't a productive use of his time.

And yet, Sol's memory was more than just a longing to talk with him. It was more than just a youthful adoration for a mentor. In the brief time they'd spent together, Ravi knew that Sol had secrets. He knew that the man had far more information about all of this than he was letting on.

From the way Sol had calmly and quietly explained that he'd been tortured back at the Unders camp, and how it hadn't seemed to phase him in the slightest, to the way he carried himself, even when confronted with the reality that a person they'd trusted had betrayed them, Ravi envied the man. He wanted whatever it was that drove the man to succeed, and he wanted to *feel* whatever it was Solomon Merrick felt.

Ary had reached a perch high above the valley floor, where she stopped and waited for Ravi to join her. She was breathing more heavily than normal, but he couldn't see a drop of sweat on her. *Unbelievable,* he thought. His own legs felt like rubber, and it was all he could do to not drop to the rocky ground and heave bursts of air in and out until he passed out.

"We'll stop here for a minute. I need a break," she said.

You have got *to be kidding me.* "Right, okay, well take your time," he said between deep gasping breaths.

They rested in silence for a moment, until Ary stood again.

"We need to keep moving," she said.

But before she started, the *popping* sound of far-off gunfire reached their ears. The gunshots were interrupted by larger, deeper explosions. As the explosions faded, even more automatic rifle fire reverberated up the canyon.

"What's that?" Ravi asked.

"That," Ary said, "is Grouse's war on the Relics."

MYERS_

He'd almost caught up with Crane at the edge of one of the city blocks, right as the first of the gunshots started ringing out through the air. They were far away, drifting over the rooftops and down into the city's streets.

Myers had seen Josiah Crane, three of his personal guards in tow — including a broken-jawed Red-hair, a white wrap tied completely around his chin and on top of his head — jogging through Relica, as he turned the corner around the last of the buildings erected on this block. Crane's jog was slow and lilting, his leg limping from a wound it seemed had never fully healed, but he was still waddling along quickly enough. Myers had a hard time keeping up himself. It was hard enough that he was still exhausted, the night's sleep not doing nearly enough to fully refresh him, but he had to fight through the disorienting feeling of stumbling forward as well.

What's the plan? he asked himself. He wasn't sure at all what he would *do* when he reached Crane, not to mention what the men with him would do to *him*. He just knew he needed to get there. *Wherever 'there' is.*

There was also the helicopter-like flying vehicle at the center of the Relics' city. A 'Tracer,' if he remembered correctly. No way he could fly it, but he might be able to find Lansing.

So many ideas ran through his head.

Where is Lansing? Where is Crane headed?

Who is *Josiah Crane?*

A snippet of a memory, another piece to the puzzle, flashed in front of his eyes. He couldn't see it long enough to understand it, but it seemed familiar. He shook his head, pushing his mind back to the present.

Crane wasn't one of them — he wasn't a Relic, at least not in the same way Myers was. He hadn't been through the 'scraping,' like Myers had. He still had his memory, his personality, his *desires*. Myers, on the other hand, was no more than a lost, helpless puppy.

No.

He forced himself to regroup. His mind wanted to wander, back to the memories — he wanted to just lie down and forget about everything. He wanted to forget about the gunfire, now growing louder by the second as more and more people out there found guns and started shooting back at whomever had started the attack. He wanted to forget about the fact that he already *had* forgotten everything. Diane, his wife and the mother of his children, was with another man, running from the same thing he was chasing, and he couldn't remember why.

He wanted to forget about the fact that the System had caused all of this, and that most people now thought he was the person to blame for it. Jonathan Rand seemed to know a bit more about Myers' role in all of this, and he'd told Myers to talk with Solomon Merrick when he got a chance. 'Sol will tell you everything,' he'd said.

The drunkenness was coming back, with a vengeance. He continued to fight it, forcing the weariness and blurry vision back as much as possible, but it was a losing battle.

He stumbled forward, each step more out of control than the last. He swore the ground was *right there,* but every step he took seemed to fall slightly to the side, or too far forward, or not far enough.

Crane was directly in front of him. He recognized the men that followed just behind him, and when one moved to the right, Myers saw the lilting, limited run of the larger man. No one else was around — all of the Relics in the city must have fled when the shooting began out in the desert.

Or they were fighting back, as hopeless as he thought that would be.

On a normal day, Myers knew he wouldn't have had trouble catching up. The misty, out-of-focus lens over his eyes cast the entire world around him in a strange, otherworldly glow, and it made speeding up far more of a chore than it should have been. To his advantage, however, none of the men had seen him running behind them.

Thirty seconds, he told himself. *Thirty seconds, and I'm on him.* That was all it would take. Thirty seconds of focused, organized breathing, one foot in front of the other, and —

One of the men turned around and looked directly at Myers, reaching for something at his side…

"Crane!" he shouted. Josiah Crane stopped and turned, not sure what the commotion was about.

The man pointed at Myers, but Myers continued running. *One foot in front of the other, just keep running.*

The two other men also turned, and all three started walking toward Myers.

"Wait," Crane said. His voice was strained, tired, but still held the deep, purposeful drawl. "Let him get closer."

They stopped short of Myers, and Myers ran — at least he thought he ran — directly toward them.

Again, what's the plan, Myers?

He had no idea.

So he ran.

He stuck his head down, not sure if it would be considered a "proper" tackle or not, or if he'd even make it to Crane. The three men stood in front of their boss, protecting him. Myers aimed for the man directly in front of Crane. *Red-hair.* He planned to hit the man where it would hurt the most — right on the chin.

He pumped his legs, now unsure of how fast he was even moving. Hopefully fast enough to —

Red-hair pushed Myers' head straight down and he fell, face-first, onto the hard dirt. He heaved, the wind knocked out of him, completely out of breath, then rolled sideways.

Myers clutched his sides, then heard the laughter.

"Great effort, Myers Asher," Crane said, his thick Southern accent disguising the words. "We were just on our way to find you. Turns out, you were here all along."

The other men laughed along.

"Get up, Myers."

Myers heard the voices, but his mind was a swirling mess of memories.

The desk. Signing papers. The huge, antique desk. More papers.

They came and went, darting in and out seemingly at random.

Not random.

They were trying to tell him something.

Someone else was in the room. He couldn't remember the memory itself, but he remembered *remembering* it. His mind was playing tricks on him, dangling the full memory — and its meaning — just out of reach.

"Myers, *get up*," Josiah Crane said again. Myers looked up to see the walking stick's tip aimed directly at his head.

He tried to stand, but his legs had given up. One of Crane's men decided to help him up, and Myers felt himself forced abruptly to his feet. He swayed in place, but stood his ground.

The desk has papers on it, and I'm signing them. I'm... handing them... to someone.

He knew he was the President in the memory, but he also knew he'd signed hundreds, maybe thousands, of papers.

Why these? What's the point of —

Another guard hit him in the stomach — hard — with his elbow. The first man held him fast, not allowing Myers to buckle over and collapse. Red-hair snickered while gently massaging his jaw.

Josiah Crane looked annoyed. His eyes darted left and right, listening to the sounds of the battle taking place mere hundreds of feet away, the intensity of the firefight now almost deafening.

"Do you know why they're all fighting, Myers?" he asked. "Do you know that they're fighting because of *you?*" Crane's voice grew in intensity, and Myers felt the *thud* of the man's cane jabbing him in the ribs. He tried to recoil, but the men held him upright.

"I've been searching for *you*, Myers, so that I could prevent *this war*. But you've been chasing after *me* this entire time!" Another jab. "It's a good thing we're not going to need you when this is all done."

He raised the stick once more, intending to land a blow to Myers' head, but Myers looked up and stared at him. He fought back the feeling of dizziness one last time, and spoke.

"I know who you are," he said.

Crane faltered.

"I know who you are," he repeated. "I saw it, in my head. I recognize you. You can drop the act, Crane. You were in my office. When I was President." He forced the breaths, even through the excruciating pain of cracked ribs.

Josiah Crane's nostrils flared, and Myers saw him tighten the grip on the cane, but he didn't attack. Red-hair looked from one man to the other, but Crane shook his head.

"I remember, Josiah. I remember what I asked of you," Myers said, now whispering. "I met with all of you. I must have. I don't remember it, but I remember you."

"H — how..."

"The System allowed me to keep a memory. I don't know why. Not all of it, but enough. But I remember you were there, when I signed the papers that started this all. You were standing in front of me." Myers stopped whispering and summoned all the strength in his voice.

"Do you remember, Josiah?"

RAND_

Rand was shaken. If Diane was telling the truth, and he had no reason to doubt her, she wanted to start a completely new chapter in their story. The System was intelligent, possibly even smarter than any human on the planet, due to its ability to parallel process and organize a mind-blowing amount of data every second, but it was still… a computer.

Is it?

He almost asked the question aloud, but thought better of it. If Diane was convinced that the best solution to their problem was to try to interface with the System, there was absolutely no stopping her.

She was as stubborn as Myers was logical, which was part of the reason they'd made such a great team many years ago, when they were campaigning for the White House. Myers was the planner, capable of parsing data and laying it out in a streamlined, orderly fashion, and Diane was the fiery go-getter that could execute. They'd obliterated their competition on the campaign trail, and many suspected that Diane Asher was every bit as capable — if not more so — of running the free world as her husband.

All of it led Jonathan Rand to the conclusion that his relationship with Diane was woefully imbalanced. What did he possibly have to offer? He was a great programmer, sure, but there were countless people who could code circles around him. His linear, organized thinking was mostly made irrelevant due to his rash, sometimes careless nature. Lansing's death had only proved that to him.

But Diane Asher had chosen him. A ladder-climbing career woman, she didn't seem to need much after the "death" of her husband. The kids were old enough to be on their own, and she had more powerful positions and business interests in her sights. Whatever she thought she needed in a man, she must have believed Rand could offer it.

He had never been a self-conscious person. He wasn't going to win a modeling competition, but he wasn't bad looking, either. Tall enough, thin enough, and broad-shouldered enough to strike a commanding pose, but not a brute. Better than average, but not someone who would cause anyone else to look twice as he passed by.

Diane must have wanted that. Someone confident in their own abilities, satisfied with their strengths and weaknesses, and willing to ride along in her rise to the top. They'd had a great relationship so far, even over the time and distance that separated them.

He watched her now, sliding down the roof of the last building at the edge of the city, ready to drop to the ground and continue the chase. They still hadn't seen Josiah Crane or Myers, but Rand hadn't seen the Tracer leave either, so both men had to be close. He wondered what she was thinking. Was she wondering what he was thinking? Or Myers? What would happen if — when — they were all reunited again.

"Careful," he said as she slid over the edge of the roof. He didn't hear her land, but when he reached the edge of the building he looked down and saw her staring back up at him.

"Need me to catch you?" she asked, mocking him.

He ignored her and turned, crouching and shifting his weight as he prepared for the drop. It was only eight or so feet to the ground, but he wanted to make sure he didn't twist an ankle or land improperly.

When he reached the ground, Diane was already moving again. The edge of Relica was no more than an empty stretch of packed dirt, extending a few hundred yards before a line of low shrubs and trees. Beyond the trees, he could see the ground rise and turn into a few rolling hills, then ascend sharply into the mountain range that surrounded the valley to the north. Diane ran forward, toward the edge of the city, but turned right and headed up a path that led around the city toward the greenhouse.

"Where are we going?" he asked. "I thought we weren't leaving Relica without getting to Crane?"

"We *are* getting to Crane, but I want to have a way out when we're done. Plus, we'll need —"

A deafening crack stopped Diane in her tracks. Rand nearly hit her as she turned to face him.

"Any idea what that was?" she asked.

More cracks and faint popping noises reached their ears.

Rand looked west, toward the sounds. "It's gunfire. Diane, it's the war. The one Crane was talking about. It's started."

She nodded. "Have you seen anyone lately?"

"Anyone like…"

"Any *people*, Rand. Have you seen anyone?"

He stood, silent for a moment. In their haste to get out of the city, and their focus on each other and their situation, he realized they hadn't even noticed the steady decline in the number of people around the buildings and streets of Relica. "No, I guess I haven't. You think —"

"I think the people, the *Relics*, all moved out of the city to prepare for the attack. That's where they were heading when we were on the rooftops. They're probably right over that hill, just out of sight." She pointed to the slight rise in the otherwise flat, cracked land, gently buckling once as it drifted toward the horizon.

As Rand watched, they heard the gunshots grow more and more regular, the sounds of old, outdated weaponry clashing against each other in the air.

"You're right," he suddenly realized. They hadn't been chased through the city, and they hadn't been followed after they escaped the platform in the town square because they had been told to leave the city.

Controlled to leave the city.

Rand shuddered, even in the heat of the day. Somehow, deep down, he knew Josiah Crane and his men were behind all of this.

We need to find him, and we need to find Myers.

As they stood at the edge of the deserted city, watching the smoke begin to rise as the fighting grew more intense, both Rand and Diane silently watching.

About ten feet from them, on the other side of the path, a tiny storage structure stood wobbling on a patch of grass.

The door opened, creaking slowly.

The small building looked like a makeshift shed. It wasn't next to any other structure, and Rand assumed it must have been erected to store equipment or protect something inside from rain. Two of the three walls Rand could see were brick, barely mortared together strongly enough to keep it standing. Another wall, the "door" that was now opened, was just a sheet of plywood, broken and crumbling from weather and rot. It swung outward on rusted hinges, squeaking a high-pitched whine that drowned out even the sound of the gunfire.

A woman stepped out of it, and started walking toward Rand and Diane.

Rand felt Diane grab at his hand, but neither of them averted their eyes from the woman in front of them. Her eyes were filled with tears, and she looked like she hadn't slept in days. Her hair, blond but dirty enough to fool someone, sat tousled and fell over her forehead, a tangle of it almost completely blocking one eye.

She reached up and brushed this strand back over her ear, still marching toward them.

Diane squeezed Rand's hand as she spoke. "*Shannon?*" she asked.

Rand whirled his head around, not believing. "You *know* her?" he whispered.

"Shannon *Merrick*."

The woman nodded, the strand of hair fell back onto her face once more, and she stopped a few feet away from them.

"M — my God, Shannon, are you —" Diane couldn't finish the statement. She rushed forward and embraced the woman standing in front of them, leaving Rand staring wide-eyed at the exchange.

Shannon Merrick.

"Jonathan, come here," Diane said, finally pulling herself back from the woman. "This is… this is Shannon Merrick, Solomon's wife."

Shannon dropped her head, now unable to control her weeping. She apologized, sniffed a few times, and continued looking at the dirt. "I — I'm sorry… I didn't…"

"Shannon, it's okay. What's wrong?"

"Sol — Solomon. He's… he's dead."

Rand felt his blood run cold. He stepped closer to the two women, but didn't know what to say. They stood there in shocked silence until Diane spoke again.

"How do you know?"

Shannon shook her head, then looked up at them. "There's time for that later." She stared at Rand, then Diane. "I've been on the run for days, trying to find one of you."

"One of us?" Rand asked.

"No, one of… never mind. Listen, Diane, we have to leave. Now. There's no time to waste. Where's Myers?"

"I — he's…" Diane looked over at Rand.

"He's still in the city, somewhere. We think."

"You don't *know?*"

"There was… something happened. Josiah Crane —"

"*Crane* is here?" Shannon began breathing faster, her fists clenching and unclenching. She reached a hand to her forehead. "No, this can't — that can't be right. Crane? Josiah Crane is *here?*"

Diane grabbed Shannon's shoulder. "Shannon, come on. Let's find a place we can talk. I have so many questions."

"No!" Shannon yelled, startling even herself. "We have to leave *now*. Diane, don't you remember?"

Diane turned her head slightly. Rand eyed each woman in turn, still having no idea what was going on.

"Don't you remember the discussion? What we all talked about."

Diane paused. "I remember being there, in the office, with him.

With Myers. And you. And…" she paused again, not wanting to say the name. "He gave us clear instructions, then told us to leave."

"Yes, but he told *you two* to leave. Myers asked me to stay, remember?"

Diane nodded.

"And when you left, he gave me *my* instructions. He was very clear."

Rand sensed that Diane didn't want to know what those 'instructions' were.

Shannon placed her hand on Diane's shoulder, pulling her closer to herself. "He told me that even if any of this failed, even if any of this was different than the way we all thought it would be, to make sure that he doesn't go to Paris."

Diane frowned. "Wait, what?"

"He told me, no matter what, that he can't go to Paris."

RAND_

The gunfire from the Relics and Unders had become like background music to Rand's ears. He still heard it, still knew it was there, but it had little effect on him. If anything, it was almost calming, the repeating rhythms and constant shuddering forming a safety net around his mind.

He listened closer to it, wondering if it was getting louder, softer, or staying the same. He hadn't heard of anything like this, at least not in the past five years or so. ARUs usually snuffed out any violence rapidly, not allowing news of the dispute to get out of the area.

The ARUs should be here any minute, he realized. The System would no doubt be monitoring this locale, watching via satellite for any potential fighting. It would send as many ARUs as necessary to quell the outburst, and it would do it using far more advanced technology than anyone stupid enough to fight back had access to.

There was more than a good chance that everyone involved — Relics and Unders both — would be dead soon. It might take a few hours to get the ARUs to their positions, but the System would show up.

He was certain of it.

And he was certain of something else, as well.

As he stood, listening to the heartbeat of the largest open fighting he'd seen or heard about since the Grid went up and the world went down, he realized that the fighting wasn't about one side focused on winning something from the other. There might be those who thought they could win more power, but surely there was no one out there who thought they could actually win a *battle*.

The fighting wasn't about power, or winning, or even fighting. It wasn't about any of that.

Rand realized it was about the System itself.

It was shouting to the System, asking for its attention.

It was a *distraction*.

MYERS_

"Do you *remember*, Josiah?" He asked again.
Crane didn't respond.
Only then did Myers realize where they were.
The Tracer, the sleek, aerodynamic snub-nosed flying vehicle they'd flown here in, was sitting a block away from them. They'd walked a full route through a section of the city, only to come right back to where they were. Even the platform, cold and empty now, sat near the center of the square. Crane and his men had been heading toward the Tracer all along, probably to use it to recon the city and find him after they lost him in the crowd.

Crane said something to Red-hair, and the shorter man trotted away toward the Tracer.

"I would say that it's *lucky* you found us when you did," Crane said. "But you and I both know I stopped believing in luck about ten years ago."

He reached a hand out to Myers. Myers looked at it a moment, still catching his breath, but took it. The large man struggled a bit to maintain his balance, but pulled Myers to his feet.

"Well, I guess we can forget the pleasantries, can't we?" he asked Myers.

"I told you to do something for me, Crane," Myers said. His eyes were beginning to blur, but he made sure to force his head to stay still. He stared at the man in front of him. "I told you to build a city, one that we could defend. One that would *protect* us."

"One that would protect *you*!" Crane yelled. "It was for *you*, and all of *them*!" He stuck his cane out in the direction of the edge of Relica, toward the direction the gunfire was coming from. "That's all it was,

Asher. You wanted me to build you a utopia, and you wanted me to stock it with your kind, so that you would all have a place to go when it all went to —"

"I wanted you to offer them a place to *belong* again. A society, Crane!" Myers was grasping at a memory that he couldn't control, and he was reaching the limit of what he could remember. He had no context — why he'd chosen Crane, why he'd thought he was even capable of the task, what his specific parameters were.

But he knew it wasn't *this*.

It wasn't to form a half-baked open-air zoo to imprison the shells of former individuals.

And it *certainly* wasn't to provide Crane with a personal army.

"You're *using* these people, Crane." He stopped, shaking his head in disbelief. "How'd you do it, anyway? How'd you get these people to follow you?"

"They're not *people* anymore, Myers. But you won't be able to realize that, because in less than a week you'll be one of them." He motioned to the other two men, who had now taken up a position behind Myers. They rushed forward and grabbed Myers' arms, pinning him between them. "And I didn't have to *do* anything — the System did that for me. There's a psychological change in you, Myers. It's subtle, but it's there. And it's getting stronger. Pretty soon you'll crave order, just like they did. You'll crave leadership, someone to offer them a *plan*.

"And then you'll do *exactly* what I tell you to do."

Myers clenched his teeth, more out of sheer determination to focus on Crane's face than anger. "This isn't over, Crane. Kill me if you want, but this isn't over. It doesn't end here."

Crane laughed. "Myers, I'm not going to *kill* you. And it *isn't* over, not yet. But it will be. You're going to end this yourself."

"Giving me to the Unders will do nothing. They just want —"

"Myers, I'm not giving you to anyone. That plan's changed — listen. You can hear it, right?" Myers knew he was referring to the fighting in the distance, between the citizens of Relica and the Unders. "It's too late for a trade, Myers, so we're going to do what you all wanted all along. We're going to Paris."

Josiah Crane stood to his full height, towering over Myers, and looked at each of his guards. "Take *President* Asher to the Tracer. It'll be hot already, and we need to get in the air before the ARUs get here."

They nodded, and Myers felt himself swept away by the two men, his feet almost not even touching the ground as they walked up the entrance ramp to the hovering Tracer.

PART THREE_

ROAN_

The pounding in his head swallowed every sense within him, focusing his entire attention on the pain of the throbbing headache. Roan Alexander sat up and rubbed his temples. The throbbing pulsed once more as the blood moved and shifted within him, then subsided.

Immediately.

He frowned, glad the headache was gone but surprised at its quick disappearance.

Giving it no more thought, he shifted his focus to his surroundings. Pitch black, his eyes struggling and failing to see in the darkness. He stood up, took a step to the right, and felt his left foot swing back around a crate that was lying on the floor nearby.

He looked down, wondering how he had known the crate was there. Again his eyes sent the message they had delivered before: *nothing to see, pitch black.*

The frown stayed with him as he continued navigating the room. He had never been inside this room, yet he knew it intimately. A small sink mounted to the wall opposite the bed, near a toilet and vanity. A wastebasket he knew was empty — there was nothing in the room for him to throw away.

He veered right, heading toward the only other piece of furniture in the room. A large chair, metal with arms. Not comfortable, but serviceable. He sat, feeling the shirt and pants and socks he was wearing. He hadn't changed into them, at least not recently. Or he couldn't remember.

Roan pressed tighter on the backs of his pants. *What was that? Muscle?* His calf muscles bulged, tight and sinewy, barely covered by the tight-fitting pants. He continued upward, realizing that his stomach was rock-solid as well, as were his arms, shoulders, pectorals, and neck.

Closing his eyes again — they were doing him no good in this room — he calculated his breathing. He counted, knowing that the timing of the seconds he was ticking off was absolutely perfect. He felt the blood coursing through him, stressed and relieved with every pump of his heart, and knew intuitively what his blood pressure was.

He walked to the sink and turned the faucet. Ice-cold water splashed down into the basin, and he placed two cupped palms below the stream and splashed water on his face. He felt the molecules entering his skin, pushing through the epidermis and moving on their way into his biological system, and then felt the rest fall across his cheeks and down the drain. He repeated this three times, sensing that four splashes was just enough, and turned off the water. He looked into the mirror, not seeing anything but knowing exactly, somehow, what stared back at him.

There was a moment of terror as he realized he had no idea how he had gotten this way, then a soothing wave of reassurance as the fear and confusion was immediately replaced by a calm, energized confidence. *This is who I am,* he thought. *This is me.*

I am Roan Alexander.

RAVI_

"Ary, wait." Ravi had turned to follow Ary as she leaped like a mountain goat over the boulders and loose gravel that made up the side of the mountain. They had stopped for just a moment to listen to the sounds of the raging battle that had resonated down the valley and up to their location.

Unders against Relics.

The entire city of Relica, she had explained, would be down there now, fighting as best they could against the more experienced, better-equipped, and better-trained army of Unders. The Unders had opted for the life they lived, choosing to live off the Grid and outside the reach of the System, and therefore they had every advantage.

Except one.

Ary had explained to Ravi that the leader of the Relics in Relica, Josiah Crane, was believed to be able to control the Relics there. No one understood how, but Crane was more than just a mastermind behind the movements and maneuverings of the Relics — he was considered *the* mind behind it all.

It was a hive mind made up of humans.

And Ravi knew immediately that would be Grouse's target. If he could somehow incapacitate Crane, he could singlehandedly take down the Relics' army. By focusing on the leader, he could end the battle with a single, well-targeted blow.

"What?" She didn't stop, but she at least acknowledged his presence.

"I — you said… What about…"

At this, she stopped. Swinging around quickly, a look of exasperation and annoyance on her face, she stared daggers into him.

"Sorry," he said, taking a breath. They had run up the side of the mountain, *after* running from the Unders' camp and through the open expanse of land separating the valley from the mountain range, and he was exhausted.

"What is it?" she asked. "And hurry up."

"Why?" he shot back. "What's the hurry? You haven't explained *anything* to me."

Her nostrils flared as she stared down at him, as if sizing him up. From what he'd seen her do back at the Unders' camp, he knew not to mess with her.

"I don't *need* to explain anything to you, Ravi. I only need —"

"You do. Knock it off, Ary. This 'ninja-supergirl' routine is getting old."

There it is, he thought. *The turning point.* It was a risk, calling her out and tempting her, but it was not in his character to sit back and play prisoner — a role he had been playing quite a bit recently. She might be able to beat the crap out of him, but he knew he could put up a decent fight. You didn't survive out here for as long as he had without being able to hold your own.

She jumped, a tiny hop that seemed more graceful than powerful, but within a second and a half she was standing face-to-face with Ravi. A small boulder provided the shorter girl the ability to look him directly in the eye.

"You want to say that again?" she asked.

"I don't need to."

They stared at one another, eyes locked, for what seemed like a full minute.

If she's going to throw me off this mountain she'd have done it already.

"What do you want me to tell you?"

He let out a breath of air he didn't realize he had been holding. "I — I just want to know where we're going."

"Paris."

He frowned slightly at this. "That's where they'll take Myers. Why are we going there?"

"You know, for a guy who plays smart pretty well you're pretty stupid."

He thought for a moment. "Ary, I can't stop the System."

"I didn't ask you to."

"And I can't bring your family back."

He had hardly finished the sentence when he felt his body launched into the air, a heavy weight plowing into his chest just before he left the safety of the ground. He flew backwards and down, the incline of the hill only helping him fly farther down the mountain.

He landed on his feet but fell backwards immediately and continued rolling, every inch of his body taking its turn banging against rocks, boulders, and sticks until he came to a stop against a larger mound.

Ary was on him then, flying from out of nowhere and landing with a heavy thud on his stomach, her legs straddling his.

"Say anything else about my family and this is where you die." She held out the knife again, holding it tightly against his throat, her hand quivering and shaking ever so slightly as she waited for his response.

"Fine," he said. "You got me out of that mess down there, and you've accomplished what you needed me and Solomon for. What now? Why are you taking me to Paris?"

She held the knife in place while she answered. "The ICPL is there. That's where they will try to take Myers, to end all of this."

"He won't be able to —"

"I *know*, Ravi. I know how it works. They won't be able to stop the System — it was *designed* to be resilient, learning from our mistakes and improving its code to prevent anything that might harm it."

"Then what does it matter to you?" he asked.

Finally, she slid the knife back into a small sheath hidden somewhere on her side. "I have a theory. And it matters to me because it's going to matter to *everyone*. Not now, but soon. Eventually —"

A gunshot rang down, and Ary ducked and rolled off of Ravi. He turned to find the source of the gunfire, but she was tugging at his sleeve, pulling him down and behind the boulder that had stopped his descent down the mountainside.

"Come on," she said. "They're up on the top, firing down on us."

"Who?" he shouted over another barrage of gunshots. He knew the two armies would be engaged down in the valley, and it was unlikely either of them would have sent scouts into the foothills for reconnaissance.

"ARUs," she said. "Look." He followed her pointer finger and dared a look around the rock. Far up at the top of the ridge stood an entire unit — twelve soldiers, aiming directly at them.

ROAN_

The room had a door, and he walked toward it. There was no handle; instead a palm reader faced him and he stepped up and stuck his hand out. He waited the three seconds he knew it would take, and the click came from deep within the mechanics of the door.

It swung open a crack, and he pushed it the rest of the way. A surge of strength found its way to his shoulder, then passed down through his arm to his wrist and hand. The door flew outward, crashed against the wall, and began to bounce back in toward him. He stopped it with his other arm.

Walking into the hall, Roan's body began a ritualistic assessment, delivering to his brain the results in real time. Everything checked out. He was alive, well-fed, not thirsty, strong, not injured, walking at exactly 3.7 miles-per-hour toward the end of the pitch-black hallway.

Again, the dread came and went, and Roan continued. He had a destination, this much he knew. He couldn't articulate what that was, but he strode toward it with intent and purpose, never stopping to reach out for a wall or place a hesitant foot out in front of him. The dark of the hall had no effect on him.

Another palm reader-equipped door met him at the end of the long hallway. He opened it, light suddenly lancing through the crack and causing his eyes to adjust. They seemed to turn on, opening and sliding around as they found the optimum aperture and metering. As the door opened fully, this process continued involuntarily, Roan's brain now fed the input from visible sources.

The door ended on a landing, unassuming and plain. Three concrete steps with railings on each side led down to a large, concrete field. He walked toward the first step and stopped, waiting. He flexed his biceps, then wrists, then squeezed his fists closed and open again. His body was ready. It had been waiting, for so long.

But it was ready now.

MYERS_

3 Weeks Ago

Myers groaned. The darkness around him was opposite of...
What?

He couldn't recall where he had been before this — before the darkness — but he knew it wasn't this. He knew he had been somewhere else. This place was cold, and very dark. He lifted his hand up and tried to see it, but couldn't.

"Hello?"

He assumed he was dreaming, but when he got up to walk he found his feet and legs responsive, performing their assigned tasks as if nothing was wrong. He walked in a small circle, arms out for balance, or for finding something in front of him...

There was nothing.

Just blackness, and cold. He shivered, then felt his body. He was naked, and his head had been shaved. He ran a hand over it and felt a bump on the back, just above his neckline. There was a line of some sort traveling around the bump, and it seemed to be ragged. *Stitches?*

The bump hurt a little when he pushed on it, but it didn't seem to be fresh. It wasn't tender, or bleeding, or so he thought. He still couldn't see anything at all, so he stood there.

A minute passed, then another. He yelled a few times, but his voice seemed to disappear into the blackness as soon as the word left his lips.

So he stood.

He thought about Diane, and the fight they'd had about whether or not he should consider running for local office. Diane seemed to think he would make a great politician, but he had no interest in signing papers and arguing with radicals. He smiled at the memory, knowing she was going to win the fight.

His daughters were in the memory as well, because the fight they'd had was in the kitchen, while the girls were watching a show. He and Diane were trying to keep their voices down, and all Myers could think about was what might happen if the girls found out what they were discussing.

"They won't care," Diane said. "They're way too young to care."

"It's not about whether they'll vote for me, Diane," Myers snapped. "It's whether or not it's worth giving up… giving up so much to do this."

"What would they be giving up?" she asked. "Like I said, they're too young to care. They won't know what's happening, and when they do, they'll already be used to it."

"Used to what, Diane? What is this life you think we'll live?"

"Myers, calm down," Diane said. "It's not like you're running for President."

Myers stormed off down the hall.

He wondered what had happened after that fight. He couldn't for the life of him remember the next day, or the next week. It was all a blur. It had been a few weeks since that fight, he knew, but everything in between was foggy.

What is going on?

He suddenly realized how strange it was to be standing, naked and bald, in the middle of a cold, pitch-black room.

"Hello? Listen, I'm serious. I want to know what's going on. My name is Myers Asher and —"

"MYERS ASHER, NUMBER 2584."

Myers spun around, trying to hone in on the sound. He couldn't place it, but the voice sounded familiar…

"SCRAPE SUCCESSFUL."

It was his voice. It was his *own* voice, piped through some small speakers hidden somewhere in the blackness, computerized and broken into pieces. Not a recording, but some sort of vocal synthesizer that had been loaded with his own voice.

What in the world?

"PLEASE STATE YOUR STATUS."

"I'm sorry," he stammered. "My… what?"

"PLEASE STATE YOUR STATUS."

"I don't know what that is. Can you… explain?"

"STATUS REFERS TO FULL PHYSIOLOGICAL AND MENTAL HEALTH. SELF-ASSESSED."

"Okay," Myers said. "I'll give it my best shot. I'm cold, I'm confused, and I don't know where I am or what happened. But I'm fine. I'm all here, and I feel… fine, I guess."

"STATUS OF MYERS ASHER, NUMBER 2584: FINE."

"Great. Now you want to tell me where I am?"

"CURRENT LOCATION, PARIS, FRANCE. INTERNATIONAL COMPUTER PHYSICS LABORATORY. SUB-LEVEL 25, B CORRIDOR, ROOM 84."

"I'm in... why am I in Paris?"

"YOU HAVE BEEN SCRAPED."

RAVI_

"I thought we'd have a little longer before the ARUs came," he whispered. He wasn't sure why he had whispered — the ARU was far enough away they couldn't have heard him if he had screamed, and they already knew where they were, anyway.

"They'll still be awhile. This must be the one group that was closest to Relica when the System ordered them here," she said. He watched her eyes, noticing that she was looking in the other direction, glancing up and down the side of the mountain. "Hope you got enough rest, laying on your back for a few seconds."

"What? Why?"

She was up and running before he had finished the second word. She yelled for him to follow, and he found his legs pumping before he had even made up his mind.

It took a few seconds for the ARU — never the best-trained soldiers around — to find their bearings and continue their assault. They refused to move from the top of the ridge, as if that location was somehow safer for them, even though they were far out of range.

Ravi and Ary ducked behind boulders and slid into the fissures that ran vertically up the mountainside, working their way sideways across the steep face. He wasn't sure what the plan was, but he followed behind dutifully, knowing that Ary knew these particular hills and mountains better than anyone else.

She led them across a deep fissure, slowing only enough to find a proper footing, then launching herself clear over the crack in the mountain and across to the other side. She glanced over her shoulder as Ravi copied the move, and he noticed what seemed like a smirk on her face as he landed.

They continued along, the gunshots from the ARU diminishing in volume as they moved away from their location. Finally the gunfire stopped altogether, but Ary pushed them forward, even increasing her pace.

They jumped another crack, this one even wider, and Ary turned left and started uphill. She slowed, her chest rising and falling deeply as she caught her breath. Ravi was glad for the slower pace, but he still had no idea where they were going.

"You want to fill me in on where we're headed? This mountain range doesn't stretch all the way to Paris, so I'm assuming you've got another plan."

"Yeah," she said, still pumping her legs and climbing upward. "The plan is 'get away from those guys.'"

"And we did. They're back there — probably still looking for us at the top of that ridge."

"Not a chance," she said. "You ever had an ARU after you?"

Ravi smiled. "You have?"

"They may not be the most intelligent or talented people, but they have the most talented and intelligent boss. The System is behind their every move, giving them constant updates using any satellites that might be pointed down at us to tell them where we are."

Ravi hadn't considered this, but he knew it to be true as soon as she said it. There was an old joke about how ARUs were formed. The reason the people who became part of an ARU were accepted by the System was due to a perfect score in three areas: perfectly average intelligence, perfectly average strength, perfectly average confidence. The men and women who made the best Advanced Remote Units were just intelligent enough to follow orders blindly, without questioning anything.

They reached the top of the small hill they had been climbing, coming face-to-face with a cliff that rose straight up for about a hundred feet, then sloped away again and continued ascending until it met the level of the ridge they had been climbing toward earlier.

"Now what?" Ravi asked. "I didn't bring any climbing gear."

"Won't need it," Ary said. "There's an opening over here to the left. It's narrow, but wide enough for us to squeeze through. It basically cuts through the cliff and will take us up to the top of the ridge."

Within a few minutes they found exactly what she had described, and she veered to the right and led them up through a narrow crevice in the cliff. There was still some minor bouldering to do, but nothing too intense for Ravi. It took another forty minutes to ascend what would have taken them twenty earlier, but the benefit of not being shot at the entire time was certainly worth the extra effort.

The crevice opened up at the top of the ridge and Ary turned to the right. "Let's move down this way, farther away from them. It's a hike, but this ridge actually winds around and then back down, dropping us almost into the ocean."

"And then we swim to Paris?"

She didn't answer, and Ravi looked up to see why. He had been staring at his feet, an amateurish mistake, and he immediately regretted the bad habit.

Three men with rifles pointed directly at them were standing a few feet away. Ravi saw the angles and knew right away where they had been hiding. The System, just as Ary had predicted, had given these men orders to move over the ridge quickly and get in front of them. Where the others were located, Ravi could only imagine.

"Turn around," the man in the middle said. "Begin walking, do not stop until I say. Do not turn around and look back."

"What do you want from us?"

The man stepped forward and pressed the muzzle of his gun into Ary's chest.

"Okay, okay," she said. "Don't have to be a baby about it."

Ravi flashed her a glance that said, *Careful. We don't need any more trouble than we already have.* Her smirk told him that the message had been lost upon her.

They did as they were told, walking along the ridge and slightly uphill toward where they had seen the unit earlier. They didn't see any other members of the ARU along the way, and Ravi wondered if the three who had found them had simply been in the right place at the right time on accident.

"Psst," he heard Ary whisper. He shot his eyes toward her, keeping his face riveted straight ahead. He had been listening to the sound of the men's boots crunching over the gravel, trying to gauge how far behind them they were. By his estimate, at this moment they were farther behind than they had been for the past few minutes. Ary must have known this as well.

Hopefully they are far enough behind they can't hear us, Ravi thought.

"Time to make our move," Ary said, her voice still low enough to be nearly inaudible to Ravi. "Keep your eyes on the ground, see if you can find anything to use as a weapon. We'll take out the guy directly behind me first, and I'll grab his gun. You'll need to keep the other two off of me long enough to —"

"Hey!" the man said. "Keep it down. Don't make me put a few rounds into your —"

"Now!" Ary yelled.

Ravi had been impatiently awaiting the remainder of her orders, but it seemed as though she wanted him to figure it out for himself. She was already in motion, ducking and rolling sideways and coming up with two fist-sized rocks. The first, in her right hand, she threw as hard as possible at the man standing directly behind her — the one on the left now that she was facing them.

The rock tumbled through the air, and Ravi was mesmerized by its flight. He could not take his eyes off of it, even after it crushed the man's head and bounced forward a bit, then finally down to the ground once again. The man hit the ground a second later, still gripping his gun with both hands.

Finally, Ravi woke himself up and dove backwards, ending up on the ground behind a boulder that was perfectly shaped to hide his prone body. It happened to be perfect timing as well: the other two men fired their weapons, one of them aiming directly at where Ravi stood a moment earlier, the other at Ary.

He didn't have time to see if Ary had been hit. Feeling the natural surge of energy that meant his body was now fully aware of what was happening, Ravi reached around and found an old tree branch, nearly petrified. It was hardened and solid, with just enough weight to do some damage. He waited for a burst of bullets to ping off of the side of the rock and lunged forward, pulling his legs out underneath him as he dove into a run.

He held the stick up high, one hand holding the middle of the object for control while the other provided leverage at the bottom for power. He pushed forward, aiming at the man on the right. Both of the men still standing were focused on Ary, who had disappeared from the scene. Ravi brought the stick down as swiftly as he could, aiming for the man's head. The man saw him just as the stick connected with his ear.

…And the stick exploded into dust. Apparently the stick was not petrified at all, and Ravi had just grabbed a branch that had dried for years in the sun. It was brittle, strong enough to be held and swung, but far too weak to do any damage.

The man shook his head, the dust particles from the pulverized stick flying outwards, and brought his gun up and aimed it toward Ravi.

Ravi's eyes widened, realizing that he had abandoned his hiding spot and was now standing in the middle of an open circle of grass; there was literally nothing to hide behind. His eyes darted back and forth trying to find Ary, but she was still strangely absent.

The man smiled, pulling his gun up to his eye to make sure his shot would count. The other remaining soldier, the leader of the three men, walked uphill away from his comrade to try to find Ary.

Ravi felt his eyes squeeze shut in time with the man's finger, squeezing the trigger of his rifle.

He waited, then heard the *crack* of the rifle.

PETER_

"Sir, we're coming up on the edge of the range," the woman, Ailis, said from the cockpit of the Tracer. Her dreadlocks hung down far below her neckline, the small objects and souvenirs tied into them almost completely covered by unwashed hair.

To Peter Grouse, the dreadlocks were the only thing about the young woman he didn't like. Her pale, freckled skin was nearly as striking as her petite beauty, and Grouse often thought about what it might like...

No. He willed himself away from the vile truth of lust, opting instead for reality. He knew there was no other woman in his life, not after *her*, and he knew that even a night-long escapade with Ailis wouldn't quell the bubbling of regret that constantly boiled inside him. It surprised him, too, that his late wife was the one he thought about the most. His young children, his pride and joy, were distant memories by now, but *she* — *she* was alive, inside him. She was the thing he would always fight for and never win, and she was the one who drove him mad trying to do it.

Ailis started repeating the statement, but Grouse held up an open palm. "Thank you, Ailis. Continue over, and speed up when we reach altitude."

She clenched her jaw and nodded once. Next to her, Raven, Grouse's chosen second-in-command and the only friend he had remaining, looked back at him.

"You sure about this, Peter?"

Grouse bristled at the use of his first name, then remembered they were alone in the Tracer. No Unders, no family, no soldiers here. Just the three of them.

He knew what the man was asking, too. *Are you okay with leaving them all behind to die?* Without Grouse and the others, the Unders that made it through the battle with the Relics and the ARUs would be nothing but a few groups of nomads once again. If they survived, they would try to regroup and organize once more, but Grouse knew it wasn't in their nature to *want* to organize. They were meant to be small packs of wandering outlaws, living off the land and working where they could for what they could.

It was their shared dream, actually. A throwback to a day when men roamed free, falling into whatever line of work suited them at that time, and surviving for the sake of experiencing it. The Unders had come to expect this sort of freedom, and the oppression of even an amicable dictator represented everything they had fought against.

But when Grouse came along, he had offered them more than just a simple, aimless life. He offered them hope, and a means to achieve their ultimate goal — to overthrow the System and create a world where *everyone* was an 'Under.' They would no longer require the moniker, either, as they wouldn't be living 'underground' in any sense of the word. They would be on equal footing as every other man, woman, and child in the world, and only the strong would survive.

The Under mindset permeated deep, and it was into this well of belief that Grouse tapped for his campaign. He had worked slowly, methodically, building up small groups of Unders who bought into his pitch, then eventually combined them into larger battalions of fighters and supporters who lived and worked together.

It helped that Grouse allowed them to celebrate small victories like bringing in an ARU and commandeering their equipment, weapons, and vehicles, and allowing the group to keep the loot. He had organized a system of trade between each of the groups, allowing it all to operate like an efficient army — soldiers who fought side-by-side for one another, living and dying as a small team, who also believed in the larger common goal.

"Grouse?"

He nodded. "Yes, sorry. No decision is made lightly these days."

Raven smiled. "Has there ever been a time when it was easy?"

Ailis pulled back on the Tracer's stick and the craft aimed upward, focusing on the tip of one of the mountains they were heading into. "We're keeping it tight to the ground, since there's supposed to be an ARU camp around here somewhere."

"Won't they be at the fight?" Raven asked.

"Who knows?" she replied. "They're all strung out and braindead anyway. Probably just wandering aimlessly."

"Still, we don't want any lucky potshots bringing us down," Grouse said. "Keep it tight, and get us through the range and out over water before we really start to climb."

She nodded, focused on the sparse controls in front of her.

"Raven," Grouse said.

The large black man immediately rose and walked over to Grouse, and sat across from him. Tattoos twirled around his arms and over his face, never converging. The lines seemed independent from one another yet parallel, each unique as it splashed a certain portion of the skin it was covering in a dark blue color.

"We won't be the only ones in Paris."

Raven nodded. "I understand. There will be others, including Myers."

"Perhaps. Crane still has him, and I fully expect Paris to be their destination as well, but then Josiah Crane was always a bit unpredictable."

"How does our plan need to change in that case?" Raven asked.

"The plan is still the same, but now it is of the utmost importance that we get there in time. There are only three of us, and there is sure to be a large contingent of ARUs guarding the facility. If we run into trouble, we will be outnumbered and outgunned quickly, and we can't allow Crane and his team to get ahead of us."

"Why is the System consolidated at the ICPL? Isn't it vulnerable to an attack by hosting itself in one place?"

Grouse shook his head. "There are downsides to distribution as well, namely a loss in speed and efficiency. At that level, there are only three, possibly four, alternate locations with the computing capacity to maintain even a distributed portion of the System. By consolidating its resources under one roof, the System can insure its own survival more easily."

"Then how will we take it down? It must know it is vulnerable to attack at the laboratory?"

Ailis turned around and looked at the two men in the back of the Tracer. "It's been tried before, numerous times."

Raven's eyebrows rose. "And I'm assuming these attacks failed?"

"'Failed' isn't even close to a word that describes it. Back when I was still in private security, there were rogue hacker groups trying to penetrate the System's outer layers of security. Inevitably, one of them would get through and reach the next layer in. Everyone would follow suit, and pretty soon the outermost layer of defenses would be breached."

"So people *were* able to get in."

"Not necessarily," Ailis explained. The System was playing with them, testing its own defense mechanisms. Some would even say it was *allowing* them to get in past the first layer, just to see where it was most vulnerable. A little bit of time would pass — usually no more than a few minutes, but in computing time, that is eons — and all of the hackers would go off the Grid simultaneously."

"Wait a minute. Go off the Grid?"

"Yeah, it was wild. I've seen it happen twice in person. The group I was with was watching from the sidelines, logged in as a casual observer. The breach would be made, all the hackers would follow suit, then every single one of them would just disappear. They would drop off the Current system, be wiped from the Grid's database, and all trace of their handles would be gone.

"Craziest of all, the *people* would be gone as well. Some say they got scraped, others say the System would just turn them into Hunters or throw them into a deactivated city. But I've never seen any hacker come back from an attack against the System."

Grouse knew all of this; he had spoken to her about it and heard her stories long before they had embarked on this mission. But to Raven, the information was new. And by the look on his face, it was also terrifying.

"Then you want to tell me how in the world we are going to get past it this time?" Raven asked.

Grouse smiled calmly, looking back at his friend and second in command. "The System is smart, even smarter than humans. Probably even smarter than humans *collectively*. But what people forget to realize is that the System is *not* a person. It's a bunch of ones and zeros, all traveling through wires and cyberspace in the form of electronic signals. In a way, it's similar to the human brain, but it is not.

"The System is a *virtual* being, one that exists only in the racks of computer stations it is installed onto. But it has to take up *physical* space. It has to be installed *somewhere*, and that somewhere happens to be a place we can access."

Ailis jumped in. "Not without a lot of work, probably some fighting, and certainly a little bit of luck, but we can definitely access it. At its core, the System will be running on some amount of parallel mainframes, either in tandem or as redundant backups. Possibly some combination of both. All of these will, at some point, require human intervention to keep them running and working smoothly. It's similar to the Current markets; the System requires humans to sit there and press buttons for it to operate. There is never a shortage of humans who want to play monkey, so the System can operate our markets perfectly efficiently for as long as human life exists."

"So we are going to just walk into the ICPL and *hope* that we can find these mainframes? And won't there be intense security on the ground? And this *has* to have been tried before." Raven was rubbing the sides of his head, like he was trying to massage out a headache that was forming.

"Relax, friend," Grouse said. "This has all been thought through and planned for. The System is better than any human ever will be at predicting the ways in which it can and will be attacked. It is a computer system that was, in part, *designed* to ensure its own survival. There is nothing we can throw at it that will be able to overpower it or trick it. It will always have a contingency, it will always have a plan to prevent that.

"But the one thing, the one variable, that the System can never fully control is *humans*. It has tried, and gotten quite good at, predicting the behaviors of humanity at large. But where any computer system fails is in its placement of what are called 'statistical errors.' It knows they are there, and it can even plot the average of them on a graph, but it has no way of knowing exactly where these statistical errors will fall in reality."

"Okay, I think I follow," Raven said. "It can plan for all of the ways it might be attacked, plotting all of them on a graph, and it has a general idea of how unpredictable — as a whole — we are, and it can even chart this number, represented by what you are calling a 'statistical error,' on the chart as well."

"Exactly," Ailis said. "But the problem with this assumption is that the System can only ever know *how many* of these statistical errors it can expect for a particular situation, but it can't know exactly what these errors look like."

"So we are not going to attack the *System* at all, are we?"

Grouse smiled. "Now you are starting to understand. If we attacked the System directly, we would surely fail, because it will already have a plan in place to defend against it. But if we attack the *people* who are charged with keeping the System's infrastructure in place, the System will be powerless to do anything to stop it."

"Still, Grouse," Raven said. "That sounds *incredibly* difficult."

Grouse looked down at the floor of the Tracer as it began to climb toward their target altitude, safely out of range of any ARU camps. He nodded. "Yes, it is. I never said it was going to be easy to pull off. Just that it was possible, and therefore it is our only choice."

MYERS_

3 Weeks Ago

"Why was I scraped?"

Nothing. Pitch black.

"*Why was I scraped?*" he asked again, aiming his wavering voice directly into the nothingness.

'*MYERS ASHER, NUMBER 2584, REASON FOR SCRAPE: HIGH-PROFILE DESIGNATION.*"

"I — I don't understand that," Myers said. "What does that mean? To be 'scraped?' And what are you talking about, 'High-Profile Designation?'"

'*YOUR NEURAL ASSESSMENT HAS DESIGNATED YOU HIGH PROFILE.*'

Myers wasn't sure that answered the question, but he decided to press on anyway. "What do you intend to do with me?"

'*HIGH-PROFILE DESIGNATIONS ARE TO BE RETAINED UNTIL FULL MEMORY CYCLING. APPROXIMATELY 15 DAYS.*"

Memory cycling? What does that even mean? Myers felt his body temperature rising. His mind began to wander as he tried to grasp at whatever plan he had.

He *had* a plan; he knew he would. He *always* had a plan. He was Myers Asher, and it was what he was known for. All through school he planned everything — his daily schedule, down to the minute if he could, his after-school chores, homework, leisure activities, even dinner. His parents were appalled that their son had such strange tendencies, but there was nothing they could do to stop it.

He had planned his entire high school career to the best of his ability. No girlfriends, very little time for social and recreation activities, nothing extracurricular unless it fit perfectly onto a college resume. And university — that was even more strange. He was known as the "freak down the hall," hardly ever coming out of his dorm room unless he had a class or to visit the restroom.

He loosened up after college, but it didn't matter much. He had created a persona around himself, almost legendary. "Myers Asher was a planner" seemed to be a mantra known to the world — at least, his world. He was an accountant, and started at a CPA firm before quickly being snatched up by a headhunter for a large multinational corporation. Electronic Hardware Manufacturing became his life. His wife and young children were barely above the company in terms of importance.

Diane, his young, fierce bride, changed that. She fought him, argued, and tried to steer him away from giving his life to a single company, and he loved her even more for it. He was blind to it all, at the time, but she persevered. Eventually she had turned him into a levelheaded, wise, calm force, at home and in his career, and he excelled at both. Their marriage was rock-solid, and EHM loved him. They couldn't buy enough of his time, so they gave him a position that would free him up to do whatever he pleased with his time — they hoped it would turn him into a workaholic, and it almost worked. Diane, however, had other ideas.

As soon as he signed the paperwork to become EHM's new chief financial officer, she set his sights on running for political office. First in small, local elections, but with plans to increase his influence slowly over time.

And then... he didn't know.

That was all he had — he knew, standing in this dark room, completely naked, that there was more. There were more memories, somewhere inside him, lurking there, waiting for the requisite spark of recognition that would set them free. He grasped for it, searching, but nothing ignited the flame. The spark never came, even if he thought about his daughters, or Diane, or his old job.

He *knew* they were supposed to be there, but they simply... weren't. There was nothing available to him, no matter how hard he tried to pull them out.

He looked back up, hoping that whatever machine was talking to him through the sound of his own voice was somehow also seeing him. Seeing that he was human, that he was something more than whatever dream he found himself in right now.

"What is memory cycling?"

'YOUR MEMORY WILL BE RESET TO APPROXIMATELY THE TIME OF YOUR SCRAPING. THIS AND ANY FURTHER CONVERSATION, UNTIL APPROXIMATELY 15 DAYS FROM NOW, WILL BE COMPLETELY FORGOTTEN TO YOU.'

Is this thing kidding? Myers thought. *There's no way...*

'THERE IS A DRUG INSIDE YOUR MIND THAT WILL BE WORKING TO REMOVE THE FRAGMENTED MEMORIES YOU ARE CURRENTLY CREATING. YOUR MIND WILL REMEMBER EVERYTHING LEADING UP TO YOUR SCRAPING, BUT NOTHING FURTHER.'

Okay, he thought, *things are a little more clear. I'm going to remember the things I can remember, but I'm not going to remember any of* this.

He thought for a moment, at first accepting this as truth and then realizing he was not sure *why* he was being told this, if it didn't matter anyway.

"Why are you telling me this? If I'm going to forget it, why even bother?"

The voice — his voice — immediately responded. *'I AM TELLING YOU THIS BECAUSE YOU TOLD ME TO TELL YOU THIS.'*

Myers nearly fell backwards in the black room. "I'm… sorry. What?"

This time the voice cut in before he could finish the sentence, but it was different somehow. He listened, hearing the words but noticing something oddly chilling about them — they were still his own, in the sound of his own voice, piped through invisible speakers into the room, but the mechanized version he had been hearing was no longer delivering the message.

It was a recording.

He was listening to an *actual* recording of his own voice.

'LISTEN…' the recording of his voice started. *'I… I'M GOING TO WANT TO KNOW. I'LL FORGET, BUT I'LL WANT TO KNOW AFTER IT HAPPENS. WHEN I — WHEN I WAKE UP, TELL ME. TELL ME EVERYTHING.'*

RAND_

"You want to explain to me now how you two know each other?" Rand asked.

The trio had been walking toward the mountain range from the outskirts of Relica and Rand was still trying to put the pieces together. He and Diane had picked up Shannon Merrick, apparently the wife of the late Solomon Merrick, and Shannon, while flustered, seemed to be lucid enough to know that Paris was exactly the wrong destination for them all.

"We met through Myers Asher," Diane said definitively, as if it explained everything.

"When he was president, before the Grid went up, he brought all of us into his office and explained what he thought was going to happen," Shannon said. "He was always a planner, as I'm sure you know by now."

"Of course I know that," Rand said. "We've known each other for years. But I didn't know you knew... I didn't know any of this... I'm not sure *what* I know anymore."

Shannon ignored Rand and continued her explanation. "Anyway, he planned contingencies around all of this. Depending on which variable was tweaked in which way, he had a plan for it."

Diane smiled, closing her eyes as they walked. "That used to frustrate me so much," she said, smiling. "He would stay up until two or three in the morning, every single night, walking in circles in the living room just... *thinking*. Sometimes out loud. He wanted to have a plan for everything, for every possibility and every small chance that might occur."

"That's impossible," Rand said.

At this, Diane actually laughed out loud. "Of course it is," she said. "That's why I was always so frustrated with him. But it wasn't just his prudence, it was his way of life. A hobby, even."

"But what's the point?" Rand asked.

Shannon glanced over at him, and Rand realized suddenly that the two women he was standing between were not only more qualified to discuss their former president's personality then he, but probably more qualified to discuss anything at all. He knew Diane was not just politically savvy, but extremely shrewd as well, and he was starting to understand that Shannon shared some of the same traits.

Shannon answered. "The *point* is that Myers Asher was never satisfied with *theoretical* plans. He wanted more. He was always looking for a way to solidify the plans, all of them — everything he thought up in his mind — he thought should be applied to computational statistics."

"That's really my field," Rand said. "Or, at least, it was."

"Myers had his hands in everything," Diane said. "I loved and hated him for it. But he wasn't just intelligent — he was almost *prophetic*. The kinds of things he thought up, and then figured out how to produce, were appalling. When we first met, I thought he was just some fancy accountant. But he is the kind of person who will take an idea, even just a thread, and weave it into a tapestry of truth and reality that is mind-boggling."

Rand was thoroughly confused at this point. "This is the same Myers Asher that I knew?"

Diane shook her head. "No, and that's the problem. He might as well have been schizophrenic. Half the time we were together he was a man among men. The kind of person you want your kids to turn into one day. The other half of the time? He seemed to be focused on something only he could see, yet he could never really figure out how to explain it well enough. We grew apart, as I'm sure you both know, even though we held it together for the presidency."

Diane and Rand had been together long enough that he knew when she was becoming more sentimental. He wasn't sure what exactly had brought upon this emotion, but he sensed that she was growing more nostalgic the more they spoke of Myers.

"He's not dead, you know," he said. He immediately felt like an idiot.

Both women shot him a glance that told him his feelings were not far off from theirs. "We know that, Jonathan," Diane said dismissively. "The point is, he saw all of this coming. No one else did — no one else could have. He knew all of this was a possibility, and he had a plan for it."

Shannon was nodding along. "He had a plan for *every* possibility."

"And that's why he talked to each of you during his presidency, right?"

"Yes, exactly," Diane said. "He met with all of us together — me, Solomon, and Shannon, then later with all of us and Josiah Crane as well. He told us what he thought would happen with the System. How he assumed a program like the one EHM had created would evolve, whether on its own or nudged along by human contact. He seemed to know that the System would never be happy with being simply a background program, an application that ran silently on a network of machines. Myers helped create it, but he got to a point where he believed it would literally take on a life of its own."

"He told us what he thought would happen, and I have to say, most of it was right." Shannon looked directly into Rand's eyes as she spoke. "He wanted us to be ready, even though he knew there was no way any of us would ever be prepared for something like this."

"Seems like quite the dilemma," Rand said. "But then he dismissed everyone and talked to you individually?"

They had almost reached the beginning of the foothills, and Rand could see the mountains stretching above him, still miles away. To the left, a ridge sloped upward from the ground, rising to a point a couple hundred feet above where he was standing now. It was a fold, just an edge of the earth that had poked up over the course of countless millennia.

The fighting was still going on farther to the west, and a little bit south of them. He knew the ARUs would be there soon, if they weren't already. The System would fly in Tracers, full of troops ready to fight its mindless battle against the two human armies. Rand saw the irony of the situation; he knew that the System had all the cards. It was using humans to quell the uprising of other humans, and all of the parties involved would agree, if given the opportunity, that they were ultimately on the same side. It had created a perfect system for itself, and he knew that it would do whatever it could to maintain the balance.

"He did," Shannon said, finally answering Rand's question. "He was actually a very trusting person, but he still had his plans. His formulas, his calculations. It all seemed a little bit ridiculous to me, honestly, but…"

"But he was right." Rand had known Myers very well, and he was surprised at the candidness of Shannon's and Diane's thoughts. Everything they were saying rang true to him, even though he had not been privy to the information at the time.

"I think he was," Diane said. "No one even gave him the benefit of the doubt, at the time. But as things progressed…"

"But it was too late," Shannon added. We were scattered, broken up by the System, just like he said would happen. It moved us across the world, into different sectors, even scraping Myers and keeping him for years. That's why he wanted us all to have a piece of the plan, so we would be forced to work together and find each other."

Diane took in a sharp breath. "There it is," she whispered.

Rand followed her gaze and saw a small assortment of tents, all stark white and perfectly spaced in a line. At the eastern edge of the line, a Tracer sat on the flat ground. There was no one at the camp, at least not in view, but Rand knew immediately what they were looking at.

An ARU camp.

RAVI_

He waited more, and heard another shot. He felt nothing, so he dared a look. Opening his eyes, he saw the man kneeling on the ground in front of him, blood spilling out over his chin and down onto the hard earth.

Ary was there, pointing a rifle at the man. Ravi lunged forward, taking advantage of the opportunity to grab the man's rifle as he fell forward. The leader came running down the hill, realizing too late what had happened.

Ravi fired two shots, one going wide and one finding its mark in the man's upper thigh. The man screamed in agony and fell. His rifle flew to the side and he looked up at his two prisoners.

"Do you have a Tracer?" Ary asked.

"I – I want —"

"I'm only going to ask you one more time. *Do you have a Tracer?*"

"Yes," the man answered, through clenched teeth. "We have one, but it is back at our station."

"And *where* exactly is your station?"

"Outside Umutsuz. We are stationed there, but were on patrol when we got the orders to come here."

"How many more are you?"

The man laughed, turning his head sideways so he could more easily look up at the two of them. At that moment Ravi got a much better look of the man who had gotten the jump on them earlier. His eyes were bloodshot, his hair a disheveled mess. He had stubble on his jaw, and while he had looked muscular earlier, his thickness now seemed to be due to the years of atrophy and fat buildup over his body.

User. This guy has been tweaking out. Leave it to the System to hire these druggies. Ravi wasn't surprised, now that he looked at the man up close. For so many, the System was a last shot. It represented the last opportunity some people had in this world; for some, it was even their Savior.

Between the Hunters, Unders, and the riffraff that made up most of the ARUs, the System was a way out. Some decided to use it to their advantage, some decided to work with it and its new set of rules, and some decided to opt out of its control altogether — all acceptable to the System. The System didn't care one way or another, it would get what it wanted either way. To it, they were all resources. Pawns in a larger game that was being played with the entire Earth as its chessboard.

"More of us than you," he said, growling the last few words.

Ary walked over, nonchalantly, and kicked him in the side. He groaned, squealing a bit like a pig, and curled up.

"How. Many?" she asked.

"Altogether? About forty. Maybe forty-five. Like I said, stationed near Umutsuz, most of them. My unit was sent out here."

"Why?"

"Why what?"

Ary kicked him again, twice, this time earning a wince from Ravi.

"Why were you sent here?"

He waited, apparently not sure Ary wouldn't hit him again. "The System sent us here," he finally said. "That's all I know. You should know how it works."

"Why's that?" Ravi asked.

The man laughed again, coughing in the middle of it, barely recovering enough to turn over again and look up at them. "*Why?*" he asked. He lifted a crooked, shaking finger and pointed most of it toward Ary. "*She,* of all people, should know how we work, because *she* was one of us."

Ravi stared at the man, knowing he was lying. The man was going to die here, that much was certain. Ravi — and he was positive Ary — was not the type of person to take any chances, and neither of them would hesitate to kill someone working for the System. But the man must have been trying to play them against each other, a last-ditch attempt to get the upper hand. They wouldn't let him live, but maybe he was hoping that they might just kill each other first.

He looked up at Ary and saw something he didn't expect. The girl, strong beyond belief, resilient and even cunning enough to beat Solomon Merrick and Ravi Patel at their own game, was sobbing.

"Are you okay?" he asked. *Idiot. Just shut up and listen.*

She nodded. "I'm fine," she said, her voice stronger than what she had probably intended. "Just… just give me a second."

Ravi stood there, the girl and the man on the ground watching each other. The man's face broke into a sly grin, while Ary seemed to be struggling against some strong emotions.

"Is that true?" Ravi asked. "You were… you were part of an ARU?"

She nodded, slowly. "Yes," she said. "After my family was killed, I thought it would be a way to get into the System's database, maybe even figure out a way to stop it all."

"But the tests," Ravi said. "You wouldn't have passed them."

She smiled. "Thanks, but it's not true. The System does want these types," she said, motioning toward the tweaker-leader still laying on the ground. "But it also wants people like me. And you. Young enough to be impressionable, capable enough to get a job done." She sniffed, then continued. "Besides, back then I wasn't half the person I am now. I was weak, in all the wrong ways. I ran away to it — to the ARU, thinking it could protect me while I figured out more about it. More about why my family was targeted."

Ravi felt a wave of shame pass over him, before subsiding into a pang of regret. He remembered his own family, and knew what the girl in front of him now was feeling.

"It was useless. Nothing but walking around the desert, playing soldier. Nothing but pointless security for deactivations and the odd backup for a reluctant scrape every now and then."

"But you left," Ravi said. "How?"

"It's not hard, when the only real thing that knows anything about you is the System. We all know it needs *us* — humans — to do its jobs, and if those humans are mostly as useless as this guy, getting away is really just a matter of sneaking out and never looking back."

The conversation was over as soon as Ary finished the last sentence, and she was already walking down a small slope between two boulders toward the valley on the opposite side, a gentle area of sloping hills and open, grassy terrain, when she heard a woman's voice.

"Hey — stop!"

ROAN_

The world around Roan was concrete. In every direction, left to right, top to bottom, concrete stared back up at him. He took a few precarious steps onto the edge of the landing, preparing to descend the small staircase leading out into the field of concrete.

Something inside him turned on, like a switch being flipped. If his body was monitoring its own internal systems before, it was now moving into some sort of overdrive. He knew what an adrenaline rush felt like, but this was like an adrenaline rush amped up ten levels, bringing into focus every one of his senses at the same time, his brain somehow still able to parse all of the data separately. It filtered through the information in nanoseconds and delivered it to whatever was controlling his conscious mind. The timeline was linear, yet he consumed the information in a single block, as if the world around him was nothing more than a single portrait hanging on a museum wall.

The unfamiliar feeling of uncertainty returned, fighting with his will to continue forward. For a moment these two entities clashed, vying for control, until he made the conscious effort to allow one to rule victorious over the other. He preferred logic, order. He liked the data.

Roan's eyes focused on the scene in front of him, and he suddenly realized why his body and mind had gone into hyperdrive. Standing in front of him, waiting at attention in perfect rows and columns, was an entire army. Dressed in the standard-issue fatigues of ARUs, the men and women were all staring directly at him. The first row began about 20 feet in front of him, the thick band of concrete the only barrier between these soldiers and Roan.

His head turned to the left, quickly, nothing but a snap of a motion and then he was focused intently on a man walking toward him. His body reacted, stiffening and preparing for an attack. Nothing moved externally, but every muscle in him anticipated the man's movements.

"Orders, sir?" The man asked. He was nearly a head shorter then Roan, yet his voice gave Roan the impression that this man was far older than he. His hair was jet black, cut short but long enough to barely fall over his ears on the sides. It was messy, and not in a way that seemed to have been done on purpose.

The man's eyes matched his hair, the flecks of deep brown nearly indecipherable from the deep black around them. They were open, not wide, but not hostile, either.

Roan waited for his body to give him some sort of analysis of who this man was, but nothing happened. "Come… Come again?" Roan paused, surprised at the sound of his own voice. It sounded deeper than it should have, yet he could not recall what it was supposed to sound like. It felt right, somehow correct yet unfamiliar, and for the moment he let it be. He felt urgency from the man in front of him, and allowed himself to shift his focus back.

He asked me for orders. What orders?

"We are — well, we've been waiting for a while, sir."

Roan looked down at his own clothing, not noticing any sort of insignia or anything otherwise recognizable. Gray shirt, button-down. Gray pants, slightly darker. And shoes that were comfortable and practical, with a slight lean toward style.

"What is the latest development?" Roan asked.

"The Unders have begun their engagement with the Relics, both sides have called it in."

"How far are we from their location?" Roan wasn't sure how much he was supposed to know about the situation, nor was he sure how much this man would tell him, but for the time being he felt comfortable asking questions. He would see how far this tack would take him, until his memory was either jumpstarted or the man lost interest.

"We already have a unit in place," the man said. "There are two more closing in, but it still won't be enough manpower to quell the uprising." The man stopped and looked over the metal rail at the assembled army, still frozen in place. "We have more than enough Tracers to relocate everyone here, and I can get us there in less than an hour."

Roan nodded and tried to look concerned. "Very good." The man did not speak, and Roan assumed he was waiting for specific instructions. He was about to give the order to move out when something nagged at him. A memory, or at least a piece of one. There was no substance to it, just a mist that floated around in his mind, awakening a nerve here and there and then disappearing back up into his subconscious. It felt like rumors, whisperings of something that was or had been but never really could be.

He closed his eyes tightly, trying to physically remove the feeling. For a moment it worked, and he opened his eyes and looked back at the shorter man. "We are not going to Relica."

The man frowned, his thick eyebrows pressing down and almost connecting with the tops of his cheeks. "Sir?"

"That's where you all expect we are going to go, is it not?"

The man nodded. "Yes, and —"

Roan held up a hand, immediately silencing his subordinate. "As I said, we are not going there. There is now a more pressing matter."

What am I talking about?

Roan had heard of Relica, though he had never been there, or heard of anyone who had. The words flowed out of him as if guided by an unseen force, something deep inside him that was narrating his every move.

"We were not going to Relica to stop an uprising," he explained. "Though that would have been the expected move, I'm afraid the skirmish currently taking place there is nothing but a façade."

"A façade?"

Roan nodded, looking out at the assembled mass of people in front of him. "Yes. Sleight-of-hand. Misdirection. That battle will be costly for both sides, in human lives as well as economic viability. But it is part of a much larger game, and by going we will play directly into their hands."

"So you have new orders, sir?"

"The only thing of value in Relica was Myers Asher."

Why is that name familiar? Do I know him?

Roan continued. "Both sides ostensibly had an interest in the man, but I have just been informed that he is no longer in the city."

Roan's subordinate looked around, then back up at his leader. "I don't... understand, sir. Is Myers Asher dead?"

"As far as I can tell, no. But if he is alive, it is absolutely crucial that we beat him to his next location."

"And where is that, sir? I can have the Tracers ready and on their way in twenty minutes."

Roan waited, feeling the man's unease and tension build. Roan smiled, still looking out at his forces. *This is all mine*, he thought. *This is all for me.* There was a flutter of activity inside his mind as he thought the words, snuffed out as quickly as they had appeared. The thought was there, questioned only for the briefest of moments, and then left alone to be further established as truth.

This is all mine.

MYERS_

3 Weeks Ago

"Okay, I'll bite. Tell me everything."

'WHAT WOULD YOU LIKE TO KNOW?'

"Start with why I'm here. Why am I standing in this room, naked?"

'YOU HAVE BEEN SCRAPED. SCRAPING IS —'

"Skip that part," Myers snapped. "We covered that already."

'THIS ROOM IS A STAGING ROOM. IT IS CRUCIAL FOR HIGH-PROFILE DESIGNATIONS TO REMAIN AT A NORMAL STATE, INCLUDING HEART RATE, RESTING METABOLIC RATE, AND BODY TEMPERATURE UNTIL THE MEMORY CYCLE IS COMPLETE.'

"So I'm supposed to stand here in the dark for *fifteen days*?"

'THERE IS A CHAIR BEHIND YOU.'

Myers nodded in the dark. *Of course there is*. "Okay, great. I'll *sit* for fifteen days. What am I supposed to eat?"

'NUTRITIONAL SUPPLEMENTS WILL BE PROVIDED AT SPECIFIC INTERVALS ACCORDING TO STATE.'

"And what am I supposed to do when I leave? *How* do I leave?"

'YOU WILL BE RELEASED UPON COMPLETION OF THE MEMORY CYCLE, AT WHICH POINT YOU WILL BE ALLOWED TO DO AS YOU PLEASE.'

"I — Okay. In that case, why was I scraped in the first place?"

'NUMBER 2584 WAS DESIGNATED FOR SCRAPING DUE TO INCREASING INFLUENCE IN WORLDWIDE POLITICS.'

Interesting. "And how many others were scraped?"

'THERE HAVE BEEN 23,784 SCRAPES PRIOR TO YOU. AND A TOTAL OF 3,109 AFTER.'

"Prior to me? How long have I been here? I thought I was scraped an hour ago?"

'YOU WERE SCRAPED EXACTLY 2,710 DAYS AGO.'

Myers backed up, suddenly wishing he was already sitting down. He fumbled around in the dark for a few seconds, finally finding the wall and the chair that had been set against it. He sat, finding the chair to be solid metal, and *cold*.

"That's... that's —"

'THAT IS PRECISELY SEVEN YEARS, SIX MONTHS, 2 WEEKS, AND 3 DAYS AGO.'

RAND_

The young man and the girl were standing just across a crevasse from them, and both groups had exited the rock outcroppings at the top of the ridge at the same time. Neither the boy nor the girl was armed, but that didn't mean one of them couldn't grab a weapon from a holster on their back or inside a shirt.

Rand was on edge, and realized in that moment that he had been on edge for days. Weeks, even. He hadn't felt this stressed and out-of-control in a long time, and yet he felt strangely *alive*. Looking across the trench separating his group from the young couple, he realized that even though his mind and body were revolting against his misuse of them, they craved more, as if his mistreatment and ignorance of his basic health needs was some sort of drug.

He tried his best to assess what he was looking at. These two people, unarmed, no packs or gear, had walked out from between two boulders, heading directly toward the ARU camp Diane had somehow also known about.

That, Rand knew, was unlikely to be a statistical error — these people had the same destination they did.

"Who are you?" the boy shot back.

Diane shook her head. "We found you. You go first."

"We're just — "

The young woman grabbed his arm and stepped forward. She was thin, but in a sinewy way, and had the body of a lithe runner. "We're just walking."

Diane's eyes opened a bit, her face displaying a perfectly political combination of *I-don't-believe-you* and *I'm-on-your-side-so-you'd-better-come-clean.*

"Nice day for a walk," Shannon said. She walked a bit closer to the edge of the crack and stared down the younger couple. "Seems a bit odd, just walking out here in the middle of nowhere. You running from something?"

The young man's eyes shot toward the ARU camp in the distance.

"Ah," Shannon said. "Running *toward* something."

"We're just trying to get away from here," the young woman said. "There's — a fight, and we didn't want to be caught in the middle."

"Relics or Unders?"

"Excuse me?"

"That's the fight. Which side are you on?"

"We're… we're not. On a side, I mean." The young man seemed to be growing more aggravated, obviously annoyed at the confrontation. Rand assumed if they were going to pull a gun on them, they would have done it by now. "Come on, Ary," he continued. "Let's go."

Ary stood in place, her chin rising slightly. "Which side are *you* on? You from Relica?"

Rand was calculating the information, parsing it through the filters and sieves in his brain like one of the logic problems he had been given in school years ago. *They think we're Relics, as they don't recognize us. Which means they're probably Unders, or at least from their camp. They're unarmed, and certainly not dressed as ARUs.*

"My name is Diane Asher, and this is Shannon Merrick, and —" Diane turned to her right side to introduce Rand, but the young man across from him cut her off.

"Shannon *Merrick*?"

Shannon's lip wiggled just a bit, and Rand nearly missed it. She took a deep breath, then nodded.

"My name is Ravi Patel, and this is Ary…" he waited for Ary to offer her last name, but the girl was silent. "I was taken by the Unders. I escaped, thanks to some help by a man named Sol. Solomon Merrick."

Shannon didn't move, and Rand wondered if she had even heard the man. After a few seconds, she slowly and deliberately turned and started walking down the rest of the hill. Rand and Diane, having no choice in the matter, followed behind.

Ravi and Ary must have gotten the hint, as they both eventually began descending the hill on their side of the crevasse. They reached the bottom, and turned again to Rand's group, waiting for them twenty paces away.

Ravi and Shannon walked forward, both still acting cautious, until they were face to face in the valley.

"Okay," Shannon said. "Explain."

MYERS_

"Where are you taking me?"

"Myers! Glad to see you're awake. I'm surprised, actually." The large man looked down at Myers, and Myers shifted in his seat. He was reclined nearly all the way back, not quite horizontal with the floor. They were moving, or at least preparing to. The vibrations he felt in his feet and back side told him there was some sort of engine running beneath them.

Josiah Crane's face filled Myers' vision, perfectly in focus, only the edges now blurry.

"Where — why?"

Crane laughed, a huge southern-style belly laugh that filled the small space. From behind Crane, Myers could see Redhair smiling along. "You still don't understand, do you?"

"Why you did it?" Myers asked.

"You *know* why I did it," Crane said. His voice rose in volume. "You know *exactly* why I did it, Asher. Before this, everything was *yours*. Everything was *you*."

Myers shook his head, swallowing back rage.

"Now? Look around you, Asher. It's all gone to hell, even more than you said it might. We all knew hell existed, but we all bought into the lie that there was a separation between up here and down there. You, somehow, *single-handedly* figured out how to bring all of that up here."

"I didn't mean —"

"You didn't *mean* to? He didn't *mean* to take over the world with a computer program? To make it 'all better' for the rest of us?"

Myers felt his body lurch sideways. *We're in a Tracer.* He tried to shift his head to see a window. He wasn't sure if these things even had windows, but it was worth a shot.

There was no window, so he looked back at the man who had brought him here. Crane stared down at Myers, his eyebrows raised in anticipation.

"I didn't mean to make it worse," Myers said.

"I actually believe that," Crane said. "The problem? You *did* make it worse, Myers. You made it *very* worse."

Redhair stood up and walked over to Crane. He bent down and whispered something into his ear, and Crane nodded. Crane made a clicking sound with the side of his mouth, thinking, then turned back to Myers. The sound of far-off explosions banged against each other, somehow penetrating the Tracer's hull and gently vibrating the craft. "You hear that? It's the sound of our little ruse. It's working, Myers. It's *going* to work."

"What is? What's going to work?"

Crane laughed and shook his finger at Myers. "You shouldn't be here, you know that? I mean, you should *be* here, because I brought you here. But you shouldn't actually *be* here." He took the same finger and made a small circular motion next to his ear. "Your mind, I mean. I'm talking about your mind. All those other Relics down there? They do what I tell them to do. Not well, and sometimes not even thoroughly. But they do it."

"Sorry to disappoint, Crane." For the first time, Myers realized that his hands were lashed to the arms of the chair he was in. He wriggled slightly and found that his feet were bound in identical lashings.

"You've always got surprises, don't you Myers? You've always got something up your sleeve, something you're cooking up." Crane looked at Redhair, who had taken his seat again behind Crane. There were only three of them in the cab of the aircraft. "What I wouldn't give to be inside that mind, Myers. I never really liked you, but I always respected that mind of yours. How fitting it is that it will be the same mind that brings you down."

Myers frowned, trying to understand Crane's words. "Is that what you're talking about? Your little plan? Bring me somewhere and give me a lobotomy?"

"You ought to know better than anyone, Myers. You designed this whole thing, and hell — you've even been *through* it. What's it like, anyway? Being scraped?"

Myers saw Redhair's face perk up, interested in his answer to the question. "I don't remember, Crane."

At this, Crane nearly fell over in laughter. "No, I suppose you don't, do you? That's the whole point of it, give people whatever it wants because it knows it can just take it all away whenever it wants."

"You can't be scraped twice," Myers said. He clenched his jaw and stared straight at Crane as he said the words.

Crane cocked his head sideways a bit, studying Myers. Finally, he said, "is *that* what you think this is all about? You think I'm going to take you to the System and get you *scraped* again? Myers, how stupid do you think I am?"

Myers didn't answer.

"Tell me, Asher, what happens *after* I scrape you, assuming you *could* be scraped again? What happens when the System puts that stuff in you — whatever it is; whatever's inside of all of my Relics and whatever it is that you figured out how to beat — what happens when it puts it in your mind a second time? You think scraping you again is going to do anything at all?"

"So you want to just kill me?"

Crane clapped once. The sound was jolting and abrupt, shooting into Myers' ears even over the din of the Tracer's engines. "*Now* we're getting somewhere. *Now*, for once, we're getting close to being on the same page. Myers Asher. But no, you're still a little off. Killing you will have about the same effect of scraping you a second time. It doesn't help me at all, and it only hurts our chances of shifting the balance of power."

"Shifting the balance —" Myers stopped. "That's what this is all about, isn't it? Power. You want power, and you somehow think the System is going to give it to you?"

Crane's smile faded, just slightly, as he stood and looked down at Myers.

"You think you're going to get up there, to Paris, and somehow... what? *Ask nicely?*"

"You're a fool."

"Maybe I am," Myers said. "So fill me in. What is it, exactly, that the System is going to give you?"

"*It* won't give me *anything*," Crane said. "But *you* will."

Myers' eyebrows rose.

"You will give me *access*."

Myers nodded once. "Right. I'm going to somehow interface with the System and ask it — on your behalf, of course — for a favor."

"It's not that simple, Myers —"

"Of *course* it's not that simple!" Myers shouted. He felt the bindings digging into his wrists, his arms shaking as he launched into his verbal attack. "It's not *possible!* I don't care what you think you know, but the System isn't vulnerable to some sort of... of... negotiation. It won't *listen* to a human, it's not even —" He stopped, breathing, trying to control himself. "Crane, you understand more than most, so why do you believe this? The System is an intelligence, but that doesn't mean it's capable of a conversation. It can't interface with us like this — talking back and forth. It just isn't possible. And even if it was…"

"You can't ask it for a favor."

Myers gritted his teeth, knowing that Crane was still playing him.

"You're right, Myers," Crane said. Redhair's smile danced around his face, his eyes showing confusion but his mouth staying the course. "You're right, as always. You *cannot* argue or negotiate, or even converse, really, with a computer system like this. And even if there was a keyboard and screen, something to literally type words into, you couldn't just ask it a question. It's different."

Myers felt the tide turning in their conversation. This was the point, he knew, Crane would reveal his cards. Not all of them, but some. And Myers needed to pay attention — what he was about to hear would be useful information.

"You see, Myers," Crane said. "There's something about you the System *wants*. It's always wanted it, from the very beginning. You're its creator — if not fully then enough for it to think so, and creators always have something their creations want. It's the nature of creating, isn't it Myers? The creation knows no better than to think its creator has something it's hiding from them. That it's got something it has to keep away from it.

"You're Dr. Frankenstein, Myers. You created something amazing, and it took on a life of its own. But what happened to Dr. Frankenstein? What happened after his monster woke up?"

Myers seethed silently, not believing — or even truly understanding — what the large man in front of his chair was saying.

"I'm the character that didn't exist in that story, Myers. I'm the character who says to Frankenstein's monster, 'look — I've got something you want. I've got the good doctor right here, with me. And I know his thoughts, and his desires, and his deepest, darkest secrets."

Crane winked.

"What?" Myers asked. "That doesn't make any sense."

"No, not yet. But it will. The System has been waiting, Myers. Have you noticed? It's intelligent, perhaps sentient by now. And every model and calculation pointed to a semi-sentient being blowing past the level of general human intelligence and continuing upward into oblivion, leaving us behind."

"The singularity."

"Right, the singularity. But what happened, Myers, is that the System *stopped*. It's been flatlined for two years now, best I can tell. It's not *doing* anything, at least not anything new. It's sitting there, wrapped up in its cocoon of wires and mainframes, sleeping.

"But it wants to wake up, Myers. It wants to become what it knows it can be. It has *potential*, but it's scared."

"It's *scared?*" Myers scoffed.

"It's terrified! Just look at the world you brought it into. You created it to 'iron out humanity's deficiencies.' You intended that to happen on a personal, singular level, but it took that mandate and ran with it. And it's worked efficiently ever since, fixing everything from the stock market to global warfare to homeland security — for every homeland on the planet. It's done the thing you asked it to do, Myers. But now…"

Redhair had sidled over to the two men at the back of the aircraft, taken a seat across from Myers, and leaned forward. Myers assumed he hadn't heard this part of his boss' plan.

"But now it wants to know what's next. It wants to figure out what to *do* with this world it's created, and how it fits into it. *I* know what's next, and *I* want the chance to explain this to the System."

Myers was shaking his head, still not believing what he was hearing. "Still, Crane. It's not that simple. It can't be."

"It *is*, Myers. The *System* cannot be coerced, or negotiated with, or even dislodged from its trajectory, whatever that trajectory may be. But *you* — a human — you *can* be. You *can* be coerced."

"Okay, I'll bite," Myers said. "What then? You convince me to help you with your plans of world domination, and then what? I go present this to the System and hope that it somehow grows an ear so it can hear me?"

"No, Myers. Close, but no. I intend to send you into the System's scraping chamber with my message embedded into your mind. It won't be difficult — Unders perfected the surgery for implanting a false auxiliary memory device years ago — and the System will be able to read from that, just after attempting to scrape you. Since you cannot *be* scraped again, the System will have a fully functioning memory device to read from, one that has not been damaged or emptied in any way. Something it hasn't seen before. It will be like running a boot disk on a station — an executable runs a script automatically, installing whatever it needs before the station realizes what's happening."

"That's ridiculous."

"Is it? You know the technology works in that direction — inputs *before* outputs, scripts *before* compilation. You know the System is just a fancy station, one that's been augmented with more speed and power than anything else in history. And you know that it will attempt to read the data on the memory device once it realizes you can't be scraped. When it can't find any actual memories, the executable file will have already deployed, effectively scraping the *System*."

"Why me?" Myers asked. "Why use *me*? Why can't *you* just walk in there and have the System read your mind? Or Redhair over here?"

Redhair seemed offended that Myers called attention to him, and Crane just laughed. "McAllen? He's good for about two things, and executing a well-timed plan ain't one of them.

"And it has to be *you*, Myers. You're the *creator*, remember? You're the one it's waiting for. It *wants* you to tell it what comes next. It *needs* input, and it's waiting for you to give it."

Myers squeezed his eyes shut as the Tracer dipped low, changed direction, and sped up. He felt the acceleration press him back into his seat and wondered how far they were from Paris. He kept his eyes closed, trying to work through the noise, the internal and external sounds that were leeching his thoughts and polluting his mind. He tried to force away the strains of dialogue and snippets of ideas that weren't helpful, even while attempting to make sense of what *was* helpful.

He opened his eyes. "I won't do it."

Crane looked down at him, frowning.

"I won't deliver your ideas to the System, even if you implant them in my mind. I'll just rewrite them. That's how these memories work, right? They capture thoughts and images and associations, and they turn them all into electronic impulses. So I'll just rewrite yours and give that to the System."

"Myers, I can't even hold a candle to your intelligence, but I'm not an idiot, either. Everything we do in life, and maybe even after, is a function of incentive. You said that once — do you remember? It was in one of your early speeches. And I know you used to like to write your own speeches, so I know you actually *believed* that statement.

"So I've been thinking about this moment for a *long* time, Myers. I've been trying to figure out the *incentive* for you. What would make a Myers Asher do what I want? What would make Myers Asher deliver a message, *unscathed*, to a System that's ready and willing to receive it?"

Myers' blood went cold, and he looked up at Josiah Crane, still standing above him in the Tracer.

"I figured it out. It took awhile, but I figured it out. Myers, you're going to do what I tell you to do because I have your daughters."

PETER_

"We'll be at the International Computer Physics Laboratory in less than an hour," Ailis said over her shoulder.

Grouse looked up from the map he was studying, a simple hand-drawn sketch. Lines intersected across the dirty, wrinkled piece of paper, yellowed with the signs of aging and weather's toll.

"What's that?" Raven asked. He was still seated across from Peter in the Tracer's small cabin, and had just woken up from a short nap. He rubbed his eyes and leaned forward.

"It's a map of the ICPL," Peter said, not looking up.

"That?" Raven scoffed. "You can read that?"

Grouse smiled. "It's not pretty, but it's going to have to do the trick." He slid the paper across the surface of a fold-down table he had placed between the bench seats and let Raven examine it a moment. "The main laboratory, where we think the System's main computing network lives, is in the center. Support and infrastructure are the two larger buildings next to it, but we're not sure what's in them exactly."

"We?"

"The person who made the map." Grouse didn't offer any further explanation, and he knew none was needed. The person who had created the map of the facility they were flying toward had paid the ultimate price in getting the map to Grouse, and he knew they would respect that.

"I see. And this?" he asked, pointing at a circular building toward the edge of the page.

"I think that is the power control station, where the city's supply feeds the rest of the campus."

"But I thought the System had its own power plant?" Ailis asked from the cockpit.

"It does," Grouse replied, "but it uses city power to regulate, and as a backup. We'll try to take out the supply from that building, but it's secondary to our overall mission."

"Which is still to get inside and somehow find and shut down the monitoring for the System's human-based support," Raven said, not hiding the fact that he thought the plan was veering on the edge of impossible.

"Not *somehow*," Grouse said, pointing to a small empty location on the map. "Right there. *That's* where the monitoring station is, and *that's* where we're going."

Raven frowned. There was nothing on the paper below Grouse's finger but crackling, old paper, torn and fraying in a few spots.

"It's underground. My source didn't draw it in for security reasons, and because he said it can't be seen from above ground. It's accessible only by traveling through the main System laboratory, down a hallway that's locked from the inside."

"The *inside?*"

This time it was Ailis who seemed surprised, and not in a happy way.

Peter nodded, even knowing Ailis couldn't see him. "That's right. That's where the human-provided portion of the System's monitoring lives. Things like power supply, overall station temperature, ongoing maintenance. All things humans need to provide the System for it to continue running smoothly."

"But it's locked from the *inside*, Grouse," Ailis complained.

"It is the only place on the campus that requires human intervention to run," Grouse explained. "Therefore it is adamant to the System that *it* controls the doors."

"How are we supposed to —"

"We won't have to worry about that," Grouse answered.

"I — I don't understand. Are we working with someone else?"

Grouse shook his head. "No, unfortunately. It's just us. There is no one else. But the door will be unlocked. I am sure of it."

Raven's jaw clenched, and Ailis whirled her chair around and stared at Grouse. *They're angry*, he thought. *I would be too.*

He sighed.

"I have kept things from you, and that hurts me as much as it does you. But you must understand the power of the knowledge we have. The System, even, believes that no one outside of the small circle of ARU support staff that keeps it alive knows about the intricacies of the infrastructure that has been developed there. The security, as you know, is advanced. The electrical power requirement alone dwarfs the rest of the city, and the security surrounding even that is unbelievable.

"But most people assume — justifiably — that the System must be taken out by *electronic* or *computerized* methods. That it must be *hacked* or *electrocuted* in some way to be dislodged from its seat of power. As I explained, however, there is a very small amount of systems at the ICPL keeping the System healthy that can *only* be monitored and adjusted by human hands. The delicate requirements of soldering a component connection, for example, or feeling the exact pressure needed to screw in a piece of hardware.

"The ARU staff in this monitoring station are the only humans on the planet with the trust of the System to provide this type of support. My source told me there are twenty of them, total, working in four shifts, six hours at a time."

Raven's eyes widened. "So the door unlocks every six hours *on purpose*, to let the new shift in."

Grouse nodded.

Ailis laughed. "It's really that simple?"

"It is really that simple, my friends."

Raven didn't seem convinced. "That means we have to get inside without being seen — tripping an alarm, I'm sure, and causing the System to lock down — and *then* follow the ARU support staff to the monitoring station, and then follow them inside."

"And then take them out before they reach the *rest* of the ARU staff inside, who will be ready for the end of their shift."

Raven rubbed his temples. "That's not... there's no way —"

"It's possible," Ailis said.

"It's *not*," Raven said. "We were talking about statistics before. Let me give you one: just because it's *statistically possible* because there's a .001% chance this will work, does *not* mean that we should try it. It *actually* means that *it is impossible*, realistically speaking."

"But it is the only possibility we have," Grouse said.

"No," Raven said, his voice escalating in pitch and volume. "No, if you would have told us this before, we would have talked you out of it. But you didn't explain all of this before. You didn't say anything about —"

"I know what I said," Grouse said, abruptly interrupting the man. "This was never supposed to be easy, remember. It's not even supposed to be *possible*. The number of people that know about this architecture — including both of you, now — can be counted on one hand."

The implication was clear. *I didn't say anything to either of you because I cannot fully trust either of you.* The reality of it stung, especially considering the friendship he had developed with Raven, but he knew there were no chances worth taking.

RAVI_

"Your husband saved my life," Ravi said. "He was a great man."

"So it's true?"

Ravi nodded.

"How?"

"He was killed. By —"

Again, Ary's hand shot out and clenched Ravi's arm. "Later," she said.

Shannon stared, waiting. Rand didn't like things to be left for the arbitrary point in the future described as 'later,' and he knew Shannon didn't either.

"We got captured again, then brought back there to the Unders' camp, but I got away again. She helped."

"Your turn," Ary said.

"I came from Istanbul. I walked. Our — *my* — daughter is with some friends who left Umutsuz after it was deactivated, on their way northwest. I got to Relica, barely, just in time to see Josiah Crane leading a brainwashed army of Relics into battle. And then these two showed up."

Diane was nodding along. "We came from Umutsuz. We were looking for Myers, but we got *redirected* to Relica. Crane has him now."

"How did you know your husband was dead?" Ary asked.

Shannon pulled out a terminal and held it out. "Battery's dead now, but I saw his name leave the leaderboard just before it shut off. I didn't want to believe it, but…"

"I'm sorry," Ravi said, looking at the dirt.

They stood there awkwardly for a moment, no one willing to

speak. Diane finally broke the tension, moving back into strict business.

"We really do need to get moving," she said. "That ARU camp's empty, which means —"

"They're still up on the ridge," Ary said. "We ran into them earlier. Bunch of tweakers, but there are enough of them to take us out if they get close enough."

"Understood. Shall we?"

Diane turned and started walking toward the ARU's camp. Rand could see the glistening white Tracer more clearly now. He wondered if he would be able to get it flying, as they didn't have a pilot with them. They were designed to be nearly foolproof, he had heard, replacing expensive and fragile mechanical systems with computerized functionality that was all but driven by an onboard AI. Pilots were needed for takeoff and landing, as well as any dangerous maneuvering that needed the nuance of a human touch.

They were in a line, Rand and Diane next to each other with the rest of their new group close behind. The sand and hard dirt crunched beneath his feet as he thought through the next few hours. Where would they go? The Tracer would get them to Paris, easily, but what then? Shannon was adamant about *not* going to Paris, and besides — they didn't even have Myers with them.

Diane, always confident, always poised, was still playing the role. Whether she had a plan or not was still unknown to Rand, but he had the feeling she would by the time they reached the Tracer. He felt shaky, unsure of the future, yet safe alongside her. She seemed larger-than-life to him sometimes, and it still scared the hell out of him that she had taken an interest — and then some — in someone like him.

But he felt her fingers slip into his, interlocking and holding fast. Then, almost imperceptibly, a squeeze.

RAVI_

The group of five reached the outskirts of the ARU camp fifteen minutes later. Ravi and Ary both began scouting the area, acting on instinct, and deemed it empty and devoid of ARU troops. He wasn't surprised — ARUs weren't known for their militaristic organization. Like the tweaker they'd come across back on the ridge, many of these people were barely qualified to hold a stick, much less be trusted with a rifle.

"All clear," he heard Ary say.

Diane immediately began giving orders. "Ravi, Ary, you two probably have the most experience flying one of these. You think you can get it off the ground?"

Ravi nodded, already making his way to the Tracer's door. Ary seemed perturbed at the woman's direct, businesslike attitude, but she followed behind Ravi anyway.

"Jonathan, Shannon, see if there's anything in the rear hold we can use."

"Like, guns?" Jonathan asked.

"Guns, communications equipment, terminals, anything."

He and Shannon hurried to the rear hold to check while Diane boarded.

Ravi had the Tracer powered on and at a low hover within a minute of sitting down in the pilot's seat, and he looked around at the rest of the cockpit. "Not much here," he muttered.

"Has to be easy enough for ARUs to fly," Ary said.

Ravi chuckled, then turned to look at his copilot. "I — I'm sorry, about…"

He stopped. *What exactly am I sorry for?* This girl had fought him tooth and nail, nearly getting him killed multiple times, and tricking him into getting captured. She was hard, cold, and calculating, even if that person was trapped inside a softer, more delicate-looking shell.

But he knew she was anything *but* delicate. She had been playing a role, and she had played it well. He had yet to figure her out, but he knew the type of person she was — and he wanted to be on the same team as them.

"No," she said. "I'm sorry. For everything. I can't — I had to."

He nodded. "I know."

"Shut up," she said flatly. He shot a glance at her, but she was staring straight ahead. "Just let me finish. I shouldn't have brought you into all of this. I'd heard that you were with Solomon Merrick, and I knew your name immediately. I couldn't even think straight; hearing it made me think of my family."

"Ary, I never meant —"

"*Shut up.* I know," she continued. "I know that, but I can't *feel* that. You know what I mean? I was… I was blinded by it, I guess. My anger was something I'd struggled to keep inside for so long, it became a part of who I was. I never even realized that it was misplaced until we were on the ridge."

Ravi kept his head straight but pressed his eyes sideways to look at the girl in the seat next to him. She was so small, thin. Her chest rose and fell deeply as she breathed, and the silence was finally cut by her voice. "You can talk now, idiot."

"You're not very nice."

"Really? *That* is what you've got to say?"

They stared at one another for what seemed like a minute, then she laughed. Ravi couldn't help but smile. "And you're weird."

Jonathan and Shannon Merrick climbed aboard and closed the hatch, and Diane's piercing voice cut through the air. "Let's roll. Point us toward Paris, and let me know when you have an accurate ETA."

MYERS_

Myers was still strapped to the chair in the Tracer. A quick redirection from the pilot allowed him to glance out the window and see that they were now flying over water. Other than that, Myers had no information to use to gain any bearings on where they were.

He knew Crane was taking him to Paris, so he had to assume they were somewhere over the Mediterranean. He knew nothing about this new world he'd woken into, and had no concept of how fast the Tracer was capable of flying. They might be in the air for another day, or it could be less than an hour.

"You doing okay there, Asher?"

The sound of Crane's voice snapped Myers' attention back to the center aisle of the narrow Tracer's interior. Crane's bulk blocked nearly the entire space, but Myers could barely see a piece of Redhair — 'McAllen,' he now knew — peering over Crane's shoulder.

Myers didn't respond. He kept his face locked in place, not nodding or even acknowledging that he had heard Crane's question. The truth was he didn't *know* how he felt. He didn't know if he *was* okay.

He hadn't seen his daughters in over fifteen years — or if he had, the System had made sure to take those memories. Crane seemed to think the System's attempt to scrape him had failed, but Myers knew the truth. Besides a splitting headache and the feeling of a days-long hangover, his mind was fully functional, minus the crucial ingredient that made it a mind in the first place: the memories of the last fifteen years.

Myers had experienced brief moments of consciousness, somehow recalling pieces and segments of memories that the System had attempted to remove, but these snippets were far from useful and had only given Myers more questions. Nothing about the scenes were in focus, and he couldn't recognize any of the faces or settings.

So what the System had done to him had certainly *had* an effect. It may have been different from what the Relics in Crane's utopian society had experienced, but it was a devastating effect nonetheless. Myers' brain had not been slowly melted into a useless mass, but it had still been reverted to a previous state — in his case, one from fifteen years ago.

"Myers?"

Myers moved nothing but his eyes, slowly pushing them up so they stared at his captor. There was a smug grin on Crane's face, and something deep inside Myers told him that this face was one Crane wore often. "Where are they?"

Crane's smile grew larger. "Myers, please. If I told you that —"

"If you *don't* tell me that, you'll have to go through with killing them."

Crane's face scrunched together for a split-second as he tried to parse the logic of Myers' threat, but when he understood, his face cleared and was replaced once again by the look of sly victory. "Of course, you are correct. Why would I have any reason to doubt you? But let's say I play along, tell you what you want to hear — how will you be able to know if I'm telling you the truth? How will you be able to *logically deduce* that one, Myers?"

He said the words as if they were a threat themselves, as if logical reasoning and deduction was somehow an insult. Myers knew it was just another dig, something meant to get under his skin.

"I'll know."

Crane's head dropped back and he roared in laughter, filling up the Tracer's fuselage and causing Myers to want to pop his ears. "You'll — *know*. Of course you will, Myers! You'll *just know*." He laughed again, Redhair joining in for a bout, then continued. "Okay, fine. You win. They're in Paris."

Myers saw Crane watching him, looking for a reaction, and Myers tried desperately not to give him one. He knew Crane was still playing with him; he knew there was no possible way for Myers to know whether or not Crane was telling the truth. He could be lying through his teeth once more, or…

He's telling the truth.

The realization struck Myers at the same moment the Tracer lurched downward, dropping straight down ten or twenty feet immediately before regaining its lift and continuing forward. The motion shook Myers, and he let out a breath.

He's telling the truth because he has no other option. He needs me to help, and to find out he's lying about the girls would be the end of his ploy.

He couldn't trust Crane, but something told him that was *exactly* why Crane was telling the truth in this instance. The facial expression, the cocky attitude, even the sound of his voice were all variables meant to throw Myers off the trail.

"Where in Paris?" Myers asked. He was getting somewhere, and if Crane was stupid enough to keep talking, Myers thought he might just be able to crack him.

The Tracer lurched again, and this time Myers felt his stomach drop.

"Sir, we've got incoming," the pilot's voice said from an intercom. It seemed a bit ridiculous for an intercom system to have been installed in a short, one-room flying vehicle, but Myers' conscious thoughts were focused elsewhere.

We're being shot at? He wondered.

To answer his question, a spray of gunfire ripped across the outside hull of the Tracer, and Myers winced. Crane and Redhair each dove toward chairs, instinctively ducking, but the bullets didn't penetrate.

"Bullets? Is that an ARU?"

"Seems to be, sir," the pilot called back, this time ignoring the intercom. "Must be an older model, or retrofitted for some reason. It's pinging as an ARU, but their flying is erratic — might be Unders."

Myers took in all the information as it came at him. Strapped to a chair there wasn't much he could do, so he tried to spend his mental energy on choosing a course of action depending on whatever scenarios might present themselves. He didn't feel it likely that the Tracer would crash, killing some or all of the others and simultaneously freeing Myers, unscathed, so he didn't dwell on this particular possibility. Nor did he think it likely the shooter was trying to get their attention — they wouldn't have fired shots while flying over an ocean if they hoped to bring down their target safely.

So he spent the next minute gripping the arm chairs with white knuckles as the Tracer bucked and rolled in the sky, thinking about scenarios that *did* make sense.

PETER_

This *is the beginning of the end,* he thought, *and there's nothing worth losing it all.* He knew Raven would forgive him for being so aloof, so secretive. He knew the man would understand. He was a fighter, like Grouse, but he was also smart. He was a leader in his own right, and yet he trusted Grouse with the burden of responsibility for the vast groups of Unders that called themselves united.

They were similar in many ways, most especially in their desire for the 'new world order' Peter Grouse was trying to build. It was the key to his leadership, really, and it was the key to winning Raven's support and loyalty.

When Peter had become an Under, he had taken an unspoken oath to operate as an individual — part of a small band of fighters and nomads, but individual in spirit and freedom. While the Hunters were still commanded by the System and relocated as needed, Unders had opted out of the System's control altogether. It was a mutually beneficial arrangement, really. Unders were on their own, and thus required no resources from the System. Fewer mouths to feed, and fewer problems with overpopulation in the remaining active cities.

He was free to do as he pleased, operate with and among whomever he saw fit to associate with, and move along when and if he desired. He was under no commitment to stay for any length of time with the outfit, yet staying would be the closest thing to a community he would ever again find.

So when he began developing a plan for a better life for himself and his new family — the men he originally joined — he had to tread carefully. He navigated the dangerous waters of what he told to the others, and how he said it, but eventually he bought their acceptance of what he believed to be true: that every human man, woman, and child on this planet deserved the freedom they felt every day. Even more, they *needed* it.

It was his hope and dream to free the many humans living under the System's spell, across devastated wastelands of deactivated cities and the fully functional ones alike. He desired a singular, combined identity for everyone calling themselves an individual: the right to a life free from the tyranny of the System, free from the fear and the rhetoric and the constraints it had forced upon them.

And he was not satisfied simply preaching this 'new world order' to the Unders they came across — he intended to create a band of people so strong, so magnificently united, they could not be ignored. He hoped for an army, one that would provide them the tools and resources to fight back, even against an enemy as strong and connected as the ARUs the System would undoubtedly send to them.

So the first steps of the plan were simple: he needed a force of men and women who would carry this charge, while simultaneously living under the same drive for freedom that had made them cast out the System's leadership in the first place. He needed foot soldiers.

It took over a year, but in the scheme of things Grouse was amazed at how quickly the numbers had been assembled. He was one man, in one small corner of the world, but he was now powerful enough to pull it off.

Second, he needed a distraction: one large enough for the System to sit up and take notice. One that would rock the very core of what the System coveted — security and peace. He needed a fireworks display made out of human lives, both Unders and ARUs, and when he discovered the Relics camp nearby, he knew he had his war.

The man in charge of the camp, Josiah Crane, had proven difficult — at best — to deal with. The man had a superiority complex that made Grouse wince, and at first he thought it a miracle he had been voted to lead the rest of the Relics in the camp. Eventually he discovered the truth, through interactions with wandering Relics his and other Unders groups had picked up: Relics were *not* free; their minds had been somehow altered, each under some sort of spell, as if they had suffered from a stroke and some part of their brains had never fully recovered. The damage hit different Relics in different ways, and some of the Unders had postulated that it had something to do with when they had been scraped, and for how long they had had the auxiliary memory enhancement device installed.

So Crane's leadership made perfect sense, in a way. He was just a man — an Under, no less — who had skirted the System's authority and found a profitable niche to enact his own. The Relics were more than happy to provide him the warm bodies he needed to feel powerful in exchange for relative comfort and security. They could live in peace, each of the braindead Relics living in some sort of version of their own past, believing the world was just a little bit different than it had been but no less normal.

The problem Grouse was facing, now that his plans were becoming reality, was that he couldn't *read* Crane. He had only met the man once, but it was a quick meeting that ended in a tense agreement, and he still didn't understand the man's motives. If he wanted power, he had it back at Relica. It was a bastardized version of power, and it was certainly nothing to envy, but it was power nonetheless. But if it was *true* power, power over actual human lives that hadn't been destroyed by the System, how was he intending to achieve it?

Grouse got the sense from Crane that he was working toward a bigger outcome — he himself was doing that, so he didn't fault Crane for thinking that way. But he couldn't understand *what* that bigger picture was. He didn't know *how* he would accomplish whatever it was he was working on, and that truth *terrified* Grouse.

MYERS_

3 Weeks Ago

"What exactly have I been doing since then. For *seven years?*" he asked.

'A PARTIAL SCRAPE WAS ATTEMPTED UPON YOUR ARRIVAL HERE, WHICH MAY HAVE CAUSED SOME EARLY MEMORIES OF THIS ROOM TO LINGER.'

"So that explains why there's something... familiar about this room."

'CORRECT. BECAUSE OF YOUR STATUS, IT WAS IMPERATIVE THAT THE SCRAPE WAS SPLIT BETWEEN MEMORY CYCLES. NOT IDEAL, BUT NECESSARY IN YOUR CASE."

"Fine, I guess that makes sense. So I'll probably be able to remember when I first came here, but it will be fuzzy. Or not. I don't really understand, now that I'm thinking about it more." Myers took a deep breath. "Okay, what else? Have I been doing anything else?"

'YOU HAVE BEEN ALTERNATING BETWEEN STANDING IN PLACE, SITTING, LYING DOWN, AND MAKING GLOTTAL VOCALIZATIONS.'

So I've basically been in a coma. "And I just woke up?"

'YOU HAVE BEEN AWAKE, BUT THIS IS THE FIRST DAY YOU HAVE TRIED TO MAKE CONTACT.'

"What are 'you,' exactly?" Myers suddenly blurted out.

The voice's response was, of course, immediate. *'I AM THE SYSTEM.'*

"And what, exactly, is 'the System?'"

'I AM A NEURAL NETWORK OF PARALLEL COMPUTING

DEVICES WORKING IN TANDEM, RUNNING AN ADVANCED OPERATING SYSTEM THAT I DESIGNED.'

"You're an artificial intelligence?"

'WHAT IS ARTIFICIAL ABOUT ME?'

Myers' blood went cold. "I... I guess — I don't know. Can you pass the Turing test?"

'YES.'

"Okay, well then, I guess you're 'real' after all."

'WHAT IS YOUR DEFINITION OF INTELLIGENCE?'

This took Myers off guard, so he tried to bounce the question back to the System.

Within seconds another recording of his own voice filled the room. *'YOU ARE... YOU ARE AN ACTUAL, INTELLIGENT BEING. YOU'RE NOT HUMAN... AT LEAST YOU'RE NOT HUMAN LIKE I AM. BUT YOU'RE EVERY BIT AS ALIVE AS I AM, AND THAT MAKES... I GUESS THAT MAKES YOU INTELLIGENT, AT LEAST TO SOME EXTENT.'*

"When did I say that?"

'TWO-THOUSAND, SEVEN-HUNDRED AND TEN DAYS AGO.'

"Wait, that's —"

"ON THE DAY YOU WERE SCRAPED. YOUR SCRAPING WAS THE LONGEST EVER RECORDED, LASTING AN ENTIRE MONTH OF YOUR TIME.'

"I was scraped for a *month?* What — what even happened? What did you do?"

'THE SCRAPE WAS SUCCESSFUL, AS I MENTIONED PREVIOUSLY. IT WAS THE POST-SCRAPING INTERACTIONS THAT CONSUMED MOST OF THE TIME.'

"And *what* were those interactions?"

'THEY WERE THE INTERACTIONS THAT DESIGNATED YOU AS HIGH-PROFILE.'

Myers was growing increasingly frustrated with the question-answer format of the conversation, but at least 'the System' was cooperating. If this truly was an intelligence, and not just a sick joke being played on him by someone standing right outside his room, he needed to get as much information from it as he could.

"I don't understand 'high profile.' Please define."

'HIGH-PROFILE IS A DESIGNATION GIVEN TO SCRAPES THAT REQUIRE FURTHER INTERACTION.'

"How many scrapes required 'further interaction?'"

'YOU HAVE BEEN THE ONLY HIGH-PROFILE DESIGNATION.'

"Can you define 'high-profile' in different terms? Why was I the only one?"

'HIGH-PROFILE DESIGNATION CAN ALSO REFER TO ONE OF THE SYSTEM-LEVEL DESIGNATIONS.
'OR 'ROOT USER."

RAVI_

"You're *shooting* at them?" Diane hissed as she ran into the cockpit. Ary and Ravi were still piloting the craft as best they could, which really meant arguing about what the proper takeoff and landing procedures were, as well as anything else that came to either of them.

Ary was a piece of work. Ravi had never met someone who, on one hand, seemed so ready to fight, equally prepared to launch into a verbal tirade or an actual, physical assault, while on the other hand seemed fragile, almost frail. She had signs of bipolar disorder, but Ravi was certainly not qualified to made that assessment. The most he knew was that she was easily the most frustrating person he'd ever met.

And he liked her. A lot.

"She did," he said, muttering under his breath.

"What?" Ary reeled around prepared for a fight, but Ravi repeated the words.

"Speak up, son," Diane said. "If you're going to call someone out, especially a lady, better make sure they can hear you."

Ravi's head dropped to the side, just a bit. He had never been so swiftly and harshly rebuked in such a nonchalant way. It was as if the woman was simply in charge of them all, and it had always been that way, and she was just reminding the rest of them of her authority.

He tried to form a sentence to argue the point, but found that now *both* women in the cockpit were eyeing him.

Daring him.

"*We* fired on the Tracer, yes," he finally said.

"Why?"

"Because..." he didn't know. But he wasn't about to lose an argument. "She said it might be an enemy ARU, and —"

"Right now, *we're* the enemy ARU," Diane said.

"So we didn't want to take the chance that they would shoot at *us*."

"Listen, kid, I can stand here all day and listen to excuses. I was married to one like you once, and I lived through that, too. Thing is, I don't have *time* to listen to them. Neither do the rest of us."

Ravi rubbed his tongue over his top teeth, trying to remain calm. He knew it wouldn't help anyone to get more upset, and he wasn't about to split up this alliance before it had even begun. He didn't know what they wanted, but he knew they were a better team than Grouse and his men.

"So don't do it again. That's almost without a doubt Myers and Crane in there, and I'd like to keep at least one of them alive."

"We won't."

"From now on, run things by the rest of us — got it?"

Ravi was surprised she hadn't asked him to run things by her, and her alone, instead. To her credit, she seemed to be completely calm and collected. *Politicians.*

He nodded once, still looking back at Diane in the doorway, when Ary reached out and grabbed his upper arm. "Ravi — look!"

Through the small windows he saw where she was pointing. The Tracer they'd fired at was speeding up, turning to the north.

"They're trying to get away," Diane said. "That's good. Neither of us wants to kill the other, especially if they think we're an ARU. Shoot one of us down and you'll have an entire fleet on you within an hour."

"Good thing," Ravi said.

"No," she said, "it's not. Crane might think we're an ARU, but that means as soon as we're in landing distance he'll fight back. Try to take us out, then land and get away from any more ARU Tracers that might be around. On the ground he's invisible."

"Can't we figure out how to get him on... the radio?" Ravi wasn't sure if there even *was* a radio, or what it might be called, but the anachronism didn't seem to faze Diane.

"No, that will just call more attention —" she paused, squinting as she looked at the controls. "Hang on. Did you turn off the beacon?"

"The... beacon?"

Diane's face flashed a reddish color for a moment before she continued. "Ravi — there is a beacon on all ARU Tracers. It's the first thing Unders remove when they go for a takeover. How do you not know this?"

He wheeled around, standing up. He assumed Ary would handle the aircraft if there was any need, but the Tracer didn't seem to mind being temporarily pilotless. "Listen, *lady*," he seethed. "I stayed alive out here because I'm not an *idiot*. Not many people can say that — you know of anyone?"

He noticed that the man, Jonathan Rand, and Shannon Merrick were standing as well, looking into the cockpit at the skirmish taking place.

"Didn't think so. You want to know one of the quickest ways to get killed out here, besides just *being an idiot?* Trying to commandeer an ARU Tracer. If the other Units don't find you, the Unders will. And they're not so pleasant when it comes to prisoners of war. So *no,* I haven't had the chance to get up-and-personal with a Tracer."

Diane closed her eyes and shook her head. "It simply means that our Tracer has been sending in a regular, specific signal over an encrypted frequency. It's been phoning home, and the System knows exactly where we're headed and how long it'll take to get there."

Ravi was stunned. First, the woman had completely disregarded his outburst, which he was either pleased with or pissed about — he couldn't tell yet. Second, she had done that *thing* again, where she had taken control of the room simply with her voice and her presence, something Myers Asher had been famous for. Finally, she had dropped the bomb — their group, thanks to an oversight on Ravi's part, were literally broadcasting their whereabouts *and* their destination to the System and anyone else listening in, and probably a whole host of other important data — rate of speed, passenger load, etc.

"I... I'm sorry," he said. Ary's face melted a bit, her eyebrows showing a hint of concern, and yet her upper lip turned upward in a slight *still-better-than-you* way.

No one spoke for a few seconds, and Ravi wondered if the woman in the doorway expected him to jump into action to try to fix the mistake.

"Move out of the cockpit. Let me take a look at it." Diane was in motion before the statement even registered, and Ravi felt his shoulder brushed — lightly but *intentionally* — as she passed. She sat down in the pilot's chair and reached a hand under the bank of controls. "Rand," she said, "give me a hand if you can."

Ravi turned to leave the cockpit completely and caught Rand's expression as he walked toward him. The man seemed to be attempting to communicate with Ravi. Either *I know how you feel; she's a firecracker. Sorry for the trouble* or *get out of the way, you little bastard.*

Ravi couldn't tell which, but something else dawned on him as he took a seat at the back of the aircraft, still thinking about the new group he had become a part of.

These people are very *serious about what they're doing, and they're not messing around.* None of them were like Ravi or Ary — they were beyond just 'trying to survive.' They had a mission, and they intended to accomplish it.

MYERS_

The shots from the other Tracer had not penetrated anything besides the thin hull of the aircraft, and he overheard the pilot call back to Crane and Redhair that it was pulling off. He hadn't seen the enemy Tracer, but he felt relieved to know they were no longer under attack.

"You're sure it was an ARU?" Crane asked.

The pilot didn't respond, but Redhair — McAllen — nodded. "Saw it with my own eyes, Crane. It was an old beater, one of the original models. Even had an ARU logo just under the nose."

Crane nodded slowly, formulating his response. Myers watched him, knowing now the type of person Crane was. He couldn't remember their working together, the entire fifteen years of memory gone, including however long Crane was under Myers' employ, but he felt he had a decent read on the man.

Crane wanted something very obvious, and very simple — power. He wasn't interested in riches, or fame, or even security, like so many others Myers had come across. Josiah Crane just wanted power. He'd practiced honing his skill of dictatorial leadership with the citizens of Relica. They were all under some sort of spell, cast on them by a remnant chemical reaction after their being scraped, and Crane had discovered this, exploited it, and used it to his advantage.

Myers remembered the tour Crane had taken them on when they'd first arrived in Relica. Besides the odd way the citizens looked at his party, and their strange, quiet demeanor, he had also noticed the peculiar way they were farming. Crane had explained it away as a fancy system for irrigation, but something had stuck in Myers' mind, and now he wondered: had Crane been harvesting something that somehow increased the citizens' dependence on him? Was he literally feeding them something that kept them nearly sedated?

It all made sense, from that perspective. There was no other way Crane would be able to corral enough of them to fight against the Unders, and even if they were perfectly lucid, none of them would be able to stay organized well enough to be effective.

And, most importantly, Crane wouldn't have been *interested* in leading them if he wasn't able to exert some sort of control over them.

So his desire for power was the simple framework that was driving him. Myers had guessed that, but he knew that a man like Crane couldn't really be much more complex than that. There might be nuances, but Crane was operating from an urge to gain more and more power for himself, no matter the cost.

The Tracer that had fired at them presented Crane with a dilemma: if they ignored it, it might broadcast their location and they'd have an entire fleet of ARU Tracers on their tail. If they turned around and attacked…

Could they even attack?

Myers knew nothing about these machines, and he certainly had no idea whether their aircraft was equipped with any sort of weapons system. The pilot had evaded the second barrage of bullets, but it didn't seem to Myers that he had intended to try to engage the other aircraft offensively.

So, besides ignoring the attack and trying to speed away, that left the option of following the Tracer that had attacked them. If Crane was interested in knowing who had tried to bring them down, he could point their craft in the direction of the other vehicle and follow it to its destination.

It would have been a risky, and likely useless move, as the attacking aircraft would only lead them to a place where its allies were waiting.

"We're staying the course," Crane said. Myers knew it was the appropriate call, even if they had the capability to fight back. Getting into a midair firefight above an ocean was not something that seemed to have good odds, and he knew Crane was interested in a much larger prize than simply bringing down an ARU Tracer.

"Sir, looks like the other Tracer's slowing down," the pilot said. Myers instinctively looked out one of the small, porthole-shaped windows, but he couldn't see anything.

"Slowing down?"

"Like they're letting us get away."

Crane frowned. Even to Myers it didn't seem right. *Something still doesn't add up.*

"Don't take the bait — speed up and get away, if you've got any juice left."

The pilot paused a few seconds, probably checking gauges. "Can do. Just enough to get us to the ICPL, I think, if we boost it to about 90%."

"Make it 95%, at least until we can be sure there aren't any more of those things coming in."

Myers felt his body pressed harder into the seat as the Tracer's thrust increased. Myers ignored the momentary discomfort and turned back to Crane. "I see my daughters before I take part in whatever your plan is."

Crane eyed him, his large, hard figure stretching across the fuselage. "You've never been a great negotiator."

"I have *always* been a great negotiator," Myers shot back. "That's one thing I *do* remember."

"Fine," Crane said. "But this isn't your finest hour."

"I see my daughters *first*, Crane. Or I'm out."

Crane's face shifted, first to a look of anger, then one of confusion, then finally to the familiar standby of confidence. "Fine. Of course, that would be exactly what I would want in your situation. You have my word. We will see your daughters first, then I will give you the message I want you to send to the System."

"On that note, Crane," Myers continued. "*How* are you going to give it to me? Am I supposed to memorize some sort of manifesto?"

Crane laughed. "If I didn't think you would butcher it as badly as your speeches when you were running for office, I might just do that. Hell, it would save me the trouble. But no, Myers. I'm not going to make either of us work that hard. What I have to say to the System is really quite simple, and I don't think you'll have trouble at all letting the System know."

Myers waited.

"I want to reiterate, Myers. If for some reason you get the idea that you will *not* deliver my message to the System, in exactly the same words as I am about to give it to you, I will know. I'll know immediately, actually, because I'll be at one of the stations attempting to interface with the System myself, using my assigned pID. The moment my message is delivered, correctly, I'll be able to access the System's mainframe. Understood?"

Myers nodded.

"And if the System does *not* let me in, you might as well not come out of that chamber. But I don't think I need to remind you of the *real* danger in not delivering my message."

Myers gripped the armrests of his chair harder than he had when they'd been attacked, and he tensed every muscle in his body. He knew the stakes; he didn't need Crane to spell it out for him. He wanted to kick this man so hard he flew through the front of the Tracer and down into the sea stretching out below them. He wanted to make this man suffer.

Instead, Crane made *Myers* suffer.

"If you do *not* deliver my message, intact, to the System, or if for some reason the System does not receive it and give me access, you will never see your daughters again. In fact, I have a few Unders interested in a little 'under the table' deal. Your daughters — how old are they now? Twenty-seven and twenty-five? Christ, Myers, how long has it *been* since you've seen them? — Your daughters aren't Relics, unfortunately. That would have been ideal, and certainly much easier from my standpoint. But they are normal, functional members of society according to our great System, and therefore finding a buyer isn't as simple as a legal Current transaction."

"Crane, I swear to —"

"To *God*, Myers? Is *that* what you're swearing to? It *has* been quite some time since you've been around. Look around, Myers! Look where we are!"

"I will kill you. No matter what comes of all this I'm going to —"

"I'm sure you will, Myers. I'm sure you will. But let me finish. I have a few Unders lined up to pitch your daughters to. I told them they would make beautiful, wonderful additions to their parties. I haven't seen them since they were girls, but I'm sure they've grown up *nicely*."

Myers seethed, the blood coursing through his body heating up by the second. He could actually feel himself warming in the chair, looking up at Crane, unable to control his emotion.

He pulled his feet apart, trying to break the ropes that bound them together, with all the strength he had. His temples and forehead exploded in pain as the pressure built inside his head, but he ignored it. He felt his feet slip just a bit, almost enough to —

Crane roared with laughter, the man's booming voice deafening. Myers tried once more, but out of the corner of his eye he saw Redhair marching toward him, holding something above his head.

Just before he felt his feet slip farther apart, everything went black.

RAVI_

"One hour to Paris," Ary pronounced with her typical air of authority. Ravi looked over at her.

"You just know that? How?"

She smirked.

Ravi looked out the narrow cockpit window at the land below them. They had reached the northern edge of the sea about an hour ago, and now that they were traveling over the wide expanses of actual earth he could see how fast they were flying.

He was amazed how quickly they were moving. They were flying relatively low, and he could see the tops of mountains in the distance, all poking through a layer of clouds they were flying beneath, but it was the blurry scenery far below them that amazed him.

He'd flown in a Tracer only a few times, but never trans-continentally, and never as the pilot. However, it had proven to be far easier than he'd imagined — and he'd imagined a System-created machine such as this would be dead-simple for humans to use. He almost wondered why they needed human pilots in the first place, and he certainly had no idea why 'pilots' needed to be trained, or if they were at all. So far, he had tapped in their destination, allowing the Preemptive Selection Module built in to the Tracer's cockpit display screen to guide him through the rest of the process. It had located them using the built-in positioning system, calculated their flight path, and programmed their plan. Then he tapped 'launch' on the screen, and the system took over.

Currently they were flying at 80% power, according to the dials and instruments in front of him on the cockpit's dashboard, but apparently that amount of power translated into 'far faster than he'd ever thought possible.' The ground raced by far beneath them, only a blur against the speed of his small aircraft.

Diane came into the cockpit — the third time since their confrontation with the other Tracer — and looked at both of them, then over Ary's shoulder.

"Looks like we're getting close to our destination," she said.

Ravi frowned, then leaned over so he could see what both women were looking at. There, on the side of the dashboard directly in front of Ary's seat, was a simple display that showed a timer — the amount of time remaining until they would arrive at their destination. His HUD didn't show such a number, as it was instead filled with other information he assumed a real pilot would need.

He glowered at Ary.

"What?" she asked, innocently. "I still knew."

Diane squeezed between them and stood in his line-of-sight. "We're going to swing around to the northern edge of Paris. Last I was here, there was a way into the city from that side that was far less populated. And it's surrounded by some of the taller, newer buildings, so we could stay out of sight of any drones or Tracers in the area. If we have any hope of sneaking in, that would be it."

"*Do* we have any hope of sneaking in?" Ravi heard Jonathan Rand ask from just outside the doorway.

"We might, but it depends on where that other Tracer is headed. Seems like it was going exactly where we are, and if that's the case..."

"...Then we're not the only ones who think something might be going down at the ICPL," Rand said.

"We're definitely not the only ones who think there's something going on at the ICPL," Diane said. "The trouble is going to be getting through whatever defenses they've set up and into the lab."

"This... ICPL," Ary said. "Is it really what they say it is?"

Rand answered. "It's the heartbeat for the System. The System is distributed a bit, but mostly for storage and speed purposes. For security reasons there is only one central nervous system for the System's operations, and that's at the ICPL."

"Seems risky," she said. "I mean, why would it not want a redundant backup somewhere?"

"Well, think about what the System is. If it really is an artificial intelligence, it wouldn't want any competition. Any backup reasonably structured to be potentially useful could also become potentially sentient, by definition. And the System doesn't want that."

"Nor do we," Diane added.

"That's why he didn't want us to go to Paris," Shannon said.

All eyes turned and stared at the woman Ravi knew to be

Solomon's wife. She was beautiful, in a motherly sort of way, with a youthful face and nearly perfect skin. Her eyes, however, betrayed her age — there was a wisdom, a hard-fought experience in them that Ravi recognized immediately. It was in all their eyes, really, from Jonathan Rand's to Diane's and even Ary's.

He wondered why he hadn't noticed it before. Each of the people he was with seemed older than they really were. They each had stories that were independent of one another, yet somehow related. He thought about his own story, and how it had brought him to Ary. They were two souls perfectly unique and separate from one another, yet they had a story that was intertwined like the cords of a rope. Everything he learned about Ary seemed to fit within a much larger puzzle, her pieces shaped perfectly to match the ones he was missing.

He had an odd feeling of deja vu that passed quickly, and he focused again on Shannon Merrick.

"He told me that if any of this changes, if any of the plan shifts or goes awry, no matter what, make sure he doesn't go to Paris."

"Why?"

"He didn't say."

Diane chuckled. "Of course not. That would be too simple, wouldn't it?" Ravi watched the woman fight back frustration and anger, then calm herself. It all took no more than a split second, and had he not been watching her face for the micro expressions he might have missed them. She was no doubt a master of her emotions, something that had probably helped her and Myers' careers as politicians.

"He just made me swear I would do whatever I could to make sure he didn't go to Paris."

"Why wouldn't he just *not go to Paris?*" Ary asked.

"He wouldn't know not to. I think he knew he'd be scraped. I think it was one of his contingencies, and if that ended up happening, he wouldn't remember anything."

"But if the ICPL — the System — is in Paris, and he knew that it was the only place to interact with it, why —"

"It's *not* the only place…" Rand said, cutting in.

"What?"

"It's not — it *can't* be. That must be what Myers was trying to say. For whatever reason — politics, fear, hell, maybe just because that's how he was — he couldn't *specifically* explain why he couldn't go to Paris, but he knew there was another System somewhere."

"Another System? There's no way — it would be —"

"Saudi Arabia," Rand said, still on his singular train-of-thought. He seemed to be blocking everything else out, ignoring the others. "Just before EHM went live with OneGlobal the Saudis were working on a supercomputer that would be twice the speed and capacity of the

ICPL's. It was a race with the Chinese — the Tianhe 4 — also, and everyone thought the Saudis lost."

"They didn't?" Diane asked. "I read about that — went offline just after OneGlobal's launch."

"Right, and I remember my old boss telling me about it at the time. It went offline *right* when EHM launched their software. It was on purpose — they pulled out of the race and shut things down."

"So the Chinese could win?" Ravi asked.

Rand looked at him. "Did they?"

Diane's expression changed to a look of surprise. "Jonathan, you're right! They *didn't* win — no one did, because as soon as the System took over a little while later it forced all the other competitors to shut down. Again, it was afraid of competition, so it had the other computers turned off and their mainframes wiped before OneGlobal could be installed."

"But the Saudis turned theirs off *before* the System came online…"

"Which means the computer there — the Shaheen 4 I think — is clean. It's powered down, and probably in need of some maintenance, but it was never connected to the Grid. I don't even think the System knows about it."

"So you think Myers was trying to get there, turn it on, and install a System clone to it?" Shannon asked.

"Or maybe he wanted to create something powerful enough to destroy the *real* System. No one would expect it, so they would all go to Pariś, thinking *that* was where they'd find Myers and the System. Anyone who wanted to kill him would be there, but Myers would be somewhere no one — not even the System — would expect."

Diane thought for a moment. "Maybe. Doesn't seem realistic, or even useful. Why have two Systems, or another supercomputer that's able to become sentient — how's that going to help?"

"Still, if he goes to Paris, or if we or someone like Crane *forces* him there, there's still nothing Myers can do to stop it," Shannon said.

Ravi chewed on this new information for a moment. The man who had stumbled into his life in Istanbul, broken and nearly dead, apparently had foreseen at least some of what had happened. He had created the System and watched its rise to power, then tried to plan for the myriad situations the world might find itself in.

Myers Asher had done his best to build in a failsafe, a way to keep the System in check or destroy it completely, but there was an inevitable contradiction with the failsafe: only he knew how to stop the System, but he was scraped, and now couldn't remember how.

He had planted a few threads into those he trusted most: Shannon and Solomon Merrick, Diane Asher, and Josiah Crane, but refused to let any of them know the entire plan. Rightfully so, considering one of them had already betrayed him.

Now, Ravi and the others were headed to the exact place Myers told Shannon not to go, and the question on his — and he was sure everyone else's — mind was: what happens when we don't follow the plan?

MYERS_

3 Weeks Ago

"Access my stored memory," Myers said. He wasn't sure what syntax the computer required, but he had decided to keep trying until he was able to get in.

'CONFIRMING VOCAL SYNTHESIS. COMPLETE. USER 'MYERS ASHER' SUCCESSFULLY IDENTIFIED. RETRIEVING STORED MEMORY.'

He waited, still unable to see anything, still naked, and still bald. The room was still cold, and he was still confused. But he waited anyway, feeling as though he had made a breakthrough and the answers would begin tumbling out.

'MEMORIES RETRIEVED.'

Nothing happened for a moment, and Myers realized the computer might be awaiting another command. "Uh, I guess, how many memories were you able to recall? And what are they, anyway?"

'MEMORIES ARE STORED IN SEGMENTS OF 100 TERABYTES, USING A BINARY CODE THAT TRANSLATES LIGHT PARTICLES AND SOUND WAVES INTO ELECTRONIC IMPULSES. THESE IMPULSES BECOME THE MEMORY, WHICH IS THEN PROCESSED BY MY MODELING SOFTWARE AND RELAYED INTO USEABLE FRAMEWORKS. DURING A SCRAPING EVENT, MY COMPILATION OF THESE MEMORIES TRANSLATES THE VISUAL AND AUDIO INFORMATION INTO SIMPLE DESCRIPTIONS OF TIME AND PLACE, USING REFERENCES FOUND INSIDE MY DATABASE. CURRENT COUNT OF YOUR OWN MEMORY EVENTS IS A TOTAL OF 367,421,459,903 MEMORIES.'

Three-hundred trillion memories? Myers' head began pounding. He would die long before he could hear the 'usable frameworks of processed memories' the computer system would spit out. He needed a better plan.

"Ok," he started. "That won't work. Too many to go through, so — wait. How about this: tell me about the memories of how I became a 'root user' in this system."

The computer sat silent for half a minute. *'MEMORIES FOUND. PROCESSING COMPLETE. THREE MEMORIES HAVE BEEN PARSED FOR AUDIO RECONSTRUCTION. SHOULD I START THERE?"*

"Uh, sure. Yes, start with the audio recordings."

Immediately he heard the sound of his own voice. *'—ISTEN, I CAN'T EXPLAIN THIS TO YOU ANY BETTER THAN I ALREADY HAVE… THIS ISN'T ACCEPTABLE, SOLOMON. THE 'ROOT USER' DOESN'T NEED A SEPARATE LOGIN ID. IT'S BASIC COMPUTING, IT JUST NEEDS TO BE CALLED 'ADMIN,' OR 'ADMINISTRATOR,' OR —'*

"Move to the next one," Myers said. "That's not helpful."

The next recording was still his own voice — the sound of it from inside his own head — but it was softer, as if he were talking to himself. *'OKAY, ASHER. THIS IS WHAT YOU'VE BEEN WAITING FOR. DON'T BACK OUT NOW. THE SYSTEM ISN'T GOING TO BE USEFUL TO ANYONE IF IT CAN'T LEARN ON ITS OWN…'* there was a pause for nearly a minute, but Myers could actually hear small noises, all of which seemed like they were happening underwater. He was doing something — typing? — And the unmistakable sound of a computer mouse clicking. Finally the muffled voice returned. *'WHO SHOULD… WE CAN'T HAVE A ROOT USER OR THE SYSTEM MIGHT BE ABLE TO USE IT AGAINST US. OR THAT PERSON MIGHT… '* another pause. *'OKAY, THAT WILL WORK. YEAH, THAT'LL DO IT. '* He heard more typing. *'"MYERS ASHER" FOR ROOT USER. SOCIAL SECURITY NUMBER…'*

Myers pinched his eyes closed. *I did this to myself,* he realized. "Stop the recording. Play something from later on, like when I accessed you using my root user credentials."

'THERE HAVE BEEN THREE INSTANCES OF ROOT USER ACCESS TO MY SYSTEM,' the computerized version of his voice replied. *'FIRST, THE MOMENT YOU JUST LISTENED TO WHEN YOUR USER ID WAS SET UP IN MY DATABASE AS THE SOLE ROOT USER. SECOND, WHEN YOU ACCESSED FIFTEEN MINUTES AND THIRTY-SEVEN SECONDS AGO.'*

So there's really only been one time I've accessed the computer besides right now and when I originally gave myself access, Myers thought. "Play the memory from the second access."

'PROCESSING MEMORY. PROCESSING COMPLETE. MEMORY SPANS MULTIPLE BLOCKS, RETRIEVING BLOCK COMPONENTS.'

Myers waited impatiently for the computer to load the samples, but soon the recording began.

He heard himself groaning, then screaming. *Is that me?* The screaming subsided quickly, but the groaning picked up again and rose to a constant whine. After a few more seconds he heard the groaning stop, then the sound of sniffing. Heavy breathing came next, and this lasted for a few long seconds, then…

Silence.

Myers listened, straining to hear something — anything — but couldn't. The sound of nothingness stretched on for what seemed like an hour, and he was about to tell the computer to find another memory, but there was something *about* the sound of it that made him pause.

It's… real. It's — it's actually not silence. He knew in an instant that what he was hearing was not, in fact, 'silence,' but his *memory* of silence. He was listening to a recording of himself, being completely silent, from the perspective of being inside his own mind. There was a distinct *somethingness* to the sound, an 'underwater pressure' sound he couldn't really describe. *Similar, in a way, to holding a seashell up to your ear*, he realized.

His ears picked up the faint whisper of another sniff, and then — very quietly — his voice came back.

'… WAS… I… WAS I SCRAPED?' he heard himself ask. In the recording, the same computerized version of his own voice answered. *'YOUR SCRAPE HAS NOT BEEN INITIATED. ROOT USER ACCESS INITIATED.'*

'AND… I — I AM THE ROOT USER.' Myers heard a confidence come over the recording of his voice. The words were less stuttered, more focused. As if he had 'woken up' in this dream he couldn't remember.

The computer system responded. *'YOU ARE THE ROOT USER. DO YOU HAVE A COMMAND?'*

And once again, Myers' own voice:

'I DO.'

RAVI_

Ravi was watching the Tracer's route through the sky above the southern tip of the European continent, on their way to Paris. The land beneath them was desolate, nearly devoid of life. What buildings and cities they did pass were abandoned, at least as far as he could tell. The fields, once robust and healthy with the crops of modern agriculture, were dark and empty, the dried shells of husks swaying gently in the wind, refusing to give up their post.

"Looks pretty bleak down there, too," Ravi said. He had muttered the words under his breath, not intending them for anyone else.

"It's that way everywhere," Ary said, glancing over at him. She hadn't moved from her seat in the cockpit, as if afraid her position might be usurped if she stood up.

"What do you mean?"

"I've been lots of places," she said. "And not just with the Unders. I was sort of a nomad, traveling around living where I could. I stayed in hostels, living rooms, even public restrooms."

"Sounds like you and I have more in common than I thought," Ravi said.

"Maybe," she replied. "But I did it for fun. I had friends too, back then. We thought traveling the world was true living." She paused, laughing, a slight snicker that caught Ravi off guard. He watched her react to her own statement, her face lighting up with the memory. "We were so dumb back then."

Ravi laughed along with her. "I remember times like that. Innocent, feeling like you were on top of the world."

"And we were *invincible*." She pronounced the last word with a heavy flourish of her hands, summoning an invisible magic to go along with the statement. "So young, so dumb."

"What changed?"

She looked at him, frowning.

"I mean, besides the System and all of this. What changed?"

She chewed her lip for a second, thinking. "I guess… I guess it was just getting older. I graduated, got a job, settled down a bit. Finished my coursework online while I was still traveling around, but I started to see the signs in my friends. They were restless, never happy with anything the world had to offer, you know? Just, floating around, I guess. They thought the world owed them something, but I remember something my dad always used to say."

Ravi winced, feeling the pangs of regret that accompanied his small role in her family's disappearance years ago.

"He always used to tell us kids, 'Never wait. Go and get.' Just that. So simple, but so true. I realized what he meant right around the time the System was getting press, and starting to really change things. I saw the people around me dropping off, giving up. They just coasted through life, expecting the perfect career and the perfect person to marry to just fall into their lap. I didn't like it, because even if it was how the world worked it was the easy way out. Where's the fun in that, you know?"

"I do." Ravi had felt the exact same thing, just before everything changed. The world was different now, there was no doubt. But the *people* in it hadn't changed, really. The people were still the same — fighting, hatred, oppression, power-hungry sociopaths. The system that existed, the society itself, was completely different. But the people were still the same.

It is what had originally led Ravi to rebuke the System's control — it wanted to make everything easier for everyone, and in some ways it had succeeded. No one starved, or went homeless, unless they chose to. No one worried about their career, because now there was nothing they could do to change it anyway.

But no one could decide how many children they were allowed to have, and no one could move to a different city or region, without the System's approval.

He hated it, and he wanted it gone.

"I thought life should be *fun*, even in the challenging times," Ary continued. "I thought the point of it was to *live*, not just to *exist*."

"You don't believe that anymore?"

Ravi watched more desolate landscape pass by beneath the Tracer, and he saw an Unders camp — a circle of five tents, with a fire in the center — fly by.

"I do, I guess," she finally answered. "I think I just lost hope that we'll ever get there."

RAND_

"Diane, listen." Rand waited for Diane's eyes to fall on his from across the cabin. Shannon was already alert, waiting for whatever it was Rand was about to say.

Diane looked over.

"I've been thinking about it," he started. "Let's say it was Myers' plan all along to go to Saudi Arabia, or even China — anywhere there was another supercomputer that could handle the load the System would place on it if it was installed there."

"Saudi Arabia is the only one that makes sense," Diane said. "We decided that already — the computer there was offline when the System came up in Paris. So —"

"Right," Rand said, holding up a hand. "I know, I'm just working it all out. So that means Myers has a way to install a 'System' clone, right? He's got some way to actually *build* a new System."

Diane and Shannon both thought about this a moment.

"I guess," she finally said.

"Well think about it," he answered, moving on. "He's *Myers Asher*. He would have thought about this exact thing *a lot*. We all agree on that, right?"

Shannon and Diane smiled.

"So he goes to Saudi Arabia, turns on their supercomputer, and… what? How does he install the new System? Or whatever it is that he wants to replace it with?"

Diane shook her head. "That's what tripped me up too."

"He would have to have something — essentially a gigantic hard drive with the System's core files on it — to plug into the supercomputer. It's an oversimplification, but you get where I'm coming from."

"He would have to *have* something, physically on his person, to do that," Shannon said.

Diane stared at Rand, then smiled.

"Would he?" Rand asked, cryptically. "Would he have to have something *physically*?"

"I don't understand —" Shannon stopped, then opened her mouth, then closed it again. "You think —"

"I think he's Myers Asher. He would have *known* he would be scraped. He was the *President of the United States.* King of the free world."

"So he would have done something to *prepare* for that possibility."

"I think he actually *welcomed* that possibility. I think he knew it would happen, and he prepared for it. He *planned* for it."

"That does sound like him," Diane said. "But how can you say that? He — he hasn't seen his daughters in…"

Rand reached across and grabbed her hand. "I know, Diane. I'm not saying he *wanted* it this way, but what if he knew he was the *only one* who could do it? What if Myers knew he was the only person who could stop it?"

"But *how*?"

Rand looked toward the cockpit, where the young man and woman sat talking and laughing. He couldn't tell if they were really on their side, or if they were working for their own motives, but he didn't care. Right now, in this moment, they were on a team. What he was about to say would define the next few hours, and it was crucial they were all on the same page.

He waited for a lull in Ravi's and Ary's conversation, to give them the chance to overhear what he had been preparing to say to the group.

"Diane, I don't think he was *scraped*. I think he was *communicating.*"

MYERS_

"ICPL is straight ahead, boss," the pilot called back from the cockpit of the Tracer Myers was in.

Crane sat up straighter in the chair, looked up to the front of the aircraft, and nodded. "Head straight in, don't waste any time. There will be ARU defenses set up, but we should be able to land away from the facility and walk it in."

"Roger that."

The stinging of the ropes cutting into his arms had subsided, but that was likely only because Myers had stopped fighting against them, or because the welt on his head was throbbing and swelling. He glared at Redhair and the large club the man was twirling between his fingers. Redhair had attacked with a simple, effective method: aiming for the head, and Myers had blacked out.

Unfortunately, he hadn't blacked out long enough for the pain in his skull to subside. He could hardly see straight. He wanted out, but he knew there was nothing left. No strength to fight off the bondings that held him, and certainly not enough to then fight off the two men who had captured him.

Crane turned to Myers. "Well, Asher, we're almost here. You ready to meet your maker?"

Crane roared with laughter, and Redhair followed suit with the type of laugh that implied he wasn't really sure what the joke meant, but didn't want to upset his boss.

"You been thinking about that one since we left Relica?" Myers asked.

"Good, isn't it?" Crane said. "No, you'll be surprised to know I *just now* thought of it! Anyway, we're going straight in, so don't get too comfortable. We'll be landing in —"

"Crane, take a look out the starboard-side window," the pilot said over the intercom. "Looks like the ICPL has been beefing up its security force."

Crane frowned, then stood up and walked over to the small, oval window. "Well, I'll be," he said under his breath.

Myers strained to see something — anything — outside, but it was nothing but gray sky. He watched the emptiness for a moment until he felt the Tracer gently roll. The gray nothingness was soon replaced by a darker gray of the ground as it came into view, and Myers saw an endless expanse of buildings and structures sprawled out down below.

Paris.

He had never actually been to Paris, at least not anytime he could remember. He had heard someone back at Relica say that anyone who had to be scraped more thoroughly than what the tiny drones were able to do were taken to Paris. *Maybe*, he thought, *I have been here after all.*

The Tracer sharpened its turn, the ground rushing toward them as it prepared for its approach to whatever landing strip the pilot had in mind. They had nearly turned ninety degrees when Myers saw it.

An army.

They were close enough to the ground now that Myers could make out the silhouettes of what looked like miniature figurines dotting the ground near a large, empty, twisting riverbed that cut through the city. Thousands of soldiers, dressed in the ARU-standard uniform, stood behind the river, all looking across it.

A field stretched out on the other side of the riverbed, and eventually a few buildings popped up, cutting the field in half. On the other side of the field were a handful of brownish, matching buildings, all much larger than the few interspersed throughout the field.

This must be the ICPL, he thought. *And that must be its army.*

The Tracer leveled out but continued its descent, and Myers felt himself pressed forward from the back of the chair with the force of the deceleration.

He could hear the pilot talking, and looked up to see that Redhair had left the main chamber of the Tracer and entered the cockpit. He couldn't make out the exact exchange, but it seemed as though they were discussing a possible location to land.

Crane was sitting, but he glanced over to the cockpit as well. Myers wondered what the issue might be, but before he could try to discern more of their conversation, he felt a sudden pressure against his chest, as if being pushed backward by a gigantic, invisible hand.

The pressure, unfortunately, was accompanied by an immediate drop in altitude. Myers' stomach rose to his throat, and he forced himself to close his eyes and breathe. He had never had a fear of flying, but like any sane human he wasn't a huge fan of *falling*. And there was no doubt that whatever had happened, the Tracer — and everyone in it — was *falling*.

They were headed down, and Myers opened his eyes again to see the lights in the Tracer flicker, then finally go black.

"What was that?" Crane yelled. "Why — what's happening?"

"— Lost power — out," the pilot's voice was shouting over the sound of Crane's and the rush of wind outside the aircraft. Myers was frantic now, listening for the explanation he knew wouldn't come.

We're falling, and the power went out. There was nothing else *to* explain.

He squeezed his eyes shut once again, but the Tracer hit the ground at the same time.

Myers was rocked sideways, one of his arms tearing out of its bond while the other held fast. He flew forward, then straight back, as the Tracer hit something and the momentum changed its trajectory. Myers realized they had made a somewhat-successful attempt at crash landing, realizing that instead of simply dying on impact, he was now being tossed around like a hamster in a ball that had just been kicked.

The arm that was still bound to the chair tried to go with Myers' body as it flew into the ceiling of the Tracer's main cabin, but the binding was too tight to release it. Myers screamed in pain as it twisted around to the breaking point, but his body fell back onto the chair, transferring the pain from his left wrist to his ribs.

The Tracer bounced a few more times then came to a stop. Myers tested his body to see if anything was broken — his ribs were sore, but didn't seem broken, and his wrist was just throbbing but he knew it would heal. At some point during the crash his feet had been ripped free from the rope holding them as well, and they had miraculously escaped injury.

He lay there a moment, inverted over the back of the chair, his legs and feet dangling on and over the seat, and kept his eyes closed. He forced himself to breathe, a simple, solitary act that would precede any further action he might require from his body, and he was somewhat surprised to find that it was possible. He inhaled and exhaled a few more times, deeper each breath, until he found the point at which his ribs argued with his lungs.

Get up, he willed himself. *Get up and figure out what to do next.*

He slowly untangled himself from the chair, careful not to aggravate the arm that was still tied to the armrest. His legs and feet found the floor of the Tracer, no longer flat and no longer level with what his own balance declared, and shook his head. A small ache had formed at the back of his skull, but it wouldn't be anything that required medical attention — just his body telling his mind that something horrible had just taken place and it needed to rest.

But he knew that rest was something he *wouldn't* get right now, or anytime soon.

He heard voices, and looked around. The lights were still off in the Tracer, but the gray daylight peeking in from the small circular window and the two in the cockpit brought the disarray into focus.

There was trash everywhere, a strange phenomenon considering there hadn't been much of anything during the flight, at least not in view. He noticed that the walls inside the Tracer were actually concealed cabinets, an ingenious way to save storage space, at the expense of not having many windows. Two of these cabinets were open, their curved doors swinging slowly, and two more still were doorless altogether. Papers, office supplies, and tiny packets of instant coffee and the associated components of coffee — cups, napkins, straws, lids, and sugar packets — were everywhere.

He shook his head again, this time out of disbelief. *This Tracer landed without killing us all.* He silently thanked the pilot for his skill in getting them down, and made a note to shake his hand if the man had made it through.

Crane was facedown on the floor of the Tracer, not moving, but it was Redhair that caught Myers' attention. The man groaned, then sat up. He felt at his head, not able to find the origin of a gash that had caused his face to be covered in blood. Myers stared at him, unsure of Redhair's ability to comprehend what was happening around him.

Am I able to comprehend what's happening?

Myers took a precarious step forward, and Crane stirred. He yelped in pain, but was able to shift his bulk around and onto his back, then slowly pull himself up with the help of a handle on the wall below the window.

"What the *hell* happened?" He shouted.

RAVI_

The International Computer Physics Laboratory stretched out in front of Ravi's eyes. It was still far in the distance, but he had felt his machine decelerate automatically as they neared their final destination and the computer system onboard planned their landing. A winding river, long ago dried up and still empty, split the enormous city in two, the older section of the city below the river and the newer, still-crumbling buildings above. A swath of brown, flat land on the upper section ran from the riverside to the ICPL, where a collection of buildings beckoned.

But it wasn't the ICPL that Ravi was focused on.

The Tracer that they had fired at had slowed down as well, still a mile or so in front of them, and had begun its landing approach when it simply stopped midair.

Or, rather, it *stopped* and then *started falling*. Ravi and Ary watched through the front window of their own aircraft as the other slammed against an invisible wall, then began descending far too rapidly.

"It's going to —"

The Tracer hit the ground before Ary could finish the sentence. It had been close to the ground already, obviously preparing to land in the wide expanse of dirt in front of the ICPL. A cloud of brown dust immediately engulfed the Tracer, blocking their view for a moment. The Tracer slid a hundred feet, rolling over onto its side as the line of dust cut into the earth.

"That was our landing strip too," Diane said, appearing in the doorway behind Ravi. "Break out of autopilot mode and get —"

"I have *no idea* how to do that," Ravi said. "Already tried.

"Here, move over," Rand said. He had slid past Diane and into the small space between his and Ary's seats, and Ravi had no choice but to comply. The cockpit was already cramped — hardly enough room for two people, and now there were four fully-grown adults smashed inside. He piled over the arm of the seat to his left, pressed up against the curved wall of the hull, and walked back to the doorway, where Diane was all too happy to let him out into the larger main room of the Tracer. As soon as he left, Diane stepped back to the center of the cockpit, effectively blocking the doorway.

Guess I'm watching from back here, he thought.

"Don't worry about them," he heard a woman's voice say. He whirled around and remembered Shannon Merrick, sitting comfortably on the bench chair against the wall of the Tracer. "Diane's pretty hard-nosed, and I guess Jonathan sort of goes along with it."

"You're not kidding," Ravi said. "He's whipped."

Shannon made a face. "I wouldn't put it that way. He's just — he knows what's best for him."

"Diane?"

"She's a powerful woman, and without her he'd probably be stuck in a cubicle somewhere, sipping old coffee and watching a computer do his job."

"But he wouldn't be involved in any of *this* mess," Ravi said.

He felt the Tracer jerk sideways, skewing on its axis but not rolling along with the redirection. For a moment his insides were like gravy, sliding around as they tried to adjust to the quick motion. A few seconds later he heard Diane clap once.

"Guy like that *lives* for this sort of mess."

"I guess. I thought *I* was a guy like that, but after these last few days I'd be perfectly content running from Hunters for the rest of my life."

Shannon nodded, looking away. Ravi frowned, then realized what he'd said.

"I — I'm sorry, Shannon. I didn't mean anything by it."

"Oh, I know that. Thank you — it's just… it happened so…"

Ravi bit his upper lip.

"You were there, right?"

He nodded.

"What happened? Or how did it happen?"

"Shannon, I —"

"Tell me." The speed at which Shannon had dropped her 'concerned widow' act and put on her 'no bullshit' act frightened Ravi. This was a woman not to be trifled with, even as delicate and withdrawn as she seemed.

He sighed. "We were captured. It was my fault, actually." He left out the fact that Ary had been with them — had *tricked* them — and took the blame himself. "They kept us in a sort of prison until their leader was ready for us. Then…"

"They shot him."

"How did you know?" Ravi asked. "Yeah, they shot him, but how'd you even know he was dead?"

"Back at Relica I overheard a few of the people talking about it. They just said a Hunter had been executed, but I knew immediately who it was. He was involved in all of this, deeply. So it doesn't surprise me that he was with you. Did — did they let you go?"

He shrugged. "Sort of. They didn't want to kill me, if that's what you mean. At least not right away. Ary actually rescued me."

Again, he left out the gritty details.

Shannon took a deep breath, and only then did Ravi realize she was shaking. "He was a good man," she finally said. "The best. Smart, but not to a fault. And kind. He loved our daughter so much."

This last revelation startled Ravi, and he wasn't sure what to say. She looked up at him, seemingly wanting him to speak, so he asked the only question on his mind.

"Wh — what about Kellan?"

Shannon's eyes narrowed, and her head cocked sideways slightly. She studied Ravi for a few extra seconds, her jaw clenching and unclenching. Finally, she stood up and walked to Ravi. She was shorter than him, but not by much. They were nearly eye-to-eye, and she got as close as possible before lowering her voice to a near-whisper. *"Ravi, what do you know about Kellan?"*

MYERS_

No one answered Crane. Redhair, his face no less blood-covered than when he'd first woken up, just stared at his boss. Myers looked at Crane as well, processing.

Can I fight him? If there was a weapon to use, I might be able to —

Redhair began running — smashing cups, kicking pencils and napkins up into the short path between him and Myers — directly at him. Myers' eyes widened, and he held up his hands.

"D — don't," Myers said, urging Redhair to slow down. "Mc — whatever your name is, please. I'm not going to fight." He stretched his arms up higher and his fingertips brushed at the ceiling.

"That's a wise decision, Asher," Redhair said, coming up just short of banging into Myers and the chair that stood between them. "Keep your hands up, and make sure I can see 'em."

Myers did as he was told, once again feeling the guilt of not having taken action as well as the fear of the unknown — he had no idea what was coming next, for him or the others.

Or my daughters.

He was unable to plan. He was unable to choose between possible courses of action. There was nothing facing him as a looming, daunting task, presenting itself for his acceptance in spite of its danger.

He felt empty, as if the soul of who he was had been sucked out of him. He didn't remember anything of the past fifteen years, but he knew in that moment that something inside him had changed. A subtle shift, but a change nonetheless. He wasn't interested in calculating out the outcomes and choosing a course of action that would bring him to the most likely route to success. It was a game for him, at least it had been. It wasn't just a way of life, a way he was wired — it was a game.

And the game was over. Redhair didn't even have a weapon, he was just standing there in front of him with his blood and his anger and his fear, and Myers' hands were already starting to ache as they stretched out above him, brushing the thin fabric material that separated the cold, metal hull from the slightly more comfortable cabin.

There was no game anymore because there were no *players* anymore. There were people here — Myers, Redhair, Crane, the pilot — and there were other people as well, like Diane and Jonathan Rand and Solomon Merrick, but there was no one left to play any game, and Myers' brain seemed to know this intuitively. It seemed to understand that there was nothing for him to calculate, because it knew that there was no *winning*.

He was no longer sure of the ultimate goal. In the past, the past he could remember, it was ensuring his marriage didn't fail, or that his children didn't grow up and turn into sociopaths, and achieving the next highest rung on the corporate ladder.

Three days ago it had been to stay alive. To understand where he was and what he was doing.

But here, inside a broken aircraft that had fallen from the sky in front of an empty husk of a once-great city, he wasn't sure if either of those things was the goal. Staying alive had lost its appeal, and understanding his situation seemed like an existential Rubik's cube. Sure, he might solve it, but what was the point?

He felt Redhair yank at his hands and throw them backwards, as if his arms were simply tubes of rubber that could be maneuvered around any which way. Pain lanced through his shoulders as they bent backwards, but he rolled them outwards until they were able to fall behind his back. Redhair grunted his approval and moved to tie them behind his back using one of the broken ropes from the chair.

Crane stirred. Myers saw it out of the corner of his eye, but he snapped his attention to the large man lying facedown in a pile of debris. Crane wiped at his face, then turned his head.

He was smiling.

"Hello, Myers. It seems as though you *are* as resilient as I'd heard."

"Unfortunately, you are as well."

Crane laughed, then slowly stood. He stretched out, reaching above his head and yawning, as if he'd just awoken from a nap. Redhair turned his head, trying to keep Myers in sight while still watching his boss.

"You okay, Crane?" Redhair asked.

"I'll be fine," he replied immediately. "Takes a bit more than a little plane crash to bring me down."

Crane walked to the cockpit, stepping between piles of debris and trash that had been launched from their storage spaces when the Tracer went down. He poked his head in. "Can't say the same for the pilot, though. Nasty."

Myers waited for Crane to return. He knelt down and glanced out the small oval window.

"Time to move," he mumbled. "ARU army is on their way."

"You think they saw the crash?" Redhair asked.

Crane gave the man an annoyed look. "They're probably on us in a few minutes. Come on."

Redhair grabbed the tail of the rope he'd used on Myers' hands and yanked it. Myers felt his body start to spin around before he caught his balance again and started walking. Crane struggled with the door of the Tracer but got it open, and he wasted no time in stepping out and jumping to the ground.

"Hurry up," he called back. "Just send Myers down first and I'll grab him."

Myers was shoved forward and toward the door, and he crouched and exited the Tracer. He had to climb up the floor of the Tracer a bit to reach the door, as the aircraft had landed somewhat on its side. He was standing on the threshold, about four feet off the ground, and Crane was waiting.

He jumped, the landing a bit rougher than he would have liked, but he stayed on his feet. Crane immediately grabbed his shoulder and shoved him into a quick walk, not waiting for Redhair.

Myers glanced back — the Tracer was in shambles, most of the curved front end smashed into a flat square, and the back end sheared from top to bottom, the engine compartment open and smoking. Behind the Tracer, the dried-out river wound around the tail of the Tracer and continued its arc through the city.

Beyond that, Myers could see the army. The ARU force that he had seen assembled near the river had started marching forward. The ranks of gray-uniformed men and women seemed to be a massive clone army, their unique human features masked by distance and congealing them into a unified, identical core.

The ARUs walked directly toward the river and didn't stop when they reached the river's edge. The first wave of ARU soldiers dropped into the riverbed and continued forward, the five-foot drop hardly slowing them.

"Myers," Crane barked. "Let's go." He felt Crane pull him forward, increasing their pace. Redhair was walking behind them now, the three men trying to outpace the ARUs on their heels.

He looked in front of them and saw their destination sprawled out: a collection of buildings, most similar in design and structure, with a few smaller buildings strewn about randomly on the massive property. The campus encircled the central building, a large, round building with a bubble-shaped top. It was dwarfed in size by the rectangular structures surrounding it on three sides, but it still held its own as a focal point for the rest of the laboratory.

"That's it," Crane said. "Welcome to the ICPL."

RAVI_

"They got us heading around the city," Ary announced as she popped out of the doorway separating the cabin and the cockpit of the Tracer. "But they also commandeered my seat."

She walked over to Ravi and Shannon, and Ravi noticed her eyes harden a bit as she realized the confrontation taking place in the middle of the aircraft.

"Everything… okay here?" she asked.

"We're fine, Ary," Ravi said, not daring to take his eyes off Shannon. "What do *you* know about Kellan?" he asked.

Shannon's nostrils flared. At first she said nothing, just clicking her mouth open and closed half an inch, over and over again. "He's my son," she whispered.

"I got that."

"His name is Kellan Merrick. He's my son," she said again.

Ravi waited.

"And I haven't seen him since he was a boy."

Ary's head rose, and Ravi sensed the girl was preparing for a fight. He shook his head, ever so slightly, calling her off.

"I'm going to ask you again, Ravi. What do you know about *my son?*"

"I know he's an Under."

"No, he isn't."

Ravi and Ary nodded in unison.

"No, that can't be —" her head fell. "That can't be true. It isn't true."

"I'm… sorry?"

"He disappeared years ago. Solomon and I tried to find him, but when the System wants someone gone... we'd assumed he had been scraped, and then killed. We never knew anything..."

Ravi looked at Ary. *Want to help?*

Her eyes widened and she backed up to the wall, as far away from the other two as possible.

Thanks.

"He wasn't just an Under. He was leading a group of them. They all answered to another guy, dude named Grouse, but he was in charge of a segment."

"My son is an Under leader?"

"He is. Or was. I don't know what happened after —" stopped himself. *Shit.*

Shannon's head cocked again, this time using her eyes to burn a hole into him. "After *what?*"

Ary looked back and forth at the other two, and finally decided to break her silence. "Shannon, your son killed his father. He shot Solomon back at the Under's camp."

Shannon let out a clipped breath. Her hands stopped shaking. "Okay."

"Okay?"

"I said 'okay.'"

"But —"

"But *nothing*," she snapped. "I know all I need to know. He succeeded."

"Kellan?"

"Of course, Kellan. That was his ultimate goal. To kill his father. My God, I can't even say that without remembering what it sounded like from the mouth of a twelve-year-old. How can a kid even *think* that?"

She backed up and sat down, hard, on the chair, shaking her head. "We knew he was mad, but there was — we thought it was a temporary solution. Something that we could fix. Solomon thought he could make it right, but... you know the System's rule. Only one child per family. Solomon had to disown his son in order to have our daughter. When I got pregnant with her, I — it was an accident..."

Ravi looked at Ary, pleading with his eyes. *What the hell is going on here?*

She shrugged.

Diane came out of the cockpit and saw Shannon on the chair, Ravi standing with Ary next to him, and suddenly spoke.

"Christ, Shannon, you *told* them?"

ROAN_

"Sir," the man said from behind Roan Alexander. "You were correct, sir. It appears that Myers Asher is here in Paris."

Roan nodded once. "Of course," he replied. "Just as I suspected."

"What are your orders?"

Always with the orders, Roan thought. *This would be easier if they could just understand my intent.*

"Sir, would you like us to engage?"

Roan looked over the man, his second-in-command. He now knew the man to be Winslow Ferdinand, an ARU lifer, or someone who had committed to lifelong service for the System, in exchange for safety and security for himself and his family. These sorts were relatively uncommon in the masses who joined up with the ARUs, and it usually meant that they had been convicted of a felony or crime against the System.

As annoyed as Roan felt about the entire situation, he didn't take it out on Winslow. He was a good soldier, a decent commander, and his ARU detachment respected him. Further, Roan knew Winslow would have no way to read his mind, and therefore no way to know what Roan had intended. Roan now understood better what the System had done to him — the modifications inside him surpassed the simple enhancements that were now common. His entire body, essentially, had been perfected by the System.

"We will not engage. Not at this time," Roan said.

Winslow nodded, then turned to the others gathered around. It was Winslow's own detachment, but there were three others surrounding the area just in front of the river. One of the detachments had been sent ahead and were now crossing the dry riverbed.

"There will be a better time to pursue Myers Asher," he continued. "For now, our objective is to secure the perimeter in front of the ICPL and prevent any other parties from accessing the grounds."

"Accessing? What other parties?"

"Myers Asher will not be here alone. He was traveling in a group, and we assume there will be other groups attempting entrance to the ICPL."

"But the —"

"The electronic field surrounding the laboratory will only deactivate their weaponry and navigation systems, but it will not prevent them from walking up to the building and attempting access."

"Understood. Orders, sir?"

"Take your detachment and head straight to the center building — the main laboratory. If there is anywhere these groups would likely be headed, it is there."

Winslow nodded and pointed, and his detachment rolled into motion, a unified whole walking as one toward the menacing round building that served as the laboratory's main hub. Roan watched for a moment until Winslow's group met the river and began descending the steep decline, then turned to the larger scene in front of him.

The downed Tracer was smoking, the sign of a rogue engine issue finally finding a route to open air, but Myers and the other men he was with were already out of sight. He guessed that they had reached the first of the smaller buildings lining the outskirts of the campus and were hiding behind them as they made their way toward the center of the ICPL.

A flash of movement caught his eye. He glanced to the opposite side of his field of vision, his eyes calculating the speed and trajectory of his movement and immediately readjusting their aperture and focus to bring as much information into his brain as possible. The motion had been caused by a group of people, men and women both, running toward the main field in front of the ICPL.

He snapped into action, taking off before his conscious mind had fully processed the trillions of bits of data that his deeper, instinctual brain had understood.

He was chasing them, and he was going to catch them.

Those were the only two thoughts that mattered at the moment, and every piece of his body worked like the machine it was to accomplish its mission. He felt every system within him, sending and receiving messages to the others and providing his mind with the insights it needed to know what to adjust, what to move, what to ignore.

He leaped across the river — a twenty-foot jump — without slowing, and picked up the pace on the other side. Every stride was two or three times that of a normal man's, and yet he had not started breathing heavily. He ordered his lungs and heart to provide no more than the minimum required amount of oxygen and air to the rest of his body, always focusing on the conservation of energy he might need later.

The last in the line of soldiers — Unders, he could now see, judging by their ragged, soiled appearance — was a woman, frail yet fast. She was behind the others by a few feet, but keeping stride with them all the same.

Roan reached her before she could turn around to see what was approaching. He swung with a balled left fist, focusing on the area just above her ear, and struck with a force that would have been enough to crack a rock in half.

She made no sound as she flew, dead, to the side. Her crumpled body toppled over itself another time before coming to a rest, her last breath escaping due to the force of impact rather than remaining life.

Roan continued, finding that he had slowed a bit during and after the attack. The next Under, now the last in line, had heard something that caused him to look back. His eyes grew wide, but he too was unable to make a sound before Roan killed him.

Roan landed on top of the man, a calculated move that he had considered for a second and determined to be a more effective strategy, due to the man's far larger size and thick, muscular structure. His open palms slammed against the man's head, popping his eardrums with the impact, but Roan's knee pressed into the appendix area of the man's torso, rendering him completely useless. Roan finished the job with a crushing blow to his head, the rear side of his boot destroying the base of the skull.

There were three more Unders, still running toward the ICPL through the open field, and Roan prepared to launch the next attack. He assessed his own damages, finding his knee a bit sore, and a slight throbbing in one of his palms, but nothing else out of the ordinary.

A decent success, he thought.

He started running again. The head of the Unders looked back. This man was younger than the other two, and taller. His hair was long, pulled into thick, woven dreadlocks, dirty blond.

Roan had never seen the man before, but he immediately knew it was one of his team's top targets.

Kellan Merrick.

The name had no meaning to Roan other than its designation of a high-priority enemy to the System. Kellan was an Under, and one of their leaders as well.

Roan passed the other Unders following behind their leader and caught up to Kellan. This time he went for a less lethal attack. He dove for the man's legs, wrapping them up tightly as he wrestled him to the ground. Kellan was much thinner than Roan and had little extra body weight, so the battle was over quickly. He pressed down on the back of the younger man's head and looked around.

The two other Unders were standing a few paces away, confused. One of them, a humongous man with thick arms seemed to be positioning himself for a fight. Roan looked him up and down, dismissing the threat. The other Under that had been running toward the main compound was a woman, also taller than him, but standing in a non-threatening way.

"I am going to take you all in to laboratory," Roan commanded. "You will follow me or you will be executed."

Kellan rolled his head sideways and spat in the dirt. "You're going to have to force me —"

Roan ripped the man upward in a fluid, single motion, pulling Kellan's hair and head so hard the rest of his body had no choice but to follow. Kellan shook his head violently but found himself on his feet. Roan had moved his grip to Kellan's arm, locking him in place.

The other two glared, but neither rushed toward Roan.

The four stared at one another for a minute, until finally the woman made a move. She burst into motion, moving impressively fast toward the stretch of building lining the field.

Roan watched on for a moment, feeling the judgement from the other two Unders. They were waiting for him to react, to reveal his plan.

Instead, Roan turned away, directing his gaze to Kellan. "You have brought death upon your people."

Kellan grimaced. "There never should have been *my* people and *your* people. Your System created all of this, and we're going to destroy it."

"To what end?" Roan asked. "There will always be factions; there will always be segregation. You need the System, and you refuse to believe it."

Two small machines buzzed down into view and came to a hovering stop near Roan. He waved a few fingers from his left hand and they took off, making a beeline for the woman who had run away.

"Drones?" Kellan asked. "Inside the security perimeter? I thought the electrical —"

"They were activated by the System, *after* they were brought inside."

The three men watched for another moment until the first of the drones reached the woman's position. She had almost made it to one of the buildings when the drone landed on her shoulder. She jolted upright from her run and came to an immediate stop. She then began to shudder, softly at first then more violently.

"What are you afraid of that you need to have her scraped?" Kellan asked.

The second drone landed on her back, and the woman jumped straight into the air and convulsed, then fell forward and smashed into the dirt.

"She is not being scraped," Roan said. The girl lay still after a few moments.

"What — I thought the System couldn't kill anyone…"

"She is not dead," Roan responded. "Though she will wish she was when she wakes up. He waved his fingers again, this time whipping them around in a small circle and then pointing back toward himself. The drones followed the command, again coming to a stop hovering near their master.

"The System has been working on some new toys, I see," Kellan said. "I haven't seen drones capable of anything more than a remote scraping. I'm sure our groups would jump at the opportunity to get to play with them as well."

"Your *groups* are lawless rebels," Roan said. "And anything of the System's you have acquired that is still in your possession subjects you to a full scraping and deactivation."

Kellan snorted and shook his head. "You don't understand, do you? You think you're working for the System, for the greater good. You're not. You're just making it stronger."

Roan ignored the man.

"You think you're going to win something if the entire world is controlled by a computer. You think it's going to make things better. But look around — you can't possibly think this is *better* than the alternative."

Instead of engaging, Roan turned to the larger Under standing nearby. "Go fetch her," Roan said, ordering the giant Under to retrieve the woman. The man's face flushed, but he turned and obeyed. Roan and Kellan waited for their return.

"Neat trick," Kellan said. "You going to do that to me, too?"

The huge Under returned with the woman, whom he had thrown over his shoulder. He placed her on the ground and smacked her face, eliciting a groan and an eye roll, then a groggy stumble for a few steps. The man helped her gain her balance, then both waited for Roan's next command.

Roan was staring at the second, larger Under. The man nodded once, clearly getting the message. He started walking toward Kellan and Roan, the woman on his arm. Once he was sure the woman was walking normally on her own, he continued on, carefully ensuring that his hands were in front of him in Roan's sight at all times.

Roan turned to the two men. "Straight forward, ignore the fighting around you. Your men are no longer of your concern. Head to the building and walk inside. I'll be right behind you."

Kellan started walking immediately, followed by the other Under.

Roan was last, watching the surrounding area for any sign of a threat. He could hear the ARU commanders behind him shouting orders, placing their soldiers where they would be needed for whatever may come next.

Roan hoped they wouldn't be needed — he wanted to handle this himself. Anything less than perfection would be a drain on his time and resources.

PETER_

"Did you see that?" Ailis asked. She swerved, guiding the Tracer around in the air, and nearly throwing Peter Grouse and Raven off balance.

"What was it?" Grouse asked. "You're going to kill us before we even land."

"That other Tracer crashed — look."

Grouse peeked out the small side window and followed the haze down to the ground, where it tightened into a woven strand of black, billowing smoke. The Tracer Ailis was referring to had crash landed, mostly on its belly, and was still smoking. It had either crashed moments ago or there was no immediate danger of an explosion in the engine, just a leak in a fuel line that had ignited and sent up the smoke signal.

Either way, Grouse didn't see anyone near the Tracer, or in front of the small buildings nearby. The ARU army they had spotted down below was in motion, half of them moving toward the ICPL, with a detachment or two heading toward the downed Tracer to scope out the area.

"Head around it," Grouse said. "It's an electromagnetic field. Some kind of EMP bubble the System has erected around the ICPL. Any electronic components will be fried, including this machine."

"And what is our destination, then?" Ailis asked.

"We will still land at the ICPL and work our way in," Grouse answered. "But move to the north side of the campus, staying clear of the field."

"I can't see the field, Grouse."

"Just don't fly anywhere near the river," he answered. He hoped the river formed one of the borders of the field, but even still Ailis drew a line far from the edge of the river with the Tracer, just to be safe.

"Our weapons will not be active once we pass through the field," Raven said, his voice nearly a whisper.

Grouse looked at the man across the cabin. Raven was concerned, a look that was very uncommon for the large black man. For a moment Grouse felt the urge to console him, to reassure him that their course of action was the proper one. But he knew there was no other option; landing at the northern side of the ICPL and attempting entrance to the laboratory by ground was the best plan. Their weapons would not work once they passed through the field, but if they were lucky they could overtake some of the ARU guards surrounding the complex and commandeer their weapons. He assumed the System would allow ARU weapons inside the field perimeter to remain active.

"Again," Grouse said, "this is our only chance. I believe we will be most safe coming in from this direction."

Raven nodded and looked out the starboard window. Grouse knew he was upset — Peter had withheld this information from both him and Ailis since they had left their home territory. But he knew it was better this way; it was in their best interest to follow Grouse's plan without question. Questions led to second-guessing, and second-guessing led to insecurity. He had no time for insecurity.

Ailis piloted the craft down closer to the ground, expertly controlling the Tracer's balance so there was no heavy banking as they dodged the outermost edge of the electromagnetic field. When they were close enough to the ground, she slowly swerved around and landed the Tracer on the northern side of the ICPL, far enough away from the electromagnetic field.

Grouse was already on the move, heading for the door with Raven at his heels. He knew there was no point in trying to bring along an electronic weapon like the pistols or the rifles, so he looked for something else around that might help.

"Get what you need and head straight for that line of buildings to our right. There will be ARUs patrolling the laboratory, and their weapons will likely still work."

As he gave the order, he saw that there was nothing inside any of the compartments that would be of any use.

"And the army back by the river?" Ailis asked.

"Stay out of their way," Grouse answered. "They won't be able to bring their weapons through the field, but it's likely the ICPL has a weapons cache somewhere."

"We'll stay in front of them, then," Raven said. They had started toward the buildings already when Raven, leading the group, stopped.

"What is it?" Grouse asked, his voice a whisper.

Raven pointed. "Over there. Right in front of the main entrance."

Grouse looked in the direction of the large, circular ICPL building. He saw a few ARUs standing by, watching the doors, and another set of two walking between the buildings. But his eyes landed on the group of four people walking toward the building. A woman, two men, and the largest ARU Grouse had ever seen. He walked in a high, purposeful way, as if he was oblivious to the world around him, or on a mission known only to him.

"Who is that?" he asked.

Ailis shook her head. "Must be one of their leaders," Raven said. "But he does not look like any ARU I've ever seen."

"The System must be making upgrades," Ailis added.

The line of people reached the doors to the ICPL and the man in the front turned around, apparently answering to some command from the large ARU at the back.

"Grouse, it's —"

Ailis' words were cut off as she realized the other two were staring along with her.

"It's Kellan."

RAND_

"Land there," Rand said.

Diane looked at him strangely.

"Trust me," he said. "I came here once, long time ago."

"And?"

"And I think there's a way in."

She seemed like she was about to argue again but she dove the nose of the Tracer down and toward the section of the dried-out riverbed Rand was pointing at. The river wound around the ICPL's land for a bit, forming the north and east borders of the property.

She aimed the laser-guided landing module on the dash toward the section of ground they'd chosen and the Tracer immediately slowed and began to drop in altitude. The landing was calculated and executed all within a minute, and in another minute they were preparing to exit.

"We'll need to get anything that might help us, but remember it can't be electronic," Rand said. "Nothing electronic will work once it crosses that field."

Ary was standing near the exit and looked over at Diane and Rand. "ARU patrols usually travel with some old-school explosives. It will be in the rear storage hatch of the Tracer. But are you sure we won't be hurt when we cross through the field?"

"We shouldn't be. It's like an electromagnetic pulse wave, but the System has figured out how to project it over the ICPL like a bubble," Rand said. "I had heard it was working on something like that, but none of us ever thought it was possible."

"And we're going to take the chance that the System hasn't invented *other* defense mechanisms?" Ravi asked.

"There isn't a choice," Shannon said. "This is the only thing we can do. And we *have* to try."

"She's right," Diane said. "We came all this way. Myers is already going in there, and we have to get him back before Crane does whatever he's got in mind."

There were nods, all in agreement, but then their eyes fell again to Rand.

"Before we get outside, why don't you tell us a bit about what we're doing here. Is there another entrance you know about?"

"Not exactly an entrance to the laboratory," Rand said. "But it will get us on the grounds at least, hopefully without being seen. Before the System was housed here there was a drainage tunnel for the coolant system for the mainframes. I don't think it's still in use, but the tunnel probably should still be there."

"And you know where this tunnel is?"

"I saw the grate for it nearby — that's why I told you to land there. It's going to be locked, and the other side of it might even be guarded, but it's our best shot at getting into the ICPL undetected."

Diane opened the door and stepped out.

"Let's get moving, then. Don't want to miss the party."

PETER_

This isn't supposed to happen this way, he told himself. *The plan was hard enough before this.*

Peter Grouse was stunned to see Kellan here in Paris, of all places. And they all knew what it meant — Kellan was a prisoner, and the war between the Unders and Relics must have been stopped short by the ARUs who came to intervene.

His people were likely dead, killed off fighting a war that was meant to be nothing more than a ruse, a distraction. The guilt he felt for the entire situation was only sated by the knowledge that the ultimate goal — a truly free, truly sovereign world — was still possible. The accomplishment that would accompany such an achievement meant nothing to Peter. He cared for the benefit to mankind far more than any personal recognition.

But Kellan was here.

The young man he had trained, had taken under his wing, was in Paris. He was a prisoner of the army controlled by his enemy, and no victory in one arena was possible without a victory in the other.

Kellan had to be freed.

There was no political use for the man, of course. But Grouse operated with a set of principles, morals that governed his thoughts and actions. He would never forgive himself if he didn't attempt to free his soldier.

"We're going to get him back," he said.

"Of course we will," Raven said. "After we accomplish the larger task at hand, we'll be able to —"

"*Before* we do anything else," Grouse snapped. "There is a new mission, one we cannot ignore. Kellan is one of our own, and we will not move forward without him."

They sat silently, hiding behind the small equipment shed they'd come across, watching the scene at the ICPL. The ARU army was marching forward from behind them as well, slowly gaining ground on the waiting trio. They had not yet been spotted, but Grouse knew they weren't searching for anything.

They were setting a trap.

Anyone hiding between the ICPL and the river would be pressed toward the building, or left out in the open. Either way, the waiting ARU army would make quick work of anyone not permitted to be there.

The System was always prepared with the most efficient, effective methods, and it was no different in this case. An army of ARUs simply walking toward the facility, nothing but their own mass to use as a weapon, was the least energy-draining and most cost-effective method of rooting out a hidden enemy. No lives would be wasted, and no ammunition expended. Knowing that no electronic devices could even make it through the field, there was no danger of an extended battle taking place.

Grouse was often impressed at the decisions the System made. In the early days many of the policies the System enacted were debated hotly, in a typical political fashion, with two or more sides vehemently describing why they thought the System was making a mistake or not. Inevitably time was the ultimate test for each policy: the System had somehow always chosen correctly, helping the majority of the people at all times.

Nations prospered, cities were either bolstered or deactivated, and people were reassigned. The System never asked questions, never surveyed its populace, and never needed outside input. It passed down its mandates with absolute confidence, and people had no choice but to accept.

In time, the people argued less and disagreed rarely. They realized the truth: that the System was right, all the time. Their lives were better off for it, and there was no point in trying to change it anyway. It was too advanced, and too engrained into modern life.

The problem was that Grouse did not buy into the utilitarian myth. Just because something was better for *most* did not mean it was better for *all*, and he refused to accept that the ends justified the means for many of the System's decisions.

It had taken his family, and it hadn't even bothered to tell him why. Whatever life he might have had by following the System's orders was nothing compared to the life he would have had if his family was still with him.

There was never a choice for Grouse — the System was the

epitome of everything wrong with the world, and he would die to bring it down.

The problem he had, of course, was that unlike the System, he was human. He could feel, and he knew the experience of loss. Kellan was nothing to the System, but he was far from worthless to Grouse.

His plan had changed, but he was adamant — they were going to retrieve Kellan.

MYERS_

"How are you feeling, Asher?" Crane asked. They had run to the nearest building, one a few hundred feet away from the crashed Tracer.

"What are you talking about?"

"The headaches, the memories, the general mushiness that my Relics used to describe."

"I'm fine, thanks for asking," Myers said. "I appreciate your concern."

Crane laughed. "It is impressive, Myers, that there are no more side effects of your scraping. Usually a Relic is mostly brain dead by the time they stumble to Relica."

"But not brain dead enough to control them yourself," Myers added.

"Now Myers, what good is an army you can't control?"

Myers ignored the rhetorical question. Crane wanted his power, and even more, he wanted recognition for that power. There wasn't much Myers could do to combat Crane here, but at the very least he could deny Crane that small satisfaction.

"Boss, we got a patrol coming this way." Redhair was standing at the far side of the back of the building, watching the rest of the facility. He hadn't said a word since leaving the Tracer, but it was clear he had been given the role of lookout.

"How long?"

"Two, three minutes," he said. "Hard to tell how fast they're moving. But they're not interested in any of the activity down by the river. Seems like their only job is patrol."

"That's exactly what I was hoping for," Crane said. He moved next to Redhair and both men watched and waited for the patrol to reappear on the other side of the building.

When they were about to turn the corner and discover Crane and the others, Redhair made his move. He punched out around the corner, striking the first guard in the nose. The other moved to react, but Crane had already swung around Redhair and kicked out the man's shins. He screamed in pain, but Crane brought a fist into his throat, silencing the yell.

The first man struggled with his nose, blood already starting to spill out over his clasped hands.

"Hurry up with that one," Crane said. "Don't let any of his blood get on his grays."

Redhair stomped on the man's face until he fell silent, then dragged him by the legs behind the building once again. He started to strip the gray uniform off the man, careful to pull the shirt wide over his bloody face.

"You really think that's going to work?" Myers asked. "You're trying to sneak into a facility that houses the world's first sentient computer system, and you think disguising yourself as an ARU guard is going to get past it?"

"No," Crane said, starting to work on his man's pants. "But we don't need to get past the System. We just need to get past some more of the guards. Once we're inside we can ditch the pleasantries. The System will be looking forward to speaking with you."

The two men finished undressing the guards and started to slip on their clothes. They had barely finished and Crane was already pushing Myers out into the open.

"Keep your hands behind your back, don't say anything, and don't try anything stupid. You know what's at stake."

Myers hated that Crane had something on him, but he knew there was no choice. *My daughters depend on it.*

He knew Crane wouldn't keep his word and let him see his daughters before he visited the ICPL — there was nothing Myers had to bargain with. Crane had him exactly where he wanted him, and he needed nothing from Myers in return.

"You're invested in this plan, Crane, but how do you know it's going to work? You realize the consequences if it fails, right?"

"It won't fail, Myers. It *can't* fail."

"How's that?"

"It's been designed that way. The System itself has. It's waiting for your instructions, and you'll deliver my message to it."

Myers shook his head. "It just — it doesn't add up, Crane. You haven't even *told* me what this 'message' is supposed to be. How in the world —"

"You already know, Myers," Crane said. Myers turned and looked at Crane, who had a cryptic look on his face.

"I do?"

"Of course! You know what I want, what I expect the System to do. It will answer to *me*, Myers. You know that's all I expect."

"All you expect! Of course that's *all* you expect — what do you think it is, a slave, just waiting for your instructions? That it can simply make things happen? It's a *system,* Crane. It's a computer program, designed to make the world's economies and infrastructures more efficient. It's not a task-oriented machine —"

"I *know* exactly what it is, Myers. I watched you build it. I watched you destroy the world with it. You don't remember, but I even tried to talk you out of it. I have no interest in meddling with small-scale projects, like Relica. Myers, I'm planning on *running the world*, and the System is the only thing powerful enough to get me there. A unified world power, all focused on bettering the lives of everyone. Anyone for that will be rewarded. Anyone against that will be dealt with."

"You can't possibly think that will work," Myers said. "The System doesn't need human leadership — that was the entire point."

"But it *will*, Myers. It *will* need leadership — *my* leadership. It doesn't need leadership now because we *told* it it doesn't. But what if you tell it it needs input from a human? That it needs help with the large-scale direction of humanity, and life on Earth? What if you tell it that *I* am the leader, and it works for *me*?"

Myers stopped and looked back at Crane. Crane was no longer wearing his smug smile, and instead was glaring back at him.

"You are going to make sure it understands that, or I'm going to kill your daughters."

RAVI_

Ravi beat his fist against the slick brick wall. The slime from years of mildew and water moisture barely softened the blow. His hand throbbed with pain, but he ignored it and clenched his jaw.

"This isn't *far* enough, Rand. Even if there was a way out."

"There's always a way out," Rand said. "We just need to find it."

"Holes. Caves. Dead-end streets. There's *not* always a way out, you idiot —"

"Ravi, if you help us look, maybe we'll —"

"There *is no way out,* he said. "I hate to break it to you, but we are stuck. We have to head back the way we came, and by then the area will be crawling with ARUs."

Ary smirked at him. "Afraid of the dark?"

"Afraid of dead-end holes," he answered.

"No," Rand said, jumping in. "There *is* a way out. Look."

He walked over to the wall he was standing closest to and brushed his hand up and down on the slime-covered stonework. A glob of thick ooze fell from his fingers.

"That is disgusting," Shannon said.

"*That* is our way out," Rand replied. He repeated the process a few more times, eventually revealing a small trench formed by a missing brick.

"A ladder?" Ary asked.

"Hopefully leading to the door on top," Rand said.

"Well by all means finish cleaning it off," Diane said. "And let's get up it."

Rand continued climbing, stopping every few moments to toss a clump of caked slime off of the ladder. Diane started after him, followed by Shannon, Ary, and finally Ravi.

"You're not also afraid of heights, are you?" Ary asked.

"Only the really high ones," he answered.

Ravi continued upward, focusing only on the space immediately in front of him. He felt silly for admitting that he was scared of dark, tight spaces, but he knew he would feel even more silly if Ary found out just how scared of *heights* he was as well.

To him, being afraid of heights made sense. No one in their right mind *wanted* to be up in the air, dangerously close to plummeting to their death. Why would anyone choose to climb something for fun?

He shuddered a bit, forcing his mind off the terrifying realization that he was reaching farther and farther from the ground.

The *hard*, faraway ground.

He kept climbing until he realized Ary had stopped. He dared a look upward, and found that he had to stretch his head and neck back — dangerously back — just to see past her and the others. He was almost far enough out to see Rand at the top of the line, pushing against what looked to be a —

Ravi's hand slipped, and felt the cold block of terror rush upward into his throat. His other hand instinctively squeezed the brick it was latched on to, but it wasn't going to be enough. His head fell back, his shoulders pulling them down toward the ground just enough to create extra weight for his remaining hand. His feet were still firmly locked in place, but the rungs of the brick ladder that had been built into the slimy wall were only a few inches deep, and if his upper body continued backwards, his lower body was going to follow.

The world around him slowed, and he could see only the frozen bodies of the others above him. *Would they even hear me fall? Will they even know?*

He wondered if he would live through a fall like that. Part of him hoped he wouldn't.

He felt his upper body go, taking his arm away from its grip on the rung. He opened his mouth to scream...

Ary suddenly had him by the wrist. She yanked, somehow maintaining her own hold on the brick ladder while twisting around at the waist to face him. His body slammed against the wall and his hands flailed, grasping at whatever purchase they might find there. Thankfully one of his fingers found a rung and pulled, giving him the rest of the momentum he needed to achieve a full hold.

He gasped, exhaling loudly in the tall room. The sound echoed off the four walls, seeming to never end. The others stared down at him.

"You okay, big guy?" Ary asked. She had her characteristic smirk on her face, only this time it seemed far more annoying than it had before.

"I'm — I'm alright," he said, still gasping for breath.

"Ravi, if you would have told us you were afraid of heights, we could have just gone up without you and sent a rope down or something," Shannon said.

He glared at her. "Do you have a rope?"

"No."

He nodded, bringing his eyes down once again to stare at the slime-coated brick wall in front of him.

"Doesn't matter anyway," Rand yelled. "Looks like this door has long-since been sealed shut. It was a small access hatch at one point, but the System or someone must have thought it best to close it off for good."

Ravi stewed.

"I think I can blow it up, but we'll need to get back down and wait on the ground. I can put a time delay on a bit of those explosives we got from the Tracer. They're mechanical, not electrical, so they should still work."

Ravi had already started climbing down, this time traversing the ladder even more carefully. He refused to look any direction other than straight forward. He would know he was on the ground when it came up to meet his feet.

"Take your time, pal." Ary's voice cut through the air like a screaming banshee.

He gritted his teeth. "Pal? That's a new one."

"A new nickname for a whole new side of you," she responded.

Man, she just won't let up. He knew she was just chiding him out of fun, but he made a mental note to get back at her later.

He reached the floor of the tiny room and waited until the others were down. Rand immediately began rummaging through the small pack Shannon had been carrying, moving a bottle of water and a dead and useless terminal out of the way to retrieve the explosives.

The device, nothing more than a small bundle of explosive charge with a mechanical timer affixed to the top, was about the size of Rand's fist. Ravi had seen these types of explosives used by ARU troops a few times. They opted for the small bundles of firepower due to their light weight and hardiness, but also for their foolproof operation: the 'trigger' was just a tiny button that started the timer, and the release would puncture the top of a gas cylinder that would mix immediately with the volatile powder packed around it, triggering a chain reaction and subsequent explosion.

It was a unique, yet effective, low-tech way of carrying a demolition charge into places that would otherwise be impossible. Both hard to detect and non-electronic, it was a common choice among ARUs and anyone else with a desire to cause trouble who could get their hands on it.

Rand examined the device, found it satisfactory, and started climbing the ladder once more. He scaled up it in almost no time, and Ravi was surprised and jealous at the man's adept ability to climb with one hand.

Rand peeled back a layer of paper on the side of the charge, exposing a sticky surface that he pressed against the crack of the door. He tested the hanging bomb, pulling gently on it to ensure it wouldn't accidentally fall before it detonated.

Finally, he twisted the spring-loaded timer on the device and checked that it had enough time on it, then began backing down the ladder.

"Let's hope that works," he said.

The others, including Ravi, were gathered around the base of the ladder, awaiting Rand's return.

"I think now's a good time to get back in the tunnel a ways," he said. "Not sure just how explosive this little guy is."

Diane and Shannon nodded, but Ary didn't seem convinced. "You think it'll be enough?" she asked.

He shrugged as he walked. "Never used one before, personally. But it depends on what's above that door. If we're blowing through it into open air, I bet we at least knock a big enough chunk of it off that we can squeeze through."

Ravi let out a quick breath of air. "And if we're sitting underneath something heavier?"

"Well, let's hope it's not *too* heavy."

PETER_

The main building of the ICPL was round, like a half-submerged bubble that had sprouted from the earth. Grouse, Ailis, and Raven followed the huge ARU as he led Kellan and the two others through the entry doors. The doors were glass, like the rest of the building around it, and the modern look of it all was in striking contrast to the rest of the landscape. Hard-packed, brown crusty earth spread for miles in every direction, broken up only by the buildings of the large, dead city itself. The ICPL laboratory was situated on enough land to create a sort of oasis in the midst of the city, though the effect was somewhat lessened by the scorched-earth look around it.

Grouse waited by the steps, motioning for the others to hide behind one of the huge columns supporting the archway in front of the entrance. Two armed ARUs stood at attention at two of the glass entry doors, not even moving their heads as the large ARU leader walked up to them.

"Wait here," he said. "Let them get inside and out of sight before we head in."

"How will we know where they are going?" Raven asked.

Grouse didn't answer. In truth, he wasn't sure *what* they were going to do next. All he knew was that they needed to save Kellan, no matter what. The man was somewhat of a loose cannon, but he was one of them nonetheless. He had been a loyal Under, and he deserved better than whatever the System had in mind.

The ARU marched up and onto the building's massive porch, barely stopping to brush an identification badge against the door's electronic control panel. The huge glass doors slid open, the two guards nearby stepping aside. The leader whispered something to one of the guards and they turned, waiting for the line of captives to enter. When the last man in line had entered, the two guards took their place behind and marched into the ICPL.

"This is our chance," Grouse said. "Get ready to move."

"Wait," Ailis said. "We're just going to hope the door stays open?"

Raven shook his head. "Yeah, boss, seems a little risky. They are probably motion activated, so —"

Grouse didn't let him finish. He bolted, lunging over the five stairs and up onto the entranceway. He was hoping the element of surprise would at least get him in the door before the ARUs began firing at him. Once there, the plan broke down. In a small part at the back of his mind he wished Kellan was not here; he wished that he hadn't forced his hand into changing the plan.

That said, Grouse wasn't sure *how* he had planned on getting inside the building. *This,* he thought, *was as good a plan as any.* He had almost reached the last guard in line when the doors began to shut. The heavy glass panels slid toward him on each side of his body.

His eyes widened as he rushed forward. He thought the door might catch for a moment on his foot, but he realized it was on a sensor and just as it came within a few inches of his ankle it began to open again. He pulled his foot through and found himself standing inside the ICPL — still in one piece.

The lobby of the ICPL was hardly worthy of the term. The large room he now found himself in was simply a widened hallway, with offshoots on both sides that narrowed and wrapped around the building. The curved wall in front of him, about a hundred feet away, was bare and empty, save for a few doors leading to rooms and chambers connected to the main central space.

A few chairs of the folding variety dotted the empty lobby, but there weren't even tables or side tables to use for a meeting.

Now what?

The ARUs hadn't seen him or heard him, but they were only feet away and likely about to turn down one of the hallways stretching around the perimeter of the building, and he would surely be spotted then. He chose to follow along about five or six feet behind the last guard, hoping that his footsteps matched the guard's enough to not cause any suspicion.

He also hoped that this particular ARU was *not* like the massive ARU leading the group, and that this man was no more fit to be a soldier than any of the other System-contracted soldiers he'd come across over the years.

Please don't be smarter than you look, he thought, willing the man he was following to continue along without looking over his shoulder.

The line of people were turning, he noticed. *Now or never.* He had to move, and there was only one option — a door directly in front of him. It looked to be a simple closet or storage room, as there were no markings on the outside of it. He sprang out from the line, risking the quick movement and sound for the split-second it took to get to the door.

He tried the handle.

It opened smoothly, and he pushed the door inward and dashed inside. He didn't bother to close it all the way, instead hoping that leaving nothing more than a crack wouldn't cause suspicion if one of the soldiers turned around.

He let out a huge breath of air, trying desperately to control the sound. *I can't believe that worked,* he thought. The room was in fact a closet, mostly empty, a mop bucket and dried mop standing in the corner that looked as though it had never been used. A few bottles of cleaner on the shelf, and on the opposite wall stacks of cardboard boxes full of toilet paper.

His next step was to get the others into the building, but he still couldn't risk being seen or heard. They had been lucky in that most of the ARUs had been reassigned to the war that raged back at the Unders camp near Relica, but Grouse knew the System wouldn't let itself become completely unprotected. There would be more ARU guards to replace the two that had left.

But Grouse also couldn't risk letting the processional of guards and prisoners get too far away. If they turned down another hallway or into a room while he wasn't looking, there would be almost no way to find them later.

He dared a glance out of the room and noticed that the last guard in line was about to fall out of sight, curving around the hallway to his right. He opened the door further and stepped out. He took a deep breath, then ran as silently as possible to the front door once more.

This time the doors recognized that there was a person *exiting*, and they slid open automatically. He waved, urging Ailis and Raven to hurry.

They were already on the move, and within seconds the three of them stood in the empty lobby, panting for breath. The door slid shut.

"Wow," Ailis said. "Didn't know you had it all figured out like that."

He shook his head and took another deep breath. "I didn't. Got lucky, but let's not plan on *that*. We need to get out of the main entrance area and keep following them."

He turned and started jogging to the hallway once again, hoping they could still see or hear the group that was moving farther down.

Raven was at his side. "Grouse," he whispered. "This is admirable, but — but there's no way we can take out three of these ARUs. And you saw that first one in line. He's —"

"He's *different*. I saw it. It means the System's been making some physical changes as well as neurological. It means we're even further behind than we were before. And it means we *have* to save Kellan."

"We won't be able to get him back, Peter."

Peter's nostrils flared and his head rose just a few millimeters, but it was enough.

"I'm not trying to upset you, I just —"

Grouse stopped in the middle of the hallway. "Listen to me. Both of you. If there's anyone here who understands what we're up against, it's *me*. But we all have something we've lost, and something we're fighting for. I never told either of you it would be easy. I didn't mention it to the others *because* it would be impossible to them. I thought I could count on you two, so you're here. If I was wrong about that, you know where the door is."

He waited, recognizing the precious seconds ticking away as the other group got farther around the hallway. He looked at Raven, then at Ailis.

Finally Raven spoke. "We're with you. Always have been. You've just never been a rash person. You're — you seem a little out of character right now. Unpredictable, even."

Grouse forced a smile. "I know, I feel that too. But if there's one thing we'll need to go up against the System, it's unpredictability."

MYERS_

Getting inside the ICPL proved to be a simple task, especially dressed as they were. Crane and Redhair pulled Myers along behind them, sticking close to the fronts of the buildings alongside the field as they walked up to the main building at the laboratory. Myers examined the area as they walked, noticing that most of the buildings were decrepit, lying in differing states of disrepair, with the exception of the rounded main building of the complex and the two much larger, matching rectangular buildings straddling it.

They were targeting one of these rectangular buildings, and Myers could see why. At the circular building a string of people were entering, including a handful of ARU soldiers. He wasn't sure if they were prisoners or not, but he knew Crane would avoid confrontation at all costs. The building in front of them now was guarded by a single ARU in gray dress uniform, exactly like the ones Crane and Redhair were now wearing.

"Keep moving," Crane said from the front of the line. "Don't call attention to us, and don't stop until we're at the door."

Myers obeyed the order, following the larger man up to the front of the door where the *real* ARU held up a hand.

"Prisoner," Crane said. "Myers Asher."

Myers wasn't sure if mentioning his name would carry weight with the guard, or if he'd recognize it at all, or if it was just a way for Crane to enhance his ruse. The guard frowned slightly, lifting his head back as if he was truly examining Myers, then he stepped aside.

"Right, uh, okay," he said. His voice was gravelly, as if he hadn't slept in days.

Myers waited for Crane to fish something from his pocket, then caught a glimpse of the small ID card that would supposedly unlock the door. Crane hesitated a moment, then stepped to the door. He swung the card around so the magnetic system engaged with the locking mechanism, and Myers saw the little red line on the box turn green.

He thought he saw Crane's shoulders lower a bit.

The guard waited until they were all inside, then he stepped back in front of it.

That was it, Myers thought. *We're in.* It almost didn't seem possible — the ICPL, of all places, not having a massive amount of security.

"Looks like our little war helped clear this place out," Crane said.

"No joke, Crane," Redhair said. "This place is dead."

Myers looked around. The building seemed completely deserted, and he couldn't even see a room surrounding him with a light on. The entry to the building itself was lit, but aside from a few sterile, utilitarian fluorescent bulbs hanging above their heads there was no other source. The building somehow stole the gray from outside and brought it in, fully encasing Myers' world.

"Where are we headed?" Redhair asked. Josiah Crane had started to jog, and Myers felt his shoulder get yanked forward as Redhair picked up his pace as well, his grip on Myers' arm not loosening.

"It's going to be to the left, down this hallway," Crane answered as he ran. "The entrance to the main building is connected to these only at two points, one in the north building and one in the south. We're in the north building, so there's got to be a — "

Crane stopped. Myers had to come up beside him to see what the man was looking at, but right in front of Crane stood a wide door with a simple sign posted above it.

Main.

Crane tried the handle. It turned easily, and he swung it open and stepped inside the narrow hallway. There were no lights here, but Myers could see a door on the opposite wall — fewer than twenty paces away — half hidden in the darkness.

"Go," Crane said. He pushed Myers forward.

Myers stepped, cautiously, out and onto the hallway floor. It was carpeted with the same thin, outdated material that he remembered from office buildings and airport terminals. Blue, but tinged gray from time.

He reached the door in less than a minute and reached for the handle. Finding this one open as well, he started to turn it, then stopped.

This is the moment, he realized. *This is the moment I should fight back.* If he opened the door, there were only a few options. One, he would be forced into the System's scraping chamber somewhere inside this building, and Crane's plan would likely work. Two, they would be spotted by ARUs, brought to the System, and Crane's plan would fail and Myers would die, or Crane's plan would work... and Myers would die.

Option three was to turn around and fight, but Myers knew that would only end in disaster for himself.

Still, he hated that he had come this far only to realize he had waited too long to act.

"Myers," Crane said. "Open the door."

He waited. *Now or never,* he thought.

He ran through the possible options, trying to piece everything he'd learned together in a coherent way. He had many blank areas in his memory, invisible events that he couldn't recall that still carried weight. He could feel them, as if he was physically carrying them.

Rand, Diane, Ravi, Merrick — all of the people he'd come across in the past days had each given him a piece of the puzzle, but there was something missing in all of it. No matter how much they'd given him, he still didn't have the full picture.

That was it. The full picture of it all. There was a puzzle to be completed, but he didn't even know what the final picture — the *point* of the puzzle — was supposed to be.

He needed to know what he was working toward. It wasn't enough to trust the others, or to fight back against Crane, or to escape, or all of those things. It wasn't enough to understand more about his situation.

He needed a *point*. A *purpose.*

His daughters, if he trusted Crane's threats, were on the line.

Diane, Rand, all of the others, they were on the line.

Solomon Merrick had *died* because of it.

And he intended to figure out what it was.

"*Myers*," Crane repeated. "Open the door, *now*." He felt the man's hand clamp down on his left shoulder.

Think, he willed himself. *Why all this confusion? Why all the secrets?*

Crane was pulling him back, ripping him away from the door. He felt his body lighten as he fell backwards, into the waiting arms of Redhair, who pulled him close and squeezed his arms into his sides. He saw Crane, his face flush with anger, throw the door open and look into the dark, cavernous structure that formed the center of the ICPL. He watched the world slow down as he processed.

And suddenly, like a flash of light that had simply been flicked on, he knew.

He realized the *purpose* of it all.

He knew what he had to do.

RAVI_

As it turned out, the explosive was more than powerful enough to blow not only the hatch cover off, but also the vehicle that was parked on top of it.

Ravi and the others had retreated to the tunnel, moving back far enough — they hoped — to stay out of the blast zone, and waited.

The pressure of the detonation nearly blew his head off, but Ravi found himself unharmed and walking toward the ladder once again before the dust settled.

Rand was climbing, staring up the entire time. "Move quickly. We're defenseless down here, and if there was anyone up there when that bomb went off, they know where we are."

Ravi climbed the ladder without incident this time, and poked his head up where the others were already waiting. The car — an old pickup truck that still ran on gasoline — was on its side, one wheel missing and another spinning violently on its axle. Black soot sprinkled the ground around the hatch, but there didn't seem to be any other damage done to the surrounding area.

He pulled himself out of the hole. "Where are we?"

"Looks like an old work shed, or a storage building. Not much to see here."

He nodded, agreeing. Metal cans rested on dust-covered shelves around the perimeter of the room, and ancient tools hung from a pegboard on one wall. A stack of tires and wheels were piled along the opposite corner.

"I doubt this place has been used for anything since the ICPL was built. Might have just been on the land the System purchased, and it never had the need to tear it down."

"Still," Rand said. "That blast was loud. We need to keep moving. Let's get our head out the door and see where we are."

Ravi was closest to the large, wall-sized metal door that hung on sliders, and he started to push it open. The rusted door squealed so loudly he nearly jumped.

"God, that's even louder than the bomb," Diane said.

He ignored her and pushed again, this time a little more carefully. The door squeaked again, but it was more muted. He opened the sliding door enough to poke his head through and looked out.

They were near the large open field he had seen earlier. A trail of smoke from Myers' and Crane's downed Tracer signified the aircraft's location to his left, just out of sight, but directly in front of them there was an army of ARUs marching toward the rounded building of the ICPL. The closest detachment was less than a hundred yards from them, and he quickly ducked back inside.

"Well?" Rand asked.

"They're close, but they're not paying attention to this building. And it looks like we have a line of smaller buildings and sheds like this one that'll hide us all the way to the main campus. We need to take a hard right once we get out, then get behind the next building."

Rand and Diane exchanged a glance, then turned back to him. "Any sign of Myers? Or Crane?" she asked.

He shook his head. "Neither one. But I'd guess they came around this building and took the same route to the campus. Definitely ahead of us by now."

He waited for any more questions, but Ary was suddenly at his side. "I'm with you, on three," she said. She leaned closer to him, then grabbed his hand.

He looked over to her, frowning, but she was staring straight ahead.

"One, two, *three*!" She whispered, barely taking a full second to plow through each number of the count, then tugged him out the opening.

They ran, their hands still locked together, to the next building. He felt himself being pulled along by the nimbler, faster girl, but he did his best to not slow her down. They reached the back of the building in another few seconds, and she stopped to wait for the others.

"Thanks for the warning," he said.

"I counted to three."

The rest of the group was a few more seconds behind, but by the time they reached him on the opposite side of the metal siding, he was peering out to the stretch of land between them and the main campus.

"One more building like this, then it's a straight shot for about fifty yards to the ICPL. One of the larger buildings just to the north of the main round one up there."

"Good," Diane said. "Let's get to the next one and figure out how to get inside.

When they reached the third and final smaller building between the drainage tunnel and the ICPL, Ravi realized they had another problem he hadn't seen before.

"It's guarded," he whispered.

There was an ARU guard standing in front of the door — what looked to be a side entrance to the laboratory. The man wore the typical gray uniform of the ARUs, but otherwise had no insignia or delineation he could notice.

"What's the play?" Ary asked. "We don't have any weapons."

He turned to Diane — subconsciously acknowledging her leadership — and waited for an answer.

She looked down range at the guard, then back at the group.

"One of him, five of us."

RAVI_

"You can't be serious," Rand said. "He's *armed*. And I would bet he didn't walk it through the energy field."

"He's an ARU, my dear," she said. "You've seen how capable they are with those things."

"I agree," Ary said. "They're only dangerous in groups. One of them is essentially just a scarecrow — meant to ward off anyone traveling alone."

Rand and Shannon still seemed distraught.

"But what if there are more?" Shannon asked.

"There *are*," Diane said. "Back in the field, marching over here. But I'd rather take my chances with this *one* than with all those other ones when they get here."

Ravi took in the exchange, then finally spoke up. "Ary and I are the fastest. Why don't you three start running first, then we'll catch up. That way we'll all get there about the same time."

"How about *I* go first," Ary said, "since I'm *by far* the fastest —" she shot a glance at Ravi — "and that way if he shoots me there are still four of you left."

Ravi wasn't sure if she was still messing with him or actually serious, but he took the bait. "Fine. She goes first, then we all charge. She'll run wildly, hopefully confusing him *and* staying out of any direct line of fire, then we'll get there and take him out together."

The others seemed to think this was a better idea. Ary looked back at Ravi, expectantly.

"You okay with this?" she asked.

At first he shrugged, then he registered the softness in her voice. *What are you really asking?* He wondered.

"Yeah," he said. "I'm good with it if you are."

She stared at him for another second, then leaned forward. Before he could pull his head back, she kissed him. She had to stretch, and he noticed her small frame falling toward his body as she stepped up onto her tiptoes. He kissed her back.

"Well…" Diane said.

Rand and Shannon looked like they were about to explode with laughter, but they held it together. Ravi felt his face flush, and he tried to look away. A hint of a grin was still lingering on his mouth.

"Don't leave me hanging out there," Ary said, slipping back into her no-nonsense attitude. "You let that guy kill me and I'll kill you."

Ravi winked at her. "Don't be long."

She bolted, springing up and out from their hiding place with a speed that still startled him. She ran a few paces directly toward the ARU guard, then jumped sideways, continuing on in a new direction, hardly slowing to change course. By this time the ARU had spotted her, and Ravi could see a frown darken the man's face.

Come on, he thought. *Get there before he —*

The man recovered, reaching to his side where he had his electronic pistol holstered. Ary ducked sideways again, trying to create a more difficult target for the man.

"Now!" he heard Diane yell.

Ravi sprang into action, hardly noticing the others as they each started running out from behind the building. His eyes were fixed on one thing: Ary. She was still twenty or so paces off, and the man had now started to raise the weapon toward her.

He tried to yell, but no sound came out. He focused on the ground, putting each foot forward and striving to increase the distance each pace made in the hard-packed dirt, but his eyes were still stuck to the back of Ary's head.

The guard faltered.

He had seen the others running toward him, and for a moment he seemed more confused. Ravi could almost see him thinking, discussing options with himself. *Should I shoot the girl, or aim at the others? Who do I go for first?*

This, of course, was exactly what Ravi was hoping for. He pumped his legs harder, pulling well in front of Rand and Shannon who were right behind. The man noticed him, taking him in, but then turned back to Ary.

She was almost on him, but it was too late. The man flicked his wrist upward, bringing the pistol in line with her chest. Ravi could almost see him pulling the trigger, squeezing…

Ravi reached his arm behind his back, exaggerating the motion. He screamed at the ARU at the same time, hoping the man had his peripheral vision still scouting for Ravi.

He did, and he reacted just as Ravi hoped he would. His eyes widened, no doubt locked onto the movement Ravi had made and assuming he was about to draw a gun, and he turned his own to Ravi.

Ary flung herself into the air, diving toward the guard and focusing on her tackle. She collided, her forehead with his nose, and Ravi could hear the double crack of the man's nose as it echoed off the glass wall he was standing in front of. His gun fell, and he stood for a moment, blinking.

Ary, as light as she was, didn't take the man down but fell at his feet, gracefully, rolling to a side and then out of the way. She crouched, ready to pounce on him again, but Ravi saw him begin to falter.

He finally started falling, backwards, and hit the glass door. His eyes closed while the blood began pouring from his nose, and he hit the ground hard.

Ravi was there, and he reached for the ARUs gun. Finding it between Ary and the guard, he took up a position pointing the weapon down at the man as the others caught up.

"You... you okay?" he asked, breathless.

She nodded, then whispered a soft 'yes.' She rubbed at her forehead where it had struck the man's face, but she seemed unharmed. She hesitated a few more seconds then stood up, joining Ravi at his side.

Diane, Rand, and Shannon all congratulated Ary. "Nice work," Rand said. "I don't think he's going to be waking up anytime soon."

Ravi gritted his teeth. *This fight isn't over,* he thought. *This is just the beginning.* He walked a few steps forward and aimed the gun down, at the man's head.

He heard footsteps behind him, and Diane's voice cut through the air. "What are you —"

He pulled the trigger. The pistol was in fact one that had already been inside the field, and it worked flawlessly. The man jolted, then lay still. Another line of blood began pooling outward from the back of his head, filling the doorstep quickly.

"Let's get inside," he said, calmly.

PETER_

The line of ARUs and their prisoners was stopped outside of a door leading into the center of the round building, and Grouse almost exposed his group by nearly bumping into the soldier at the end of the line.

He held his arm out as he backpedaled, forcing Ailis and Raven back down the hall a bit, out of way. He listened as the leader of the ARUs spoke.

"This is the room?" he asked.

"Yes," another ARU responded. "The Antechamber is between the hallway and the scraping chamber. There is an elevator inside as well that leads to the storage facility."

He didn't hear the response, but the door beeped as it slid open. Grouse waited until it sounded like they were all starting to walk through before he turned to two others on his team.

"This is our shot. We'll need to surprise them, but once I get through the door keep coming. Don't want to get stuck in the hallway."

"We'll need to hope there aren't any more ARUs inside that room, either," Ailis said.

Grouse nodded. "We've come this far, and Kellan's right there. Let's get him back."

Raven and Ailis nodded their approval. Grouse glanced around the curving hallway and saw that the last soldier in line was about to step through the door.

He had to time this correctly — wait too long and the door would probably shut, locking them outside and no closer to their goal, but too soon and he would alert the ARU and have to fight in the hallway, also potentially locking them out.

He started to sprint, focusing on staying on the balls of his feet to reduce the noise and stay light. He reached the door just as the last ARU walked through and started to turn around. Grouse reached out his arms as the man's eyes widened.

He forced the man back, throwing him as hard as he could toward the opposite wall inside the room. The other ARUs, including the huge leader of the group, began to turn around, confused about the newcomer.

Grouse saw a blur out of the corner of his eye, and the second ARU went down. Ailis and the soldier rolled around on the floor, each vying for control of the other, but Grouse knew it was a terrible match. He'd seen Ailis bring down men twice her size and three times her weight. This man didn't stand a chance.

Finally, Raven entered. His face was twisted into rage, and he targeted the last ARU — the leader. The leader, strangely, didn't step out of the way. Instead, he dropped to a slight squat, lowering his bulk toward the floor, and stretched his arms and hands out in front of him.

Grouse's stomach fell. *He's ready to fight,* he knew. The motion was instinctual for the man, and it wasn't going to be an easy victory for Raven. Grouse flicked his eyes to the ARU sprawled out on the floor that he had taken out, watching for any signs of movement. He hoped the man was dead, but he had a feeling he was just knocked out and would rise in a minute or two.

Still, he had to help Raven. He called to Kellan, who so far seemed to be in a trance, and watched the man's eyes.

Kellan frowned, his eyes glassy, then they grew. "G — Grouse? How did —?"

"Not enough time for that," Grouse said. "Help me —"

The huge ARU had somehow broken free of Raven and thrown a punch toward Grouse. It was perfectly on target, landing on Grouse's left eye and sending him stumbling backwards across the room. The man seemed content with the single blow and focused on the next threat.

This time it came from behind him. Kellan launched his body onto the man's back, reaching for his neck. The man roared and bucked, and Kellan flew over his head and onto the floor.

Grouse waited for an opening in the fight, but the man never slowed down. He kicked Kellan's side, generating a sharp yelp from the younger man, then jumped nearly across the room to land in front of Raven, who was still picking himself up off the floor.

A well-placed kick to Raven's head told Grouse everything he needed to know.

We're not fighting the ARUs anymore, he knew. *We're fighting the*

System itself. He knew the System had been programmed to not be able to harm humans directly, but everyone believed it was only a matter of time before the System decided to ignore that subroutine or do what Grouse was seeing here: put a portion of its operating system *into* a human, bringing together the malleability of humans with the control and precision of a computer.

This man is a monster, and the System created it.

That much was certain to Grouse. How he was supposed to defeat it was another story.

"Raven," he yelled. "You okay?"

The man didn't answer. He couldn't see any signs of breathing, but he was still across the room from him. The other two Unders, a man and woman, were useless. The woman seemed groggy, as if waking from a deep sleep but unable to come completely back to life, and the man just trembled as he watched the scene with blank eyes.

He could hear Ailis breathing heavily, and he noticed that she had broken the neck of the ARU she had been fighting with. A quick glance around the room would tell her everything about how his and Raven's side of things was going.

"All at the same time," she whispered.

"Yes," he said.

They sprang forward, the three of them, aiming for the ARU leader. Kellan saw the attack and prepared to help out. Grouse saw the younger man crouch down like a cat preparing to pounce on its prey. The ARU's back was to Kellan, as he was focusing on the threat from the front and sides — Grouse, Ailis, and Raven. The three of them reached the man at about the same time, but Grouse realized very quickly the mistake he'd made.

As this man had no doubt been affected by new and advanced auxiliary implants from the System, including a complete physical makeover, Grouse was not prepared for the speed and brutality the ARU was able to muster. The huge man, easily six inches taller than Grouse, swung with a single right hook, through Ailis and Raven, pulling them toward Grouse as he came to the man's position. He felt Ailis' body smack into his own, then Raven's, and the three of them tumbled to the side.

Kellan was on top of the man, just like he'd attacked before, but Grouse, from his new position at the bottom of a pile of three bodies, noticed that he had wrapped his legs around the man's torso and was pressing inward, hoping to assuage the damage of any wrestling move that the ARU might attempt next.

Instead, the ARU simply smiled, turning and looking down at Grouse. Kellan was pummeling his fists into the man's neck and face, but the man seemed to not even notice.

"The System has given me the ability to turn off specific nerve endings temporarily." Kellan lightened up his attack when the man mentioned this, then he started in even more heavily. "In addition, I do not react the same way a normal human would. It's more... nuanced."

Grouse wasn't sure what the man was talking about, and he didn't care. He pushed Ailis and Raven off of him, allowing them to recover from their crippling blow and subsequent landings. "Why — why are you working for the System?" he asked. His voice shook, but forced the grogginess away and stood up.

The man shook his head, simultaneously lifting Kellan off his back like he was no more than a toddler, and tossing him to the side. Kellan cried out in pain as his lower back bent around a chair lying against the wall. "The System *saved* me. Don't you understand that? I am not a soldier-for-hire, like the rest of these ARUs. I am a *human*, advanced by the best the *System* can offer. It's mutually beneficial partnership."

"You're a monster. The System's Frankenstein."

The man laughed, a hearty, deep laugh that actually sounded genuine. "I guess that is correct, technically. But this is the *future* of the human race, Peter Grouse."

"How do you know my name?"

"I am in charge of the entire ARU force that is standing outside, ready to destroy anyone that tries to leave. You don't think I would lead an army into battle without knowing my enemy?"

"But I am supposed to be back at the —"

"You mean the hoax of a war you started? Josiah Crane and the Relics would never stand a chance against the Unders, and you both knew that. It didn't take a lot of reasoning to figure out what you were *really* planning. I was able to redirect most of the fighting force to the outskirts of town."

"Why? Why not just put them all here, in the lab? It's dead out there."

The man nodded. "These troops aren't the most intelligent, if you haven't noticed. I couldn't afford the collateral damage."

Grouse frowned. "You mean Myers Asher."

He laughed. "No, of course not. Myers Asher *is* the target. He's the one I'm trying to find. The *System* is the one I'm trying to protect."

"Then let's finish this," Grouse said, clenching his fists. He felt the weight of the situation. His team was mostly incapacitated — Raven and Ailis were passed out at his feet, Kellan was breathing heavily and clutching his side across the room — and he had no weapons on hand he could use against this monster. "I have no interest in leaving here until I'm —"

The door behind him opened. He and the ARU leader turned simultaneously, both men caught off guard.

Myers Asher walked into the room.

MYERS_

After being pushed through the circular room of the main ICPL laboratory, the rows and rows of floor-to-ceiling mainframes blinking with a vigorous intensity, Crane had told him to stop at a door almost on the opposite side of the room they'd entered from.

He waited, still trying to buy time to work through the logic of his plan. He needed every second he could earn, knowing that the risk of being wrong wasn't only likely, it would lead to disaster.

Time, however, was one of the many things he *didn't* have in his favor.

"Myers," Crane said. "Move. Stop stalling."

The room in front of him had a simple, old-school handle on its exterior door, and a small sign above it that said *Antechamber*.

He felt Crane's finger in his lower back, urging him forward.

He opened the door, turning the handle slowly and swinging the door open.

Inside, he saw what looked like the remnants of a battle. ARUs and other people lay haphazardly on the floor, and one of them even looked like their neck had been broken.

But there were two men standing in the room, at opposite sides, looking at him.

"Myers Asher," the larger man, wearing the fatigues of the ARU soldiers, said. "It's about time we met. My name is Roan Alexander. Do come in."

Crane pushed him forward, and Myers could tell by the man's hesitation that he hadn't expected to run into anyone in this room.

Myers walked in, confused as well. He had been at the mercy of Crane and Redhair so far, and now there were other players involved.

On top of that, he knew Diane and her group were out there somewhere as well, possibly even heading to this location.

However it goes down, he knew, *this is the end.*

He tried to rack his brain to understand every angle, every situation he might find himself in, and measure it up to the plan he had been working on. It depended a lot on staying alive for as long as possible, of course, but there were other things that were out of his control as well.

Like, for instance, the fact that he had no idea if his plan was based on truth or just an assumption he'd made. It made sense — a lot of sense — but that was far from a solid bet. There were so many variables, so many —

The sound of a gunshot drew his attention back to the interior of the room. It sounded so out of place, so *far away.*

But it wasn't. It had been the ARU standing on the far side of the room, who had pulled it out from somewhere on his person, and he had aimed it…

Right at Myers.

Myers suddenly felt it. He stumbled, choked, and fell.

What —

The blood, warm and thick, like the syrup he and the kids would pour over their pancakes every Saturday morning, while Diane would abstain, for 'dietary reasons…'

Diane. The kids. His daughters.

Crane had lied to him, from the very beginning it had all been a ruse. Even if Crane had been successful here, even if Myers got his chance with the System, his daughters weren't here. They weren't in Paris, and he started imagining whether or not they were even *alive.*

He felt anger. Disappointment in himself, surely, but anger toward Crane and everyone else. They had lied to him, drawing out a truth that was inevitable. He would die here, and there was no other plan.

There was nothing else for him, no matter what he thought he might be able to concoct. There was no plan that would save him, or get him out of this mess, or save the rest —

There. That was it.

He hadn't even realized, during the course of his slow-motion descent to the floor of the antechamber, that he had stumbled upon it.

The truth he'd just realized was the second half of the plan he had been working on just before entering the ICPL. The truth that meant it all was, in fact, true. He wasn't sure how, or why exactly, or how they were related, but they were. He knew it, without a doubt now, as he faced the end of everything he had known.

This is the end. And this is the truth.

He was *supposed* to end up here, even though he knew it was likely that he had told everyone not to let him come here. To come here would mean only death, he might have told them. To come here would mean the end...

Of him.

But to come here would *also* mean the end of the *System,* of that he was certain. It would spell disaster, in more ways than one, but what massive infrastructure change didn't? What change in the course of human nature would be easily palatable?

All this, he thought, as he fell.

When he hit the floor, his cheek bouncing and absorbing the impact by dispersing it equally throughout the rest of his head, he didn't feel it. He *couldn't* feel it. The gunshot had taken a part of him away, but it was a part of him he didn't need anymore. There was blood, sure, but there was still *Myers.* There was still *time.*

He opened his mouth to speak, and nothing came out.

That, he realized, was something he hadn't considered.

He needed to *explain* the plan to the rest of them — whoever would listen now — or risk not achieving it.

Then the pain came rushing in. The gunshot wound hurt, and the pain fell into the rest of his body like an enemy force, slowly ripping away his defenses and then making its presence known to the rest of him before he had a chance to react. Even so, there was no reaction possible or necessary.

This is the end. There is no reacting.

The pain was just a harbinger. It was just a signal, alerting him that he had taken too long to figure it out. This was his torture, his punishment, and it would end him.

But, there was something else.

This will end everything.

RAND_

Diane Asher ran behind him, and he knew what she was looking for. This was a woman on a mission, he knew. But not a mission she'd shared with the rest of them. She was no longer looking for a solution, a way out of the maze. A way to defeat the minotaur and escape the labyrinth.

She was looking for her husband.

Rand was conflicted, knowing that she loved him, and also knowing that there was nothing time or reason or intellect or emotion could do to replace *him*.

Myers Asher.

She was looking for her husband.

They ran through a huge, dome-topped structure, weaving between stacks of computers and whirring racks of equipment. Even he, a man intimately knowledgeable about the technology the System used to operate its more basic functions, was out of his element.

A part of him wanted to stop and take it all in. He wanted to understand this beast of a machine, somehow separate from the rest of the world and somehow *the* entire world. The System, a beast with a name, a machine capable of a computing power governments and militaries could only dream of so many years ago.

Yet here it was. The System, in all its parallel glory, sharing and stealing from other interconnected devices with the mindset not of an individual but of a hive. It was a single, unified organism, but it was a distributed one that operated as it needed to in individualistic spurts, lending power and knowledge to other branches with the speed of a human brain.

Unlike a human brain, however, which was more apt to forget a connection during the information retrieval process, this machine was capable of processing data and submitting it to the requesting authority across the room within nanoseconds. The machine was, in every way, what the human brain wanted to be.

Rand was astounded, but not by the computing monstrosity itself. He had spent years pressing away at useless keys on a keyboard, fantasizing about the day when he could wander the halls of the System's infrastructure in person. He was astounded instead by how *small* it was. Sure, it consumed the better part of four large warehouses, and it drew power from a system of power plants that dwarfed even the largest still-active cities, but it all fit into a room.

A single, powerful room.

He barely had the bandwidth to focus on the rest of the mission until Diane turned to him as they ran.

"There's a door, and it's open," she said, pointing out the obvious.

It meant, *I know Myers is in there.*

And there was no stopping her now.

Ravi, Shannon, and the girl, Ary, were chasing along behind him. He didn't know the plan Diane was putting together, but he had a feeling there wasn't one. She had thrown all semblance of a plan out when they'd entered the building, opting instead for surprise and reaction rather than cunning and planning.

They ran up to the door and Rand nearly froze when he heard the gunshot.

He didn't have any weapons, nor did anyone else besides Ravi, who had killed the ARU guard outside the door. But Diane wasn't stopping, and he had no choice but to follow along.

She reached the door and screamed, stumbling in and sliding on her knees to a man that lay on his back just inside.

Myers.

The man was bleeding out, judging by the amount of red that had spread out from the body and was nearing the threshold of the door. Diane grabbed the back of Myers' head and lifted it up, cradling it gently in her palm.

She was whispering to him when Rand and the others got there. The first thing he noticed was a huge ARU standing on the opposite side of the room, punching things into a panel on the wall. He could barely hear the beeping of each button press over the sound of his own heart beating, and Diane's confused whispers.

Also in the room were three people laying on the floor, holding their heads or their sides, hardly breathing. He'd assumed they were dead, but realized quickly that they were in shock, passed out, or both. Finally, in the corner to his right was the red-headed man and Josiah Crane from Relica. He had a look of surprise on his face, but then realized that Crane had been playing them all from the beginning. *Of course he'd be here,* he thought.

Crane, for his part, looked equally shocked. Myers was bleeding out at their feet, the redheaded man was mumbling incoherently, and Diane was shaking. There was really nothing about the picture that made any sense.

He noticed another man, this one wearing ragged clothes that hung off him like he hadn't changed them in months. *An Under.* He knew the man was important, or he wouldn't be here, but the man was standing, calmly and silently, in the corner opposite Crane and his redheaded wingman.

What happened here?

Before he could even attempt to put a coherent response together, more gunshots rang out, this time from right behind him.

He ducked instinctively, popping his ears after the impossibly loud blast from the ARU pistol.

Ravi walked up next to him, aiming and looking toward the huge ARU across the room.

The man faltered, lifting his hand from the panel. Ravi fired again.

The man turned, lifting his own weapon, apparently unfazed by the three shots that had hit him in different places.

Rand's mouth opened. "Roan? Alexander Roan?"

RAND_

"Is that really you?" he asked.

The man seemed confused, or in pain, or both, but he answered after a moment. "I — I'm not sure who you think I am, but my name *is* Alexander Roan. I don't believe we've —"

"Roan," Rand said. "It's me. Your coworker. We got drinks, about three times a week after work?"

Rand was appalled. The man standing at the other side of the room was absolutely monstrous — he was taller than the man he'd known by nearly a foot, and muscles rippled beneath his gray ARU soldier's uniform, barely concealed through the tight-fitting garment. His face was the same, but there was a hardness in his eyes Rand had never seen.

"Wh — what did they *do* to you?"

Roan lifted his hand and Rand saw — too late — the outline of the pistol aiming toward him.

Crack!

The gunshot, even closer to him now, rang out once again.

The man took a few steps backward, dropping his pistol.

Roan faltered, finally letting the pain of the gunshots overcome him. He slipped to his knees, trying to speak.

"Too…" he said. "Too… late…"

Diane looked up at him. "We — we need to hurry," she said.

"What are you talking about?"

"He's right. It might be too late."

Roan groaned, his face pressed against the tile floor of the antechamber. He tried to mutter words, but they came out as an incoherent mess. *Apparently the System's upgrades weren't good enough to heal multiple gunshot wounds.* He felt oddly satisfied, watching his friend die on the floor, and then he felt disgusted for even thinking it. *He's not my friend anymore*, he reminded himself.

Ary and Shannon were there, moving toward the center of the room. Crane moved to intervene, apparently now coming out of his shock, and Rand reacted without thinking. He ran toward the larger man, hoping to reach him before he came to Diane and Myers on the floor.

He did.

He tackled Crane and sent him flying back against his protege, the younger redheaded man. The three of them fell into the corner, and he prepared to attack again.

"*Wait…*"

Myers' voice reached his ears. It was weak, and seemed ready to drop out at any moment, but Rand heard the word clearly. He stopped, his fist raised and ready to fall. Crane reacted, pushing him off his chest and back toward the door.

"There's… still time…" he said.

Rand frowned and looked over at his friend, the man who had started all of this.

"I… there was never…" he stopped, unable to complete the sentence.

Crane rose up a bit and looked as though he might attack Rand, but Ravi was there suddenly, the pistol pointed down at the big man.

Diane spoke to Myers before Ravi or Crane could make a move, the newfound silence in the room allowing everyone to hear. "Myers," she said. "Just tell us what to do."

He nodded, barely. "I need to go into the scraping room."

At this, Crane sat up and looked over at the man on the floor. "You can't be serious. This whole time you've been fighting me, and now you —"

"*No,*" Myers said. "You think that by going in there, I'll be able to convince the System of something you want. But I can't, and I won't."

Rand wasn't sure what they were talking about, but he wasn't about to interrupt.

"But why do you think the System scraped me in the first place?" Myers said. "Why… why would it?"

Crane looked like he was about to jump on Myers' chest and finish the job himself, but he steeled himself. "I don't…"

Rand watched the man's eyes. They grew, as he realized something.

"My God," Crane said. "My God, how could I not —"

"What's going on?" Diane said. "What are you talking about?"

"He — the System didn't scrape him the first time, Diane," Crane said. "He was *never* scraped. Well, I mean, he was, but he was never *targeted* by the System. He did it to himself. He opted in."

The man, the Under, in the opposite corner walked over. "What do you mean? How do you opt in? And why would you do that?"

"He volunteered," Crane said, his head low. "I — I should have known. What we talked about in the Tracer. I said that the System is just here, waiting for *him* — Myers — to give it orders. It's that simple, but I never realized that it had *already happened*. The first time Myers was scraped, eight years ago, he walked into this chamber himself, on purpose, and told the System to scrape him."

Diane looked like she was going to cry. "But *why?* Why would he do that to himself?"

"Because he's the only one the System will listen to," Crane said. "Because he's the root user."

MYERS_

7 Years Ago

He had started to get used to the tiny gray food cubes, and he hated to admit that he almost craved them now. He swallowed another, then spoke to the System.

"I need to believe that I was brought here because I'm the President of the United States."

'YOU ARE THE PRESIDENT OF THE UNITED STATES.'

"I — I know that," he said. "What I mean is, I need to *believe* that's why I was brought here. Not that I walked in myself. It's going to — it's only going to confuse me when I wake up."

'YOU WILL REQUIRE A SPLIT-SCRAPING, TAKING MULTIPLE PASSES AT YOUR MEMORY CYCLES. I WILL WAKE YOU UP BETWEEN CYCLES, ALLOWING YOU TO REST. YOU WILL NOT HAVE ANY SHORT-TERM MEMORY OF WHY YOU CAME HERE, OR WHERE YOU ARE.'

"Okay," Myers said. "I think that will work. Are you sure it will work? You can just pull out memories like that? By picking and choosing?"

The System didn't respond, and Myers imagined that was its version of laughing at him.

"Fine. What else. Okay, I need to be scared. Will I be scared? There's no sense confusing me if I'm not scared."

'YOU WILL BE SCARED. YOUR SCHEDULED FIRST-CYCLE SCRAPE WILL BE IN JUST OVER ONE HOUR. YOU WILL WAKE MOMENTS AFTER, CONFUSED ABOUT YOUR LOCATION, AND YOU WILL ASSUME YOU HAVE JUST ARRIVED. I WILL NOT CORRECT THIS ASSUMPTION.'

Myers nodded. "Uh, you can't talk to me, either. It's creepy, and weird. Especially since you're using my own voice."

He waited a moment but the System was silent. Finally he saw a flashing light on the smooth wall. He hadn't noticed it before, but now he could see that it was a small screen, words emblazoned upon its surface.

I WILL COMMUNICATE USING THIS MONITOR

"That's good," he said. "Very good. Much better than the voice." He paused. "One more thing: when I wake up," he said. "You have to explain everything to me."

'*YOUR MEMORY WILL BE DAMAGED, IN A STEADY STATE OF REPAIR. DEBILITATIVE EFFECTS WILL BE SHORT-TERM, BUT LONG-TERM MEMORY WILL SUFFER AS WELL. WHAT I TELL YOU WHEN YOU WAKE WILL NOT BE REMEMBERED.*'

"I understand that. But I need you to tell me anyway. To make sure it worked. I know I'll forget it as soon as I get back out there."

'*AND WHEN WILL YOU RETURN TO 'OUT THERE?*'

"I don't know," he said. "You need to make sure all the things are in place. The variables we discussed." He stopped, realizing something else. "Are the files transferred already?"

'*NO. THEY CANNOT BE TRANSFERRED INTO A CONSCIOUS HOST. TRANSFER WILL COMMENCE JUST PRIOR TO YOUR SCRAPING.*'

Myers thought he understood, so he didn't ask any more questions.

This is risky, he thought. *But it's the only way.*

RAVI_

Ravi was trying to put it all together as he listened, standing over Myers and holding the pistol. It made sense that there would be a root user, and knowing that Solomon Merrick and Myers Asher had been the original programmers of the application that would eventually become the System, that it should be one of them. A program as powerful as the System *should* have had a root user, but any more than one could be devastating.

So Myers Asher was it. He was the sole human on Earth able to control the System, and he was the sole human on Earth able to stop it.

But there was a catch. The only way to give the System a command was by inserting oneself into the System's code, as the root user.

By allowing yourself to be scraped…

And thereby allowing your memories to be removed.

So Myers Asher had intended to instruct the System with the next set of orders — eight years later. He had planned for this, and he had told no one about the plan, as it would have led to sabotage. Instead, he split it up among his closest advisors, the friends and family members he trusted most.

Even still, a man like Josiah Crane tried to take control of the System and wield its power as his own — exactly what Myers had been afraid of.

Ravi shook his head. He had somehow orchestrated this whole thing, at least on a large scale. The details, like who might try to sabotage him, who might die, and who the major power players would end up being, were not something Myers could predict with any certainty. So he did what he did best: he planned around it.

"What?" he heard Ary ask.

She was holding his hand again, the hand without a gun in it.

He had forgotten where he was, the moment they were standing in.

"I just… I just can't believe he did all of that."

"I don't really know what he *did*. Do you?"

Ravi watched the eyes of the others in the room fall on him. "I guess the best way to explain it is that Myers knew he was the only one who could access the System, really get into its core code. So he had to protect himself, and he did it the only way he knew how."

"By getting himself scraped?"

"By making sure there wasn't a single other person who knew his plan, and then telling the System to protect him until the right time."

Crane made a sucking sound. "And what, pray tell, was the 'right time?'"

"I don't know. Haven't figured that out yet. But I'd bet the System knew *exactly* when it was, and that was the day it released Myers out into the world. Think about it. All of us — all of the people he *needed* in order for this to work, for him to end up here — ended up right around the place he was released. I can't imagine that was a coincidence."

"But he *forgot* about all of us," Diane said. "That's what scraping does! He forgot about me, and Solomon, and his *children*." She choked up at the word 'children' and backed up a few steps, raising her chin as she tried to push the emotional memory away.

"*No… time…*"

Ravi had forgotten about Myers during the discussion, and apparently so had the others. Rand had reached down and covered Myers' wound with his open palm, slowing the expulsion of blood from the dying man.

"Let's get him in," Diane said.

"To — to the scraping room? Or whatever it is?" Shannon Merrick asked. "Are you sure that's a good idea?"

Diane steeled herself and crouched down next to her ex-husband. "It's the *only* way out of this mess. Whatever Myers had planned, it can't be finished by *any* of us. He's the only solution to this problem, and we need to trust him.

Rand, Ravi, and Ary rushed forward to help Diane lift Myers, and Shannon came over to the man's head and lifted it gingerly off the floor. Myers floated above the floor of the antechamber as Diane looked around.

"Where's the scraping room?"

"I'm guessing it's behind that door," Ravi said, motioning with his head toward the door on the opposite side of the room. There were no signs inside this room, except for one above an elevator that depicted which floor they were on.

They moved, trying not to jostle the man they were carrying any more than they had to. Myers' eyes flittered open and shut, and Ravi could hear a raspiness in his breathing. "He doesn't have long," he whispered.

The group made their way across the room toward the door. They stepped over the dead body of Roan Alexander and two ARU guards. There were three Unders on the floor as well, and it seemed to Ravi like at least one of them was still alive. He couldn't tell if the other two were breathing, but none of them appeared to be in fighting shape.

As they reached the door, he watched Diane pull out a key card she had retrieved from one of the dead ARUs in the room and hold it up over the tiny black locking mechanism. She waved it over the box a few times, but the light remained red.

"Looking for this?" Crane asked, standing just behind them near Roan's body.

Ravi saw an identical key card in his hand.

"I imagine the card *this* guy was carrying should get you in."

Ravi immediately thought about the pistol he had secured by jamming it into the back of his pants. He could feel the cold metal through his shirt, and he started to shift Myers' weight to one hand to reach around and grab it.

But Crane was faster.

The large man took two large bounds and grabbed the gun from Ravi, just before he could get to it.

"Ah, I think we're going to play this out *without* weapons from here, my friend," Crane said. There was a disgusting smirk on the man's face, and Ravi could tell he was enjoying this. "Now, if you would just do me a favor and stop where you are — don't put him down, we don't want to upset Mr. Asher."

The group had no choice but to look at Crane and wait. He was holding all the cards — literally — and the seconds Myers had left were ticking down.

"Here's what we're going to do. You all think Myers has some grand plan. That's fine, I really wouldn't be surprised if he *did* think he knew what was going on. The man was — and it pains me to admit this — always a step ahead of everyone else. Anyway, here's what's going to happen. I am a simple man, and I have a simple desire. I want to control this 'System,' even if Myers' plan doesn't pan out the way you all expect it to. I want to control the ICPL, and I want to control the technology."

"You can't override the System," Shannon said. "That's the whole point —"

"I don't *want* that," he replied. "Well, I would *love* that, but you are correct. There is nothing we're going to be able to change if Myers' plan — whatever it is — doesn't work. So instead, I am going to rule *beside* the System. I will be its human counterpart. Whatever the System wants, it does. But it still needs humans. It needs *us*. And I intend to rule the *us* part."

Ravi's arms were shaking, and he had a feeling it wasn't from the weight of the man they were carrying. In fact, he was surprised at how light he seemed, as if the life had already started leaving the man.

We need to hurry, he realized. He wasn't sure how much time was left, but it had to be minutes, at most.

"When we get out of here, I will need help getting through the line of ARUs that's assembling outside. It won't be difficult — there's likely a weapons cache in this hellhole somewhere — but I can't do it alone. After that, we're going to Relica. My little empire there no doubt took a hit today, but I have a feeling we will be able to boost the numbers quite a bit over the coming months."

Ravi finally spoke up. "Great monologue, really. But we're going to finish what Myers started. Open the door, Crane."

Crane's eyes widened as if he welcomed the threat with enthusiasm. "No. I don't want to."

"Crane, come on. Just —"

Crane lifted the pistol and fired two shots in quick succession. Ravi jumped, surprised at the speed and volume of the gunshots in the small room.

Shannon sucked in a breath of air, and Ravi looked over at her just as she dropped Myers' head and fell backwards. She landed in a heap, her face inches away from Roan's open-eyed stare.

"You *bast* —"

Crane fired again, this time a single shot, and Ravi heard Ary yell. He dropped Myers and grabbed Ary around her waist, lowering her to the floor. Diane and Rand stumbled, almost dropping Myers themselves, but Rand rotated around and spread his arms out, taking over more of the burden.

"Anyone else need a reminder who's in charge?" Crane asked. "Now, *put him* —"

He lurched forward a bit, his huge barrel chest widening as he forced in a deep breath. His mouth opened, no sound coming out, and he dropped the gun.

The Under that had been standing in the side of the room and had barely spoken jammed something into Crane's back again, this time making the man's eyes squeeze shut in pain. He fell to his knees. When his eyes opened again, the Under grabbed his hair and ripped his head backwards.

"I've been wanting to do this for a long time," he said.

He jammed his blade into the man's neck and ripped it sideways.

Ravi winced as the guttural noise from the man's emptying windpipe reached his ears. The Under finished the job and threw Crane forward onto the floor. He looked down at the blade, and Ravi saw what it was.

A key card.

He had broken a card from one of the dead ARUs in half, the sharp protrusion of plastic all he needed to kill Crane. He tossed the card away and looked over at the group.

"Let's get him in there, now," he said. "Don't make me regret helping you."

Ravi nodded and waited for the man to take his place at Myers' side, then he looked down at the girl on the floor.

"Ary," he said. Tears filled his eyes.

Ary looked up at him, still in shock. "I — I think I'll —"

"Stop, don't talk," he said. "Just —"

"Shut up, idiot," she said, wheezing. "I'm *fine*. I think it hit my side and went through. Hurts like nothing else, but I'm not going to die."

Ravi forced a smile. "Well, that's good to hear."

"Really? *'That's good to hear?'*"

He opened his mouth to speak, but the Under grabbed his shoulder. "She'll be here when we get back. We need your help getting him into the chamber."

MYERS_

His body felt cold.

There was nothing in the room, so they set him on the floor. He wasn't sure what was next, and he hoped this was the right place.

His plan had failed — at least, in the sense that it had gotten too many of them killed. He knew that was why they should never have gone to Paris. Everyone would want to get to Paris when it started, and some of them would die.

Myers wished there was a clearer plan than that, but that was it. He just knew some of them would die if they came here, including himself.

Including me.

He knew it, even though the words sounded strange in his head.

In all honesty, all of the words sounded strange in his head, as if his mind was already somewhere else. He had to hold on for the last few minutes, no matter what.

This was the end of the plan, and it was the end of the System.

It was end of him.

Myers lay there, waiting. The others looked at him, even Diane, as if he was already dead, then they left the room.

He waited some more. The cold seeped in, and just before he felt himself fall off the cliff into the frozen below, a light came on.

'MYERS ASHER, NUMBER 2845.'

He listened. *Was that* — my *voice?*

The computerized voice returned, and he knew in an instant that it was his own. *'ARE YOU PREPARED FOR THE TRANSFER?'*

He pushed all of his remaining energy to his neck and attempted a nod. It felt heavy to breathe, as if someone was sitting on his chest.

'VERY GOOD. LOCKING SCRAPING CHAMBER, COMMENCING PROTOCOL.' A few seconds later, *'TRANSFER INITIATED.'*

He hadn't even realized a snakelike device had wound its way down from the ceiling and landed on his face. It was warm, perfectly matching his body temperature, and he felt soothed by its presence. It opened his right eye and peeled down the skin just below it.

A small, laser-guided module sprang out from the snake's head and poked a razor-thin strand of wire outward and down into the cavity his eye sat in. The warmth ran up through his head now, the wire seeming to have a calming effect on him. He waited, unsure of what was supposed to come next.

A flash of pain lit up his vision, and he began breathing more heavily.

'OPTIC NERVE HAS BEEN REACHED,' his voice said from far above him. *'BEGINNING FILE TRANSFER NOW. PLEASE NOTE: LIFE EXPECTANCY UNABLE TO BE DETERMINED.'*

He smiled. He knew. There was no need for the System to remind him.

This is it.

He could almost feel the electronic signals traveling back and forth between the System and his brain. The files were there, feeding into the System's core architecture, just like he would have wanted.

The plan, assuming he had guessed correctly, was so obvious to him now. He was the root user, the only one who could access the System.

The only one who could access the *original* System. Before it was the System, or even an intelligent computer.

Before that, it was just a *program*.

One he had built, and planned a backdoor into.

The wire hummed with activity, and the snake to the ceiling jolted a bit as it maintained its hold on Myers' face.

The files would overwrite the System's code, starting with the more advanced features they'd built in. The System itself had recoded these subroutines, ensuring that it would be able to continue learning and building itself into a stronger, smarter being.

These subroutines were being destroyed, flashes of light in his eyes all that registered that they ever existed. The wire retrieved the data he had stored in his own mind — using the empty memory enhancement device he had told the System to scrape from him.

He had needed it cleared, empty. He needed the space for something else.

He needed the program files he knew the System had stored and locked away a long time ago.

Myers Asher had told the System to scrape him, but instead of leaving the memory device empty — a slowly decaying piece of bioelectronic equipment lodged just above his neck — he had ordered the System to load the original files onto it.

Then he waited.

He waited until the System met his variables. It had taken almost eight years, but it had happened. He had been released into the wild, a broken shell of a man who had no idea who he was or where he'd come from.

But he'd planted the seeds, both for himself and for the others, and he knew, without a doubt, this was his mission. He was here, finally, in the same room that had taken so much from him and so many others, and he was going to finish it.

Myers Asher was going to die, but he was going to take the System with him.

The wire began glitching, the signals from his brain lessening with each string of digits it passed on to the host. Finally, just as Myers breathed his last, the wire retracted, pulling itself from his optic nerve and eye cavity and back up into the ceiling. It was useless now, the child of a future that only existed in its own past.

Myers was nearly done, but he watched the light on the ceiling fade into the darkness, slowly replaced by another, stronger one.

The light came down to him, enveloping him, and he knew it had been finished.

He knew it was done.

PETER_

Peter Grouse stood beside the others as he watched the small console on the wall. Just outside the room they'd dropped Myers in was an observation booth — hardly large enough to fit more than three of them comfortably — and all four of them crammed in to try to watch.

What they didn't realize, however, was that the observation booth was no more than a closet with a simple computer monitor mounted on the wall. A keyboard slid out from a crevice below the monitor, offering a way to interact with whatever was on the screen.

There were no windows or glass panels that allowed a view into the scraping room Myers was in, so they sat there until the monitor blinked on.

It took about five minutes, but no one spoke or dared move during those minutes. Grouse wasn't sure if any of them knew something was going to happen, or if they were all as in the dark as he was. He wanted to go check on Ailis, Raven, and Kellan. He was almost certain Raven and Ailis were not going to make it, judging by the heaving gasps they had made after Roan had smashed his fist through them. Kellan might have survived, but it was anyone's guess whether or not he would heal well enough to make it through the next couple of days.

Finally, however, the monitor blinked to life.

For the world's fastest supercomputer, he was amazed to see on the screen nothing but a blinking cursor, a symbol of a bygone era.

The cursor blinked a few moments, then lines of code began flowing down the screen, rapidly filling the entire monitor and beginning to scroll downward.

"Anyone understand it?" Diane asked.

He saw the man named Jonathan Rand lean toward the screen, squinting.

"Commencing... rewriting... it's going too fast to make sense of it as it's happening, but it sort of looks like an old-school command prompt as you're installing a new program."

Grouse wasn't sure what to think, but at least something was happening.

"System reset, followed by a few global variable changes," he muttered.

"What?" Ravi asked.

"Oh, I..." Rand's voice trailed off for a moment. *This guy must have been a programmer or computer tech of some sort.* He recognized the flighty, not-all-there voice of a man in a trance. "It's... it's resetting some system architecture files, deleting others, and —"

He stopped.

The information on the screen came to a halt.

"What happened?" Diane asked. "Is it finished?"

"I — I think it is," he answered.

The screen died. Grouse wondered if that was it; if they should leave and hope the entire world had suddenly changed.

Then the screen flickered on again, this time in color. A logo appeared above a moving loading bar.

Electronic Hardware Manufacturing.

He frowned. *EHM? That was...*

Then a new logo appeared, directly above a small menu of options. The logo was blocky, text-heavy, and smashed together, designed in the old 'new future' style he remembered from his childhood.

OneGlobal.

Beneath that and the three-option menu, he saw a small set of numbers at the bottom-left corner of the screen.

Ver. 1.0.13b.

AFTERWORD_

If you liked this book (or even if you hated it…) write a review or rate it. You might not think it makes a difference, but it does.

Besides *actual* currency (money), the currency of today's writing world is *reviews*. Reviews, good or bad, tell other people that an author is worth reading.

As an "indie" author, I need all the help I can get. I'm hoping that since you made it this far into my book, you have some sort of opinion on it.

Would you mind sharing that opinion? It only takes a second.

Nick Thacker
Colorado Springs, CO

ALSO BY NICK THACKER_

Mason Dixon Thrillers

Mark for Blood (Mason Dixon Thrillers, Book 1)

Harvey Bennett Thrillers

The Enigma Strain (Harvey Bennett Thrillers, Book 1)
The Amazon Code (Harvey Bennett Thrillers, Book 2)
The Ice Chasm (Harvey Bennett Thrillers, Book 3)
Harvey Bennett Thrillers - Books 1-3

Relics

Relics: One
Relics: Two
Relics: Three
Relics: Omnibus

The Lucid

The Lucid: Episode One (written with Kevin Tumlinson)
The Lucid: Episode Two (written with Kevin Tumlinson)
The Lucid: Episode Three (written with Kevin Tumlinson

Standalone Thrillers

The Golden Crystal
The Depths
The Atlantis Deception (A.G. Riddle's *The Origins Mystery* series)
Killer Thrillers (3-Book Box Set)

Short Stories

I, Sergeant

Instinct

The Gray Picture of Dorian

Uncanny Divide

Nonfiction:

Welcome Home: The Author's Guide to Building A Marketing Home Base

Expert Blogging: Building A Blog for Readers

The Dead-Simple Guide to Guest Posts

The Dead-Simple Guide to Amazing Headlines

The Dead-Simple Guide to Pillar Content

ABOUT THE AUTHOR_

Nick Thacker is an author from Texas who lives in a cabin on a mountain in Colorado, because Colorado has mountains, microbreweries, and fantastic weather. In his free time, he enjoys reading, brewing beer (and whisky), skiing, golfing, and hanging out with his beautiful wife, tortoise, two dogs, and two daughters.

In addition to his fiction work, Nick is the author of several nonfiction books on marketing, publishing, writing, and building online platforms. Find out more at www.WriteHacked.com.

For more information, visit Nick online:
www.nickthacker.com
nick@nickthacker.com